After a childhood filled with Bollywood, Monty Python, and Jane Austen, **Farah Heron** constantly wove complicated uplifting happily-ever-afters in her head while pursuing careers in human resources and psychology. She started writing those stories down a few years ago and is thrilled to see her daydreams become books. Farah writes romantic comedies for adults and teens full of huge South Asian families, delectable food, and, most importantly, Brown people falling stupidly in love. Farah lives in Toronto with her husband and kids, plus two cats who rule the house.

Find out more at:
  FarahHeron.com
  X @FarahHeron
  Instagram @FarahHeronAuthor
  Facebook.com/FarahHeronAuthor

Books by Farah Heron

Just Playing House
Jana Goes Wild
Kamila Knows Best
Accidentally Engaged

A Little HOLIDAY Fling

FARAH HERON

PIATKUS

PIATKUS

First published in the US in 2025 by Forever,
An imprint of Grand Central Publishing, a division of Hachette Book Group
Published in Great Britain in 2025 by Piatkus

1 3 5 7 9 10 8 6 4 2

Copyright © 2025 by Farah Heron

The moral right of the author has been asserted.

*All characters and events in this publication, other than those
clearly in the public domain, are fictitious and any resemblance
to real persons, living or dead, is purely coincidental.*

All rights reserved.
No part of this publication may be reproduced, stored in a
retrieval system, or transmitted in any form or by any means, without
the prior permission in writing of the publisher, nor be otherwise circulated
in any form of binding or cover other than that in which it is published
and without a similar condition including this condition being
imposed on the subsequent purchaser.

A CIP catalogue record for this book
is available from the British Library.

ISBN 978-0-349-43877-1

Printed and bound in Great Britain by
Clays Ltd, Elcograf S.p.A.

Papers used by Piatkus are from well-managed forests
and other responsible sources.

Piatkus
An imprint of
Little, Brown Book Group
Carmelite House
50 Victoria Embankment
London EC4Y 0DZ

The authorised representative
in the EEA is
Hachette Ireland
8 Castlecourt Centre
Dublin 15, D15 XTP3, Ireland
(email: info@hbgi.ie)

An Hachette UK Company
www.hachette.co.uk

www.littlebrown.co.uk

*This book goes out to my loyal fans
who have stuck with me through ten books.
I adore you all and am endlessly grateful.*

RUBY DHANJI HAD NEVER seen herself as a particularly interesting or memorable person. Probably because she wasn't all that *good* at anything. She had no advanced degrees—hell, no unadvanced degrees, either—she had no athletic skills, and she was downright horrendous at sewing and car maintenance, despite her parents being a seamstress and a mechanic. But what Ruby lacked in God-given talents, she more than made up for in enthusiasm and living in the moment. Her life was great, because Ruby *carpe'd* the fucking *diem* her way through it. Ruby didn't just enjoy things; she *relished* in them.

Three passions had risen to the top of Ruby's interests. First, she loved anything and everything coming out of the UK—except colonialism, of course. She was Indian, and British colonialism hadn't been kind to her people. But she loved the architecture of old English manor houses, loved Jane Austen, loved the Beatles, and loved modern British exports, too, like Harry Styles and chicken tikka masala. Second, Ruby loved the finer things in life: designer clothes, imported skin care, even expensive handbags. This particular passion was probably the result of working in high-end retail for years, so she was surrounded by luxury goods every day. Ruby was practical, though—even with an employee discount she would have gone bankrupt several times over if she wasn't willing to buy her luxury goods secondhand or on clearance.

And finally, despite her Muslim upbringing, Ruby Dhanji *adored* the Christmas season with her whole heart. She loved the winter aesthetic, Christmas carols, holiday movies, and watching happy families celebrating together. *Secularly*, of course—she ignored the religious roots of the holiday. As far as Ruby was concerned, if she could love most things British while still being critical of their nasty habit of randomly declaring places people already lived in as their own colony, then she could also pick and choose which aspects of a holiday to celebrate and love.

This year, the Christmas season was a little bittersweet, though, because it would be her last one in Toronto—likely her last in Canada. So, as a proper send-off to the city that hadn't always been great to her, Ruby was throwing herself a thirty-third birthday and tree decorating party on the day after her birthday—since she had to work on her actual birthday.

On Friday evening, the night before her party, Ruby left Reid's Holiday, the small pop-up store in the Distillery District where she was store manager. The district had just transformed into the annual Toronto Winter Market, modeled after European Christmas markets, and Ruby hadn't seen all the new vendors and temporary stores yet. When she spotted a new sign advertising LIVE CHRISTMAS TREES, she knew it was fate. She'd planned to set up the hot-pink tree she'd thrifted last year for her party, but a real tree would be so much better.

After buying the perfect small one (because her apartment was beyond tiny), Ruby carried the tree out of the lot by holding it in front of her so it wouldn't touch her vintage red coat. She quickly realized she should have stuck with her pink one, though, because navigating cobblestones in high-heeled shoes, a velvet miniskirt, sheer tights, and a whole-ass *tree* was tricky. She should have brought a wagon. Not that she had a wagon. She was only three feet away from the lot when she dropped the twine-wrapped bundle. The trunk bounced on the stone walkway before falling sideways, hitting a person walking near her on its way to the ground.

"Bloody hell," said a voice. "Watch it!"

"Oh no! I'm so sorry!" The man her tree hit could have been the one to chop it down in the first place. He seriously looked like he'd just walked out of a forest, with his worn blue jeans, a shearling-lined denim jacket unbuttoned to reveal a red flannel shirt, plus a blue beanie pulled down almost to his eyelids. He was Brown, like Ruby, and maybe in his mid-twenties.

"Careful with that…" He scowled, causing his hat to lower even more. "Is that a tree?"

Ruby smiled warmly as she bent to pick up her fallen tree, being careful to lift with her knees and not her back. She couldn't get laid up with a back injury now. "I'm so sorry. It's just…it's *so much bigger* than I thought it'd be!"

The man stared at her, his dark eyes blinking in slow motion. And…Ruby realized what she'd just said. Classic Ruby. She giggled at herself. "That wasn't innuendo," she said.

Although, maybe it should be? Because despite this man's

stereotypical Canadian attire (which honestly wasn't Ruby's vibe), he was *cute*. Actually, more like…classically handsome. That jawline. The smooth skin. Ruby had over a month left in Toronto—there was certainly time for a final fling with a young Canadian before she moved overseas.

But the guy wasn't laughing with her at her suggestive gaffe. Or *at* her. Okay, so the lumberjack didn't have a sense of humor. No worries; a fling was probably a bad idea anyway. Ruby held her tree in front of herself with outstretched arms again and started walking.

The guy sped to walk next to her. "Why are you carrying a tree like that?" he asked.

"This is a vintage Max Mara coat. I'd rather not get poked right now." She laughed again. Clearly her subconscious had *ideas* about this guy and his cute frown. Although it wasn't mutual. He still looked annoyed at her. In fact, he might be the surliest person in the Winter Market. Which was fair—she'd just dropped a tree on him.

"Isn't it gorgeous?" she asked. "It's so *fragrant*. Here smell it." She turned so the tree was inches from the guy's face.

"I can't smell anything," he said, nose wrinkled.

"Weird. It's so strong! This is a Colorado blue spruce. I picked it because of the strong scent, and apparently, it's a long-lasting tree—not that I need it past December thirty-first. I hope it lasts that long. Oh!" Ruby felt the branches in her hands start to buckle. In what felt like comical slow motion, she scrambled to prevent the tree from hitting the surly guy again, ending up hugging it close to her while the trunk hit the ground.

"Oh my god," Ruby said. "I'm such a klutz." She stepped

away from the tree, holding the branches with her hands, and checked her coat. She winced when she saw spruce needles stuck to the wool. This was definitely a mistake. How was she going to get this thing home?

Suddenly, the guy took the tree from her hands.

"Oh, um, thank you! But I'm fine." Ruby reached out to take it back, but he'd already hoisted the thing onto his shoulder with what looked like no exertion at all. He was strong. She looked at his broad body carrying her tree on his denim-clad shoulder. It was…hot. He *should* be a lumberjack. Although, she noticed for the first time that there were dusty white splotches all over his jeans.

"I got it," he said. Or rather, he grunted.

Ruby exhaled. "It's okay! I can carry it!"

"You've already dropped it twice, so no, you clearly *can't* carry it. Where's your car?" he asked.

Ruby raised a brow. "A car? In this economy? Who can afford that?"

The guy blinked at her again. She could almost see his eye twitch with irritation. Ruby should shut up and take her tree home. But this guy didn't look like he was going to give it to her.

"I could call an Uber?" Her condo was only a few minutes' walk from the Distillery District, and she doubted an Uber would show up for such a short ride.

"They're not going to let you take a tree in their car," the guy said, exasperated. "Why did you buy a tree without a way to get it home?"

Ruby smiled. "Because it was pretty? I'm having a tree-decorating birthday party tomorrow. Today's my birthday."

He stared at her for several seconds. "You really should have thought this through."

Ruby bit her lip. He was right. There was no way she could walk the five minutes to her apartment without dropping the tree again or seriously hurting herself. Or ruining her coat. She could call a friend, but her cousin Marley wasn't able to lift heavy things yet after her surgery, and her friend Shayne had a photo shoot today.

"It's fine. I can take it," Ruby said, slipping off her coat and hanging it off her arm. "It's only a five-minute walk home. I can—"

"Which way?" the guy said, the tree still on his shoulder.

"Which way what?"

"Which way is *home*? I need to head back to work, so let's get going."

Ruby shook her head quickly. "Is this a pick-up, because I'm not looking for chivalry here."

The guy actually huffed a laugh at that, which completely changed his face. This grump was very cute. His gaze swept from her heels to her white mohair scarf. "You're not my type. Where am I taking this tree?"

Ouch. Ruby bit her lip. It was fine—based on how he was dressed, women in vintage red coats, Michael Kors shoes, and the perfect red lipstick for their skin tone weren't his type. But to hear an exceedingly attractive man with the most amazing skin she'd ever seen say he wasn't interested based on how she looked didn't feel nice. Maybe he was one of those guys who thought girls with makeup and nice hair were "high maintenance" (cars were high maintenance…people were *worth* it). Or more likely, it was Ruby perpetually sticking her foot in her mouth that had turned him off.

Ruby pointed to the grouping of condos in the distance. "I'm in there. Thank you."

"Okay, let's go," he said, walking past her with a whole entire tree on his shoulder like he was a chimney sweep carrying a broom or something.

Ruby took a few quick steps to catch up to him while putting her coat back on. "I appreciate this a lot," she said. "Did you say you need to get to work? Which is weird because you're all dusty, so I assume you came from work? That's dust, right? Or maybe it's flour! I know a baker; she's always covered in white when she's working. She's on maternity leave right now, which sucks because her bread is the best. Well, it doesn't suck for her, because her baby is gorgeous."

Ruby was rambling. Which she did when she was uncomfortable. Seriously, with her nervous motormouth, and her permanent foot-in-mouth, someone should really remove Ruby's mouth. But then she wouldn't be able to wear MAC's Ruby Woo—a red lipstick so perfect for her skin tone that she was convinced it was named after her.

The man kept walking, focused on the sidewalk in front of him. It was hard to keep up and incredibly awkward to walk with someone holding your Christmas tree without saying anything at all.

"So...do you work around here, too?" she asked. He didn't respond. This mystery lumberjack was a man of few words. "I mean, I assume you must. Oh! Do you work at the pet store! All that dust could be cat litter! I don't have a cat—I move too often. But I want to get one. Maybe after I move to England. British shorthairs are so cute! Why do they look so different from North American cats? Like—"

"It's not cat litter," he said. "It's drywall dust."

"Oh. So, you're in, like, construction? Cool! I work in the Distillery District. It's *gorgeous* this time of year, right? I love the Winter Market so much. It used to be called the Distillery Christmas Market, but they changed the name to be more inclusive, which is great. Not that I have anything against Christmas, but I mean, I'm all for inclusivity. I'm the manager at the Reid's Holiday pop-up store. You know Reid's, right? The department store in Yorkville? They have a mini store in the Winter Market only for the season. We have lots of gift-giving options, like designer ornaments, fragrances, and skin care. And services, too, like bespoke wrapping, custom gift baskets, and private shopping services for corporate clients. You should come by! I'd be happy to wrap some of your gifts for you, free of charge. As a thank-you for carrying my tree! You don't have to shop at the store for wrapping…" Ruby's voice trailed off. She hoped he didn't think she was implying that he couldn't afford to shop at Reid's. Because she didn't mean that at all. The store was expensive, but she knew people in construction could make good money, especially if he was a skilled tradesman.

"You work in a Christmas store?" he asked.

Ruby nodded. "Reid's Holiday. I know it's not the most original name. But…seriously, you should come by with gifts you need wrapped so I can repay your kindness."

He shook his head, making his blue beanie drag against

the needles of the tree on his shoulder. "I don't celebrate Christmas."

Ruby laughed awkwardly. "Oh, I don't either. I mean, not religiously. But I love this season! We have non-denominational wrap, too. And some Hanukkah paper, and Eid—"

"I don't do *any* holidays."

Ugh. She'd offended the lumberjack. But as usual, her mouth didn't know when to shut up. "But gifts don't have to just be for holidays, do they? You must have someone in your life that deserves a 'just because' gift! I love giving people little things for no reason, you know? To show you have their back. It's like—"

He turned sharply to face her again. Thankfully there was no one behind them, or he would have hit them with the tree.

"Do you always talk this much?"

Ruby gave an awkward smile. "Yes. You're taking my tree all the way home, and it would be rude if I said nothing, wouldn't it?"

The guy stared at her for several long seconds again before turning back around and pointing to the building in front of them. "That yours?" he asked.

"Yeah. Um, you don't have to bring it upstairs for me or anything. I mean, I can have the building concierge help."

He didn't respond. He climbed the two steps to the entry and rested her tree next to the door. "You can take it from here," he said, already walking back down the stairs and away.

"Wait," Ruby called out. The guy turned back to her. He was still frowning. Such a shame. The guy was breathtakingly gorgeous when he had laughed for half a second. "Thanks again for helping me. I really appreciate it," She smiled. "I think...I think maybe that was fate. I mean, if you hadn't found me, I'm sure I would have spent the rest of my birthday in the ER with a broken back. And I meant it—if you work nearby, come see me at Reid's Holiday so I can repay your generosity. I'm Ruby, by the way."

"My mother taught me to never leave a woman struggling. Happy birthday, Ruby," he said, that small smile appearing on his face for a moment before he turned and walked away.

Ruby watched the mystery man head back toward the Winter Market. She exhaled. She knew that she could be annoying. She hyperfixated on the things she loved, and she wasn't always great at noticing when she needed to chill about her passions. Or needed to stop talking.

Ah, but it didn't matter. So, what if this bah-humbug guy was immune to holiday cheer. He'd helped her a lot by bringing her tree home. And he even said happy birthday—the first in-person "happy birthday" she'd had this year.

Ruby wasn't going to let a run-in with a surly grump get in the way of enjoying every single moment of this season.

2

"DO YOU THINK I'M annoying?" Ruby asked while laying out neat rows of shortbread on a holly-printed plate. She hadn't been able to get that run-in with the tree-carrying guy out of her mind since he'd said happy birthday to her yesterday. "Like, do I take this Christmas stuff too far?"

"There is no such thing as *too far*," her friend Shayne said. He was hanging clear glass ornaments on the Colorado spruce. "The only people annoyed about Christmas are stick-in-the-muds, and we do not concern ourselves with their opinions. Holidays exist to be celebrated."

Exactly. Ruby was not taking the festivities too far—the shortbread wasn't even homemade. True, she'd made the gingerbread men and the individual Christmas puddings herself—but that was because she wanted her tiny apartment to be filled with her favorite scents for her birthday celebration: honey, cloves, ginger, cinnamon, and nutmeg, all mingling with the scent of her spruce Christmas tree.

"Who said you're annoying?" asked Ruby's cousin Marley,

who was helping Shayne with the tree. Marley was a personal stylist and Shayne was a photographer, and they had a better eye for space and design than Ruby, so she'd assigned them to tree duty when they'd arrived at her party.

"No one said I was annoying," Ruby said. Which was technically true—the lumberjack dude hadn't actually called her annoying. He'd certainly implied it, though. "This guy helped me carry my tree yesterday, and he was obviously irritated about how *enthusiastic* I was about the season."

"Ridiculous," Shayne said, shaking his head. "Openly *liking* anything is considered selling out these days. We are surrounded by capitalism and consumerism, but people look down at anyone who deigns to enjoy any of it. Not everyone singing 'Last Christmas' is buying in to the capitalist Kool-Aid—you bought these ornaments from a thrift store, and this sweater is from Poshmark." Shayne's sweater had a vintage-style image of Santa drinking a whisky by the fire on it. As always, he looked fabulous.

"So's this dress," Ruby added. It was a vintage Badgley Mischka, and she'd squealed when she saw it on the designer resale site last month. The impeccably fitting red dress was going to be her signature look for the holidays this year.

"Why do you think this guy got under your skin? That's not like you," asked Shayne's partner, Anderson, who was helping Ruby plate food at the coffee table. He was one of the most perceptive people Ruby had ever met—probably because of his job. He was also the quietest person in the friend group, which was ironic because he was one of four hosts on a daytime talk show—one of those shows where the hosts all talk over each other to get a word in. He had the nickname Oprah in their friend chat group, despite being a small Taiwanese Canadian man.

Ruby popped a small slice of fruitcake with marzipan into her mouth before answering. The sweet and spicy flavor punctuated with the creamy nuttiness of the marzipan reminded her that there was nothing wrong with loving this season. "I know. I shouldn't care what the guy thinks of me."

Maybe it was because he was Brown and said he didn't celebrate Christmas…so it unearthed some cultural guilt that Ruby shouldn't obsess over a Western holiday, either. But that was nonsense. Ruby's mother had been quite a devout Muslim, but she'd loved Christmas, too. Mom had loved the focus on family and giving, and said that if they were going to make Canada their home, they may as well love the things that Canadians loved. Of course, Mom had gone all out for Eid and other Muslim holidays, too. Mom would have been delighted that her only daughter still loved the Christmas season.

"Was the guy cute?" Shayne asked.

Ruby nodded. "Very. Too young for me, though."

At that, Shayne beamed at Anderson, who was about five years younger than him. "Nothing wrong with a younger man. So, you were into the guy, but he didn't feel the same, so your ego took a tiny hit. No shame in that. Put the Scrooge out of your mind. This is a birthday party! Where's Reena…I can't wait until you see your present!"

Reena, her husband Nadim, and their baby Aleem were the only ones missing from this party. Marley picked up her phone, presumably to text Reena. "They're at Nadim's friend's place," she said a few seconds later. "They're on their way—it's only five minutes from here."

Shayne laughed. "They have friends other than us?"

"Shocking, I know," Marley said. "Apparently she's one of Nadim's London friends. Reena said she's been going through a rough time, so they took the baby to meet her. Babies always cheer people up."

That was true, but there was another nugget of information there that piqued Ruby's interest. Nadim had grown up between England and Tanzania, and he still had a lovely British accent. Ruby hadn't known he had any British friends in Toronto. "His friend from *London* lives near here?"

Marley laughed, plopping on the small green sofa in front of Ruby's bed. This apartment was a bachelor—which meant it was pretty much one big room. Actually, *big* was probably overstating it. "Are you going to make the poor woman read Austen to you now?"

Ruby frowned. "No. But considering I'm moving to London in like, six weeks, maybe I should meet her? Get some tips or something?"

"Why don't you get tips from Nadim?" Shayne asked. "He lived there, too."

"I've tried," Ruby said. "But he was useless. Apparently when he lived in London, Nadim only went to nightclubs or Michelin-starred restaurants. He was a super-rich trust-fund brat back then, remember?" Ruby loved to hear stories of Nadim's UK debauchery, especially since he was such a goofy nerd and devoted family man now.

"If this woman is Nadim's friend, she was probably a

trust-fund brat, too," Marley said. "Hey, do you have a star for the top of the tree? Didn't you get a Swarovski one on clearance last year?"

"Yes!" Ruby had forgotten about that star. She knelt near her bed to get at the storage boxes down there. She'd been so excited when she found it on a clearance shelf—but it was bright red crystal and was all wrong for her pink tree. Maybe a part of her knew that she'd have a much better tree this year. She found it in a box of summer shoes and handed it to Marley.

"Maybe this woman can help you get a job there, though," Anderson said. "Did you get any offers yet?"

"Sort of," Ruby said. "Two boutiques on High Street said they'll likely offer when I get there. And three more told me to call them for an interview the moment I land." She'd known it wouldn't be hard to get a job. Ruby moved a lot, and finding a new job was always the easiest part of moving. Her résumé was an impressive list of sales and management positions in the best luxury retail stores in Canada—and she had excellent references, too.

But none of the places where she really *wanted* to work in the UK had called her back.

"Nothing from hotels?" Marley asked.

"No. I've been completely ghosted by every hotel I've applied at."

After years of planning, Ruby was finally moving to the UK for one main reason: to fulfill her and her mother's lifelong dream to run their own business there—an inn or a bed and breakfast in the English countryside.

About three years ago, Ruby had learned that her mother

had set up a trust with money from her personal savings account, payable to Ruby ten years after her mother's passing. There was a letter enclosed, in which Ruby's mother wrote that she was sorry she wouldn't be there to carry out their dream together, but with this money, Ruby could do it on her own. The ten-year wait was so Ruby's father wouldn't find out about the money and try to claim it as his own, but it was also so Ruby wouldn't get it until, as her mother put it, "you know who you are."

Even with the money, Ruby knew achieving the dream now was a long shot, so she'd been approaching the plan rationally and practically. The first step had been getting a visa to live, work, and own a business in the UK. The next step had been to find a job in the hospitality industry there, so she could learn more about hotel management while looking for her own property. But it turned out that getting a job in a UK hotel as a Canadian with literally zero experience in the field and no contacts was next to impossible.

"So, are you going to work in a store, then?" Marley asked.

Ruby shook her head. "Nope. I have enough savings to last a bit—I'm going to hit the pavement the old-fashioned way when I get there. I'll walk into every hotel in London until one of them hires me."

There was a courtesy knock at the door then before Nadim and Reena noisily came in, holding baby Aleem. Everyone rushed to greet them and help get the baby and all the baby's stuff inside. And then everyone wanted to see Aleem's Santa outfit under the heavy snowsuit he was wearing. And wanted to squeeze his cheeks and then take pictures of him. Thankfully, Aleem tolerated his doting aunties and uncles well.

After the chaos the baby brought, they all sat around Ruby's coffee table. Shayne was holding the baby in one arm and a mug of Ruby's signature chai eggnog in the other.

"I'm sorry we're late," Reena said as she made herself a plate of cookies and fruitcake. "We were at Jasmine's longer than expected. Poor thing's going through *a lot*. She left her husband right after she started her own business."

"Oh, that sucks," Ruby said. "Right before the holidays, too."

"It doesn't suck," Nadim said. "It's *good*. I've only met the guy twice, but Derek is a stuck-up, arrogant douche. But it is hard for Jasmine and her kids right now."

Reena nodded. "She's got twin five-year-old girls. And no family of her own in Toronto. Jasmine is such a sweetheart." Reena looked at her husband. "I have no idea how she ever fit in with your London friends."

"We used to call her the Angelic One. I was closer to her twin, Ayesha, anyway. Hey, Marley, can I invite Jasmine to your Caroling party next month? She doesn't know a lot of people in Toronto."

"Yeah, absolutely," Marley said. She and Shayne, who shared a house, threw a big holiday cocktail party every year. Shayne and Marley had been best friends since high school and had been through a lot together.

"She'll need a babysitter," Shayne said. "No one under eighteen allowed." He looked down at baby Aleem in his arms. "Not even you, stinkers. You have to wait seventeen years for your invitation."

Reena grinned. "Hey, Ruby, did you get a date for the party yet? Because we know someone who would be *perfect* for you."

"Yes! Ruby needs a man." Shayne nodded vigorously. "The Caroling party is couples only this year!"

Ruby exhaled. She shouldn't be surprised at this. In the last year every person in this little friend group had experienced a major life change. Reena and Nadim had baby Aleem. Both Shayne and Marley, who'd previously been chronically single and commitment phobic, were now in committed relationships. And since all her friends were quite smugly in happy little families now, they were obsessed with changing Ruby's relationship status, too.

"Seriously? You're making your party couples only?" Ruby asked.

Marley gave Shayne a warning glance. "*No.* Shayne's being silly. You don't have to bring someone if you don't want to. I mean, of course you're welcome to if you meet someone, but—"

"I know exactly who!" Shayne said loud enough to make Aleem stir. Reena shot him a warning glare. "Sorry," Shayne whispered loudly. "Anderson's cousin Jonathan is single. He's very cute. Imagine John Cho in that space movie. *Star Hike* or something…"

"*Star Trek?*" Anderson asked, laughing.

Shayne nodded. "Yes, that! Jonathan is *adorable*…and single. Smart, too. He's an anesthesiologist. You know what they say about anesthesiologists, don't you?" He wagged his eyebrows suggestively.

Marley gave Shayne a confused look. "They put people to sleep?"

"They're full of gas!" Nadim suggested.

"Shush, all you," Shayne said. "They are…like useful or something."

"The guy we had in mind for her is a doctor, too!" Reena said. "Maybe she can check out their Rate My MD scores and pick between them. Or try them both out! Nothing wrong with a second opinion!"

Ruby shook her head. "Or I can try neither of them out. I'm moving in, like, a month and a half."

"That's plenty long enough for a fling with someone who understands your *anatomy*," Shayne said wagging his brows.

"I'm not going to date a *doctor*!" Ruby said. "Plus, I'm literally working six days a week in December—it's a terrible time for a fling."

"Man I am *not* going to miss retail in December," Marley said. She'd worked at Reid's, too, until she started freelancing as a stylist. They all talked about how Ruby could possibly *enjoy* working in retail at Christmastime.

"What do you have against doctors?" Anderson asked during a conversation lull.

"Oh, nothing." Ruby forced a chuckle. "They're great. Just too committed to their jobs, right? Won't make time for little old me!" She glanced at Marley.

Marley gave Ruby a sympathetic look. She knew better than anyone else in the room why Ruby wasn't a huge fan of doctors. Marley had been there thirteen years ago when their entire lives were consumed with doctors and medical facilities. She'd been there when doctors hadn't been able to prevent Ruby's mother from dying of breast cancer.

The others in the room must have caught on, though, because everyone was awkwardly silent for too long. Ruby finally couldn't take it anymore. She had to say something.

"So…Nadim, you said your friend is from London? Does she go back often?"

"Yeah, actually, she does," Nadim said. "We were telling her about your move. You'll love this, Ruby. She came to Canada for school and stayed after meeting her husband here. But her twin sister Ayesha is still back in the UK, and she's working in their father's *hotel* business."

Ruby nearly dropped her gingerbread man. "You have a friend in the *hotel* industry in England? Why didn't you tell me?"

"I had no idea Ayesha was working for her father. Last I heard she was a yacht girl in Monaco. Before that, she called herself an event planner—I don't think she ever planned any events." He shook his head, smiling. "I had some wild times with the Hakim twins."

Shayne snorted at that. "Ah, so the one in England is the *bad* twin, and the one here is the *good* twin. To be honest, I wish the bad one lived here. She sounds *chaotic*."

Nadim nodded. "She used to be. Now Ayesha's running a posh boutique hotel in Spitalfields. I'm shocked she's a responsible businesswoman now."

Ruby didn't care how chaotic this girl used to be—she *needed* to get an introduction to her. "So, their father owns more than one hotel?"

He grinned. "Yeah, he owns a bunch. All in the UK. And this is the good part, Ruby: Jasmine told us that apparently their father recently got a new property—an inn in the middle of the UK countryside. In Cheshire, near Manchester."

Oh my god. Ruby grinned. Forget the chaotic twin; she

needed to meet their *father*. This could be the foot in the door to make her and her mother's dream a reality.

"Apparently, their mother was tired of city living," Reena said, "and convinced their father it was time to semi-retire as country innkeepers."

Anderson rolled his eyes. "They probably turned it into a cookie-cutter clone of his other properties."

Nadim shrugged. "Maybe. But Jasmine mentioned that he's having trouble with staffing there—she said it's so hard to find people who *want* to be in the boring English countryside."

"I *want* to be in the boring English countryside!" Ruby said. It was her dream. She could almost taste the scones and milky tea.

Nadim grinned. "I know. Like I said, Jasmine's a bit of a mess right now…and she really has no influence in her father's business decisions, but I think we should all get together. Soon."

Reena nodded. "She'll love you, Ruby. And once she loves you, it will be easy to get an introduction to her family in the UK. They're Ismaili Muslim, too."

Ruby grinned. This was fate, she was sure of it. Ruby, as well as Marley, Nadim, and Reena, were all raised as Ismaili Muslims. It was a small sect of Islam, and followers tended to look out for each other, so knowing this family was from the same community as her was in itself a foot in the door. "Yes. We can have tea. There's an adorable café in the Distillery District. You said her business is nearby…What does she do?"

"She's a physician," Reena said. "Two young kids and her own practice—I can't imagine having two babies at once." Reena shuddered, then looked at Nadim. "Thank goodness you didn't impregnate me with *twins*. I would have left you if you did. One is more than enough."

Nadim frowned. "You'd leave me if you had twins?"

"Good point. I'd need your help with the twins. I would have done something, though. Stopped baking bread for you, maybe."

Nadim's eyes widened, then he pantomimed Reena stabbing him in the heart. Reena was a baker, and Nadim claims he fell in love with her bread before her. Ruby could believe it. Her bread was excellent.

At that, Aleem let out a wail. "He's hungry. Here, pass the little man over. He's also a fan of my food."

While Reena nursed her baby, they all talked about their holiday plans while eating Christmas cookies and drinking chai eggnog. Ruby was in a fantastic mood, thanks to this possible connection to a UK hotel family. Her thirty-fourth trip around the sun was shaping up to be her best one yet.

MONDAY MORNING RUBY WAS at the back of the store tidying the small lingerie section after the weekend rush.

The other person working today, Jenisha, interrupted her as she was straightening cashmere robes on the hangers. "There's a man here who asked for you by name." Jenisha had plenty of teasing in her voice.

Ruby frowned. "Man? What man?"

Jenisha shrugged. "He's cute. I'm not a fan of the beanie, though. I wish men would wear formal hats again."

Beanie. Was Lumberjack actually taking her up on her offer of complimentary gift wrapping? Ruby turned to look at the front of the store, and yes, it was him. She cringed. Anderson was right when he'd said on Saturday that Ruby didn't usually care what people thought of her. But this guy had gotten under her skin more than most.

"I owe him a favor." Exhaling, Ruby headed to the man, the click of her red boots reverberating over the worn wood floors in the store. She put on her best retail smile. "So wonderful to see you again! Are you here for some gift wrapping?"

The guy narrowed his eyes at her. "Are you wearing novelty Christmas ornament earrings?"

Ruby shook her head, smiling. "No, I'm wearing *designer* Christmas ornament earrings. From Milan." She'd been wearing Christmas earrings the day they met, too, but her shoulder-length hair had been down in loose waves then. Now with her hair slicked back in a tidy ponytail, the earrings were more visible.

The guy literally scoffed at that. "What's the point of expensive jewelry you can only wear a few weeks a year?"

Ruby sighed. If he didn't like Christmas, why come into a holiday store? This was easily the Grinchiest person in the Winter Market. It was a shame, because in the soft lighting of the store, the man was even more attractive than he'd been outside on Friday. He was dressed similarly—in jeans and a thick, lined denim jacket. Instead of a flannel, though, today he had a dark green sweatshirt under the jacket. His blue beanie was still pulled down low, and his smooth skin still practically glowed. Ruby agreed with Jenisha—she wasn't a fan of the knit beanie. She hated that neck-beard incels had ruined fedoras and trilbies for the rest of society, because this guy's classically handsome features would look great in a fedora. Like a Brown Clive Owen.

Ugh. Ruby needed to stop giving cute men makeovers in her head. After her last few relationships, she should know that fixer-uppers were *not* worth it.

She gestured to the white canvas tote bag he was carrying. "So, do you have something for me to wrap?"

He nodded. "Yeah. I'm terrible at gift wrapping. I didn't know there were places where someone would wrap things for you."

Ruby smiled and motioned him over to the gift-wrap counter. "Let's see what you have."

When they got to the counter, he pulled four books out of his tote bag. "They can all be wrapped together," he said. "And I *will* pay."

"Nonsense!" Ruby said. "It's on me. This is repaying a favor, isn't it?" Upper management didn't mind if Ruby comped gift wrapping for some customers, because they knew that the more time someone spent in this curated space, the more likely they would open their wallets. That's why there were so many impulse buys near the gift-wrap station, like fragrance sets and leather gloves.

Ruby looked at the four books he'd placed on the white marble counter: two popular book-club fiction titles and two children's picture books. She doubted very much they were all for the same person—unless the person equally loved Fancy Nancy and Reese's Book Club picks. She pointed to the wrapping paper samples on the counter. "Do you have a paper preference? Reid's signature colors this season are warm burgundy and rich cream, but we also have more traditional holiday colors…royal blue, rose gold, antique silver—"

The man frowned. "Aren't Christmas colors red and green?"

"Reid's selects a signature color story every year." She pointed out the glossy cream wrapping paper and the deep burgundy satin ribbon. "Soft neutrals with jewel tones are on trend this season. But if you'd prefer—"

"They're not Christmas gifts, though." His brow was furrowed. "I don't need Christmas paper."

"That's why Reid's signature colors are perfect. They're

more about *seasonality* than a traditional holiday look." She glanced at the books. "I'm sure she would love this palate."

He tilted his head. "How do you know these are for a woman?"

Ruby smiled. "Apologies for making assumptions. So, the rich cream, then?"

"Why do you call colors two words?" He pointed at the paper samples. "*Rose* gold, *rich* cream, *warm* burgundy…Why can't you just say pink, beige, or red?"

"Because this is rose gold, not pink." She flashed a winsome smile.

He harrumphed at that. This guy was a literal caricature of a grumpy Christmas hater. He was so on the nose that Ruby wondered if she was being filmed for some sort of YouTube prank. But she couldn't deny that she was egging him on a bit. He was too easy to tease, and she found that she liked the look of his confused head tilt, as well as his brows furrowed in annoyance. But she should be kinder. She couldn't forget that he had done her a major favor by carrying her tree to her building Friday.

"How about this *purple*?" she asked. The deep eggplant would work for all genders, and although she thought it was perfectly appropriate for the holiday season, she assumed he wouldn't find it too Christmassy.

He nodded. "For the adult books. Pink for the kids' books."

Ruby turned to the rolls of paper on dispensers behind her and pulled out a piece of eggplant paper large enough to wrap the two adult books together. She centered the books in the middle and started folding one side of paper up to meet the center of the books. After folding the other side of the paper to meet the first, she pressed the creases crisp with her fingernails, then taped it.

"Why are you wrapping it like that?"

Ruby forced a smile while exhaling. What could he possibly have a problem with now? This was literally the standard way of wrapping presents. She wasn't doing any of those fancy Instagram origami wrapping techniques. "Like what?"

He pointed at the paper. "You folded the tape under itself."

"Oh, this is gift wrapping the Reid's way. No visible tape makes for a cleaner look." He still looked annoyed, so she added, "It's company policy."

He didn't say anything to that and silently watched Ruby finish wrapping the adult books. Who was all this for, anyway? Wife and kid? He wasn't wearing a ring—it was a habit to check whenever a man came into the store, so she'd know what to show him. Married men tended to buy robes, pajamas, or skin care sets, while unmarried men bought sexier lingerie or fragrances. This man seemed too surly to have a wife and daughter. But what did she know—it was possible he'd found a partner as grumpy as he was. Or it was possible that his grumpiness was only for the outside world, and he treated his family much better.

She really hoped it was the latter. She grew up with a surly, short-tempered father, and she wouldn't wish it on anyone. Especially the little girl who'd be getting these Fancy Nancy books.

Without asking first, Ruby selected a wide cream ribbon to go with the eggplant paper instead of the gold she would have normally used. The cream seemed less Christmassy. After tying the ribbon in a simple bow (she elected not to add any sprigs of greenery), she moved on to wrapping the child's gift with the rose gold paper.

"I meant it, I'll pay for the wrapping service," he said. "How much is it for the two gifts?" He took out his wallet, and Ruby was surprised to see that it was a quality leather piece. She'd expected a canvas wallet. With Velcro. And also, there was something odd about the way this lumberjack spoke. He was dressed very stereotypical blue-collar Canadian, but he had a slight upper-class cadence, if there was such a thing in Canada. He was probably a generational wealth guy slumming in his denim. Hipster.

Ruby shook her head as she tied the same cream ribbon around the rose gold gift. "No, I insist. It's the least I can do after you were so kind to help me with my tree." She added a little pink teddy bear charm to the center of the bow.

"Thank you," he said. He was still frowning.

"Of course."

"You're..." He hesitated. "Different here. You're much more polite, and not rambling,"

Ruby had to strain not to laugh at that. She flashed her most charming sales associate smile. "I'm at work." She narrowed her eyes. "But...you prefer me like this, don't you?" she asked, letting a little hint of flirtation into her voice.

And the expression on his face was the best one yet. Surprised and a little embarrassed. The grump was actually blushing. Interesting. He was flattered by Ruby's flirting. This guy was, maybe, a tiny bit *into* her.

Ruby decided she wanted to prolong this interaction. She

slid his two gifts across the counter to him. "Would you like me to show you around the store? We have some lovely gift options for any occasion." She met the man's eyes. Even considered batting her lashes a bit. Yeah, this guy's aesthetic wasn't her usual type at all, but did that matter? She was leaving the country in six weeks. And as grumpy as this lumberjack could be, he was clearly strong. Built. This could be a fun way to end her days in Canada.

He looked at her with those intense dark eyes before nodding slightly, a tiny smile reaching his eyes. "Okay. Show me your store, Ruby."

The sound of her name on his lips did all sorts of things to her. "Of course," she said, "follow me."

She started at the back of the store. Reid's Holiday didn't carry a lot of clothes, since the focus was on gift giving, but they did have a small lingerie and sleepwear section since pajamas, robes, and sexy underwear were popular gifts. The mystery man didn't say much as Ruby pointed out the silk pajamas and stockings. When she showed him a cashmere robe, he reached out to run his fingers lightly over the soft pink fabric. His hands were sexy. Soft-looking, which was surprising, considering he worked in construction.

"It feels decadent, doesn't it," Ruby said, letting her own fingers graze the luxurious knit. She'd love to own one of these robes, but she needed to save money for her move. "Anyone would appreciate this robe as a gift. I love fine fabrics against my skin." She resisted the urge to say *bare* skin, but she hoped that's what he was imagining.

He turned to her, his gaze sweeping from her red patent

boots to her cream wide-legged trousers and, finally, her fitted red satin wrap blouse, and Ruby was sure she saw some appreciation in his eyes. His hand was still on the robe's sleeve. "It's quality cashmere," he said.

Ruby smiled. The man knew luxury. He liked sensual things. He wasn't nearly as grumpy as she thought, just quiet and thoughtful with a tiny case of resting grump face.

"We also have a selection of fine fragrances," she said, guiding him toward the fragrance and skin care counter.

"Oh!" the man said, surprised, "the new Le Labo men's. I didn't think it was out yet."

Ruby beamed. Le Labo was a newer fragrance house. And this new scent totally matched this man's rugged, manly vibe. "Are you a fragrance enthusiast?"

His brows knit together. "I wouldn't call myself an enthusiast. I do like cologne, though."

Still smiling, Ruby went behind the counter and took out the tester bottle of the newest Le Labo release. "I would say liking fine fragrances makes you an enthusiast. This one is *sensuous*. Let's see how it reacts with your body chemistry."

He extended his arm so his wrist peeked out from under his heavy shirt and jacket. And it was a beautiful wrist. His skin was such a warm brown, and so, so smooth. She gave him a small secret smile before spritzing the fragrance on his wrist. When she looked at his face again, he also had a small smile on his lips, mirroring hers.

Their eyes were locked for several seconds while Ruby mentally cheered for herself. She knew this subtle dance well. She and this man were on the same wavelength, each anticipating the other's actions perfectly. She wasn't being any more friendly or flirtatious than she was with any customer, but she had no doubt that the grump would be asking for her phone number before leaving Reid's Holiday today. And despite her misgivings about his temperament the day they met, or about starting a fling right now, Ruby fully intended to give it to him. Chemistry like this shouldn't be wasted.

"There. Let's give it a few moments to let it settle," she said. "This fragrance changes quite a bit as it interacts with your individual skin. In the meantime, can I show you some skin care sets? We have gift sets for both men and women." The man had some of the nicest skin Ruby had ever seen—maybe he was a skin care enthusiast, too.

But the man's smile instantly left his face. "No, thank you," he said curtly.

"Come now, this set is quite popular." Ruby held up a men's moisturizer, toner, and night cream set. "I guarantee *you* will love it. This formula was developed by a well-known designer—"

At that, the man's Grinchiest Grump in the Winter Market expression returned, guffawing at Ruby's suggestion that he would love it. Loudly.

Ruby raised a brow. "Not a fan of luxury skin care?"

"*Luxury.* You mean overpriced, right? I guarantee the cost of that packaging is more than the cost of the ingredients in that formula." The flirtation was gone from his face.

Ruby's eyes widened. What happened to them being on the same wavelength? "I assure you, only the best quality ingredients are used—"

He shook his head. "Don't be so gullible. Those cosmetic conglomerates are gaslighting you to think it's their multi-hyphen ingredients that are helping your skin instead of good old-fashioned emollients and sun protection." He waved his hands over the gift sets on the counter. "This is all overpriced, useless crap."

Ruby exhaled. Gaslighting? *Crap?* The worst part of his rant was that his voice sounded so posh and snooty now. Yeah, he'd definitely grown up in a better part of the city.

The guy had gone too far. Ruby didn't take his comment as an insult to the store or to the good people at Lancôme, either. He was insulting *her*. Ruby was a skin care girlie, and she'd met people like this guy before. People who thought anything that women value—makeup, fine skin care, even adjectives before colors—was worthless. This one was particularly bad, using terms like *emollients* as if he knew what they meant. He was probably parroting some dudebro he saw on YouTube. Men like this really thought women had little value. Maybe he was the right type to wear a fedora after all. She again felt bad for the little girl whose gift she had just wrapped.

He wasn't going to ask for her phone number, and if he did, Ruby wouldn't give it to him. He'd insulted her, the store, and the whole freaking holiday season. Time to get him out. Ruby kept smiling, though, because years of retail had not only given her supple, dewy soft skin, thanks to employee discounts, but also thick skin. "You said your mother taught you never to leave a person struggling. Did she also teach you that if you can't say anything nice you shouldn't say anything at all?"

"Oh, come on," he said, rolling his eyes. "Even a Christmas

Cheer Lady like you must admit that the markup on creams and lotions this time of year is ridiculous." He held up a box from a new line from Paris that was enriched with the essence of juniper berries. "You're paying a fortune for gimmicks and scents. It's a rip-off. All you should use is—"

Ruby finally lost her smile. "Don't *should* on me, mister," she said, maintaining her calm and pleasant tone of voice despite wanting to spray him with the worst-smelling men's cologne in the store before kicking that fine ass out. "You've come into my place of work, where I'm trying to earn a living, and insulted things I love. Christmas, luxury gift wrap, and skin care. You even managed to insult the concept of adjectives. I know this season isn't for everyone, but it's bringing a hell of a lot of people joy…something a grump like you could honestly use. Now I'm going to have to ask you to leave. I think we can consider any debts repaid and can forget we've ever been acquainted. I look forward to hopefully never seeing that grumpy face of yours again."

The man stared at her for a few moments, gaze shifting from her red lips to her holiday earrings. She couldn't believe she thought he was into her. He clearly hated everything he saw.

"Apologies," he said. "Thank you for the gift wrap." He turned and walked out of the store with his deep eggplant and rose-gold wrapped gifts (with natural cream ribbon) without saying goodbye.

"Good riddance," Ruby said once he was out of sight in the Winter Market. She hoped the Christmas music playing out there was giving him hives.

"Sooo…who was that?" Jenisha asked as she walked toward

Ruby. Her tone made it clear that she hadn't heard Ruby telling him off. Or hadn't heard him insult everything she loved.

"That was the most infuriating man I've ever met." She didn't even get the chance to smell the Le Labo on him.

Jenisha nodded. "Cute, though. How do you know him?"

Ruby shook her head. "I don't know him. He helped carry my Christmas tree, and I stupidly told him I would wrap a gift for him as payment. He's a complete ass."

"Oh!" Jenisha said. "He carried a tree! Thank you for that mental image."

The door opened then. It was Gwendolyn, the store's assistant manager. And the expression on her face made it clear she wasn't in a good mood. Gwendolyn (never Gwen, always Gwendolyn), walked around with the air of someone who didn't need to be working at all—and spoke to Ruby like Ruby was miles below her, despite Ruby being her literal manager. Ruby was accustomed to working with these kinds of divas—stores like Reid's attracted a lot of Ladies Who Lunch types who could no longer afford the lifestyle and had to work for a living. Ruby was not going to miss Gwendolyn at all when she left the city in a month.

"Jenisha, Alana Schwartz will be coming in at two for some bespoke gift baskets. Candles and coordinating scents should be pulled beforehand to make her experience streamlined. Ms. Schwartz will be having a half-caf oat latte; put the order in at Sophie's now, and pick it up at five minutes before two."

Ruby raised one brow. Seriously? Sending another sales associate to get her customer's coffee? "Gwendolyn, Jenisha has to stay here for walk-ins, as I also have an appointment at two.

And you know it's your responsibility to prepare for your own customers."

Gwendolyn exhaled, probably counting to ten under her breath about the fact that the Brown daughter of a seamstress was her superior. She opened the drawer behind the counter. "I cannot find a lint roller. The medical clinic near the day spa is renovating—I was caught in an absolute cloud of dust on my way here. How could the Winter Market allow a business to renovate now? It's a nuisance."

Oh. Was that where the surly tree guy was doing his drywall work? There was a small strip of professional offices on the street leading to the Winter Market. They were technically not part of the Distillery District, so it was doubtful the Winter Market organizers could stop the construction.

"I got the best dirt on that place from my friend who works at the spa," Jenisha said. She was completely unfazed by Gwendolyn trying to use her as her personal assistant. "So, the office was under construction a few months ago, but construction stopped suddenly. Apparently, the doctor who owns it left her husband out of the blue, and he froze their accounts so she couldn't pay the contractors to finish the job. The husband was caught completely unaware—rumor is that she's having an affair with a much younger man."

"Ugh." Ruby cringed. That was horrible. "But now she's finishing the construction?"

"Yeah, my friend says the boy-toy has been there every day finishing the work. She has kids, too." Jenisha shook her head.

"It's a terrible time to split up a family like that," Gwendolyn said. "At Christmas!"

Ruby frowned. That reminded her of Nadim's friend. Could it be the same doctor? "Do you know the doctor's name?"

"Dr. Hashim or Hakim or something like that."

Ruby exhaled. Sounded like Jasmine Hakim. But Reena said she was a complete sweetheart—would she cheat on her husband with a younger man?

Oh! Was she having an affair with the tree-carrying grump? The younger man who was finishing construction at her practice? Did Ruby just wrap gifts for Jasmine and her twins from her *affair partner*?

This complicated things. But Ruby remembered Nadim saying it was the *husband* who was the asshole in the breakup. The whole situation sounded messy. Normally, Ruby preferred to stay far away from that kind of drama, but she still wanted to get to know Jasmine to eventually get an introduction to her sister and father in the UK. "I think she's a friend of a friend," Ruby said. "I should introduce myself."

This cheating or heartbroken physician could be the ticket to making Ruby and her mother's dreams come true. Ruby was more determined than ever to take hold of the connection and make it work for her. Even if it meant more contact with the grumpy tree-carrying guy.

RUBY DID SOME GOOGLING on the Hakim family hotels during her break. The landing page for the corporation was sleek and modern, and after looking around a bit, she saw that the CEO was a handsome man in his sixties who was unfortunately named Hakim M. Hakim. What had his parents been thinking? The Hakim Hotel Group (because apparently Hakim M. Hakim wanted one more Hakim on his business card) owned several hotels, all in England: two in suburban London, and one each in Birmingham and Bristol. Plus, a new boutique hotel in London called the Raj, and the country inn near Manchester.

Ruby opened a text in her friend chat group—called Shayne Freaking Loves Olives, for some reason.

> **Ruby:** Nadim—is your friend Jasmine's office near the Distillery District? Because there is apparently a doctor with an office here going through a messy breakup and maybe having an affair with a younger man.

Nadim: Yeah, that's her. She's a dermatologist. She's having an affair? Seriously?

Ruby: I think it's with the hot tree guy. He's doing construction in the area.

Shayne: Oh my goodness, why didn't you tell me she's a dermatologist! I've been trying to get in to see one for a fucking year. I have this thing I need looked at.

Marley: Ew. Shayne we're not supposed to talk about medical stuff on this group chat. This is a safe space with no health-related discussions.

Shayne: Ruby started it. She mentioned a doctor.

Anderson: I'm with Marley. Ruby mentioned a person...that's vastly different than mentioning the weird growth on your

Ruby had no idea why Anderson didn't finish that sentence, but she was glad for it.

Nik: What dermatologist? What hot tree guy? Who's Jasmine? I have FOMO!!!

Ruby laughed. Marley's boyfriend Nik, who was currently in LA to shoot a movie, was always complaining in the group chat that he had no idea what they were all talking about.

> **Nadim:** I am not introducing any of you to Jasmine if you are going to show her your random skin growths or accuse her of cheating with the guy that Ruby threw her tree at. She's going through a crisis. She doesn't need drama from you weirdos.

Ruby exhaled. If this woman was going through a hard time, then maybe it would be a good idea not to harass her. But Ruby *had* to meet her.

> **Ruby:** Maybe tell her that you have a friend who works in the Distillery and ask if she's looking for a local friend? I don't have any rashes, and I won't tell her about the gossip I heard.
>
> **Reena:** Better idea: let's invite her and her kids to join us for the Santa Claus Parade on Sunday.
>
> **Ruby:** That's brilliant! I can get us a reservation for dinner after, too.

Despite their baby being an infant who won't remember any of it, Reena and Nadim were taking Aleem to the Toronto

Santa Claus Parade, which was the city's official kickoff to the holiday season. When they asked in the chat group who wanted to join them, everyone except Ruby made polite (or not so polite) excuses. But Ruby was determined to squeeze in all the holiday joy she could before she left the country.

Nadim: Okay, I'll ask her and let you know.

Ruby grinned. There. She was going to meet Jasmine Hakim. It suddenly occurred to her that the Christmas Grinch might have had that skin care rant because he's dating, or having an affair with, this cougar dermatologist. But despite Jasmine's questionable taste in affair partners, Ruby was determined to make this woman her friend.

On the day of the parade, Ruby took extra care in putting together the perfect outfit, since she would not only be joining the whole city in officially kicking off the holiday season, but she also needed to impress Jasmine Hakim so Jasmine would introduce Ruby to her family in the UK. Ruby decided on her red Max Mara coat and her cream vegan fur hat. Usually, this hat and coat combination was a little too on the nose (she looked like Santa), but this was the Santa Claus Parade, so it was fine. She added a black leather bag, and instead of gloves, she dug out her white vintage fur muff. Underneath she wore dark jeans, her black leather boots, and a slim red sweater. And of course, her signature red lipstick and adorable enamel Christmas tree earrings.

The weather was perfect—not too cold and clear skies, and it seemed the whole city came out for the parade. One of the things that Ruby loved about this season was that wherever she was, she could be surrounded by simultaneous joy. She could never feel alone during the holiday season because there were always so many people celebrating the same thing as her.

Ruby stopped to get a gingerbread latte before finding Nadim and Reena sitting at the corner where they'd agreed to meet. They'd brought five chairs—borrowed from Reena's parents, which were set up in a straight line with Reena and Nadim sitting together in the middle of them. Aleem was in a snowsuit strapped to Reena's chest. Ruby peeked at the baby before saying hello.

"He's out cold. Drunk on breast milk," Reena said.

"I hope he doesn't sleep through his first parade," Ruby said.

"Better than screaming through it. We're just here for the pictures—there's no way he's going to remember this."

Nadim shook his head, smiling. "No, we're here because I've never been to a Santa Claus parade and now that I have a kid, I have an excuse."

"You don't need to have kids for a holiday parade," Ruby said. "I came alone last year. And the year before I went alone to the parade in Montreal. Where's Jasmine? She's still coming, right?"

Nadim nodded. "She's on her way." He looked at his wife. "She's…um…You tell her, Ree."

Ruby frowned as she sat in the chair next to Reena. "Tell me what?"

Reena smiled a smile that told Ruby she probably wouldn't

like what Reena was about to say. "Okay, so, remember there was that doctor I wanted to set you up with, but you said you didn't want to date a doctor?"

"Reena, what did you do?"

"It's how we got Jasmine to agree to come today! She's been trying to set her brother Rashid up with someone. He's only here for a few months to help her out, so he's not looking for anything long term either. Jasmine thinks he's lonely hanging out with only her and the twins. She wants him to meet people in Toronto."

Ruby did not want to be anyone's pity holiday date. But charming and befriending *two* members of the Hakim family would give her an even better chance of connecting with their father. "Okay, what do we know about him?"

"Not a lot," Nadim said. "I've never met him. He's older than Jasmine and Ayesha, and he's also a dermatologist—Jasmine says she went into the field because of her older brother. He's only here for a few months to take Jasmine's patients while she gets back on her feet."

"Jasmine showed us a picture. He's very handsome," Reena said, grinning. "Posh British guys are totally your type."

True, but…"Wait, the dermatologist's name is *Rashid*? Like, Dr. Rash?"

Reena laughed at that, which made the baby make a noise of annoyance. "I never realized. Why go into dermatology with that name?"

Good question. Their father was Hakim Hakim, and the son was Dr. Rash the skin doctor. This family was ridiculous. Like a Monty Python skit.

"Okay, let's do this," Ruby said. "Introduce me to this Dr.

Rash—I'll be all poise and charm and make him fall in love with me so his father will give me a job in England."

"I see them," Nadim said, looking out onto the street and waving to someone in the distance. Ruby looked over and saw a petite brown-skinned woman holding hands with a young girl with curly hair and a purple coat.

Jasmine was pretty, with smooth, almost luminous skin (because she was a dermatologist), huge brown eyes, and pink lips. Ruby wasn't sure what she was expecting, but she looked the furthest thing from a cougar having an affair with a young drywaller.

But where was Dr. Rash?

She saw the second child. She had straight hair, but was wearing the same purple double-breasted coat as the child with Jasmine. And when Ruby saw the man holding the little girl's hand, she nearly dropped her latte.

"Oh my god," Ruby said. "Jasmine brought her *affair partner* to the Santa Claus Parade?" Because the man holding the other daughter's hand was, without a doubt, Ebenezer Grump himself. This was the guy who she told off after wrapping his gifts the other day.

"What?" Reena said. "That's the—"

"The guy who carried my tree home. Who I heard she cheated on her husband with."

Nadim frowned, shaking his head. "No, that's her brother."

Ruby groaned audibly. Apparently, she was about to be on a blind date with the grumpiest, most Christmas-hating guy she'd ever met.

RUBY COULD SEE DR. Rash's face drop the moment he realized he was walking toward the Christmas Cheer Lady, as he'd called her. On one hand, good. She was glad that he was irritated at the sight of her, because that meant telling him off on Monday achieved its goal. But on the other hand, if this man was also a child of Hakim M. Hakim, then the fact that he already disliked Ruby was a problem.

Jasmine reached them, so Ruby had no more time to dwell on the mysterious Grinch. After Nadim hugged Jasmine, Reena gave her a half sideways hug so she wouldn't wake the baby, then introduced Ruby to Jasmine.

"Oh, I adore that coat!" Jasmine said, while shaking Ruby's hand. "I wish I could wear that color."

Ruby smiled. She understood why Nadim had called Jasmine the Angelic One—there was a sweet prettiness to Jasmine. Her cheeks were rosy, and she had faint smile lines near her eyes. And she had the loveliest upper-class London accent. Ruby thanked her and complimented her Fair Isle knit hat while wondering why the grump didn't have this accent.

"I'm being rude," Jasmine said. "I should introduce my family. These are my daughters, Tara and Noor, and my brother Rashid. He's come from out west to help me with the girls over the holidays. Rashid, this is Nadim and Reena, and their good friend Ruby."

Okay. So, this brother was from out west and not the UK? This didn't make any sense. Ruby exhaled. She had to wipe her dislike of the man off her face. She needed to *charm* him. Ruby wasn't concerned. Years of working in the most exclusive, expensive stores in Canada had taught her to be charming to just about anyone. And maybe he wasn't as bad as she'd remembered, anyway. He came all the way from…wherever…to help his sister at a difficult time. That was kind of sweet.

After shaking hands with Nadim and Reena, Rashid looked at Ruby without putting his hand out. He was in jeans again today, but they were less dusty. And of course, he had on what must be his only hat—that blue beanie. Ruby really didn't mind the way he looked today since his clothes looked clean and fit well, but he looked the farthest thing from the posh Brit she was promised.

"Oh, we've met," Ruby said. She looked at Jasmine. "It's such a coincidence! Your brother was kind enough to help carry my Christmas tree after I foolishly thought I could walk it home last week." She looked back at him, smiling as wide as she could. "Thank you again. What a delightful surprise to see you again."

He opened his mouth, no doubt ready to remind her that six days ago she'd said she hoped never to see him again. Ruby took her hand out of her muff to shake his. Hopefully he would recognize that what she was really offering was an olive branch, not a handshake.

He stared at her hand a second, seemingly locking on to her glittery red and nude French manicure. She even caught him checking out her earrings—visible under her fur hat. The last time he looked at her like this, Ruby was sure he liked what he saw. Now she knew she'd been wrong—he thought she looked ridiculous.

Finally, he shook her hand and said a flat hello. He didn't quite smile, though. His hand was so soft—drywall was probably an infrequent activity for him. She couldn't believe this man was *older* than Jasmine.

"You were such a lifesaver when me met!" Ruby said the moment his hand left hers. "I would have broken my back carrying the tree on my own. I should have asked for your name after I wrapped..." It occurred to her that the gifts she'd wrapped were probably for Jasmine and her daughters, so Ruby shouldn't mention them. "After I saw you in the Winter Market." She smiled at Jasmine. "I work at Reid's Holiday in the Distillery District. Your brother was in the store on Monday."

"I love that store!" Jasmine said. "I've drooled over the Swarovski ornaments. The whole Winter Market is so charming. It must be such a fun place to work."

So, hating Christmas wasn't a family trait, then? "Oh, it's fantastic," Ruby said. "Your girls are so adorable! I love their names...that's Star and Light in Arabic, right?"

"It is!" Jasmine said. "Girls, say hello to Ruby Auntie."

Ruby knelt to say hello to the little girls. They had the same wide eyes, but one had straight hair, and the other curls. Neither of them smiled or even said hello to Ruby.

"They're shy," Jasmine said. "Shall we make ourselves comfortable?"

Rashid didn't object to Jasmine insisting he sit next to Ruby. He probably knew this was a setup, too. Ruby ended up between Reena and Rashid, with Jasmine on the other side of him. Jasmine and Rashid each had a twin on their lap, since there were only five chairs.

"I have chai!" Nadim said once they were all settled. He produced a large thermos and a few reusable cups from his bag. When he offered Ruby a cup, she declined, pointing at the latte in her hand.

"I assume that's, like, a peppermint hot chocolate or something Christmassy," Rashid said, with no accent other than grumpy Canadian. Why didn't he sound like his sister? An accent would make him so much more palatable.

"Ooh, I love peppermint mochas," Jasmine said. "Chai is great, too, though," she smiled, taking a cup from Nadim. "Do you girls want a juice box? I have apple or orange."

While Jasmine busied herself with her kids, Rashid leaned close to Ruby. She caught a scent on him—a spicy cologne. Not the new Le Labo. "So is that what it is? A peppermint mocha?"

Ruby bit her lip. That was bait, and she wasn't going to take it. He wanted her to admit that she loved holiday drinks. "Actually, no. I'm not a fan of mint beverages."

"If I know Ruby, it's a gingerbread latte," Reena said. So much for not taking the bait. Ruby sighed.

"So, Jasmine," Ruby said, leaning over Rashid. "Nadim tells me you two met in London. How long ago did you live there?"

"Oh it feels like *ages* ago. I moved to Canada for medical school and stayed." Her face fell a bit. She looked at her brother, who gave her a supportive little nod. "We visit, though. The girls love their nani and nana. Didn't we have a fantastic trip the last time we were in London, girls?"

"It seems wonderful," Ruby said. "I'm going to be in London next month. Girls, what is your favorite thing there? It will be my first time in the UK."

The child on Jasmine's lap—the one with straight hair—looked terrified that the strange big person was talking to her and buried her face in her mother's chest. The other one—the one with the curls, said very quietly that she liked castles, but didn't say anything else. Ruby knew that children came in all temperaments, and there was absolutely nothing wrong with being shy with strangers, so she didn't push the kids. She smiled at Jasmine. "I'll be sure to visit some castles."

"When will you be visiting London?" Jasmine asked.

"My flight is January first, but I'm actually going there to live, not to visit. I'm hoping to run a business there eventually."

Jasmine's eyes widened. "Wow, and you've never been there before? That's so brave."

"It's weird and impulsive, that's what it is," Rashid said. Ruby looked at him. He was, of course, frowning. "How can you move to a country you've never set foot in? Leave your family, your friends, and your job? Don't you need a visa? Or are you just going to show up and hope you don't get deported back to Canada?"

Well. That was super judgmental. Was this payback for her telling him she never wanted to see his grumpy face again?

Ruby counted to three in her head before responding, putting on her smile. "As you're aware, I work in a holiday store, so it won't exist by the time I leave. I could go back to my previous job at Reid's flagship store, but I haven't been with the company very long, so I don't have a lot of loyalty to them. And of course I have a visa...and I've already had several job offers from High Street boutiques, so it's not like I'm showing up with no prospects. And I don't have any close family who would miss me here."

He blinked at Ruby a few times. She was impressed she was able to say all that without losing the pleasant lilt to her voice. But the longer he stared at her without speaking, the thicker the tension in their little group grew. Ruby fully intended to tell Rashid that if she could manage to be polite for one damn parade, then he could, too, but that's when Ruby noticed the little tremble in Jasmine's lower lip while her big eyes looked concerned.

"But never mind about me, have you seen the parade before, Jasmine?" Ruby asked.

Jasmine shook her head. "No, only on TV. The girls...I mean...We're looking forward to it."

They all talked about the parade and about holiday parades they'd seen in other cities. All except Rashid. Ruby didn't understand why he'd agree to come to a *Christmas* parade, of all things.

When the parade finally started, Ruby couldn't help but watch him as much as the floats, clowns, and marching bands. Rashid Hakim was such a puzzle. It didn't take long for Ruby to solve one mystery about the man—why he'd come today.

He was here for his sister and nieces. Jasmine seemed a little... fragile. She got flustered easily and even zoned out a few times with that little tremble on her lip. Rashid was so attentive and helpful with the girls, pointing things out to them in the parade and helping them with their snacks and juice boxes, which seemed to take some weight off Jasmine. He was such an involved, doting uncle to those cute little girls that it almost melted Ruby's cold impression of him.

Almost...because Ruby was well aware that people were multifaceted, complicated beings, and being a good uncle and good brother didn't mean he was a good person.

"So," Nadim said during a long lull between floats. He was sitting on the other side of Reena and had Aleem on his chest now. "I'll ask the question we're all thinking. Why does Jasmine sound like she grew up in West London while Rashid sounds like he grew up in Edmonton?"

Rashid chuckled at that. "You're close. I've lived in Calgary for almost fifteen years. I went to boarding school and then university in Vancouver before that. I did grow up in the UK, though."

"How did you end up so far from home?" Ruby asked him. She wasn't giving up on her goal to charm him, but his smile immediately disappeared.

"As I said. *School*." He looked like he was holding in a rude comment.

Jasmine laughed. "He was obsessed with Canada as a kid. Started when he got into hockey. Our aunt lives in Vancouver, and after a trip there once, he just...stayed."

Ruby's eyes widened. She'd been obsessed with the UK for

so long, it had never occurred to her that anyone there could be obsessed with Canada.

"Why don't you have your accent anymore, but your sister does?" Reena asked.

"When I go back home, I sound British," Rashid said. "Here it's easier to sound like everyone else so I'm not asked a million times a day where I'm from."

Ruby leaned close so hopefully only Rashid would hear her. "So your accent's *fake*? And you think *I'm* weird. You're cosplaying as a Canadian because you're into violent winter sports." She cringed. She shouldn't be antagonizing him, but she couldn't help herself. This man was so infuriating.

"And I have no doubt that you'll have Union Jacks on your nails and Big Ben earrings within a week of landing in London," Rashid responded quietly, not even looking at Ruby.

That was it. Ruby was done being polite—no matter who his father was. He suddenly turned to Ruby, unsmiling, just as she was about to tell him to sod off. Their eyes locked, and Ruby couldn't look away, remembering that charged moment they had in the store when they both had their hands on the cashmere robe.

Ruby's lips parted, and she felt her whole body warm. She had no idea what was going on, but she didn't appreciate how his intense stare made her a little breathless. Why did this grump have to be so ridiculously handsome?

He finally turned away when one of the girls whined. Jasmine listened intently to her daughter, then turned to her brother. "She needs the bathroom."

Those words made the other twin turn away from the parade and nod.

"Okay, they both do," Jasmine said.

"There's a Tim Hortons over there," Ruby said, pointing a few doors away from where they were sitting. Jasmine started to gather her things.

"Let me take them," Rashid said, standing.

Jasmine shook her head. "I doubt they'll have a family room. It's fine. I can manage."

Ruby almost offered to help Jasmine with her kids, but the tone in Jasmine's voice stopped her. Determination and insistence. Jasmine wanted to prove that she could handle her kids alone. Whether she wanted to prove it to herself or to her brother, Ruby didn't know.

Nadim stood. "I'll walk you there…this guy needs a change anyway."

Ruby was alone with Reena and Rashid. And there was a gap in the floats, so there wasn't anything to look at.

"It must be so hard for you to be far from your sisters," Reena said. "My sister and I aren't even that close, but I like knowing she's nearby, you know?"

Rashid nodded. "We all visit each other a lot. And our family group chat is active." He was perfectly pleasant with Reena and saved his acerbic barbs for Ruby. Rude.

"That's so nice," Ruby said, hoping to smooth things over between them. "It must be so cool to have family in different cities."

"It's convenient," he said curtly.

Ruby exhaled. She was floundering.

At least Reena was here. She said, "Your sister mentioned that your family is in the hotel business?"

Rashid nodded. "Yes, they own several hotels. It's great, but they work so hard. Med school was a breeze compared to my father's workload. Owning a business isn't for the faint of heart." He glanced sideways at Ruby. She clenched her teeth.

Reena nodded. "I know what you mean. I own a bakery, and even while I'm on maternity leave, it's always on my mind."

Reena and Rashid talked about Reena's bakery for a bit, and Ruby may as well not even have been with them. This was useless. The man hated Christmas and was stuck at a Christmas parade with someone he disliked quite intensely. Maybe it was time for Ruby to concede defeat and stick with her original plan of applying for hotel positions after arriving in London.

Reena pulled out her phone. "Ugh. Nadim says there's no changing table in the men's room. That's so sexist." She stood up. "He said Jasmine is in line to get hot chocolate for the kids. Do you guys want anything?"

Ruby and Rashid said no at the same time. Reena smiled, then left in the direction of the coffee shop as the marching band finally reached them.

Which left Ruby alone with Rashid. Ugh.

RASHID WAS CLEARLY AS annoyed to be alone with Ruby as she was to be alone with him. At least the parade was busy now, so it was easier to ignore each other and pretend the upside-down clowns were the most interesting things they'd ever seen.

This man *really* got under her skin. Ruby knew her enthusiasm sometimes rubbed people the wrong way. But it was usually easy to brush off criticisms because she was happy with who she was. And after everything she'd been through, she deserved to enjoy her life. But Rashid's censure stung more than others'. He called her incredibly impulsive. He implied her move was irresponsible. He even insinuated she was unintelligent because she liked expensive skin care and themed manicures. It reminded her of her father—a man who also thought that everything Ruby did or liked was a waste of time. Ruby hated to be reminded of her father.

Parades were supposed to be fun. People in large gingerbread man costumes walked by waving. Clowns were handing out candy canes. People were joyful, and Ruby was sitting next to the Grinch with the Good Skin.

Finally, she couldn't stop herself. She had to say something. "You're aware that everyone disappearing like that is probably because they want us to be alone, right?"

He nodded. "Probably."

"So, you knew this was a setup then?"

He nodded again.

"Did you know that you were being set up with *me*?"

He shook his head. "I knew my sister found another date for me, despite me telling her not to. I wasn't aware it was the Christmas elf that tosses trees on bystanders."

"I *dropped* my tree on you," Ruby said. "Not tossed. And that was the first time that's happened. It's not, like, a habit."

He shrugged.

Ruby exhaled. "You're hating this, aren't you?"

"Hating what? The parade, or you talking to me?"

"The *parade*. Why did you come if you don't like Christmas and didn't want to be set up with anyone?"

He turned to her, eyes full of annoyance. Actually, a step above annoyance. His eyes were full of disdain. "Why do you care? You're *loving* this…which doesn't really make sense either. Why do you care about Christmas so much? You come from the same religion as me."

"Okay, so Muslims aren't allowed to enjoy Christmas?"

"Yes, but don't you think you're taking it too far?"

Ruby rolled her eyes. "We're surrounded by this holiday every winter. Why shouldn't we find joy in it? Or is it all forms of joy you have a problem with, not just Christmas joy?" She exhaled. She shouldn't be provoking him. He was going to make sure she was blacklisted in the entire United Kingdom hospitality industry.

"Okay but you *must* have noticed the way people celebrate the holiday is more about commercialism than anything else."

"Yes! I work in a Christmas store. My income relies on that commercialism!"

A clown carrying an iPhone came up to them. "Smile for the Christmas cam!"

The clown snapped a picture, then frowned at the phone. "No Grinches allowed! Let's try that again…smile for the Christmas cam!"

Ruby had no idea what the Christmas cam was, but if this clown wanted her to smile, she could do that. Even next to Rashid Hakim.

The clown seemed satisfied with the second picture and waved before finding another couple—hopefully a happier one, to photograph.

Ruby sat silently watching the parade. How long did it take to change a diaper, anyway? And what about Jasmine? She'd been gone even longer. "I hope your sister and nieces are okay. Santa will be here soon." Ugh. Ruby was incapable of keeping her mouth shut.

He shook his head. "I've never understood who thought the Santa Claus myth was a good idea for children. *He sees you when you're sleeping. He knows when you're awake.* Sure, let's tell little kids that overweight white men in red suits are predators stalking them. And that Elf on the Shelf thing? The girls' grandmother got it for them last year, and they screamed in terror every morning when they saw it in a new spot, staring at them. Creepy as hell. My sister had to hide the damn thing."

Ruby chuckled. He actually had a point. "I agree that elf is creepy, but Santa is wholesome! He's not a predator. He gives gifts."

"Yes, but only to kids who he deems worthy. You ever think about what kids who *do* believe in Santa think about the non-Christian kids who don't get gifts from Santa? They probably think Muslim, Hindu, and Jewish kids are all naughty. That's not the way to facilitate compassion and respect between religions."

And that was another good point. She'd never looked at it like that. "Do the girls believe in Santa?" Ruby asked.

Rashid exhaled. "Yes. They celebrate Christmas—and they love it. Their father insisted, even though Jasmine didn't want to do the whole Santa thing. But we don't tell them that kids who don't get presents are naughty—just that they don't celebrate this holiday."

"Your sister not wanting to do the Santa thing must have annoyed the grandmother who got them the elf," Ruby said.

Rashid huffed a laugh. "You have no idea. There are people in their father's family who believe that Jasmine is teaching them to be extremists. Which is hilarious because none of us are very religious. But they hear *Muslim* and believe the stereotypes. They're from a small town, but I don't think that's an excuse."

Ruby could believe it. She'd lived all over the country, and Canada wasn't the tolerant utopia that some people thought it was. "That must be hard for the girls. To be pulled in different directions like that."

He nodded. He looked less annoyed right now. Or more like annoyed at the situation, not at Ruby. Maybe he was happy to have someone to talk to about this. "It's very hard on them. They grew up with Christmas, but this year it's been taken from them, and they're confused. It's not their fault that their father is the asshole of all assholes. That's why I agreed to come today—the girls deserve a Christmas. Even if it's not my cup of tea."

Ruby smiled. It seemed this Grinch's heart was already three sizes bigger than Ruby thought it was. "That's really kind of you. I'm sorry you ended up having to spend the day pretending not to hate me."

He turned to Ruby, one brow raised. "I don't hate you. I barely know you."

"Okay, but you find me annoying."

He shrugged. "I find a lot of things annoying."

She laughed, shaking her head. "I don't doubt that. They've all been gone awhile. Hope they're okay."

He picked up his phone, no doubt to text his sister. "She says there's a big line."

They watched the next float go by—a re-creation of Santa's workshop sponsored by a big hardware store. Rashid shook his head. "Every Christmas sentiment must be sponsored by a corporation. The holiday isn't magic. It's a great big advertisement."

"True, but someone has to pay for all this," Ruby said. "Look at all the kids enjoying it. When they grow up, they're not going to remember that the Santa's workshop float was sponsored by Canadian Tire; they'll remember the elves making toy cars and sewing dresses for the dolls. They'll remember coming to the parade every year with their family and waiting for Santa to show up. If we have to put up with a bit of commercialism to get those memories, then it's worth it."

He looked at her with a curious expression. Like he saw her point, just like she saw his about the elf. Their eyes were locked for several seconds before Reena's voice behind them broke the spell. "What's worth it? L'Oréal?" Nadim and Jasmine were behind Reena. "Ooh, is he giving you skin care recommendations?"

Ruby smirked. "I know better than to ask *him* for skin care recs." She and Rashid seemed to be finally getting along, but she'd rather not be on the receiving end of another rant about luxury skin care.

Rashid chuckled at Ruby's comment.

"Rashid Uncle! We got you a plain coffee because Mommy said you don't like things that taste good," the curly-haired twin said. That was the most either of them had said all day.

Rashid laughed at that. Like an actual full, joyful laugh as he took the coffee cup from his sister. It was the first time Ruby saw a look of genuine enjoyment on his face, and it looked so good on him. When not smiling, Rashid had a classically handsome face—strong jaw and dark intense eyes. But when he smiled, he looked...cute. It was a childlike smile. His eyes were the kind that twinkled. She wished he would take that hat off so she could see if his forehead wrinkled when smiling.

After everyone was back in their spots with Nadim wearing the baby carrier with Aleem in it, they watched the rest of the parade. The girls were a little more talkative—but only to their mother and uncle. Aleem slept through his first Santa Claus parade, and it looked like Nadim might have joined his son, as his head was leaned back on his folding chair.

"He was up all night with the baby," Reena said, leaning close to whisper in Ruby's ear. "So, did you and the Grinch have words while we were all gone?"

Ruby smiled and waved at the women walking by in red and white Victorian dresses. "He's very frustrating, but we were fine," she said quietly enough so only Reena would hear.

"He's a cutie though. And a doctor."

"So?"

"So, isn't finding a single doctor the South Asian dream?" Reena said.

Not for Ruby it wasn't.

"Plus, remember what Shayne said," Reena added. "He'll know a lot about…anatomy."

If Nadim, Jasmine, two children, and a baby weren't right next to Reena she would have told her friend to get her head out of the gutter. "Pay attention to the parade, Reena. Santa's watching you—you don't want your stocking to be empty, do you?"

The rest of the parade was…fine. Ruby didn't have a reason to talk to Rashid again, which was good. She had no idea if he was enjoying the event—she assumed he wasn't—because he was pretty preoccupied with his nieces. Which was…sweet.

Ruby knew that men could be great with kids. She'd seen Nadim step up to the plate and be a fantastic father in the three months since Aleem was born. And she'd known lots of other men who were great fathers and uncles, too. But seeing a grown man be patient and gentle with children was something that Ruby always noticed. Especially if the children were girls. Ruby herself was not planning to have kids—for many reasons—but that didn't mean she didn't *like* kids. But her own father never seemed to like kids, and he was definitely disappointed that his only biological child was female. In all her years on planet Earth, Ruby had learned that the biggest red flag when it came to men was when they saw children as a giant inconvenience... or a nuisance.

Rashid Hakim had a lot of red flags, but at least one giant green one, too.

After Santa and his sleigh full of animatronic reindeer arrived with much fanfare and cheering, the parade was over. The crowd dispersing was a bit of a nightmare. Their group of eight managed to get out of the crush without losing any children—or adults, for that matter. It was only a four-minute walk to the French bistro where Ruby had made reservations for a late lunch. She'd picked the restaurant because they had tables big enough for all of them and, despite being a bistro, had a kid's menu.

But even with a reservation, their table wasn't available yet. It seemed that large French bistros were popular Sunday afternoon hot spots. They were shown to a bar area to wait for their table.

Jasmine sat on the one empty barstool with a twin on each knee, clutching their mother's neck for dear life. Reena gave Jasmine a sympathetic look—no doubt she was thinking again about how hard it would be to have two babies at the same time.

Rashid looked incredibly annoyed. "What's the point of making a reservation if we still have to wait this long? Is this place always like this?" He was looking at Ruby when he asked.

She shrugged. "I've never been here. They're popular on Instagram, though."

He rolled his eyes and looked away. Like that was a stupid reason to pick a restaurant. After a few moments of silence, Ruby asked the question she'd been thinking of all day. "So why didn't you two go into hotel management like your parents?"

"Our parents always wanted us to follow our own path, not theirs," Rashid said.

Jasmine laughed. "Yeah, and neither of us are suited for it. Our parents are quite typical—they pushed us all academically. And Rashid and I were more into biology than business. The hotel industry works for Ayesha—she's the most business minded of us."

Nadim shook his head with wonder. "I still can't really believe that. Ayesha was *such* a party girl."

Jasmine smiled. "She still is. She just found a way to be a party host for a living."

"I've wanted to work in hotels for a while," Ruby said. "It's actually why I'm moving to England."

Jasmine frowned. "You're moving because you want to work in hotels?"

"Sort of." She laughed nervously. "It's complicated. It was a dream of my mother's and mine to one day own a country inn somewhere in England. We are…were obsessed with English literature and that whole aesthetic. I'm moving to determine the feasibility of our plan."

"Did I hear you correctly?" Rashid asked, turning to her. "You're moving all the way to the UK to live some Jane Austen pipe dream?"

"Don't listen to my brother," Jasmine said, waving her hand. "I think it's a delightful idea. It's exactly what my mother wanted—she convinced Dad to buy a property in the country recently. It's so lovely. Calmer than city living. You should meet my father when you get to the UK. I'll call him—"

"Mommy," one of Jasmine's daughters interrupted with a whine. "I don't feel good."

"Me too," said the other one, holding her stomach.

Jasmine put her hand on one of the girls' foreheads. "Oh, sweetheart." She looked at Ruby. "I was afraid of this. They get stomachaches whenever they have overly rich things, like that hot chocolate.

"Do you need the bathroom," she asked them, they both shook their heads no, then the one closest to Jasmine leaned in and said something quiet.

Jasmine looked at the rest of the table. "They want to go home. To be honest, I'm surprised they lasted this long. They're exhausted. I think we may have to take a rain check on lunch."

Rashid leaned down and picked up one of the girls so Jasmine could stand, holding the other one. Ruby didn't know what to say. She wanted to urge Jasmine to stay—because Ruby wanted to finish that conversation when Jasmine was about to say she'd tell their father about Ruby. But the kids were sick. Ruby felt bad.

Jasmine apologized again when she said goodbye. "We had a wonderful time at the parade, didn't we, girls? Thank you so much for inviting us. And it was so nice to meet you, Ruby! Hopefully we'll see each other again soon!"

"I hope so!" Ruby said. "It was so great to meet you. And meet Tara and Noor!"

Each holding one little girl, Jasmine and Rashid left the bistro. Rashid, unsurprisingly, didn't say goodbye.

"Well, that went terribly, didn't it?" Ruby said as they left. Reena sat on the barstool that Jasmine had vacated. She draped a blanket over her shoulder so she could nurse the baby.

"They'll be fine," Nadim said as he handed Aleem to his wife. "Kids always have stomachaches."

"No, I don't mean about the kids," Ruby said. "I mean I was supposed to impress Jasmine. I think I can kiss that plan goodbye since her brother hates me."

Reena shook her head, looking down at her baby. "He doesn't hate you. C'mon, open your mouth!"

Ruby raised a brow at Reena.

"Sorry. Aleem's not latching on." The baby let out a high-pitched squeal that made everyone in their vicinity turn to them. "Maybe we should go, too," Reena said. "I doubt he's going to settle down." She looked apologetically at Ruby.

"It's fine!" Ruby said. "Take the young sir home. I don't mind."

Nadim took the baby from Reena. "Okay, but you stay and eat," Nadim said. "It's on us. I feel bad that we're all leaving."

Ruby waved her head. "Nonsense. I had a great time anyway. I don't mind eating alone." That was the truth. Ruby had long ago figured out that she would never be able to eat at any of the gorgeous restaurants she saw on Instagram if she wasn't willing to eat alone. "Go, seriously. I'm fine."

Reena finally hugged Ruby goodbye and rushed out after her husband and child.

Sighing, Ruby went back to the hostess station to tell her that their table for eight was now a table for one.

"My friends had to leave," Ruby explained. "Their kids were overstimulated from the parade."

The hostess nodded, looking at the monitor on the counter. "So, you need a table for one?"

Ruby was about to say yes when someone behind her spoke for her.

"Two," a deep voice said. "I'll be joining her."

She turned, and yep, Rashid was still here. *Great.*

RUBY SHOOK HER HEAD at Rashid. She still wanted—*needed*—to be somewhat nice to the man so he wouldn't bad-mouth her to the rest of his family, but she did *not* want to eat a meal with him. Alone. "I'm fine. Go with your sister. Your nieces need you."

He shook his head. He still wasn't exactly smiling, but he wasn't scowling, either. "I was buckling the girls in when we saw Reena and Nadim heading to their car. Jasmine insisted that I couldn't leave you all alone."

"I can eat alone. The girls are sick, and your sister—"

"My sister can manage her daughters' stomachaches. She's a doctor, remember?"

"Yes, but two doctors are better than one! I'm sure two dermatologists are as good as one…" She frowned. "What's a stomach doctor?"

"Gastroenterologist," the restaurant hostess said. She looked very invested in this interaction. "So, table for one or two?"

"Two," Rashid said. Then he turned to Ruby. "Unless you

really don't want to have a meal with me. Then we'll need two tables for one."

The hostess shook her head. "I doubt we'll be able to swing that. We don't actually have tables for one—so we'd need two tables for two, and there are a lot of people waiting. I have one table for two now, and since you gave up that table for eight which was really two tables for—"

Ruby sighed. "One table for two is fine. Separate bills." She'd eat with the man, but the last thing she wanted was for either of them to owe the other anything.

"Good choice," the hostess said, taking two menus from the stack behind her, and motioned for them to follow her. "My name's Claudia. Thank me at your wedding. This way, please."

They were brought to a table in front of a large window overlooking the busy street. This place totally deserved its Instagram fame. The tile floor, rattan chairs, and plethora of potted plants made Ruby feel like she was actually in a bistro in Paris. Not that she'd ever been to a bistro in Paris—or anywhere else in Paris. But that would soon change. After she moved, visiting Paris would be easy.

The table was small, though. Intimate. She opened the drink menu—Ruby definitely would need alcohol to get through dinner with Dr. Rash.

Rashid finally pulled his hat off before sitting. He had thick, wavy black hair that was a little long on the top with a tiny bit of graying at the temples...which made him look older. Or actually look his age. She squeezed her lips shut so she wouldn't tell him how much more handsome he was without that hat and quickly skimmed the offerings on the drink menu.

"Ah, they have cute winter cocktails! Should I have a black rose or a French martini? The black rose is pink, not black, but ooh…the French martini is made with black raspberry liqueur. The rich red is even prettier than the pink! They should switch the names of the cocktails, don't you think? That's what I'm getting—the French martini." She closed the drinks menu. Rashid was looking at her curiously. "Oh, wait— Do you mind if I drink? You said you weren't really religious, but I mean, there are lots of reasons why people abstain, not just religion. I drink— not that much, though." Ruby forced herself to stop talking.

"It's fine. I was going to have a beer. Did you decide on the drink because it's *attractive*?"

Ruby nodded. She wasn't going to let this guy get under her skin. No matter how hard he tried. "Yup. What can I say? I like pretty things. And descriptive colors."

The waitress came to get their drinks order then, and Ruby ordered her French martini. Rashid ordered a local microbrew.

After the waitress left, Ruby read the dinner menu. She'd looked at the menu online before making the reservation, so she already knew what she wanted—the roasted apple, chestnut, and Camembert tartine. But hiding behind a menu was a good way to avoid the small talk she didn't want to have. Her runaway mouth had embarrassed herself enough for the night.

"Did you find something suitably attractive on the menu?" Rashid asked.

"Yes. I'm having a tartine," she said, smiling. When he didn't say anything, she specified. "It's like a French open-faced sandwich. Not like the Swedish ones. They use a rustic country bread instead of rye. I'm thinking the apple tartine."

"I know what a tartine is," he said curtly. He was still looking at his menu and not at her. She had to agree with his sister: Rashid Hakim had no talent for hospitality. She felt sorry for his patients.

"The bread here is apparently really good," Ruby said. "I mean, not as good as Reena's. You should try her bakery if you're ever in Markham. Her sourdough is to die for. They also have, like, jams and chutneys, too. Reena makes a mango cardamom jam that is *so* good. I like it with Greek yogurt, but it's great on toast, too." Ruby really needed to stop talking. Why did this guy make her so off-kilter? Probably because she had no idea what he was thinking most of the time. He was probably internally disapproving of everything he was seeing in this restaurant. Or disapproving of her.

Or maybe it was because he was really hot.

"I'm glad you like bread," he said. This table was small, she couldn't not look at him. Were those lashes real?

"Doesn't everyone like bread?"

He huffed a laugh. "Not the last two women I went on dates with. One actually said I should turn in my medical license if I ate brioche. But I guess you're not like other girls."

Ruby's nose wrinkled at that. She had no idea if he was aware of the sexist meaning behind the phrase—he honestly didn't seem to be trying to insult her this time. "That's where you're wrong," she said. "I'm *exactly* like other girls." He raised an eyebrow at that, so she explained. "There are women who say 'I'm not like other girls...I like manly things like diesel and eating bread' to imply they're special for liking things other women don't like. But what they really mean is that they are better than other women because they aren't into things that society thinks are 'girly'…like diet culture, pretty cocktails, holiday romances, or even makeup. It's misogyny. The belief that feminine-coded things are less important or have less value than masculine-coded things. I love girly things. I get my nails done every two weeks, I love makeup, I work in luxury fashion, and I freaking love holiday rom-coms. There is nothing wrong with feminine-coded things unless you think there is something wrong with feminine-coded people, aka women."

Rashid didn't say anything to that. He looked at her for a long time with a practically imperceptible smile. Did he disagree with her? Was he laughing at her? She was almost positive that they wouldn't make it through this meal. Ruby didn't know which one of them was going to get up and walk away first, but she had no doubt one of them would.

The waitress came with their drinks. Ruby's martini was the most perfect dark ruby red and had a toothpick resting on the rim with three sugar-frosted raspberries on it. It was beautiful. If she was with anyone else, she would have asked them to take a picture of her holding it…but not Rashid. She did snap a picture of the glass sitting on the white tablecloth, though.

She took a sip of her drink. It tasted even better than it looked.

"Do you want me to take your picture drinking that?" he asked.

Ruby grinned mischievously. "Why? Because of how good I look with a drink that matches my holiday aesthetic?"

He exaggeratedly rolled his eyes at that. And if Ruby wasn't mistaken, he blushed a bit. He *did* think she looked good.

Beaming, she unlocked her phone and opened the camera app. She slid it across the table to him.

Puckering her lips slightly, she put the martini glass to her mouth and extended her pinky finger so her holiday manicure would be in the shot. Rashid took a few pictures before handing the phone back. The pictures were perfect. She uploaded one to her Instagram story right away.

The waitress finally came to take their orders. Ruby ordered the apple, chestnut, and Camembert tartine, and Rashid got a steak and Gorgonzola one. After the waitress left, they had more awkward silence.

"You said your sister keeps setting you up on dates. Why?" Ruby asked.

"Do you know about her leaving her husband?"

"A little." She knew that the gossip Jenisha heard wasn't true—the boy-toy was Jasmine's older brother, not her affair partner. "You don't have to tell me details, though."

Rashid took a sip of his dark amber beer before answering. "It's fine. It's been a messy breakup. Her husband was bad news for a long time. Jasmine's alone here in Toronto. Our parents are in England, and I'm in Calgary. She'd just opened her own practice...and Derek has been doing everything he can to stop her from opening it. He's even spreading nasty rumors about her to the nearby businesses."

Ruby winced. "Yeah, I heard some of those rumors."

Rashid shook his head. "He's such a petty asshole. Anyway, I took a leave of absence at my hospital and drove out here to help get Jasmine's practice off the ground. I just finished the outstanding construction, and I'll start taking her patients tomorrow until she can get back on her feet." He chuckled. "I had no idea the whole area would turn into a Christmas market for two months…or I may not have volunteered."

Ruby smiled. It was nice of him to come—she wished she had a big brother to help her when things went sideways. "That's pretty cool of you. But why is she setting you up with women who don't like bread?"

He shrugged. "My sister hates being a burden. She insists I need my own social life in Toronto and can't only hang out with her and the girls. So, she started setting me up with women she knows."

"And you don't want to be set up?"

He shook his head. "I'm not going to be here very long. Hopefully I can leave by mid-February. I'm not against dating, but let's say she *does* manage to find someone who likes me. What's going to happen when I leave? That's not fair to this hypothetical woman, is it?"

Ruby smiled her sweetest smile. "Well, she did excellently with me, then, because I'm moving in January anyway. Where are you taking me next? There's a whole Christmas village north of the city. You have a car, right?" The look of horror on his face made Ruby laugh. "That was a joke. I have no idea what your type is, but clearly, I'm not it."

He shook his head, not acknowledging her statement. "Not to mention," he said, "I want to help Jasmine with the girls when I'm not working. I can't drag a couple of five-year-olds on dates, can I?"

That was a good point. He was a handsome doctor, but Ruby doubted any single woman in Toronto would be okay with him bringing his two nieces along on every date. Even if they rarely spoke. "How is the beer?" Ruby asked.

"Very tasty. This area has great microbreweries. How's the pretty martini?"

She smiled as she took another sip. "It's excellent. Tastes even better than it looks."

After their food arrived, they ate silently for a bit, save polite small talk about how nice the food looked and how delicious it was. Ruby couldn't stop thinking about Rashid while she ate. He was such a contradiction. A stand-up guy, loyal to his sister, a doting uncle, and a man who didn't want a woman to get too attached to him because he wouldn't be here very long. On paper, he was such a catch. But he was so hot and cold. Sometimes he looked at her like he was utterly fascinated with her, and other times he was a judgmental prick to her.

"How old are you?" Ruby asked. He raised a brow at her. Maybe she shouldn't have asked so directly. "I mean, you don't have to say. I'm curious. You know how old I am, because—"

"Because we met on your thirty-third birthday. I guess it's only fair. I'm thirty-seven."

She giggled, shaking her head. "I seriously thought you were a *decade* younger when we met. Maybe I should have listened to your skin care rant—you clearly know what you're doing."

He laughed at that. He especially looked younger than thirty-seven when he was laughing.

"Why do you hate skin care, anyway?"

He shook his head. "I hate *overpriced* skin care filled with unproven additives. Like, people are slathering their face with snail mucus now—and spending a fortune on it, too. It's not only nasty, but there is no evidence it does anything. I'm not a cosmetic dermatologist, but I know that skin care is mostly water and that actual, *proven* additives are incredibly cheap—like vitamin C and retinol. But these companies gaslight you into thinking that you can only have good skin if you spend a fortune."

Ruby frowned. Snail mucus didn't work? "If you're not a cosmetic dermatologist, what is your specialty?"

"I focus on clinical dermatology. Basically, I treat medical issues with the skin, like hereditary skin diseases and autoimmune disorders."

"Do you hate it when people call you Dr. Rash?"

He blinked, staring for several seconds. Then barked a loud laugh. "Honestly, no one's ever called me that."

"No one has called you that *to your face*," she said. "I guarantee they thought it. I mean, your name, Dr. Rash, is right there. Were you surprised your sister wanted to follow in your footsteps?"

"A little, yeah. She was in med school in Calgary while I was interning, so she saw how fascinated I was in derm. I did some work at a burn clinic, and it's so rewarding to *see* the difference you can make. That's the thing with skin—it's the most visible organ. A heart specialist can't easily know that treatments are working or not working. With skin, we can catch problems quicker, and we can see that we are making a difference. Skin cancer is one of the easiest cancers to find, and that's why it has such a high survival rate."

Ruby took a long sip from her martini glass. She needed

this conversation topic to change. Now. This...this was why she hadn't wanted to date a doctor. "I wish I had siblings," Ruby said. "You're so close to your sisters. Jasmine even followed you to Canada."

"Yeah, they're great. We're all in different places now, but we talk all the time. My whole family is close."

Ruby felt a pang of jealousy. "The only family I still talk to is my cousin Marley. She and I are only children, so we grew up like sisters."

"You grew up here in Toronto, right?"

Ruby nodded. "I left when I was twenty. I've only been back for a year and a bit."

"And you're leaving again. You said you move a lot?"

She nodded, then started counting cities on her fingers. "I went to university in Montreal, then moved to Ottawa, then Halifax, then I was daring and moved to Vancouver, then Kelowna for a few years, but I realized I'm not crunchy enough for the west coast, so moved back to my first love, Montreal. Then came here just over a year ago."

"And now you want to move to England."

"Not *want to*...I *am* moving to England. I already have my ticket. The visa is sorted."

He didn't say anything to that. Ruby was surprised at how pleasant this dinner had been so far—once they stopped the medical conversation. Maybe Rashid wasn't a complete grump after all. In fact, maybe she didn't need Jasmine to introduce her to Hakim M. Hakim. Maybe Rashid could, instead?

"Hey, before your sister left, I was telling her that my eventual goal in the UK is to work in the hotel industry. My mother and I always dreamed of running an inn there, and the reason I'm going now is to see how feasible it is."

"Yes, I heard you."

"And I know your father owns hotels and inns in England. I was kind of hoping she'd connect me to him? Like even just to talk to him after I get there. Or…if he has any vacancies at any of his properties—"

"No," Rashid said. Just the one word. *No.*

Ruby frowned. So much for civility. "You don't even know what I was going to ask."

"You just asked it. You want me to tell my father all about this amazing woman I met in Toronto who fetishizes everything about the UK so much that she's dropping everything to move there on a whim. I'm sorry, Ruby, but why would I tell my father to hire someone who admits she doesn't stay in one place longer than a few years? He has enough trouble finding *serious* employees, he doesn't need someone like–"

Ruby rolled her eyes. *Here we go again*, she thought. "Someone like what? Someone who buys expensive skin care and is a self-proclaimed girly-girl? Someone who loves all the things you hate? Christmas, fruity drinks, and joy? And I'll have you know I don't fetishize *everything* about the UK. I mean, I'm not a fan of colonialism. Or the royal family. Except Harry—he's a cutie. But the rest of them can go."

Rashid huffed a laugh at that. Ruby wasn't sure if he was laughing *at* her or with her. She took a breath. Despite them getting along for most of this dinner, one thing was very clear: Rashid Hakim and Ruby Dhanji could never be friends. They were way too different. They may be able to manage a few minutes of nice, nonaggressive conversation, but eventually one of them would say something that annoyed the other and all this would start again. Maybe there was no point. She didn't need the Hakim family to get a job in England.

But it wasn't just a job. It was her and her mother's dream. She *had* to give it her best shot.

"Look," Rashid said. "I know I've been a bit judgmental with you. You…touch just about every nerve I have. I actually wonder if you were created precisely to get under my skin."

"Ha!" Ruby exclaimed, pointing at him. "You're a skin doctor! You should be able to get me out from under your skin, no problem."

He looked at her with that non-expression again. See? This is why they were such opposites. He was incapable of enjoying a joke. And she was incapable of keeping her mouth shut.

"I *do* apologize for judging you, though," he continued. "You're not as…*bad* as I first thought you were. In fact, you seem very smart with excellent points—especially what you said earlier about how people assume women who like feminine-coded things have less value. I'm going to have to think long and hard about that. I'd hate for Tara and Noor to think I see them as less because they like the color pink or makeup. But the other things I know about you? Like the fact that you speak before thinking? Or act before thinking? You're impulsive—you bought that tree without figuring out how to get it home because it was pretty. You move as soon as you get bored with a place. Now you're moving to a whole new continent, and want to work in a whole new industry, just because of a childhood dream. I do admire your loyalty to your mother and am grateful that you gave me some insights on some deep-rooted misogyny that I need to work on, but my answer is still no. I won't refer you for a job in my family's business."

Ruby exhaled. That all stung. He was wrong. She *was* committed to this dream of hers. And the worst part of his little speech is she finally detected a bit of his English accent. "No?" she asked feebly, feeling about as tiny as the sugared raspberries in her drink.

Rashid tilted his head. "You seem like a fun person, Ruby," he said, his voice a little gentler. "But if I'm referring someone to work in my father's business, then it needs to be someone I would hire myself. And from what I've seen, you wouldn't be committed. I'm not going to stop you from applying, though. I believe there are vacancies listed on the Hakim Hotel Group website."

Ruby blinked. But what was the point of applying now? If their father found out that Ruby knew Jasmine and Rashid, he'd ask his kids about her. Rashid would say Ruby's a bit odd—like always wears Christmas earrings and has perpetual foot-in-mouth disease. And she moves every one to two years and doesn't talk to her family.

Ruby knew how the world worked. She had to make a good impression on everyone in Canadian retail, because everyone talked to everyone, and for a massive country, Canada had a super small population. She'd never get a job in luxury retail anywhere in the country if she pissed off even one store owner.

And the same was probably true in the UK hotel industry. Ruby took a deep breath. "Okay, I understand. I mean, he's your *father*. If you wouldn't hire me, then why would you let him? But…will you give me a chance to change your opinion? Let's go out this season…you, me, and the girls. Your sister will stop insisting you need a social life, and I'll have a chance to fix your terrible first impression of me. And your second and third impressions, too."

He raised a brow. "You want to *date* me?"

She shook her head quickly. She most definitely did not want to date this man. "Of course not. We can be friends. Hangout buddies over the holiday season. I'd like to prove that you're wrong about me not being serious or committed to my dream."

He crossed his arms in front of him. "And then you'll ask me again to introduce you to my father."

She smiled, shaking her head. "No strings attached. I mean it. At the end of December, if you want to tell him all about the impressive, responsible, totally serious woman who's moving to his country, then I'm not going to stop you, but that will be your decision. I'll take you and the twins out, say…four times in the next four weeks. We'll do Christmassy things in the city so the girls can experience all the joys with someone who actually loves it. Just four outings. After the twenty-fifth, you never have to see me again."

Ruby was almost completely sure that Rashid would say no. Why would he possibly agree to this? He hated Christmas, and he disliked Ruby.

But he loved his nieces.

"Just as *friends*?" he asked. The way he emphasized the word *friends* made Ruby wonder if he was thinking about them flirting in Reid's Holiday last week.

"Absolutely. Only friends." The man may be hot, with a small handful of green flags, but this was now business for Ruby. She could not jeopardize her dream for a holiday fling.

He looked at her with that intense non-smile, then gulped the rest of his beer down in one sip. "Okay, Ruby. Let's do this. One condition, though: I'll pay for all the outings with you and the girls. But yeah, you and me…we can hang out this season."

Ruby smiled. *Game on.* This was her chance to show Rashid Hakim that she could be serious. She could be committed. And she would be a great employee at any of his father's hotels.

8

AFTER RUBY LEFT WORK on Monday, she took the subway and a bus for her monthly pilgrimage into the bowels of hell—otherwise known as her father's house.

Ruby would prefer to have nothing at all to do with the man, his wife, or his teenage stepson. But she'd made a deal with the devil—and since her father had fulfilled his end of their bargain, she had no choice but to honor hers. When Ruby got to the small North York townhouse where her father and his replacement family lived, she steeled her nerves and knocked on the door. Her father opened the door almost immediately.

"Rubina!" he said with a frown. "I thought you were coming for dinner...We're almost finished eating." He moved out of the way so Ruby could come in.

Ruby's father was short with a receding hairline and a thickening midsection. He wasn't the type of man anyone would expect to trade in his beautiful wife for a younger model. But that's not what really had happened—yes, Ruby's mother had been more beautiful than his new wife Pamela, in

Ruby's opinion, but he'd traded Ruby's mother in for a *healthier* wife. One without cancer.

"Hi, Dad," Ruby said, stepping into the house and taking off her winter boots. "I told you I wouldn't be able to get here until seven. I worked until six."

"At least you're here for cake," he said, motioning Ruby through his small but pristinely clean house. "I made goat for dinner. Can you believe I cook now? Come, everyone is in the dining room." His wife and her seventeen-year-old son were at the oak table. Gavin nodded to her, and Pamela stood to give Ruby a hug. "Ruby! Look at you! You should come home more often! I hope you had a wonderful birthday!"

Pamela was about fifteen years younger than Ruby's father, and objectively there was nothing wrong with the woman. She was a single mother originally from Trinidad, had brown skin and dark hair, and absolutely doted on Ruby's father. Which was probably what he liked best about her.

Over ice cream and grocery-store cake, they asked how work was and about her move, and asked if she was dating. Ruby gave vague answers that hopefully would satisfy them. She was glad she'd be cutting ties with her only parent again, soon.

She was only here for one reason—while researching how to move to the UK, Ruby had discovered that there was something called a UK ancestry visa that would allow her to both work and own a business there. Since her father's mother had been born in the UK, all Ruby needed was her late grandmother's birth certificate to apply. The problem was, her grandmother died over twenty-five years ago, and Ruby hadn't spoken to anyone on that side of her family in years. Including her father.

After contacting him for the first time in almost a decade, he agreed to track down the documents Ruby needed on one condition: He wanted to see Ruby regularly before she left the country. So, Ruby packed up her Montreal apartment and moved to Toronto last year. She'd been thinking of returning to her hometown to be closer to Marley for a while, anyway.

Ruby figured she could manage this relationship with her father if she didn't actually let him into her life. He didn't know much about her job; he knew nothing about her friends; he didn't even know about her plans to own a business in the UK. She'd hoped to keep the relationship deep enough for him to be satisfied, but nowhere near deep enough for her to get hurt by him again. But the plan wasn't really working. Because being around him—with his happy new family—hurt every time.

"So, where will you be living when you move," Ruby's father asked as he helped himself to more ice cream.

Ruby finished chewing the cake in her mouth. The frosting was grainy. "I booked a room in a rooming house for the first week. I can renew if I like it there, or I can move once I get a job."

Her father's brows wrinkled. "Did you call the numbers I gave you? I still have family in London. You can stay with them. Don't waste your money on a rooming house."

Ruby didn't know this family in London and preferred not to have another debt to pay with anyone in her father's family. "It's fine. I know I'll find a job soon—and then I'm going to want to live near work."

He was still frowning.

"It's so inspiring," Pamela said. "You're young and living your life! I wish I'd done things like that when I could."

"Rubina isn't young," her father said, shaking his head. "You really should be settled instead of moving so much. At your age I had a wife and daughter and owned a business. You should go back to college and get a real job. Even Gavin is looking at schools now—I took him on a campus tour in Hamilton last March."

Ruby looked at the stepson, who only nodded. She exhaled. Her father had never taken her on any campus tours. Also, no one called her Rubina except her father. Plus, a career in luxury fashion *was* a career. She had no doubt she made more money than the entry-level "real" jobs that she could get with a college degree—and that was because she was damn good at what she did.

And most important, did her father ever realize that the reason Ruby had never settled anywhere—in a relationship, or hell, in a city for more than a couple of years—was because of him? Because he'd never, ever made her feel wanted in his home?

But no. She wasn't going to say any of that. Because she was committed to keeping things surface level. "Yeah, maybe! I'll look at options after I move."

There was one thing Ruby knew without a doubt—she was never going to see this man and his perfect new family again after getting on that plane to the UK. She didn't need to keep this up anymore—she had her visa. Maybe she'd contact him one more time, just to see the look on his face when she was settled in England, owning her own business, and not just succeeding in spite of him, but *thriving*. Ruby would love to show her father that she was more than the person he saw.

Ruby was in the store before opening the next day to put out some new stock and told Jenisha about that awkward and painful birthday cake at her father's.

"Your birthday was like two weeks ago, wasn't it?"

"Week and a half, but yeah. I told them this was my only free night this month." She'd said that mostly because she wanted to put it off as long as possible.

"I don't get Brown parents—no matter what we do, it won't be enough." Jenisha was Sri Lankan, so she knew. "Did they even get you a birthday present?"

"Drugstore fragrance from three years ago. Still had the sticker from one of those closeout places." Ruby sighed. She hated being ungrateful. Pamela had never been anything but kind to her, and her father *had* helped her get the visa. Plus, they went out of their way to get the cake and wrap that gift, right? But he was her father. Her only living parent. He was *supposed* to do something for her birthday. He hadn't even remembered how old she was.

Ruby yawned. She'd had a terrible night's sleep. The hour she spent with her father left her feeling unsettled, like it always did. Hopefully, that was the last one. She opened another box, which turned out to be scented candles made by a top fragrance house.

"I don't need my father anymore," Ruby said, smelling one of the candles before putting it on the shelf. She didn't know why, but the scent reminded her of Rashid. "I'm going to get a referral to the Hakim Hotel Group in the UK. They are so much more influential than anyone my dad knows. All I have to do is impress Dr. Rash."

Jenisha shook her head. "I still can't believe that you're going out with the guy you called the most infuriating man you'd ever met."

"I'm just going to show him and his nieces around a bit. Improve his impression of me." She pulled another box toward her and opened it. The irony wasn't lost on her—she wanted to prove she wasn't impulsive, so she impulsively made that deal with him.

"So when is your first not-a-date, and where are you taking him?" Jenisha asked.

Ruby pulled out a couple of pearlized white ceramic Christmas trees with little glowing white lights on the tips. They reminded Ruby of these hideous green trees that her mother had made one Christmas at one of those DIY ceramics places. Which...would that be a good activity for five-year-olds?

"Dunno yet. I haven't spoken to him." She didn't have his phone number. She should have gotten it when they had dinner on Sunday.

"So, you made this great plan to impress the guy by taking him and his nieces to Christmas things, but you didn't actually, you know, plan anything?" Jenisha laughed.

"Why are you laughing?"

"Because, Ruby, it's so you. You aren't a planner! Like, you could have opened all these boxes first, seen what was in them, then planned where they would go, but instead you've been opening one box at a time and putting them on the shelf. Now you're going to have to either move the candles or put the taller Christmas trees in front of them."

Ruby scowled at Jenisha. "I plan things! Does no one think I'm capable of carrying things out?"

"I know you're capable. But a lot of times you do things without thinking them through, assuming it will all fall into place."

That was ridiculous. She'd done a hell of a lot of planning for this move—which was proof that she *could* and *did* plan. "Okay, let's finish merchandising. And I promise, I'll make some Christmas plans today."

RUBY SPENT HER FIFTEEN-MINUTE morning break in the back room of the store googling and planning her first outing with Rashid. Then, on her lunch break, she put on her red coat and cream cashmere scarf and headed to her favorite independent café, Sophie's, to get some warm drinks. The Winter Market was already busy—it was past noon, so the outdoor shopping cabins and food vendors already had a steady stream of customers. Ruby had only half an hour for lunch, so she didn't have time to look around, but walking through the market was enough to put a huge smile on her face. She didn't understand how Rashid could complain about working in the middle of this magic. Being surrounded by all this holiday cheer was heaven.

The outside of Jasmine's dermatology clinic didn't look like a doctor's office. The only way anyone would know was the small white lettering on the door that read DR. JASMINE HAKIM, BOARD CERTIFIED DERMATOLOGIST. Ruby went inside.

And…all the joy from the Winter Market left her at once.

After all the elaborate holiday decorations and old-world charm, complete with holly on the light posts, this clinic was stark, minimalist, and, honestly, a bit boring. The walls were white, and a faint paint smell lingered. The counter where the receptionist sat was glossy white. The chairs were white leather. There weren't even any paintings on the walls. Ruby was the only person in the waiting room.

She walked right up to the receptionist—a twentysomething East Asian woman with shiny dark hair parted in the middle and full lips with shiny nude gloss.

"Happy holidays!" Ruby said. "I'd love to speak briefly with Dr. Rash—I mean, Dr. Hakim. Rashid Hakim. Is he in?"

The woman didn't smile. "Do you have an appointment?"

Ruby frowned. "Oh. I mean, no. I guess he's probably busy with patients. I saw him on the weekend but didn't get his number—"

"Dr. Hakim isn't interested," the receptionist said. She looked smug.

Ruby frowned. "Interested in what?"

"Whatever it is you're selling, soliciting donations for, or asking him to join. If you'd like a consultation, you can make an appointment with $100 deposit. If you have a doctor referral, please have them fax it."

"Oh no, I'm not a patient. I'm his..." She wasn't sure what to say. His friend? His holiday date? Neither was really true. "I *know* him. Like, personally." Well, that didn't sound right, either. It sounded like she was implying she'd had sex with him. *Ugh.* Was that what the receptionist was thinking? That Ruby was his hookup?

The receptionist gave Ruby a startled look. Yep. That's exactly what she was thinking. And Ruby wasn't a fan of how shocked the girl looked at the thought of Ruby having sex with Dr. Rash. Sure, Ruby wasn't a size 2 with lip fillers, but she was attractive. She could get a man like Dr. Rash if she wanted one.

"Rebecca, it's fine. Hello, Ruby," a voice behind her said. It was him, of course. Had he heard her kind of implying she'd slept with him? She turned and…oh.

She hadn't seen him at work before. Only in jeans. And he looked…*different*. Less lumberjack, more hot doctor. No stethoscope around his neck or lab coat or anything, but instead, very, very nice business casual. Charcoal flat-front pants, a blue dress shirt that looked buttery soft, and leather shoes that looked pretty designer for someone who criticized her love of designer brands. And a perfectly tailored black wool overcoat. The gray at his temples was more visible in the bright lights, and paired with the more adult outfit, he looked like he'd earned every one of his thirty-seven years. All in all, Dr. Rash looked gorgeous. She kind of understood the receptionist's hypothetical point now—he probably was a touch out of Ruby's league.

Ruby took a deep breath, pushing down the butterflies in her stomach. He even smelled hot—he *did* smell like that designer fragrance candle. "Hey Dr. Rash…id. *Rashid*. I just came to bring you a coffee…I didn't get your phone number on Sunday. We need to talk, right? So, I can tell you my…plans?"

"I was about to eat my lunch," he said, holding up a brown paper bag. "If you don't mind talking while I eat, come into the consultation room."

She relaxed a bit when he said consultation room instead of examination room, and followed him down a gleaming white hallway. She wasn't sure what she expected from the consultation room—but it looked like a stock photo of a modern corporate office. White walls and a neat glass desk. She sat in the chair opposite his desk.

Rashid took off his coat and hung it on a hook behind his door. He sat in the white leather desk chair, opened his bag, and took out his food. The smell of grease and beef filled the room.

"You're having a burger and fries for lunch?" she asked, taking off her coat and putting it on the back of her chair.

"Yes." He smirked, looking at her. "Are you wearing Christmas earrings again?"

"They're bells. They don't ring, though—that would be annoying on my ears." She handed him the coffee. "Your niece said you don't like things that taste good, so I got you a peppermint mocha." She wrinkled her nose at the thought of mint and coffee together.

He blinked at her before giving the coffee a sniff.

"That was a joke. Sophie's coffee always tastes good. Even their peppermint."

Not saying anything, he took a tentative sip from the cup, then looked up at Ruby, eyes wide. "It *is* good. Thanks. You sure you don't mind if I eat?"

Ruby smiled, waving her hand. "No, of course not! Go ahead. I'm on my lunch break, too. No time to eat, though!"

He raised a brow. "So…what did you need me for? Please don't say you want me to look at a blackhead or something."

Ruby inhaled indignantly. "Excuse me? Blackheads don't stand a chance with the crap skin care that I waste my money on."

He chuckled, shaking his head. "Apologies again for being so rude that day. I have no idea what you are using on your skin, but it looks great."

Ruby put her hand on her chest. "Oh my god. Did Dr. Rash just *compliment* me? Compliment my *skin*?" He huffed another laugh. He seemed a lot less grumpy now than that day he came into Reid's Holiday and insulted everything there. "Does it bug you when I call you Dr. Rash?"

"No. Rashid has always been my name, and I'm a doctor. I still wonder why no one else thought of it. I mean, at my hospital everyone always teased Marcus Johnson, the urologist."

Ruby laughed out loud at that. "Maybe they called you Dr. Rash behind your back."

"Maybe. Want some chips?" he asked, indicating to his box of fries.

Ruby beamed. "You said *chips* instead of *fries*!"

"I *did* grow up in London. So, will you have some? This is way too much for me."

Ruby nodded, because how can anyone say no to fries...or chips. He dumped about half his fries on the paper his burger was wrapped in, then slid the box to her.

"Anyway, the reason I'm here..." Ruby said after eating one. "I made a list of holiday activities for us to do with the twins." She pulled out her color-coded chart. "For the first outing, we can go see the enormous Christmas tree at the Toronto Eaton Centre, then the Christmas windows at the Hudson's Bay department store, which I guarantee will blow their mind.

Then we'll have a meal—lunch or dinner, depending on when we start our day. I don't know what they like, but all kids love pancakes, and I heard about this all-day brunch place on Baldwin that makes loonie-sized pancakes and serves them in a bowl with fruit and syrup. Then—"

"You have every outing all planned out?" Rashid asked.

"Of course! I'm a planner! I only have the first outing itinerary finalized, though. I brainstormed a bunch of ideas for the other days, but I thought it would be better if all four of us discussed them together. We can do that while we're eating the small pancakes! I don't want you to think I'm like an evil taskmaster or anything. This can be collaborative. And I know you *think* you don't like holiday things, but there must be something you enjoy that's holiday or winter themed."

"I like skating," he said. He took a big bite of his burger.

Right. He was a hockey fan. Ruby's brows knitted together. "Oh. Like, on ice?"

He laughed. "Of course, on ice. I play hockey on a rec team in Calgary. I had to drop out this year, though. Because I'm here."

Ruby bit her lip. "Skating. I mean…it's not really my thing. Like, I know it's weird. I've lived all over Canada, and I can't skate, but my parents never made me learn, and I was too nervous when we had school skating days. Like why are humans balancing on these narrow blades on slippery ice…and *enjoying* it? Plus, I doubt your nieces can skate, and I don't want them to get hurt. I mean, I know you're a doctor, but their mother will be upset about cuts and bruises and—"

"You talk a lot, you know that?" Rashid said, interrupting

her. She couldn't tell if he meant *Oh, you're so cute! You talk so much!* Or *Wow, you're annoying! You talk too much!*

Ruby frowned. "I talk when I'm nervous."

"Why are you nervous?"

So many reasons. She was in a doctor's office, and she'd had mostly bad experiences in doctor's offices. She had to impress this completely baffling doctor so he'd tell his father how mature and totally serious Ruby was, and if she failed, then everyone, including Dr. Rash himself, would shake their heads and say *Oh, Ruby…she's always like this, isn't she?* And Ruby would never be anything more than what everyone already thought she was.

Not to mention this confusing man was breathtakingly gorgeous. There was so much to be nervous about—it was no wonder she couldn't put the brakes on her runaway mouth.

Maybe Dr. Rash found a gram of compassion, because he gave her a sympathetic look then. "You know what, Ruby? Don't worry about any of this. I know I said yes to your plan to take me and the girls out, but really, it's not necessary. I can take the girls out on my own."

She frowned. "You can't back out. Your sister wants you to have a social life!"

"I don't have to do what my sister says."

Ruby exhaled. She'd already annoyed the man so much that he dreaded the thought of spending more time with her. Ruby stood. "Okay. I mean, I'm sorry for…you know. Taking your time. Thanks for the fries." She didn't even finish them. And they were good, too.

He stopped her. "Wait, Red, sit back down."

Ruby turned back to him. "Did you call me Red?"

He nodded. "If you're going to call me Dr. Rash, then you get a nickname, too. Your name is Ruby, and you're always wearing that red coat."

Ruby grinned. "Not always. Just in November and December." She sat back down and ate a fry.

"Do you really want to take me and the girls out?" he asked. "Or was it just so I would say nice things to my father about you."

"I mean, yeah, partially that second one, but also..." She shrugged, smiling. "You know, I freaking love this season. If I don't do these things with you, I probably won't do them at all. My friends here are all busy. And coupled." Reena had Nadim, and of course an infant, too. Marley's boyfriend Nik would be back from LA soon, so Marley would be busy with him. Shayne had Anderson. And Ruby was alone. She knew her friends would come along once or twice if she invited them somewhere, but she'd be a third wheel.

"So, you want to be coupled, too?"

Ruby shook her head. "Like a relationship? No. Who has time for that? But my memories in Toronto, like from before I left the first time, aren't really great. It would be nice to have some nice memories before I leave it again."

He stared at her with that frankly bordering-on-unsettling gaze of his. Finally, he shrugged. "Okay, Red. Let's do it. But I'll warn you, don't plan the outings too much. You saw what happened when we tried to do the parade and lunch on the same day. The twins don't have a lot of stamina. Or patience."

Ruby grinned widely. "Yay! It's a date! But not really a date.

And I'm even better at not planning than I am at planning. I'm off Thursdays. Does that work for you?"

He checked something on the iPad on the desk. "I should be free after one. I don't think Jasmine will mind pulling the kids out of kindergarten a couple of times."

"Shall we shake on it?"

Dr. Rash smiled small, then put his hand out to shake. And wow, the feeling of that skin against hers could be downright addicting.

"Quick question," she asked after letting go of his hand.

"Yes?"

"Any ketchup in that bag?"

10

RUBY PUT MORE THOUGHT than normal into her outfit on Thursday for her first outing with Rashid and the twins. She wanted to dress festive without coming across as too *extra*. She finally decided on dark jeans and a red oversized sweater with a wide neckline that tended to fall off her shoulder. She wore a wide-strapped camisole under it so he wouldn't think she was trying to be seductive or anything. Because she wasn't. And she wore simple red hoops instead of any of her holiday earrings.

Rashid had insisted that he would drive since the girls tended to get overstimulated on the subway, so Ruby texted him her address. To which he responded, I know where you live, Red.

Ominous. She again wondered if she'd made a mistake with this plan.

He pulled up in front of her building at exactly one fifteen, which wasn't a surprise. She'd assumed he was the punctual type. What was a surprise, however, was his car. When she'd met him, she'd assumed Rashid worked in construction or was a contractor. So, she figured he'd drive a pickup. But then she saw him dressed in his doctor clothes in his sleek office. So maybe a Lexus?

But it was neither. The man rolled up in a green Volvo station wagon with Alberta license plates. It was a newer one, but still. This car was not Rashid. But maybe she didn't know enough about him to know what kind of car was him. She peeked into the back seat and saw the twins buckled into booster seats. Ruby opened the passenger side door and slid in. She immediately twisted to see the girls better. They were in their purple coats and pink boots. The one with curly hair had her hair in a ponytail, and the other had her hair down.

"Hi, Tara and Noor," Ruby said. She looked at Rashid. "I made a playlist for them. Can I plug my phone into the stereo?"

Rashid gave her a confused look. "I know they're shy and probably don't want to talk," she explained. "You know I can talk enough for all three of us, but I thought we could get into the holiday spirit with some Christmas music!" When Rashid still didn't say anything, Ruby added, "My kid-friendly favorites."

He shrugged, but she could see the irritation on his face. He did not want to listen to holiday music in his car. "Sure." He unplugged his phone and handed the cable to Ruby.

Ruby watched Rashid's eye twitch the moment the Wiggles' rendition of "Rudolph the Red-Nosed Reindeer" filled his car. Maybe she shouldn't have done this—the last thing she needed to do was to annoy Rashid even more.

But when they heard the sound of two quiet voices singing along from the back seat, Rashid smiled.

"See?" Ruby said. "Isn't this better than the awkward silence monster?"

The twins giggled at that, which made Rashid chuckle, too.

"Yes, this was very thoughtful of you, Red."

Ruby beamed, loving the expression of appreciation on his face. Rashid still looked distractedly hot. Ruby decided it was the lack of hat. Rashid had sexy hair. The kind Ruby imagined running her hand through…and she had to stop doing that. They decided to be friends, nothing more.

"This your car?" she asked. "I wouldn't have clocked you as a Volvo guy."

"Why not? It's spacious. Practical. What kind of car would you think I'd drive?"

She thought about it. He was a cautious driver, but he lived in Calgary. She thought of that blue beanie. "Subaru. But a smaller one. A bit sporty."

He chuckled. "My last car was an Impreza. I needed more room for my hockey gear, though."

Ruby smiled, satisfied with herself. Her interest in cars, despite not having one, was one of the only things she had in common with her father.

The drive to the downtown mall thankfully wasn't long, so Rashid had to endure only three Christmas songs. After he parked in the underground lot, the four of them stepped into the elevator. The girls' eyes opened wide and they clutched each other's hands as the glass elevator ascended into the large center court of the mall.

"Have they been here before?" Ruby asked. The Eaton Centre wasn't Ruby's favorite mall in Toronto, but it was kind of hard to ignore it since it was huge and smack-dab in the center of the busiest part of the city.

Rashid shrugged. "I assume. They've lived in Toronto their whole life." When they got off the elevator, Ruby pointed out the tree. It was enormous and richly decorated with red lights and gold accents.

"The tree is over one hundred and fourteen feet tall!" Ruby explained to the girls. Would kids know how big a foot was? "That's like…five of your Rashid Uncles."

Rashid shook his head. "I'm taller than them, but not *that* tall. More like…" His brow furrowed as he did the math. "More like nineteen of me. Should we go up a level so we can see the whole thing at once?"

One of the girls nodded, while the other clutched her sister's hand.

On the escalator up, Ruby leaned into Rashid.

"Which is which?"

He leaned in to answer her. So close she could smell his cologne. It was a different scent than last time, and the clean scent gave her goose bumps. "Noor has her hair down today," Rashid said.

"Does your sister style their hair differently so people can tell them apart?" She knew they weren't identical twins, but other than their hair texture, they looked pretty much the same to Ruby.

Rashid's brow furrowed at that. "I did their hair today, and I let them choose their hairstyles."

Oh. She didn't know why she assumed their mother would be the one to get them ready. Was that assumption sexist? But he was only their uncle. Maybe she would have assumed differently if he was their father?

When they got to the third floor, they walked to a railing overlooking the central court. Even though they were on the third floor, they were only about halfway up the tree. It was *huge*.

"Where do they put this thing the other ten months of the year?" Rashid asked.

"I assume in a storage space? It probably disassembles."

He frowned. "That seems like a giant waste of space. And money."

"Nonsense. It's beautiful," Ruby said. "I love all the crystals dancing. They're real Swarovski, you know."

He said nothing. But he didn't have to. The disapproval was all over Dr. Rash's face. She hoped the twins hadn't heard his bah-humbug comment.

Suddenly, loud music started playing in the mall. Louder than the normal background music. It literally made Ruby jump.

"What the…" Rashid said. "That's way too noisy." He turned to find where the classical music was coming from.

"Rashid Uncle, look!" the ponytailed twin said, pointing at the tree.

Synced to the music, a light show started on the tree. First the ornaments started changing colors, then the whole tree turned blue and glittering snowflakes started falling down it. Soon, twirly red ribbons cascaded from the top. Ruby had no idea if this was a projection on the tree, or the lights on the tree were changing to make all the images appear, or if it was literal magic...but it was *spectacular*, the crescendoing symphony and the enormous, multistory tree in the middle of a mall showing this mesmerizing light show. Ruby had no idea this was going to happen, but she was so glad she was here to see it.

Rashid was probably hating it, though. But when she looked at his face, that's not the expression she saw. He was entranced. His features had softened, his eyes focused, and his lips were slightly parted. He looked...gorgeous. The sight of his face in complete wonder was even more mesmerizing than the light show. He must have noticed Ruby staring, because he smiled awkwardly, rubbing his neck. He didn't look like he'd shaved this morning, as there was a hint of stubble there, but his skin still looked soft and clear. "Okay, that's pretty cool," he said quietly.

Ruby grinned widely. Even if the rest of the day was a bust, she'd succeeded in showing Dr. Rash a bit of holiday magic.

After the light show, the four of them went to the bookstore on the third floor. Rashid let the girls pick a book from one of the tables in the children's section. Ruby couldn't help but notice his irritation when they both picked out Christmas picture books—one of them about Santa's workshop, and the other about a little girl helping her mother decorate for Christmas. He also told the girls they could get outfits for their American Girl dolls.

While the girls were looking at the doll clothes, Ruby leaned into Rashid. "Why do they have American Girls? They're British Canadian."

He shrugged. "I bought them each the Indian doll when it came out. All their other dolls were white." He frowned. "I swear, their father's parents gave them blond dolls on purpose. Their grandmother actually said that it was too bad their skin tone is more like their mother's than their father's."

Ruby frowned. "Ugh." She hated that their father's family didn't love everything about these two girls—including their light brown skin and dark hair. "I hope they never said that to the girls' faces."

He shrugged. But now Ruby kind of understood why he was resentful that the girls still wanted to celebrate Christmas.

After they picked identical green velvet dresses for their dolls, Rashid paid for it all, and they walked over to the Hudson's Bay to see their windows.

This store had done over-the-top Christmas windows for as long as Ruby could remember. Her mother used to bring her to see them every year, and Ruby had always found them magical. There were six windows in all, and the diorama in each one told a story. This year, it was a re-creation of Santa's workshop, which made Noor, the twin who'd picked the Santa's workshop book, squeal with joy. "It's like my book!" she said. "Look, Tara, they're making elephants!"

Ruby could tell that these windows were a bigger hit than the tree for the girls. They excitedly pointed out all the small details to each other, like the little mouse family eating a meal together in a hole in the wall, and the robot assembling more robots. Rashid didn't seem as enthralled as he had for the tree light show, though.

Ruby crouched to talk to the girls. "Hey, doesn't that doll look like your American doll?"

"American *Girl* doll," Tara corrected. "Not American doll."

Ruby smiled. She was happy to be corrected if it got the girls talking to her.

As they moved toward the sixth window, Rashid leaned in close to Ruby. "Okay, these windows are cool. And so was the tree. You did good, Red."

Ruby beamed. "I made Dr. Rash feel holiday joy! I'm going to ride that high all day."

After leaving the mall, Rashid drove them to the restaurant. There was a huge crowd outside. Ruby told Rashid and the girls to wait on the sidewalk while she went in to see if their table was ready.

"Did you make a reservation?" the hostess asked.

"Of course I did." She told the hostess her name.

The hostess frowned and looked at her screen. "I don't see it. Did you call it in?"

Ruby shook her head. "No, I made it online."

After a few more moments, the hostess shook her head. "Your reservation is for tomorrow afternoon. Would you like me to cancel it?"

Crap. She screwed up. "Can I switch it to today?"

The hostess shook her head. "We're fully booked for reservations right now. If you'd like to wait for a walk-in spot, it's about forty-five to fifty minutes."

Ruby cringed. The girls were clearly tired. "I have kids with me. Any way we can get a seat sooner?"

The hostess was shaking her head when Rashid came in,

holding Tara in his arms and Noor's hand. "What's wrong?" he asked.

"Oh...they can't find my reservation," she said, forcing a smile. She couldn't let Rashid know she'd made the reservation for the wrong day. She was supposed to be impressing him with her organization skills, maturity, and all-around employability.

"She made the reservation for tomorrow instead of today," the hostess said to Rashid. "I can get you a table in forty-five minutes. You're welcome to wait in the bar." She handed Ruby a plastic disk. "This will buzz when your table's ready."

Ruby glared at her. Why had the hostess told him she screwed up? Was there no girl code?

Rashid, at least, didn't look irritated or angry. More like exasperated. Unsurprised. "Should we go somewhere else?" he asked.

"I want Santa pancakes!" Tara said.

Ruby cringed. She should not have shown them the pictures of the pancakes on the drive over.

"We can sit in the bar!" Ruby said, doing her best to sound enthusiastic. "It'll be fun. Maybe they can make Shirley Temples. Have you ever had that drink?"

"Pancakes," Noor said before hiding her face in Rashid's legs.

"Okay," Rashid said. "We'll wait in the bar."

They clearly weren't the only ones with that idea, because the bar area was quite full. Thankfully, another group got their table, so they were able to get an empty bar table that had three tall stools at it. Rashid lifted each girl onto a stool, then told Ruby to sit.

"It's fine," she said. "You sit. I'm okay."

He shook his head, his eyebrows knitting together. "I'm going to the bar. Sit. What do you want to drink?"

Ruby exhaled. She'd planned to have one of their holiday cocktails—like an eggnog martini or something like that, but after screwing up the reservation, she didn't want to see more of Rashid's disappointed face at her festive drink. She asked for a hot tea. He went to the bar, leaving Ruby alone with the girls.

Ruby tried to engage in some conversation, like asking if they were going to order the Santa pancakes and what they thought of the Christmas windows, but they were quiet. They only looked at each other, clearly terrified of the big red lady who talked too much. Which was fine. They were tired.

Rashid returned then, with a server carrying a tray of drinks behind him. The girls got red drinks that had little plastic swords with cherries on them—apparently, they did make Shirley Temples here. Rashid got a black coffee, and Ruby a hot tea.

Ruby tried to get up and give Rashid her seat, but he insisted that she sit. He still looked irritated.

"I'm sorry," Ruby said. "About the reservation, I mean." She felt terrible. Not only because she was supposed to be impressing Rashid, but now he had to stand in this dark and crowded bar with two cranky kids instead of being in the cozy dining room feasting on little pancakes. It was a stupid mistake. She'd undone all the good she'd done by taking them to see the Christmas windows and the tree.

Rashid didn't even look at her. "Why is this place so full, anyway? It's a Thursday afternoon."

"I guess because of their Christmas menu. It's been all over Instagram."

He scoffed at that. "So, because some entitled influencer was comped a meal here, the rest of us have to deal with these crowds?" He was standing near Ruby and was quiet enough that she doubted the twins heard him. They were focused on stabbing their cherries with their little swords, anyway.

"Girls, don't make a mess," he said. "The staff here is going to have to clean all this up."

A server, who was clearing a nearby table, turned to them, smiling. "Oh, it's fine. I have a son about that age—I know how hard it is to keep them busy while they're waiting. Your daughters are adorable. Twins? They certainly take after your wife!"

"Oh, they're not our kids!" Ruby said. She frowned. Did they look like her? Maybe…in that they were Brown. But that was it.

"And we're not married," Rashid said. Ruby couldn't miss the contempt in his voice, like how dare anyone assume he would choose to marry someone like Ruby. Ruby sighed. She'd been right. This was a mistake.

The server looked back and forth between Ruby and Rashid, no doubt trying to figure out the relationship between them and questioning why they all looked so miserable. "Okay. Well, I hope you get your table soon." She headed back to the bar with her tray of empty glasses.

"You didn't have to look *that* disgusted at the thought of being with me," Ruby said quietly. She should probably keep her mouth shut, but she was hurt by that look on his face.

He didn't say anything to that because Noor started whining that she spilled her drink. Then Tara complained that it had spilled on her skirt. Ruby sighed, looking around the festively decorated restaurant with the gold streamers and plastic bells covering the ceiling. Maybe Rashid was right—there was nothing *magic* about dozens of tired and hungry people squeezed into this place with dollar-store decorations waiting for their overpriced tiny pancakes because some wannabe celebrity ate them. This was her *favorite* season. And hanging out with the Grinchy Dr. Rash was taking away Ruby's joy.

She exhaled and took a sip of her tea, which...Was that cinnamon?

"What kind of tea is this?" she asked.

"You didn't say what kind you wanted, so I got you cinnamon-gingerbread," Rashid said while dabbing Tara's skirt with a napkin.

Ruby frowned. On Sunday, she'd had a gingerbread latte. Had he remembered that she liked gingerbread-flavored things? That was incredibly thoughtful.

Maybe Dr. Rash wasn't such a Grinch after all.

11

THANKFULLY THEY WAITED IN the bar only long enough for Ruby to finish her tea. The Shirley Temples—or, rather, the tiny sword fights—invigorated the girls, and Rashid seemed to lose his irritation, too. When the hostess brought them to a lovely little table in the tasteful dining room, they ordered more drinks and some pancakes-for-dinner creations.

"I didn't think it would just be pancakes," Rashid said, frowning, after the waitress left their table. He'd ordered Chicken Little pancakes, which was a stack of cornbread pancakes topped with chicken, avocado, arugula, barbecue sauce, maple syrup, and cilantro. Ruby ordered the gingerbread molasses pancakes, and both girls got the strawberry SantaCakes.

"The restaurant is called Milk and Honey Pancakes. What did you expect, fish and chips?"

He shook his head. "Oh, I'm not complaining. Just not used to pancakes for dinner."

Ruby looked at him curiously. Not complaining? Was it

possible that she was misinterpreting Rashid's rants? Or was he completely clueless about how he was seen by others?

When their drinks arrived, Rashid asked Ruby if she wanted a picture of her drinking her eggnog martini for her socials.

She chuckled with surprise. After his rant about Instagram, this offer was unexpected. Rashid used his own phone this time and took a few pictures of Ruby sipping her martini, and then some of the girls with their strawberry milk.

The food finally came. The strawberry SantaCakes were small buttermilk pancakes topped with sliced strawberries, crème anglaise, and a little Santa made from a whole strawberry and whipped cream. Ruby's gingerbread pancakes were little dark gingery rounds topped with cinnamon whipped cream and salted caramel molasses. Rashid even seemed impressed with his chicken and cornbread pancakes. They both took pictures of the food and of the girls grinning with their pancakes, too. After taking her first bite, Ruby closed her eyes and made an embarrassing sound. "Oh my god, this is the best thing I've *ever* put in my mouth," she said under her breath. The girls seemed to be distracted by their own food, so hopefully they didn't hear Ruby's hardly G-rated moan with pleasure.

Rashid heard her, though, and chuckled. She turned to him. "Seriously, you have to try this."

He shook his head. "It's basically dessert for dinner. I don't know why I agreed to let the girls order those."

Ruby smiled mischievously. "Because it's festive, and breaking the rules sometimes is a bit of harmless fun. Here, try mine. I guarantee it will be life-changing." She prepared a bite for Rashid, getting a bit of the gingerbread pancake and dipping it first into the salted molasses, then in the whipped cream. She held the fork in front of his mouth.

He started to roll his eyes, but then he suddenly stilled, looking at her with intensity. The table was small, and since they were sitting next to each other, they were only inches apart. She could smell that intriguing cologne and see the smoothness of his touchable skin. Why was he looking at her like that? And why did that look on his face make it harder for Ruby to remember that she did not like this man? Rashid's eyes traveled from her eyes to her lips, and finally to the bite of food on her fork.

She smiled slowly. "I *know* you want this."

He let out a soft laugh and opened his mouth. As she slipped her fork in, she wondered if this was his bedroom expression. If so, she envied his past lovers. It was a heady experience to be on the receiving end of his sultry gaze.

The corners of his lips upturned as he chewed the bite. "Okay, I don't know about life-changing. But I agree, that's excellent. Dessert for dinner certainly has its merits."

A satisfied smile spread on Ruby's face. Another win for her.

Overstimulated and maybe oversugared, both girls whined that they didn't want to sit when Rashid tried to belt them into their car seats after dinner.

"No! I don't want to go home, Rash Uncle!" Noor yelled.

"Great. Now the kids are calling me Rash," he said under

his breath while buckling Noor in. But he didn't sound annoyed. More like amused.

Of course, because Toronto, they were caught in traffic on the way home. The twins quickly fell asleep, though.

"Go ahead and put on more Christmas music," Rashid said. "Just not too loud so the girls don't wake up."

Ruby couldn't tell if he was serious about the Christmas music, but his mood seemed pleasant. Despite her mistake with the reservation, dinner ended up being a success, probably because the food was just that good.

"What would you be listening to if you were alone in the car?" she asked.

He shrugged, watching the road in front of him. Rashid was a very steady and patient driver, even in this traffic. "Probably a news or science podcast."

She chuckled.

"No laughing," he said, even though he was smiling, too. "I'm not that dull."

"I never said you were," Ruby said. She plugged her phone on and put some holiday instrumental music on.

They didn't talk much on the drive, but the vibe between them was different. Lighter. Maybe it was because their first holiday hangout had been mostly a success. Or maybe that electrically charged moment they had when she fed him a bite of her pancakes had unraveled something in him, the way it did with her.

Probably not. There was no way that he was as affected by her as she was by him. She really shouldn't think about that moment too much, because the last thing she needed was for her mind to get ahead of itself, imagining what could have happened if they had been alone instead of in a busy restaurant with two five-year-olds. That was an ill-advised daydream—especially since they had three more outings like this, and those would only be harder if Ruby was fantasizing about what his skin would feel like under her fingertips. Or wondering if he really did know a lot about her…anatomy.

When Rashid pulled up in front of a redbrick house about five minutes from the Distillery District, Ruby assumed it must be Jasmine's home. He picked up his phone after turning off the car. "Jasmine can help get them inside, then I'll drive you home."

Ruby shook her head. "Oh no, it's not necessary. I'll call an Uber or—"

"Rash Uncle! I have to go to the bathroom!" one of the twins called from the back seat. He quickly got out of the car, then pointed at Ruby. "You stay."

Jasmine came out in black yoga pants and a floral sweatshirt. She gave Ruby a quick wave, then she and Rashid each unbuckled a twin and led them by the hand into the house.

Ruby waited. Why was he so adamant about taking her home? Maybe he actually *was* into her, and he was expecting her to invite him up for a drink or something. She didn't mind inviting him for a drink. It was the *or something* she was worried about. As much as she was fascinated by and *very* attracted to Rashid, the point of this deal was to get a job in his family's business. Ruby had no intention of jeopardizing that opportunity by mixing business with pleasure, even though she suspected the pleasure would be off-the-charts good, based on their chemistry so far.

When he returned, he smiled at her before starting the car. "The girls will sleep well tonight," he said.

Ruby nodded. She would not have imagined their first outing would go so well. "It was such a great day. That molasses dipping sauce…I have to re-create that. So, what's next for our plan? I'm off next Thursday again, so we can—"

"Maybe we should tone it down next time? The girls were clearly overstimulated."

Ruby frowned. "But they enjoyed it! They totally felt the magic of the holiday season." She glanced at him. "And I think *you* did, too."

He snorted at that.

"Don't guffaw at me, Dr. Rash. I saw your face when you saw that tree," she said, still smiling.

He shook his head. "I do not guffaw. I don't even know what a guffaw is."

She'd never met anyone who guffawed as much as Dr. Rash. He was guffawing now, even though he was laughing.

"Seriously, though, Red," he said. "Yeah, the girls had fun, but all we showed them was crowds and manufactured cheer designed to get us to spend money," he said. "Which I did a lot of today."

"Oh. I mean I know you said you'd pay for all of this, but if it's too much I can cover my—"

He shook his head. "I *can* afford it. It's not the amount of money. It's just…The tree and the windows were cool, but you do realize that putting up a tree and decorating those windows in a literal shopping mall is all marketing, right? You say the holiday season is for creating memories with family and joy, but at what cost? Corporations are making record profits, and the difference between the haves and the have-nots is the largest it's ever been. These companies are enticing everyone to spend even more money by wrapping it all in family traditions and commercialized joy." They were at Ruby's building then, so he stopped his car in front. "We don't even celebrate the holiday. It seems so silly to buy into all this hype. It's not *for* us, Ruby." He was still smiling. His eye wasn't twitching with annoyance. His tone sounded like he was just chatting with a friend—the Grinch face was nowhere to be seen right now.

But his words felt like a punch to her heart.

Ruby took a deep breath, looking at that stupidly handsome face. "Don't tell me that I'm not allowed to feel joy because it's not my holiday. Do you even hear how exclusionary that is? I was born and raised in this city. And if the whole city wants to celebrate a holiday for an entire season, then it *is* for me, just as much as it's for anyone else who wants to celebrate it. And my memories of the holiday *are* about tradition and joy, not commercialism. I came to the Santa Claus Parade every year with my mother when I was young. And we went to see those windows, too. My mother was a seamstress, and my father's a mechanic. We certainly couldn't afford to shop at the Bay or buy American Girl dolls. But those windows and the parade are for *everyone*. They are for the self-righteous privileged people like you as much as they are for people who can't afford the fancy clothes and toys those stores sell. And I'm not going to let anyone, let alone a *doctor*, take the joy from those memories from me."

Ruby unbuckled her seat belt and opened the door to the

damn Volvo. Rashid's eyes were wide, like a deer caught in the headlights. And because Ruby was Ruby, she kept talking. "My mother *died* when I was twenty. I didn't have a father or an uncle who cared enough about me to continue our traditions when she was gone. So, no, this holiday isn't about family for me anymore. Because I may as well not have one." Her voice cracked. "But it *is* about joy. Joy, and that cozy feeling I get when I eat gingerbread, hear Christmas songs, and see children enjoying the season as much as I used to—there is no way I'm going to let a cynical grump take that joy away from me. Goodbye, Rashid. I won't torture you with any more holiday happiness."

She got out of the car and closed the door without even looking back. Screw him. Let him tell his father all about the immature, holiday-brainwashed woman who was coming to England and wanted to work in one of the family hotels. She'd survived this long without anyone supporting her, and she could continue to survive without the Hakim family's help.

12

RUBY'S PHONE LIT UP with a text about an hour after she got home from that outing with Dr. Rash. It was the Shayne Freaking Loves Olives group chat.

> **Reena:** Ruby! How did the first date with the doctor go?
>
> **Ruby:** It wasn't a date. And that man is an insufferable codpiece.
>
> **Nadim:** Oh no! Ayesha always said she had the best brother in the world!
>
> **Shayne:** Oooh, Ruby's bringing out the UK insults. What exactly happened? Spill the British tea! First tell us what you wore!

Ruby smiled. It felt good to debrief with friends after that mess. She wrote it all out, from her outfit to the tree, the windows, and, finally, his Scrooge rant at the end of the night.

Anderson: He does sound insufferable.
I hate antiestablishment rich bros.

Marley: That's not antiestablishment.
That's just rude.

Reena: Nadim, why are your people
like that?

Nadim: How is he my people?
I'm not a codpiece, am I?

Reena: No, but you're a rich British dude.

Nadim: The guy lives in Calgary.
I'm not claiming him as one of my own.

Shayne: For your next outing, pick something
less commercial. Go thrifting or something.

Ruby: We're not going out again. He's a twat.
I'll figure out another way to get a hotel job in
England.

Ruby was much too busy the next day to worry about the insufferable dermatologist. It was a Friday, and the store was the busiest it had been since the pop-up opened at the beginning of

November. And she knew it would be getting even busier every day until Christmas.

Past the time when she was supposed to leave, Ruby was still gift wrapping a big pile of cosmetic sets for a lawyer who was buying gifts for her entire office when Jenisha came up to her at the gift-wrap counter. The customer was at the other end of the store, picking out even more sets to add to the pile.

"You're not supposed to be here anymore. Let me take over. Your skin doctor is here," Jenisha said.

Ruby scowled and looked up, and sure enough, Rashid was near the entrance, holding a couple of pink cups from Sophie's Café. He really was like a bad rash she couldn't get rid of. "He's not *my* doctor."

"Well, he's *a* doctor, and he's certainly not here to see me. Sexy doctors never wander in for me. Clearly, I'm doing something wrong with my life."

Ruby wasn't sure he was here to see her, either. After she told him off last night, she figured he wouldn't want anything to do with her. Or at least he would have gotten the hint that she didn't want anything to do with him.

He noticed her then, and those intense eyes locked with her for a moment before he started walking toward her. She sighed and handed Jenisha the next makeup set to wrap, then walked around the counter to meet him.

His fitted charcoal pants, dark green shirt, and wool overcoat was a look. A look that would normally be exactly Ruby's type. Too bad his insides were nothing like his outsides.

"This is for you," he said, handing one of the cups to her.

She did not take it. She raised a brow.

"It's a new drink they had—sticky toffee pudding latte."

Oh. Well, that sounded delightful. She took it and was hit with the aroma of ginger, cinnamon, and rich caramel. "Why are you here, and why are you bribing me with beverages?"

He rubbed the back of his neck nervously. "I owe you an apology. I was insensitive yesterday. I'm sorry…and I'm sorry about your mother. That must have been hard for you to lose her when you were so young."

"Not that young. I was twenty." She sighed. He looked sincere, at least. "Thanks for the apology, though." She looked at the second drink that he was holding. "What are you drinking?"

"A peppermint mocha."

Ruby couldn't help it—she chuckled.

"Can we talk?" he asked.

She took a sip of the drink. "I'm officially done for the day. Where do you want to talk?"

"We can go back to my office? It's empty now."

No. Ruby didn't want to go back to his office, where presumably sick people went and doctors made decisions about their lives. Not to mention, talking in his office would give him a home field advantage. She shook her head. "Let's walk and talk. The market is open for a few more hours."

She saw on his face that he wanted to object to hanging out in the Christmas Market with her. But if he wanted to make up for being such an insensitive tool, then he should agree to go where she wanted.

"Okay," he said.

"Jenisha, I'm heading out." She smiled at Rashid. "I'll get my coat." She went to the back room.

Ruby used the bathroom, reapplied her signature Ruby Woo red lipstick, smoothed some anti-frizz serum over her curling-iron waves, then put on her red coat and white scarf. It was mild today, which was one of the reasons she'd suggested the market in the first place.

When she returned to the selling floor, Rashid was in the fragrance area smelling one of the men's scents.

"Why do you approve of designer fragrances, but not designer skin care?" she asked him.

He shrugged. "Probably an occupational hazard. I know too much about skin care, but fragrances are mysterious. I liked this one when I tried it the last time I was here." He held up the new Le Labo.

She took the bottle from him and sprayed it on his neck, then wrists. "I didn't get the chance to smell it on you after it settled into your biology. If you still smell good at the end of the night, then it's a winner. Let's go." She headed out of the store holding her drink, and Rashid followed.

They walked side by side on the cobblestone streets. For once, Ruby didn't feel the need to speak to fill the silence. She was still irritated at him. The things he said yesterday—that she shouldn't be enjoying the season, that it wasn't for her—stung.

Ruby didn't exactly grow up very poor, but her family *did* have less than many of her peers. Even less than her extended family—her cousin Marley's parents had a big house in Markham instead of the small Toronto apartment where Ruby grew up. And because Ruby was Brown, was a college dropout, and moved so often in adulthood that she had no long-term friends, she was used to feeling like an outsider. Feeling like she didn't really belong somewhere. His comment only rubbed salt in that wound. She *knew* all this wasn't for people like her. She knew she didn't have a family to celebrate with, and she knew all the warm feelings she was having were because corporations were trying to sell her something. But she was still allowed to enjoy it.

She peeked at Rashid. His forehead wasn't furrowed like it was when he found out she'd made the reservation for the wrong day yesterday. But he wasn't smiling, either. After they'd walked long enough in complete silence, she finally had to say something.

"You said we needed to talk," she said. "Are you going to, you know…talk?"

He chuckled. She'd seen his real smile a few times now, and she liked it more than she wanted to admit. "I don't know how to start," he said.

"Yes, I noticed. You've been through the Winter Market before?" she asked. The dermatology office was technically outside the market—but right next to it.

"Yeah," he said. He glanced around. "With my sister, when they first brought out all this holiday stuff. The girls wanted everything from those stalls." He pointed to a neat row of adorable wooden stands, each selling a different holiday treat. One had ornately iced cookies, another had mini donuts, and one made huge cotton candy animals to order.

"That's the best one," Ruby said, pointing to the stall that sold pastel de nata—Portuguese egg tarts. "The tarts are to die for."

He stepped closer to look at the tarts. "I've had them in Portugal. Let's see if these are as good. Do you want one?"

Ruby should probably eat actual food for dinner instead of a latte and a custard tart, but she couldn't say no. After he bought two tarts, they walked while eating them. Ruby had never been to Portugal, so she had no idea if the tart was as good as ones from there, but this was flaky and buttery, and the caramelized flavor from the browned top cut through the sweetness perfectly.

"It's as good as Portugal," Rashid said, popping the rest of his tart in his mouth.

"I've always wanted to go. I've never been anywhere in Europe." She wanted to say that she planned to travel throughout Europe after moving to the UK, but she knew he didn't approve of her move, and she didn't want to set him off.

"You've moved a lot in Canada. Can I ask why?"

Ruby shrugged. "After my mother died, I haven't felt tied to any one place, so when an interesting opportunity comes up, I move." She realized that saying that only made her seem flighty, but that was who she was. "I mean, none of those places meant anything to me. Montreal was my favorite, but I've never found anywhere that felt…right. Like home."

"You grew up here in Toronto, right?"

She nodded. "Yeah. Why all the questions?"

"I'm trying to understand you, Red."

She smiled to herself. Just like she wanted to understand him.

"Toronto doesn't feel like home?" he asked.

Now that was a tricky question. Ruby took a breath. "No, not really. There are too many memories in this city. Not good ones." Memories like doctors and hospitals. And her father yelling. And then leaving.

"I'm sorry again about your mother," he said, seeming to understand what she meant. "You've spoken so fondly about her. I hadn't realized she had passed. Are the bad memories why you want to leave the country?"

Ruby shrugged. "I do have some good memories here, too. Like all the holiday ones. But…I can make holiday memories anywhere, right? I can make new ones in England."

They walked by the large tree in the middle of the market. It was absolutely covered with blue and gold ball ornaments and gold bows. Halfway up the tree, big black letters spelled DIOR. Evidence that all this beauty and joy had a corporate sponsor. She waited for him to say something.

"My sister made me take about a million pictures of Tara and Noor at that tree," he said.

"You didn't mind the corporate branding in the pictures?"

He huffed a laugh. "I took them from the back of the tree."

She pointed to the Spanish restaurant near the tree. "That place has fantastic tapas."

"I love tapas. Honestly, Spain has the best food in Europe. My parents used to have a flat there—we went every summer."

It struck her how different their upbringings were. Ruby grew up in an apartment in an area full of immigrants. Her father did own his own business—an auto shop—but it didn't always do well enough to support them, which was why her mother took on work as a seamstress. They didn't really have family vacations—maybe a trip to Niagara Falls when guests were in town. They certainly didn't have a summer home in Spain.

Even now, as adults, Rashid could be considered to be in a different class than Ruby. He was a doctor; she worked retail. True, she made pretty good money selling luxury goods, but she hadn't even finished college. Ruby remembered reading an article once that said cultural differences between classes were much bigger than cultural differences between races. She could believe it. She'd dated blue-collar white men—they had more in common with Ruby than this Brown doctor. But it didn't matter that she and Rashid came from different classes, because they were nothing to each other, and it would stay that way.

She chuckled. "A house in Spain? We really come from different worlds."

He sighed. "Yeah. I'll be honest, Red. I've led a very privileged life, and I think that maybe my blinders are thicker than I realized. The truth is, my parents taught us all good values and morals, to treat everyone equally, and to be grateful for what we have, but they left us to our own devices with those lessons. We were told we had a lot of privilege compared to others, but we weren't really shown it. But you...I mean, you kind of rubbed my nose in it."

"You sound like Mr. Darcy. Your accent is even peeking through."

He gave her a confused look, so she explained. "In *Pride and Prejudice*, when Darcy apologizes to Elizabeth for being a dick, he said, 'As a child I was given good principles, but was left to follow them in pride and conceit.' It sounds like what you just said." He still looked confused, so Ruby waved her hand. "Never mind. Carry on..."

He shrugged. "All I was going to say is that if you're willing, I want to continue our deal. You said you wanted to show me that you're a responsible, non-impulsive person, and now I want the chance to show you that I *do* have manners, and I do respect you and your...worldview."

She raised a brow. "So now you *respect* me?"

He laughed at that, nodding. "I not only respect you, Red. I think I'm starting to actually...*like* you."

Ruby grinned. The truth was, she'd been starting to like him, too. When he wasn't a pretentious ass, he was kind of fun. He was smart and ridiculously loyal to his family, and he clearly listened...which was more than she could say about many doctors she'd known in the past. He paid attention to what she liked and bought her gingerbread drinks. And he was very easy on the eyes, too.

"Tara and Noor like you, too," he added. "They wouldn't stop talking about you this morning. They told their mother about the best pancakes they'd ever had, and they want to bring her to see those windows. They said they can't wait until we go out again."

Ruby huffed a laugh. "Really? They actually talked?"

"The girls are actually very chatty with their mother. And me."

Considering the complete tantrums they'd had when Rashid had been strapping them into the car, Ruby was surprised that they were so positive about their day. But that was holiday magic. Ruby of course realized that not every moment she had with her mother as a kid had been perfect. She'd probably burned cookies, cried at the parade, and been poked with pins when Mom made her annual choir dress. But Ruby didn't remember any of those bad moments. She only remembered the good. She only remembered how much she loved the season and how great her mother was for doing all those things with her.

Rashid was staring at something in the distance. Ruby looked, and it was an archway leading to the back patio of a restaurant. The patio was closed because it was way too cold to eat outside now, but the arch spelled out in blue and white lights THE HAPPIEST TIME OF THE YEAR.

"Look, Ruby," he said, looking into her eyes. "I hate the way it happened yesterday, but I'm glad I learned more about…" He hesitated. "About why you love all this so much. Maybe we won't get under each other's skin if we understand our differences better?"

Ruby looked at him. "They teach you those skin metaphors in medical school?"

He laughed. "Shush, you. So will you show a clueless doctor and his two nieces Christmas joy three more times?"

Ruby smiled. "Okay. Yes. This could be fun, now that we understand each other."

He smiled so big that it actually gave her goose bumps. The man had a breathtaking smile. Maybe she liked it too much.

"I'll try harder not to be so single-minded," he said. "If I slip, remind me of my addiction to designer cologne."

Ruby grinned, then picked up his wrist to smell it. The cologne had settled into a smoky, spicy scent that made Ruby's knees weaken. And his skin was even softer than she imagined. She stepped back and grinned. "That scent is a winner on you. Want me to put one aside for you in the store?"

"That would be great, thanks."

"You know what Dr. Rash? I don't think you and I are all that different. I've figured out something else that we definitely have in common."

"Oh? What's that?"

"Food. We both love good food. Which…look." She pointed at the stand that they were walking past. "You ever have a Liège waffle?"

"I've had a Belgian waffle. What's a Liège waffle?"

She smiled. "It's a type of Belgian waffle. Yeast based. Oh my god, they have ruby chocolate drizzled ones. I freaking *love* ruby chocolate…and no, not because of my name. Wanna split one?"

He nodded, grinning.

She ordered a waffle drizzled with ruby chocolate and sliced strawberries. After the woman handed Ruby the little cardboard tray with the waffle on a stick, she immediately handed it to Rashid to take the first bite. She grinned when his eyes practically rolled back in his head after tasting it.

"Good, right?" she asked.

"Phenomenal. I've never had ruby chocolate. It's a little fruity…and rich. It's decadent. You're going to have to get another one, because there is no way I'm sharing this." He took a step away from her and took another bite.

Ruby laughed. "But if you only eat half, you'll have room for cider donuts."

He looked at her, blinking a few moments. "Seriously, Red? Dessert for dinner, again? You're going to be a bad influence on me, aren't you?"

She smiled cheekily and shrugged. "You need a little more *naughty* in your nice little life."

"Good point," he said. "We'll need churros, too."

RUBY WAS GLAD SHE wasn't working until noon on Saturday, because she woke up with the mother of all sugar hangovers. And a bit of a regular hangover, too, because she and Rashid had ended their desserts-for-dinner night sitting in front of a fire in the Winter Market with warm cups of mulled red wine.

She ate a healthy breakfast of an egg white omelet with toast and made it to Reid's Holiday ten minutes before her shift started. The store was ridiculously busy again.

When she took a five-minute break in the back room, Ruby opened her friend group chat.

> **Ruby:** Change of plans—Operation Impress Dr. Rash is back on.
>
> **Reena:** It's back on? I thought he was a twat?
>
> **Ruby:** He's a twat who apologized. I still want him to refer me for a job at one of his father's

hotels, so I'm giving him another chance. Where
should I take him that won't make him rant about
the commercialization of Christmas?

Reena: Niagara Falls? That's a natural wonder.
I hear they do a holiday light show.

Ruby: Too far. And super commercial. Have you
even been there in the last thirty years?

Marley: Casa Loma is doing a Christmas event.

Ruby: Too…castle-like. We ranted for a while
about the royal family and British peers last night.

Ruby had been delighted to find that they had similar views on the usefulness of the royal family in the modern age. They also talked about living in Quebec, Alberta, and British Columbia, and which province had the best signature dessert, arguing between British Columbia's Nanaimo bar and Ontario's butter tart before finally agreeing that Quebec's sugar pie was the clear winner.

Shayne: I know the perfect thing…I heard about
this cute vintage/craft sale. Give me a minute,
I'll look it up.

Ruby didn't have a minute—she needed to head back to work. The moment Ruby walked back into the store she spotted

Jasmine Hakim looking at the robes in the lingerie area. She was alone. Ruby headed straight to her.

"Hi, Jasmine!"

Jasmine smiled warmly and gave Ruby a hug...which, wow, Jasmine was nothing like her brother, who had just waved goodbye after walking her to her condo last night.

Jasmine even held on to Ruby's arm a few seconds. "I wanted to come and thank you in person for taking the girls out on Thursday!"

Ruby smiled. "No problem. I had a lot of fun. Did you need help finding anything? Those robes are one hundred percent cashmere. They're *so* luxurious."

Jasmine looked back at the hanging robes in pastel colors. "They're gorgeous. Honestly, this whole store is wonderful. I love all this Christmassy stuff."

After getting to know this woman's brother for the last few days, it was a tiny bit shocking that the Doctors Hakim came from the same genetic material. "You're nothing like your brother."

Jasmine smiled. "He's a little...grumpy, but honestly, Rashid is an amazing person. You left quite an impression on him." She leaned close as if she was going to say something scandalous. "He let the girls play a Christmas album at breakfast without complaining once."

Ruby giggled. "He was probably still high on all the sugar we had last night."

Jasmine shrugged. Despite Jasmine making jokes and hugging Ruby, there was still something a little low energy about her. Like she was struggling to get her words out. She took a pale pink robe off the rack and ran her fingers over the soft knit. "My mother would love this." She looked at the price. "I'll take it. Can you gift wrap?"

Ruby smiled. "Of course." After ringing up the sale, Ruby took the robe over to the gift-wrap station and grabbed a medium box. She lined the box with tissue, placed the robe in it, folded the tissue over the robe, and affixed it with a small Reid's sticker. Jasmine picked the deep burgundy paper.

"Can I ask you a question, Jasmine?" Ruby asked as she cut off a large piece of paper.

"Of course."

"Your brother...Does he have a particular reason for being so grumpy? Like a trauma or something he's dealing with?" Ruby had done enough self-reflection to know that a lot of the reason she was so enthusiastic and extra was because of losing her mother when she was twenty. She wanted to enjoy her life, because she knew how fragile it could be. Also, having a father who didn't approve of anything about her probably played a role, too (yes, she was well aware that her unresolved daddy issues were a problem she needed to deal with at some point). But from what she could tell, Rashid's childhood was ideal. No money problems; parents healthy, alive, and seemingly great to him. She knew that Jasmine was struggling right now because her marriage had just ended, but she didn't know if Rashid was also struggling with something.

Was his Christmas hatred just because of Jasmine's ex? Or had he dated a Christmas elf who ruined him for the holiday season forever? Even Mr. Darcy's ill manners at the beginning of *Pride and Prejudice* could be traced back to the situation with Wickham and Darcy's sister. Maybe if there was a reason for his moodiness, then Rashid would eventually get over it.

Jasmine shook her head. "No, not that I know of. He's always been the most serious of the three of us. And the most principled. He's a great guy, really. He's easily the most generous person I know. I don't know what I would have done without him right now. He's just...Rashid is an *acquired* taste."

Ruby smirked. People had said the same thing about Ruby. Of course, for completely different reasons.

"Has he...dated? Any serious relationships?"

Jasmine gave Ruby a small smile. She clearly thought Ruby was asking these questions because Ruby herself was interested in dating the man. Which she wasn't.

"He's single now, if that's what you're asking," Jasmine said. "He split with someone a few months ago—not very recently though. He's not on the rebound."

Ruby shook her head quickly. "We're just friends. I have no time for dating now. I'm just curious. Why's he still single?"

Jasmine shrugged. "He works a lot. He's in a hospital system in Calgary, plus he does medical research and some consulting. I keep telling him to slow down. Private practice would give him more free time. His ex broke up with him because she didn't want to wait for a proposal anymore." Jasmine's nose wrinkled. "I shouldn't be gossiping. I adore Rashid, but... Ayesha always said he needed something to shake up his routine. Maybe coming here has done that for him."

Ruby agreed—Dr. Rash could use a shake-up. "Which ribbon do you like? The warm cream looks great with this paper."

"Yes, the cream is lovely."

Ruby tied a bow with the cream ribbon and handed Jasmine the box.

"Thank you!" Jasmine said slowly. "Mom's going to love it. I'm going to have to mail it, since I won't be seeing her..." She frowned, a slight tremble on her lips, like she missed her family. She forced a smile. "I'm so happy we met you, Ruby. I hope we stay in contact after you move away."

Ruby smiled. "I hope we will, Jasmine."

She was glad she met the Hakim family, too. Even if some of them were an acquired taste...Ruby was oddly acquiring it.

For the rest of her shift, Ruby couldn't stop thinking about what Jasmine had said—that Rashid's grumpiness was just who he was and wasn't because of any trauma. It was one thing to be a bit introverted and a bit...cantankerous, but Rashid had also been judgmental. She'd accepted his apologies because he seemed genuinely regretful, and they had a fun time eating their way through the Winter Market last night. But was this going to be a cycle for him? Treat her like crap, feel bad about it, then apologize? Would he ever *really* change? Once a twat, always a twat.

But it didn't matter if he was a twat. Her friendship with Rashid Hakim was a means to an end only and had an end date. Hell, after the end of this month, she was pretty sure she would never see him again.

Shayne finally texted Ruby about the craft show the next day. It was basically a vintage market and craft sale being held in a mansion owned by the city in the East End. She checked their Instagram and saw that the vendors were either artisans selling their own homemade items or vintage stores carrying a curated selection of gifts. Also, there would be an afternoon tea served in the formal dining room and lots of photo opportunities. It was perfect. With the focus on either handmade or resale goods only, Rashid couldn't call the event too commercial, but at the same time, it was very holiday themed. She bought two tickets online for next Thursday (children were free) and texted Rashid the confirmation page.

He wrote back right away.

> **Rashid:** I was supposed to be covering the cost of our outings.
>
> **Ruby:** It was $20, and it's going to charity. This looks like fun, don't you think? No commercialism! A vintage Christmas vibe! It will be the perfect place to get bespoke Christmas gifts.
>
> **Rashid:** It does look fun. But aren't you going to buy all your gifts from Reid's? To use your discount?
>
> **Ruby:** Oh, I wasn't talking about me.
> I meant for you. The twins will be with us, but maybe you can find stuff for your sisters? Do dermatologists approve of artisanal skin care?

> **Rashid:** What about you? Your friends don't exchange gifts?

Ruby frowned. She didn't know if they would be giving her anything. Last year they all exchanged gifts at the Caroling party, but only Marley and Shane had something for Ruby. She'd only been in town a few weeks, so it made sense. And this year she was closer to the rest of them, but they all just gave her something for her birthday. Were they close enough for two gifts within a month?

> **Ruby:** They're not really my friends—they're my cousin's. She lets me tag along while I'm in town.
>
> **Rashid:** What about friends somewhere else? Halifax or Montreal?
>
> **Ruby:** I'm not really close to other people. Saves me so much money this time of year! Lol.
>
> **Rashid:** Why did you do that?
>
> **Ruby:** Do what?
>
> **Rashid:** Add lol to your text.
>
> **Ruby:** I don't know.

Rashid: I have some patients on Thursday morning. I can pick you up at one again.

Ruby: Perfect!

When Thursday came, Rashid pulled up in front of Ruby's building promptly at one o'clock. After saying hello to Rashid, Ruby peeked at the girls. They were in red skirts with white tights and green sweaters. Their hair was styled differently again—one had all her hair pulled into a French braid, and the other had two high pigtails. She'd just need to figure out which was which, and she'd be able to tell them apart all day.

She smiled at Rashid. "They look like a Christmas card."

He nodded. "My sister looked up the place we're going and wants me to take pictures of them in the mansion."

Ruby laughed. Poor guy was being subjected to the holidays by everyone in his life.

"I have something for you," Ruby said, handing each girl a small wrapped box. "Open them," Ruby said. The girls took the boxes, but nervously looked at their uncle instead of opening them.

"Just a little something," Ruby said to Rashid. "I saw them in an Indian store and thought they might like them."

Rashid nodded to the girls, so they tore off the paper and opened the boxes.

"It's an elephant!" Tara said. At least Ruby thought it was Tara. The girl held up the red embroidered Indian elephant

Christmas ornament. Noor grinned, holding up her green elephant.

Rashid shook his head. "Ruby, you didn't need to do that."

Ruby waved her hand. "It was nothing. When I saw Indian Christmas ornaments, I knew they would be perfect for Tara and Noor."

"Because we're Indian!" Tara said.

"Exactly," Ruby said. She put her seat belt on. She was happy to bribe the girls to make them smile like that.

When Rashid didn't start the car, she looked at him. He was watching her with that intense gaze of his. He needed to stop doing that, because that look was giving Ruby thoughts she shouldn't have.

"Seriously, Rashid, it was nothing. Now let's go, before they run out of hot chocolate!"

It was a long and quiet drive to the holiday craft market, but Ruby didn't feel the need to fill the silence. She'd realized that Rashid was particularly quiet when he was focused on something, like driving. Which was fine. She wanted him to drive safely, especially when his nieces were in the car. The girls were chattering quietly behind them to each other, but Ruby couldn't make out a word of it. She wondered if they had their own made-up language. They clearly had a very close bond. Ruby felt a pang of jealousy—what would her life have been like if she'd had a sibling? But it was probably a good thing that her parents only had one child—the last thing she would have wanted was another person saddled with her family.

Ruby gasped when Rashid pulled into the parking lot of

the East End mansion. She'd seen pictures of the place, but it hadn't seemed this big, or this picturesque. The house was an old Victorian country home now surrounded by a residential neighborhood filled with 1960s bungalows. The mansion was dark brown brick, with lots of cream gingerbread moldings on the multipeaked roof. It even had a turret. Walking up to it felt like walking back in time. Ruby half expected to see a mysterious woman in a black veil in the attic window.

"Oooh, very Jane Eyre!" Ruby said, clapping her hands. "I had no idea this place existed!"

Rashid raised his brows. "I figured you would think it was Dickensian...I mean with those wreaths on every door, this could be a scene from *A Christmas Carol*."

Ruby turned to give Rashid a look. "How would you even know what *A Christmas Carol* looks like?"

"Um, because I'm a human being born in the twentieth century? Remember, I grew up in the UK. Dickens is kind of unavoidable. You girls ready to be Victorian gentry for the day?"

The twins looked at their uncle, thoroughly confused. Ruby laughed. "C'mon, let's get some pictures outside."

After taking a bunch of pictures of the twins, and then the twins with Rashid, they went inside.

"Oh, this is...perfect," Ruby said after their tickets were scanned at the door. The house was fully decorated for Christmas, but very tastefully. Natural pine boughs tied with red plaid ribbons and groupings of white pillar candles were everywhere. The fireplaces in each room were adorned with greenery, silver candlesticks, and ornaments, and the whole place smelled like winter—cinnamon, pine, and warm chocolate. There were craft vendors set up in all the rooms of the main floor, selling jewelry, pottery, stained glass, gourmet jams and jellies, woven tapestries, hand knits, hand-painted ornaments, and even handmade candles and skin care.

It was lovely. It was the exact opposite of the Winter Market—no corporate sponsors, no overpriced drinks, just artisans selling locally made gifts. Ruby had to admit that even though she loved Reid's Holiday and the Winter Market, she also loved the charm of this place. And best of all, Rashid seemed to be enjoying it, too. The four of them went from room to room looking at all the crafts for sale. Rashid bought a lot—starting with twin fairy crowns made with silk flowers and crystal beads, which the girls insisted on wearing right away. Ruby chuckled when she saw their red and white Christmas outfits paired with pink and purple tiaras. He also bought gifts for other people, with Ruby's help. Some little knit pieces, some ornaments, jellies, and even a handmade soap that smelled like cinnamon and marshmallows. Rashid's family was very lucky—he really was very generous, just like Jasmine had said.

And he was in a fantastic mood. He smiled more and talked more, and there was a lightness, almost a giddiness, in his steps as he moved from vendor to vendor. It was contagious. The girls were chattier—with each other and with their uncle. They even talked to Ruby a bit—showing her things they liked, like little clay fairies and unicorns.

"How much are you going to buy?" Ruby asked Rashid after he bought an adorable hand-knit hat with a fur pom-pom. "I thought you don't celebrate Christmas?"

He shrugged. "I want to support local artists. Plus, other people celebrate, even if I don't."

"Oh, wow, look at that…" Something caught Ruby's eye. It was a necklace made of delicate raw rubies on a copper chain. It was so unique. Of course, considering Ruby's name and her love of the colors red and pink, she'd always been attracted to rubies. She picked it up. "This is *gorgeous*."

The woman behind the table—a twentysomething Brown woman, smiled. "It's handmade. Kashmiri rubies and pure copper."

Ruby was usually drawn to more traditional jewelry, the type sold in boutiques, not this handmade, rustic style. But this piece was beautiful. The stones weren't clear, and they were a deep, kind of moody blood-red instead of the pinky-red rubies she was used to. And the copper chain they were strung on was so slim and delicate.

"Do you make the jewelry yourself?" Rashid asked the woman.

The woman shook her head. "We work with a women's collective in Northern India. All the pieces are handmade for us and are one of a kind."

Ruby wanted to buy it. It wasn't that expensive, just over $100. But she hesitated. She wasn't supposed to be spending too much before her move. But she thought about Rashid mentioning that she didn't exchange gifts with anyone. There was absolutely nothing wrong with Ruby buying a gift for herself. And she wanted something to remember this weird month—when she made an unlikely alliance with a Christmas Scrooge who turned out to be kinder than he appeared.

"I'll take it," Rashid said, handing the woman his credit card before Ruby could tell the woman that she wanted it. Ruby turned quickly to him.

"I was going to buy it," she said.

"I know you were. I'm beating you to it."

"Well, that's very rude. I'm literally holding the thing in my hand."

The woman at the table was still holding Rashid's credit card, looking between the two of them, not sure what to do. She glanced at the twins, wincing. She'd probably assumed the four of them were a family and was worried that she'd caused a fight between the girls' mom and dad. "I have another similar one," the woman finally said. "Made with Ceylon sapphires. Can I show you?"

"I'm buying it *for* you, Ruby," Rashid said. He looked at the woman. "Can you gift wrap it?"

Ruby shook her head. "You can't buy me a necklace!"

"I owe you," he said. "You bought the tickets today."

"I spent twenty dollars on the tickets! This is over four times that much! We're not supposed to be giving each other presents."

"You gave the twins elephants!"

"Those were three dollars each!"

He sighed. "Just accept the necklace, Ruby. It doesn't mean anything. A friend giving a gift to a friend. It's not that deep."

Ruby didn't want to cause a scene, so she did as she was told and handed the woman the necklace. She didn't know why she was so uncomfortable with him buying this for her—he was right. It didn't have to be that deep. It was just a necklace. And lord knew he could afford it.

Was it a pity gift? Because she said she didn't have anyone to exchange gifts with? Or did he still feel bad for being so judgmental last week? Or was this payment for taking him and his nieces out, showing him around the city?

But she wasn't taking them out selflessly—she was doing it because she wanted something from him, a referral for a job in his father's company. And now every time she saw this beautiful Kashmiri ruby necklace, she would remember that she sold herself out for a job.

Ugh. This was why Ruby hated owing people things.

But she couldn't say no now, not while the woman had already tapped his card for the sale and was wrapping the necklace in a gift bag. The poor woman looked like she didn't know who to give the bag to when she was done. Rashid finally put his hand out to take the package.

He handed it to Ruby with a smile. "Happy holidays."

Ruby took it. "Um…thank you."

He looked at the twins. "Now, how about we take a break from all that shopping and have tea and cake?"

They nodded enthusiastically.

The holiday market had a tearoom on the second floor—a bright space with chintz wallpaper and a tin ceiling. They chose a table near a window, and a woman immediately served tea to the adults and hot chocolate for the girls. The tea was served in mismatched vintage china, and the hot chocolate in paper cups. Then another woman came with a little cart offering homemade baked goods. The girls excitedly chose pale pink cupcakes. Ruby selected a gingerbread Nanaimo bar, and Rashid a peppermint blondie.

"This is nice," Ruby said. Mostly because she didn't know what else to say. She exhaled. Him buying her that necklace made things weird for her. She had no idea why.

"It is nice," he said. "After tea we can check out the vintage area?"

Ruby nodded. The rooms on the second floor apparently had vendors selling vintage gifts.

"Ruby? Is that you? What a surprise!" a voice behind her said. Ruby rolled her eyes before turning around. She knew that voice.

"Shayne, what are you doing here? Are you *stalking* me?" She turned. It wasn't only Shayne, but Anderson, too. Anderson at least looked a little sheepish that they had crashed Ruby's not-a-date, but Shayne had no shame.

Shayne gave Ruby a knowing look. "I'm not stalking you, Ruby. I'm delighted to see you, though." He looked at Rashid, grinning and putting his hand out. "You must be Rashid. I'm Shayne, a very close personal friend of Ruby's. Oh, and these must be your nieces! How adorable. Love the tiaras—you'll have to let me know where you got those. This is my partner, Anderson."

Rashid looked at Ruby curiously for a moment—Ruby didn't know why—before smiling and shaking Shayne's hand, then Anderson's. He introduced Tara and Noor and invited the two men to join their table.

Shayne pulled over chairs from a nearby table and flagged

down the tea server. "This is such an adorable little sale. We just got here—but I know we're going to buy a ton. Did you get the tiaras here? Because if so, all of Anderson's nieces are getting those. And a few of his nephews, too. I can't wait to shop with you all!"

Ruby exhaled. Maybe she shouldn't be annoyed. Shayne and Anderson cared, which was why they were here—to make sure Rashid wasn't being a judgmental ass today.

First Rashid gave her that necklace. Then these two came to check up on her. Ruby was feeling very valued right now. And she had no idea why she was feeling so weird about that.

14

ANDERSON AND SHAYNE WERE on their best behavior during tea. They didn't ask intrusive questions, didn't grill Rashid on why he'd upset Ruby last week, and, best of all, didn't show him any skin issues. The four of them chatted about the craft sale and about other similar artisan markets they had been to. After tea, they all stayed together to wander the vintage vendors on the second floor of the mansion. The vibe up on this floor was funkier than downstairs. Probably because the vintage clothing and decor were mostly from the seventies to the nineties. Ruby loved vintage shopping—finding the best secondhand stores that had designer stuff was always the first thing she did when she moved. She didn't find any Armani at Gap prices here, though. But going through the vendors' curated selections with Rashid, Shayne, Anderson, and the twins was a lot of fun.

Shayne pointed out a Little Mermaid ornament on a tree absolutely covered with old Disney ornaments. "That's probably my favorite Disney princess." He turned to Tara and Noor. "Who do you two like?"

The girls, of course, didn't answer. Rashid wasn't nearby, so Noor hid behind Ruby's leg, while Tara took her hand.

"They're shy," Ruby explained. She looked around for Rashid—who was chatting with the vendor.

"They're certainly not shy with you," Anderson said.

Huh. That was true. It had happened so gradually that Ruby hadn't noticed that the girls weren't afraid of her anymore.

Shayne crouched down to their level to talk to them. "It's okay. I don't really like new people either. I saw Ruby *eight times* before I finally said hello."

"Ruby *Auntie*," Tara corrected him.

Shayne looked up at Ruby and raised one brow. "Oh, we're going by Auntie, are we?"

Ruby waved a hand. "It's an Indian thing. All of your relatives' friends are your uncles and aunties, even if you're not actually related."

"Ruby, I'm well aware of the etiquette," Shayne said, standing. "I've been best friends with your cousin since we were thirteen. But I had no idea you were close enough to the Hakim family to be considered an auntie?"

Rashid came back to them. "Princess ornaments!" he said enthusiastically. Which was such an odd thing to come out of Rashid's mouth that she almost put a hand on his forehead to see if he had a fever.

Shayne smiled. "I was about to guess which ones were their favorites. Hmm…you have beautiful curly hair and look very courageous," he said to Tara, whose curls were in pigtails. "So I think Merida from *Brave* is your favorite. And you…" he said to Noor. "You have your hair in one braid, which makes me think you're a *Frozen* fan. Team Elsa?"

That made Noor's eyes widen. "Elsa is my favorite! Noor likes Anna better."

Shayne nodded. "I'm an Elsa fan, too. After Ariel, of course. Which one do you think Ruby Auntie likes?"

Tara immediately pointed to a Christmas ornament with Belle from *Beauty and the Beast* wearing a red Christmas cape. "Because Ruby wears red all the time."

"Rashid Uncle bought her a red necklace!" Noor added.

Shayne frowned. "He did? Why?"

"Because they're friends, and Rashid Uncle said it's not deep," Tara explained with a straight face.

Ruby exhaled. Anderson and Shayne looked like they were going to laugh.

"Oh look, they have a Mulan one," Ruby said to change the subject. "I love the song about her reflection—the Christina Aguilera one."

Noor agreed and told Shayne she also liked Elsa's songs, which made Tara jump in and say that Anna's songs were better, but not as good as the songs from *Beauty and the Beast*. Soon Shayne, Tara, and Noor were having an in-depth conversation about the best Disney songs.

Rashid turned to Ruby, an absolute look of wonder on his face. He was clearly surprised Shayne could get through to the girls. Ruby wasn't. If anyone could make a couple of shy kindergarteners comfortable, it was Shayne.

Shayne made *everyone* comfortable. What he'd said to the girls—that he hadn't talked to Ruby until he'd seen her eight times, was the farthest thing from the truth. When Ruby moved back to Toronto and connected with her cousin Marley, Shayne immediately welcomed her into their circle. And when he started dating Anderson, Anderson became as important to Ruby as Shayne. Ruby was going to miss these two so much when she left Toronto. Watching them interact with the twins now almost made her tear up.

She shook that thought out of her head. Why was she getting sentimental now? Ruby was used to leaving places, not looking back at them. There was no reason why this move should be harder than the others, even if she was moving farther than she ever had.

Ruby only bought a pair of starburst earrings from the vintage sellers, but again, Rashid bought a lot. He bought Disney ornaments for the girls, an old edition of a Hans Christian Andersen anthology, a gorgeous 1920s faux emerald brooch, and a gray tweed jacket that Shayne insisted was made for Rashid. Shayne was right—the jacket made Rashid look devastatingly handsome. Like, country gentleman hot.

While Rashid was paying for the jacket, Shayne and Anderson cornered Ruby alone.

"Okay, girl. Talk," Shayne said. "He bought you a necklace? Also, why are those girls attached at the hip to you?"

"What? No. They like *you*, Shayne."

"Everyone likes me," Shayne said. "I'm a goddamn delight. Why the necklace?"

"And why does he look at you like you're the best Christmas gift he ever had?" Anderson asked.

Ruby huffed a laugh. "He doesn't. He bought me a small ruby necklace that I liked. We're friends."

"Okay, but—"

"Shayne, come on. Maybe he's not as bad as I thought he was, but there is no way I would want anything more with Rashid because—"

"I know, because you hate doctors. But that doesn't mean—"

"My mommy is a doctor," Noor said behind them. And yep, the girls were listening, along with Rashid, who was holding a paper bag that Ruby assumed had the tweed jacket in it.

Ruby recovered quickly and smiled. "And I like your mother very much. Shayne's being silly. Come on, the next room has some old crystal glassware. Anderson, didn't you say you like vintage crystal?"

Rashid was quiet on the drive home again, but this time Ruby was worried. She had no idea if he'd heard her say so emphatically that she and Rashid were only friends, and she'd never want anything more. She hoped he hadn't heard. Not that she *did* want more from him—but after he was so nice all day, even bought her that necklace, she didn't want him to feel bad.

He said the necklace didn't need to be deep, and it was just a friend giving a friend a gift, but how could they even be real friends when she was only hanging out with him because she wanted something from him? And the more she got to know Rashid, the more she realized that she *didn't* want this friendship to be fake. She didn't want to use him. He was too kind for that.

The girls fell asleep again on the drive home, so like last week Rashid dropped them off at Jasmine's house before taking Ruby home. When he pulled up in front of her building, she gathered her nerve. "Um, do you want to come up for a bit? I mean, there's something I want to talk to you about. Just…a few minutes. It's kind of cold to talk in the car."

He smiled at her. "Yeah, there's something I need to talk to you about, too. Where should I park?"

He was quiet while parking his car and on the elevator, which Ruby was kind of getting used to. But, of course, since no one was talking, Ruby was overthinking. Why had he agreed so easily to come up to her place? Did he think she was flirting? What did he want to talk to her about? Was he going to kiss her? Would she let him?

Ruby cringed a little when she opened her door, realizing this would be the first time Rashid would see her tiny apartment. Jasmine's house was big and probably expensive. Rashid probably also had a big place back in Calgary. And here was Ruby bringing him to her little postage-stamp one-room apartment.

"This place is…" he said, taking in her apartment with the old, mismatched furniture and the peel-and-stick teal chintz wallpaper she'd put on the wall behind her bed.

"Tiny?" she asked.

"I mean, yes, but that's not what I was going to say. It's very you. Colorful and lively. Ah! Look, it's my old friend, your tree!" He kicked off his shoes and headed toward the window where the Douglas fir was set up with all her thrifted ornaments. After looking at it for several moments, he turned to her.

"This is the same tree, right?"

She frowned. It was a tiny bit drier, but still doing pretty well. "Yeah. Why?"

"It looks different. I don't think I've ever seen the same tree before and after it was decorated. It reminds me of that scene in *A Charlie Brown Christmas* where they make fun of his crappy tree, but all it takes is some lights and tinsel to make it look festive."

Ruby gave him a knowing smile. "So you *have* seen Christmas movies, then."

"Shush, you." He sat on her sofa. "What did you want to talk to me about?"

"You go first," she said, joining him on the sofa. It was the only other place to sit.

"Okay. I couldn't ask you in front of the girls, but how do you feel about *The Nutcracker*?"

She frowned. "Like the movie with Keira Knightley? It was okay. I've only seen it once, though."

"No, not the movie, the ballet."

"Oh! I've never been to the ballet." Her family could never afford something like that when she was young. She'd always wanted to go, though.

"My sister bought four tickets a while ago—for her, Derek, and the girls. Jasmine doesn't want to go now—too many memories. They went last year, too. But the girls still want to go. I know you're supposed to be planning our activities, but do you want to go to the ballet for one of our Christmas outings?"

Wow. Seeing the *Nutcracker* ballet was a total bucket list thing for Ruby. "When are the tickets for?"

"Wednesday night. I know Thursday is your day off, but maybe you can switch?"

Ruby shook her head. "I wouldn't have to. I'm only working until five on Wednesday."

He smiled. He looked so hopeful. Ruby wondered where her surly friend went. "So, you'll come?"

Ruby exhaled. She didn't know what to say. She *did* want to go…but ballet tickets were expensive. She didn't want to take advantage of him. Or his nieces, who were starting to like Ruby. Maybe he should take someone who didn't want something in return for his friendship.

Rashid frowned. "You don't look excited. Hey, are you worried that I'm upset about what Shayne said earlier? That you don't like doctors? It's fine. A lot of people don't like doctors. We literally poke and prod people for a living."

It wasn't the doctor thing. Somehow, Rashid had completely changed her opinion about doctors, anyway. He was thoughtful, he listened, and he cared. He was an incredibly compassionate person—exactly what a doctor should be. She shook her head. "No, it's not that. It's…this deal of ours, that I would take you and the girls out for holiday things so I could change your mind about me. Today you kept doing nice stuff for me…the necklace, and the ballet ticket…You know I'm only doing this for my own self-serving reasons, right?"

He nodded. "Yeah. So I'll help you get a job at one of Dad's hotels."

She frowned. "You don't mind that I'm using you?"

"You're not using me. Friends do things for each other."

"Okay, but I don't like the idea of you spending money on me when this was just a deal we made."

He shook his head, irritation on his face. "Ruby, the necklace wasn't expensive. And Jasmine already bought the ballet ticket, so it would be wasted if you don't use it. The money isn't a big deal."

"Spoken by someone who's never had to worry about money in their life," Ruby said quietly.

He looked at her silently. And Ruby felt terrible for saying it. She didn't know why she was so hung up on this, why she couldn't let herself get a little spoiled by her new friend for a while. His eyes were open. He knew her intentions, and he didn't care.

But Ruby *did* care. She understood the value of expensive things, probably because she hadn't been able to afford them for so long. She'd started to like Rashid. A lot. And she liked Jasmine and the girls, too. She didn't want to be taking advantage of their generosity.

"I'm sorry, Ruby," he finally said. His expression was remorseful, and it only made her feel worse. "You're right. I was insensitive." He exhaled. "How can I make you feel more comfortable? I want to do nice things for you, but I can take the necklace back. Return it, or give it to someone else."

Ruby bit her lip. Would that help? She didn't know. If she gave the necklace back, and if she paid Jasmine for the ballet ticket, then she wouldn't feel weird about using this family for their connections, because their relationship would be transactional only—she would take him and the girls out, and he would hopefully refer her for a position at his father's company.

But that wouldn't be a real friendship. What did Ruby want more? A friendship, even only for a few weeks, with a man who was kind and smart, and who wanted to do nice things for her? Or did she want him to refer her for a job in his father's business?

Honestly? At this moment, Ruby wanted the friendship more. A month ago, she didn't know about the Hakim Hotel Group, and she was fine with pounding the pavement in London to get a job. She could go back to that plan easily—she'd done fine professionally for years without connections, and she didn't need any now. She'd rather have the person who gave her the beautiful ruby necklace and the trip to the ballet. She'd rather have her new friend.

Ruby shook her head. "No. I was thinking...After today, and after last Friday at the Winter Market, I want to..." She took a breath. This could be a big mistake. She could be throwing away her best opportunity to make her and her mother's dream a reality. "I want to cancel our deal. I don't want you to ask your father to hire me. Just forget it all, okay?"

Rashid looked at her with a confused expression. "But we still have two dates left! What about *The Nutcracker*?" He grinned playfully. "Don't make me do something aggressively festive without my Christmas buddy."

"Are we?"

"Are we what?"

"Christmas buddies?"

Rashid gave her a confused look. "Yeah, we're friends. We had fun today...didn't we?"

Ruby nodded quickly, mostly because Rashid looked

genuinely hurt. And she didn't want to hurt him. "I had a great time today. But you said you bought me the necklace because we're friends, and the girls are more comfortable with me now, talking more. But I feel like I'm taking advantage of you all. I mean, the point was for me to make you change your impression of me, and—"

He cut her off. "Ruby, are you saying you were being fake? Like you don't really like me, Tara, or Noor?"

Ruby sighed. She couldn't be fake if she tried. Ruby wore her heart proudly on her sleeve—as evidenced by her enthusiasm and excitement about everything she loved. Not to mention her foot-in-mouth issues. She looked down at her hands. "No. I meant it when I said I was growing to like you. And I adore the girls."

"Ruby, look at me."

She did. He was so close…right next to her on her small sofa. His dark eyes focused on hers. She half expected him to touch her, put his soft hand on her cheek or leg. And she would let him. Rashid wasn't a cranky person at all. He had strong opinions and didn't keep those opinions to himself. He was like Ruby that way. Only their opinions were sometimes opposite.

"Ruby, it's okay. You're not using me. I'm helping you, and you're helping me. I had a great time today. And the other times we went out, too. My sister was right—I need to have friends of my own. Friends help each other, and do nice things for each other, too. Like I bought you the necklace, and you put aside that cologne for me. And you found all these fun things to do with the girls. And I can even help you in your career. Because friends help friends."

Ruby swallowed. She didn't know what to say, so she said nothing.

"Ruby, I'm glad we've spent this time together. I'm glad you gave me another chance after I was such a…"

"We've been using the word *twat* in my chat group," she said.

He laughed. "I assume that's why your friends crashed our outing today, then? To make sure I wasn't being a twat?"

She nodded.

"Well, I must agree. I was a twat. I'm glad you put me in my place. I had no right to call you frivolous, impulsive, or absent-minded."

Ruby shook her head. "But I *am* those things. And love a lot of things that you don't care for. Like designer clothes and skin care. How can we be friends?"

"Most of your designer stuff is bought secondhand, though."

"Sometimes thirdhand. What about my expensive skin care addiction?"

"I never said you were perfect."

She snorted, then hit him on the arm with a pillow, which made him laugh. She couldn't believe how much this man laughed—she didn't know what she was thinking when she thought he was stoic.

"Okay, I'm adding violent to your list of faults," he said, taking the throw cushion from her. "No one else would put up with either of us this month, please don't make me take the girls to *The Nutcracker* alone."

She grinned. "Okay. We can be friends, but no strings, okay? This isn't so I can get anything from your family."

He nodded. "Deal. Or rather, no deal. You'll come to the ballet?"

She nodded. "I've always wanted to see it. Ooooh, I know exactly what to wear—I thrifted this red and black boucle coat last month. Very Jackie O. It's perfect for the ballet."

"I don't know what that means, but thank you."

She nodded. "Hey, I was going to order a poke bowl or salad and watch a movie tonight. Want to join me?"

He stared at her. Oh god, maybe she shouldn't have offered that? Was she taking this friendship too far?

Finally, he nodded. "Okay, but no dessert. I'm still feeling the blondie and Nanaimo bar. And no Christmas movies."

She grinned. "Okay on the food, but I *only* watch Christmas movies in December." She made a sweet face and batted her lashes a bit. "Pretty please? After we were talking about Dickens, we should watch *A Christmas Carol*. The Muppets one is one of my all-time favorite movies."

He raised a brow. "Seriously? I'm not sure I want to experience the Muppets' take on Dickens."

"You'll love it. Trust me. Would I ever disappoint you?"

He laughed. "Why do I get the impression that I won't ever be able to say no to you in this friendship? Okay, let's watch the Muppets."

15

"OH MY GOD, I can't believe Gonzo is Dickens," Rashid exclaimed after about a minute of *The Muppet Christmas Carol*.

"Believe it," Ruby said, stirring her spicy salmon poke bowl. "This movie is closer to the source material than most adaptations—just with frogs and pigs." She was sitting on the floor with her bowl on the coffee table, while Rashid was on the sofa, holding his. They'd ordered from Ruby's favorite poke place, and Ruby got hers with salad instead of rice. She didn't want to go anywhere near carbs for the foreseeable future.

"You're loving this, aren't you?" she asked twenty minutes into the movie. His eyes were glued to her TV.

"Honestly, if every Christmas movie had Kermit in it, I'd watch them all."

Ruby grinned. Maybe she should dig up some of the lesser-known Muppets Christmas movies. After a few more minutes, she joined Rashid on the couch. Her butt was starting to hurt on her hardwood.

"Young Ebenezer is hot," Ruby said after the scene when

young Scrooge told his fiancée that they'd have to put off their wedding because he needed to make more money first.

"When you called me that, did you really think I was as bad as Scrooge?" Rashid asked.

Ruby frowned. She'd never actually thought Rashid was a Scrooge. He was smart with his money, but he was far from miserly. The number of gifts he bought at the craft sale today was proof of that. "No, you're not cheap. You bought me a necklace for no reason." Then she remembered Jasmine telling her that his last ex dumped him because he wouldn't propose. Was this scene hitting close to home for Rashid?

"I didn't buy you the necklace for no reason. You're a friend, and you liked it."

She shrugged. "You're generous. I'm sorry I called you Ebenezer. It was the first person I thought of who hates Christmas. You're really more of a Grinch than a Scrooge."

He frowned. "I'm not sure that's much of an improvement."

Ruby nodded emphatically. "It is. Believe me—I'd much prefer you to be covered with green fur than turn into a crabby old white man. A crabby old man in *finance*, too! I swore off finance bros a long time ago."

They watched silently while they finished eating. Rashid laughed at the funny bits and was appropriately somber at the sad bits.

After the Ghost of Christmas Future showed Scrooge Miss Piggy and Kermit mourning Tiny Tim's death, Rashid didn't exactly shed a tear, but his expression told her he was moved. Ruby had tears flowing, though. She always did for this scene. "Michael Caine is acting the hell out of this role," Rashid said.

"How is he keeping a straight face talking to literal puppets? He's crying over a dead frog! I'm practically crying over a dead frog!"

"I told you you'd like this movie."

He laughed. "I'm shocked at how good it is."

She wiped her eyes. "You know, this was the only movie death I could watch for years after my mom died."

"Because they're Muppets and not people?"

Ruby shook her head. "No, it's because I know how the movie ends. This is just a dream."

Rashid turned to look at her. "Can I ask you a question? You not liking doctors…does that have anything to do with your mother's illness?"

Ruby sighed and paused the movie. She knew he'd ask that question eventually. "I don't actually *hate* doctors. It's just that my mother had more than one doctor minimize her symptoms before she was finally diagnosed. She was told to lose weight when she complained of back pain or shortness of breath. Really, her breast cancer had already spread. Maybe they would have listened if she was white, skinny, or male."

Rashid shook his head, eyes full of compassion. And a touch of anger. "Oh, Ruby, I'm so sorry. That's horrible."

"I know you wouldn't do that. I mean, you listen to your patients, right?"

"I try to," he said. "I know gender bias is a big problem in medicine. And racial and body-type bias, too. I believe all physicians have a duty to examine the preconceived notions that we bring to our practice so we can treat all patients with the same care and empathy. I sat on a task force in Calgary that was working on ways to encourage physicians to examine their biases. I know I can be…difficult in my personal life, but I work hard to be empathetic and nonjudgmental in my work."

She believed him. Maybe if Mom's doctors had been like Rashid, Ruby could have had more time with her. Maybe Mom would have suffered less.

They were silent for a while. Ruby had learned to sit with silence instead of always wanting to fill it, thanks to this man.

Finally, she smiled at him. "I think you're one of the good ones. And I don't dislike *all* doctors. My surgeons in Montreal were fantastic."

He looked at her with a curious expression but didn't ask for more. Of course he wouldn't ask why she had surgeons in Montreal. He was respectful of her privacy. But good friends should be honest with each other, so she wanted to tell him the truth about herself. If he was going to know her, he needed to know all of her.

"Mom's cancer was genetic," she said quickly. "We have the BRCA1 genetic mutation."

His face fell. "Oh, Ruby, I'm sorry." He was a doctor, so he would understand what that meant. He would know that her BRCA1 mutation meant Ruby had a much higher than average chance of developing breast and ovarian cancer, and a high risk of other cancers, too. Like skin cancer.

"I mean, it's fine," she said. "It's not a big deal to me. And I mean that." Ruby didn't tend to tell a lot of people about her medical history—first, because it was none of their damn business, but also because she always got pitying looks for it. She understood that different people coped with things differently, and there was nothing wrong with that at all, but her genetic mutation didn't have a lot of impact on who she was, other than the fact that her boobs were now fake. Losing her natural breasts was nowhere close to being as hard as losing her mother, and she hated being pitied because of her unlucky genes.

Rashid seemed to understand, though. He didn't look pitying, just empathetic. "So, the surgery you had in Montreal was..."

Ruby smiled. "I had a preventative mastectomy with silicone implant reconstruction. I also had my fallopian tubes removed, since most ovarian cancers start in the tubes. I plan to get my ovaries removed in a few years. I never wanted kids anyway."

He tilted his head. "Really? You don't want kids? Like, ever?"

She put her hand to her chest with indignation. "*Procreation?* In this economy?"

He huffed a laugh. "Seriously, though. You're great with the girls. You'd be a fantastic mother."

Ruby shrugged. "I mean, I like kids. And who knows, I may change my mind and adopt, or go the IVF route. But I didn't have the best childhood. After my mom passed, I decided it's probably best if my bloodline dies with me. What about you? I assume you want a whole brood?"

He shook his head. "I don't know. I used to. I wanted a wife and kids and all that. But I worked long hours for years, and I saw other doctors miss their kids' music recitals or come into the hospital on their kid's birthday, and I don't want to be an absent father. I figured I'd wait until I had a private practice. But now..." He exhaled.

"It's not too late for you," Ruby said. "You're fantastic with your nieces. If you want kids, you still can have them."

"Yeah, maybe. I don't know, though. I mean, the world is pretty messed up. I don't know if it *needs* more children in it.

I can be a favorite uncle instead. Or I can adopt or foster a kid who needs me."

They were silent for a while. Ruby wanted to say that if he wasn't entirely sure if he wanted kids, then he shouldn't have any. She knew what it was like to have a father who didn't really want a daughter.

But Rashid would never be like her father. She smiled at him. "Let's finish the movie. Wait until you see how excited the bunny gets when Scrooge sends him to buy a turkey. You're going to want to adopt *him*."

After she put the movie back on, Ruby watched Rashid instead of the movie. She could tell he was really into it. It seemed her Christmas hater was on the road to his own Scrooge-style redemption. But on second thought, Rashid didn't need a redemption. He was fine as he was. With Dr. Rash, you needed to get a little underneath his skin to see his warm and soft core.

After the movie, Ruby put a music playlist on, then put the kettle on for tea. She brought two mugs of oolong back to the sofa. "Do you want to watch another one? *Love, Actually* is controversial, but it's also one of my favorites."

He raised one brow as he took a mug from her. "What are you trying to do to me, Red? I'll give the Muppets a pass because they're the Muppets. But I have to draw the line somewhere. No Hugh Grant."

Ruby was downright offended at that. "What's wrong with Hugh Grant? His rom-coms are *iconic*. *Bridget Jones's Diary* is my favorite modern Austen interpretation! And what about *Notting Hill*! Nineties Hugh Grant was so hot!"

"Okay, so I'm gathering that all one needs to be attractive to Ruby Dhanji is to be white and British?"

She shook her head. "Wrong. I happen to have huge crushes on Chiwetel Ejiofor and Himesh Patel, too. Have you seen *Yesterday*?"

"I think you're going all the way across the pond to find someone just like me," Rashid said, using a London upper-crust accent.

Ruby laughed and reached over to grab the cushion he had taken from her earlier and hit him again. He chuckled, snatching the cushion back. They tussled for the cushion for a minute, laughing, then he grabbed her by both arms, stopping her from being able to hit him again. Within moments, though, his laugh was replaced by a slow smile.

They were so close. He was leaning over her with his hands on her arms, and all his power was on her. Their legs were pressed together. But it was his hands that had all her focus. So strong and so soft. The smile on his face faded and turned to something altogether different. She'd been tamping down this attraction that she'd been feeling for him, mostly because she thought it was one sided—she doubted he was feeling the same thing. But she was wrong. He *was* feeling this. It was clear as glass. He wanted to kiss her as much as she wanted to kiss him.

The tension was so thick between them that Ruby didn't have a chance in hell of ignoring it. She'd never felt a charge like this. Electricity this strong. "All I Want for Christmas Is You" came on, and all Ruby could think was that it wasn't someone *like* Rashid that she wanted; it was *him*.

Smiling, she lifted her chin to close the distance between their faces and kissed his lips briefly. He was frozen for about a second, and Ruby assumed she'd made a grave mistake. She was about to laugh it off and apologize for her impulsivity when Rashid made a little growling sound and wrapped his arms around her, slamming his lips against hers.

And holy hell, it was good. He nibbled at her bottom lip a moment before pulling her even closer. Soon they were kissing without inhibition, exploring each other's mouths with lips, tongues, and teeth. She had one leg draped over his, and his arms were caging her in. Ruby didn't remember the last time—if ever—she'd been kissed like this. There was no awkwardness. No hesitation. He was assertive. He knew what he wanted: *her*.

She half expected him to throw her over his shoulder like he'd done with her Christmas tree a few weeks ago and toss her on her bed. And she wouldn't stop him. Hell, she was seconds away from *asking* him to take her to bed right now.

But that was only three weeks ago that he carried her tree home. And it was just under four weeks until Ruby was leaving town. This wasn't supposed to happen. Ruby wasn't supposed to find someone who made her feel respected, valued, and *wanted* right before she left the city. The last thing Ruby needed now was to complicate her life. They were both in Toronto temporarily—two trains passing on their way to their final destination.

It took everything in Ruby to pull away from him, but she had to. She untangled her body from Rashid's and sat back on her knees on the sofa, facing him, catching her breath.

Rashid looked as shell-shocked as she felt. Neither of them said anything. She knew she'd have to speak eventually, because lord knew he wasn't going to. The Mariah Carey song was replaced by a sadder instrumental melody. Ruby exhaled slowly. "Sorry," she said.

He nodded, then looked a little confused. "Are you apologizing for kissing me, or for stopping?"

"Um, the first one. Actually both. But I wouldn't have had to stop if I hadn't kissed you in the first place, so the second is a bit of a moot point, right? I mean—"

"Ruby," he said in the tone he used when he wanted her to stop rambling. She pressed her lips together and nodded. "Don't apologize," he said. "I mean, I didn't exactly push you away when you kissed me."

No, no he didn't. "I know. It's just...I like you a lot, like so much more than I thought I would when we met, which is a bit of a...*wow*. But I'm leaving soon, and I don't think...I mean, it's not a great time to start something with someone."

He nodded. "Yeah, I'm only here temporarily, too."

"Exactly. Plus, if things get weird between us, we won't be able to take the girls out, and we still have two more Christmas outings."

He nodded. "You're right. We should just be friends."

Ruby wasn't sure how she felt about him agreeing so easily that getting physical was a bad idea. Maybe she was wrong, and he wasn't really that into her. Maybe it was just that she was there, and not that she was *her*.

But she couldn't be upset if it was what she wanted. "Okay. Friends."

He smiled. "Deal." He didn't put out his hand for her to shake like he did the first time they'd made a deal. Which was probably for the best. She wasn't sure it was a good idea to touch that skin again.

16

RUBY DIDN'T SEE RASHID for a few days after that scorching kiss, but she did text him several times. She wanted to make sure there was no awkwardness between them. So, she texted him things she thought might amuse him, like a plaid tree skirt that looked like one of his flannels, a new men's cologne they got in the store, and the menus for a few restaurants near the ballet where they could go on Wednesday. He was chatty over texts, too—chatty for Rashid, at least. He sent light and pleasant responses, like oh that's hilarious or looks tasty! Ruby wondered if he was also overcompensating to make sure she knew they were fine after she kissed him on Thursday. Or, rather, fine after she'd *stopped* kissing him.

But she couldn't stop thinking about him and that kiss. It had been mind-blowing. When she closed her eyes, she could almost feel his body pressed against hers again. Feel his soft lips. Feel his smooth face rubbing against hers. Smell that spicy cologne…and *him*. She couldn't believe she'd put a stop to whatever they were starting. Not jumping into bed with Rashid

Hakim on Thursday night had to have been the most responsible, least impulsive thing Ruby had done in a long time.

It was better they stayed friends. *Safer.*

On Sunday, Ruby worked until five, and even though it had been snowing steadily all day, the store was very busy. After being on her feet for almost nine hours two days in a row, she wanted nothing but sweatpants, a cup of hot oolong, and her fuzzy blanket at home. But when Ruby walked out of the store, a voice behind her startled her.

"Rubina. I was waiting for you."

She exhaled. Steeling her shoulders, Ruby turned to face her father.

She hadn't seen or heard from him since that awkward cake at his house after her birthday.

"Can I talk to you? You live close, right? We can go there."

Ruby shook her head. "I just got off work. I'm exhausted." There was no way she was going to bring her father to her apartment. She knew he'd criticize the size, the wallpaper, and the *everything*.

"Rubina, I came all this way. I even had to *pay* to come onto this street. What a waste of money."

Ruby shook her head. "It's just because of the Winter Market." Ruby was too tired to argue. "I'm exhausted and sore. I just want to crash."

"After everything I've done for you, you won't even have a coffee with your father?"

Ruby exhaled. "Okay. Let's have a coffee. Follow me."

Without saying a word, she walked to a Tim Hortons just outside of the Distillery District. It wasn't her favorite café in the area, but she knew her father wouldn't care about Sophie's single-origin beans or artisan teas. After they silently waited in line, her father ordered a small decaf, and Ruby chose one of their holiday items—a gingerbread oat milk latte. He paid for their drinks, miraculously not complaining about how expensive Ruby's was, and they found a table near the window.

In the bright overhead lights, her father looked rough. She'd been struck at how old he looked when she saw him last month, and now he looked even older. But he *was* old—the man was over sixty. And still working stooped over car engines. Was his body failing him? Was he thinking of retiring?

"Okay. What's going on?" she asked. She took a sip of her drink. It was surprisingly good.

"Pamela lost her job after we saw you last."

Ruby winced. "I'm sorry to hear that. What a terrible time to lose a job."

"She's having trouble finding more work."

"It's only been a few weeks. And companies don't really hire this time of year, do they? Did she get severance?"

"No." He didn't elaborate. Ruby didn't know where her dad's wife worked or even what she did for a living, but to leave a permanent job without severance meant either she was the one who quit, or she was let go with cause. Her dad didn't seem to want to explain which it was. Ruby took another sip of her latte.

"Are you going to leave her while she's facing hardship, like you left Mom?" Ruby had been nice and polite every time she saw him all year, but she was too tired to put on her mask right now.

Her father shook his head, disappointed. "Rubina, that's not fair. I didn't leave your mother because she was sick. I was—"

"You were faced with having to work more hours because Mom couldn't bring in money while on chemo. And you were mad that you had to cook and clean, too. I was *there*, remember? I heard your arguments."

He didn't say anything for a while. He didn't have to. There was no denying what had happened.

Finally, he said something. "I thought, since you're a manager at that fancy store, you might be able to help Pamela get—"

Ruby shook her head. "I'm only there a few more weeks. I can't make any hiring decisions now." She *could* refer Pamela for a position at the flagship store, which could get her to the front of the hiring line, but there was no guarantee she'd get a job. Many people would give their right arm to work at Reid's. "What does Pamela do, anyway?"

"She's a bank teller."

"I wish I could help, but if she doesn't have experience in high fashion, Reid's isn't for her. She could try getting clothing store experience in a store in the mall and work her way up."

Her father frowned. Ruby wasn't sure if he believed that she couldn't help his wife. "Maybe you can give us a loan then?" he asked. "The mortgage on our house—"

"You can't afford your mortgage after she's been off work for only *three weeks*?"

He scowled. She knew that expression too well. "Rubina, I'm your father. Is that how you talk to me?"

Ruby sighed. "You know I'm planning a big move—I've been saving for it for years. I don't *have* money to loan you."

"What about the money your mother left you?"

Ruby froze. He wasn't supposed to know about her trust. "How did you find out about that?"

His eyes narrowed, which almost made Ruby shudder. "A little bird told me. That money should have been mine."

Ruby shook her head. "The trust was in *my* name only. You weren't supposed to know about it."

"Where do you think she got the money?" he asked. "*I* was the one who worked every day—her little sewing projects earned peanuts. She stole it from our bank account. I should have hired a lawyer and fought for it when I found out about it, but I didn't want to hurt you. I did that for you, Rubina. Because I *understand* the meaning of family." He sounded so angry. Ruby hadn't heard him sound like this since she was a little girl, back when she would hide in her closet so he couldn't yell at her.

But Ruby wasn't a little girl anymore. She could fight fire with fire, now. "Bullshit," she said. A woman sitting at the nearest table turned and looked at her, but Ruby didn't care. "You didn't come after the money because you knew you'd *lose*."

He shook his head. His anger seemed pathetic to Ruby now—not scary. He was a small, petty man. "You never called home, never visited for years," he said. "Then out of the blue you ask for help to get the UK visa. I thought, I shouldn't help her, she neglected her family for too long. I thought about saying I would only help for half the money. Not even all of it— just my share. But Pamela said no, I should help my daughter. Pamela is a good person, Rubina. She made *me* a better person. I thought if you saw us and saw how I've changed, you would do your duty and help your family. But you're still a selfish, irresponsible girl."

Ruby shook her head, anger heating her blood. "You are *not* my family."

"I'm your *only* family. Your *father*, Rubina. Are you really going to let me lose my house? What about Pamela? What about your brother, Gavin?" He shook his head.

"Gavin is my *step*brother, and I've seen him only a handful of times. And Pamela is nothing to me. I'm truly sorry she's unemployed, but I'm even more sorry she has to be married to you. I hope she has an escape fund hidden from you like Mom did."

Her dad clenched his teeth. He looked like he wanted to hit her. Like hell he'd changed. Poor Pamela and Gavin. "I should have known you'd never help me. You don't care about your family. Your own father might be homeless. You with your designer clothes and big inheritance. You are as materialistic and impulsive as always. And your mother was a thief. I can still hire a lawyer to get my money, you know."

Ruby shook her head. "Don't you dare talk about my mother. The wife who you *left* while she was in cancer treatment. The one who had to move in with her sister's family for the last months of her life."

"Rubina, I left because she *told* me to leave."

Ruby didn't acknowledge his statement. They had an audience now; several people in the café were watching them. "And what about your *daughter*? I dropped out of college to take care of Mom after you left. And after she died, I was alone. I didn't even have a degree to get a decent job. I started working at Old

Navy and sleeping on friends' couches in Montreal and worked my way up to Reid's. So don't you *dare* talk to me about abandoning family." Ruby stood. "Fuck you, Dad. Never come see me again. Never talk to me. Pretend you have no daughter. You did that for twelve years, so it shouldn't be a problem now."

Ruby was pretty sure she heard someone clapping, but she picked up her bag and left the café, leaving her coffee and her father behind.

Ruby was shaking as she walked away from the coffee shop without checking to see if her father was following her. It was cold out—and snowing hard. The tears running down her cheeks were probably turning to icicles. The sidewalk in front of her was blurry, but she didn't stop walking. She didn't even know where she was going.

What was she doing in this city? She wanted—*needed*—to get the fuck out of it. There were too many memories here, too many people she never wanted to see again. Ruby was used to taking off when bad things happened. After Mom died. After she found out she had the BRCA mutation. Thank goodness she would be out of Toronto soon. For good. This huge city—the biggest in the country—made her feel more alone than anywhere else.

But that wasn't true anymore. For the first time that she could remember, Ruby had a real support system. Not only her cousin Marley, but she also had Reena and Nadim, and Shayne and Anderson. She had friends—*real* friends—who cared about what was happening to her. And for the first time in her life, Ruby wanted support. She wanted to lean on someone and tell them about the terrible thing that happened. She didn't have to be alone when she was hurting anymore.

And she knew exactly who she wanted to talk to. Ironically, it was someone who also called her irresponsible. But now, after knowing him only a few weeks, it felt like there was no one in the city who understood Ruby better. She called Rashid.

"Hey, Red. What's up?"

"Do you still think I'm selfish?"

"What? Are you okay? You don't sound like yourself."

Ruby sniffed. "My father was waiting for me when I left work. He wants my mother's money because his wife lost her job, and they might lose their house. He said I was selfish and irresponsible when I said no. I told him to fuck off." Her voice cracked.

"Where are you?" he asked.

Ruby looked at the intersection she'd wandered to. "King and Parliament."

"Stay there, Red. I'm coming to get you."

"No, it's a snowstorm. You don't have to—"

"I'm already out the door. Be there in five minutes." He disconnected the call.

The Volvo pulled up eight minutes later. Ruby was frozen by then—she was not dressed for standing on a street corner in a blizzard. She got into the passenger side, and Rashid immediately gave her a supportive smile. "Your father did a number on you, didn't he?"

"What do you mean?"

"I've always thought that you had the most enthusiastic eyes I'd ever seen. You always look so happy and excited to be doing whatever you're doing—even if what you're doing is yelling at me. You've lost that look."

She shut her eyes a moment, then looked at Rashid. "I knew I shouldn't have let my father back into my life." She sighed. "I'm exhausted. It's been a long couple of days."

"Where do you want to go? I just finished cooking dinner at home. You're welcome to join us."

Ruby raised a brow. "You cook?"

He laughed. "Of course I cook. I live alone. If I didn't cook, I'd be eating takeout or frozen pizza every night."

"What did you make?"

"Turkish meatballs, bulgur pilaf, and salad. Come, have a family meal with us. Jasmine and the girls would love to see you."

Ruby couldn't say no to that, because it sounded delicious. And if she didn't go, she'd be eating a frozen pizza and stewing over that meeting with her father. She'd have to face the fact that she didn't have an immediate family. Maybe that was why she wanted to spend the evening with a family that cared about one another. And cared about her, too.

"Okay. I'll have dinner with you guys."

He smiled wide. "Excellent. Let me call Jasmine and tell her you're coming. Everyone will be thrilled."

Ruby smiled.

17

"RUBY AUNTIE!" TARA AND Noor were in the entryway squealing the moment Rashid opened the door.

"Hi, girls!" Ruby smiled at them.

"Do you want to see our tree?" Noor asked.

"We put the elephants on it!" Tara added.

"Let Ruby Auntie take off her winter things first," Rashid said, motioning the girls to get out of Ruby's way.

After Ruby took off her coat and high-heeled boots, the girls led her into the living room. Jasmine's house looked recently renovated, despite being an old house. And it was gorgeous. The design was minimal but cozy, with lots of blond wood and cream contrasted with lush textures and brass light fixtures. And yes, in the corner of the room was an enormous Christmas tree decorated with mismatched ornaments highlighted with pops of red and green glittery balls. Ruby stepped closer and easily found the Indian elephant ornaments.

She didn't know why she was surprised to see a tree here—this was Jasmine's house, not Rashid's. And as far as Ruby could tell, Jasmine wasn't Christmas-averse like her brother. But Rashid did live here right now, and the whole house looked warm, festive, and cozy. She couldn't imagine grumpy Rashid spending his downtime in this space.

Even looking at him now—in his sweats with stocking feet, with a small smile on his face as the girls showed Ruby their favorite ornaments on the tree, like the Disney ones from the craft show and some Popsicle stick ones they made themselves. She was again seeing another side of Rashid Hakim. He wasn't a grump dressed like a lumberjack. Or a pretentious doctor, either. He was just Rashid, a man in sweats who'd come to rescue her when she was feeling alone. The man who looked at his nieces fondly and reminded them to be polite to guests. And the man who'd apparently created the phenomenal food smells in the kitchen.

Jasmine came down the stairs with her hair in a messy ponytail. "Hi, Ruby. I'm so glad you're joining us for dinner. My brother makes the *best* meatballs. Aren't Rashid Uncle's meatballs the best in the world? Can you show Ruby Auntie the dining room?"

"Come," Noor said, taking Ruby's hand and guiding her to a dining room off the kitchen. The room was bright, with a long solid wood table and bright yellow place mats with white dishes already on them.

"You sit there, next to me," Noor said, pointing to a chair on one side of the table.

"And next to me, too," Tara added.

Jasmine and Rashid joined them, each carrying a serving platter. "They've been arguing about who gets to sit next to you since Rashid called," Jasmine explained. "We had to rearrange so you could be between them. I hope you don't mind."

"No. Not at all. Thanks for having me. I didn't really want to be alone tonight."

Jasmine smiled again. "You're *always* welcome here." She paused. "I mean it. Even if Rashid leaves, whenever you're in Toronto, come see us anytime."

Ruby glanced at Rashid, and he also had a welcoming smile on his face. Ruby exhaled. She was feeling so low, what, half an hour ago? Like she'd wanted to get on a plane and never come back to this city. But now? Being welcomed by these four people whom she'd only met a few weeks ago? She felt a sharp prickle behind her eyes, like she was going to tear up again. "You guys are amazing."

Dinner was delicious. The meatballs were lightly spiced and oven roasted on a bed of peppers and potatoes, and the bulgur pilaf was a revelation—nutty, with rich flavor brightened by fresh herbs. It was all so comforting. "This is excellent," she said as she broke apart another tender meatball with the side of her fork.

Rashid smiled. "You sound surprised that I can cook."

"Honestly, I am." She knew a lot of men who cooked well—Marley's boyfriend was a fantastic cook, for example. And Nadim wasn't bad, either, although Reena was the better cook in that relationship. But men who cooked, and enjoyed it, always seemed remarkable to her. Like it was the ultimate green flag for Ruby. Maybe because her father couldn't even make his own tea when she was young.

But apparently her father cooked now. Cooking and

spending time with a kid who wasn't even his. The only thing he wanted from his biological child was her money. She swallowed.

"Red, you okay?" Rashid said. He was across from her at the dining table.

Ruby nodded and smiled. "Yeah, I'm good. This is delicious. I'm pretty much only good at making desserts."

"Rashid Uncle," Tara said. "Why do you call Ruby Auntie Red? She doesn't have red hair. My friend Kennedy has red hair, and her daddy calls her Red, even though I think her hair looks orange, not red. But Ruby Auntie's hair is black like yours."

Rashid smiled at his niece. "It's because of her name. A ruby is a precious red gemstone. Plus, haven't you noticed that Ruby Auntie always wears red lipstick?"

Noor nodded. "And she has a red coat." She turned to Ruby. "I like the name Ruby."

"My full name is Rubina, but I like Ruby, too."

"My name means star," Tara said. "And Noor means light. Mommy picked our names."

Ruby smiled. "They're beautiful names. Your mommy picked well."

After dinner, while the kids were in the bathroom washing their hands and Jasmine was loading the dishwasher, Ruby said thank you again to Rashid. She told him she'd call an Uber and get out of their hair for the night. Rashid shook his head. "Stay," he said. "After the girls go to bed, we can talk."

Ruby waved her hand dismissively. "Oh no, it's not necessary. I feel so much better. You've been so great and—"

"You're not imposing, Ruby. And we both know you need

a friend right now." When Ruby didn't say anything, Rashid put his hand on her arm, looking at her with those warm, dark eyes. How had she ever thought he was cold and unfeeling? Her entire body flashed to that scorching kiss a few days ago. This man was the furthest thing from cold. And he had the kindest eyes she'd ever seen. "If you don't want to talk, we can watch a holiday movie. A rom-com, even."

Ruby raised one brow. "Is Rashid Hakim seriously offering to watch a holiday rom-com with me?"

"Really?" Jasmine asked, coming back onto the dining room. "He wants to watch a *rom-com*? Isn't this the third sign of the apocalypse?"

Ruby laughed. She liked Jasmine. She liked Rashid. And she liked the twins, too. "Okay, I'll stay."

While Jasmine was upstairs putting the girls to bed, Rashid put on a kettle for some tea.

"Orange pekoe or masala chai?" he asked.

"Masala," Ruby said. When it was ready, they took their mugs to the living room. Ruby sat on the sofa, Rashid on a white armchair opposite her.

"So, what happened?" Rashid asked. "Why did you see your father? I thought you had no relationship with him?"

Ruby let out a slow breath. "I've been seeing him occasionally for the last year. I needed his help to get a UK ancestry visa since his mother, my late grandmother, was born there. He agreed to find her birth certificate only if I would see him whenever he asked before I left." Ruby paused. "It's part of the reason I moved back here. He said he wanted to fix our relationship. Now I wonder if the whole thing was a ploy to get my mother's money."

Jasmine came into the living room then with her own mug of tea. "The girls were exhausted. I'll leave you two alone so you can talk," she said, picking up a book from the coffee table.

Ruby shook her head, patting the empty seat next to her on the sofa. "No, it's fine. I mean…" She exhaled. "You can stay. We're just talking about some family issues. I don't have the best relationship with my father, and he kind of ambushed me today."

Jasmine shook her head. "Ugh. I'm so sorry. Family stuff is hard—especially this time of the year." She sat next to Ruby.

While drinking the excellent masala chai, Ruby told Jasmine and Rashid about the money she inherited from her mother. "I didn't know about it until this law office contacted me a few years ago. Mom set it up so I wouldn't get the money until ten years after her death. She left a letter saying she wanted me to use the money to make our dream a reality."

"Oh, wow," Rashid said. "You didn't know she'd been saving?"

Ruby shook her head. "No. I did know…" She glanced at the Christmas tree, eyes welling with tears. "I didn't realize she'd saved that much. She'd been stashing away money so she could leave my father, but then she died before she could use it."

"Your mother sounds like a special person," Jasmine said.

"She was." Ruby sighed. "I don't even know how my father found out about the money, but for the last year he's been acting like he's a new person. He cooks now, and he took his stepson to visit colleges. But he hasn't changed at all. Today he said he was going to talk to a lawyer to get his share since I told him I wasn't going to give him a penny." Her voice cracked.

Jasmine reached over and squeezed Ruby's arm a second.

"Oh, Ruby. That sounds awful. Do you think he has a case?" Rashid asked.

Ruby shrugged. "I doubt it. The trust was in my name. But there was one thing he said—that my mother *told* him to leave. I always thought he left because he couldn't handle her illness."

Jasmine smiled small. "I hope she was tired of being around the whiny man-baby while she was sick, so she kicked the fucker to the curb so she could take care of herself instead of him for a change."

Ruby looked at Jasmine, eyes wide. That was the first time she'd heard Jasmine swear. Actually, that was the first time she'd heard Jasmine say something negative about another person.

"Do you believe him that she asked him to go?" Rashid asked. "Maybe he just didn't want to look like the bad guy."

Ruby shrugged. "I don't know." She thought for a second. "Actually, I also kind of hope he *was* telling the truth. Because that means my mother had a lot more power at the end of her life than I realized. I hope she threw the garbage out herself."

"Exactly," Jasmine said. "What was your father like? I mean before her diagnosis. What kind of parent and husband was he?"

Ruby thought for several moments before answering, the warm mug of chai in her hand helping clear her thoughts. "He was angry. Short-tempered. He was always stressed with his business, and he took it out on us. He wasn't abusive—I mean, not physically, but he was a yeller." She swallowed. "I used to be afraid of him. I...I never really spoke much at home because he would tell me I was rambling, and I needed to stop talking nonsense all the time. He said anything I liked—clothes, makeup—was frivolous and that I was irresponsible." She viscerally remembered forcing herself to be silent so her father wouldn't snap at her. And asking to eat dinner at friends' houses so he wouldn't yell at her not to speak at the dinner table. She always suspected that the reason her mother would take her to malls and stores every weekend even though they couldn't afford to buy anything was so they would be out of the house when he was home.

"Jasmine," Rashid said. "We can...I mean, if this is hard for you, Ruby and I can go somewhere else."

Ruby looked at Jasmine. Her eyes were glassy, but she had a determined look in her jaw. "No, it's okay." She exhaled, then smiled sadly at Ruby. "You could be talking about Derek. My husband."

"Soon-to-be ex-husband," Rashid clarified.

Ruby blinked. She'd had no idea why Jasmine and her husband had separated. But now it made sense. Especially the girls and their quietness. Their fear of talking when Ruby met them. Ruby realized that one of the reasons she was so drawn to those little girls was because they reminded Ruby so much of herself as a kid, being afraid to talk even though they had so much to say. Ruby's eyes filled with tears again. Those poor girls.

Jasmine nodded. "It's fine. People have said that they don't understand how I could leave him. He never laid a hand on me or the girls. We seemed like a perfect family. He was a yeller. I mean, he had a stressful job. I get it."

"It's no excuse," Rashid said, almost through gritted teeth. "The whole fucking world is a big ball of stress. He was *abusive*. He tried to isolate you from your family."

"I know," Jasmine said. She looked at Ruby. "I moved to Calgary after Rashid did and met Derek there. We moved here after I finished med school. Derrick's family is all in Ontario, but I realized that we came here because he didn't want me to live close to any of my family." She suddenly smiled apologetically at Ruby. "Sorry. You came here to talk about your issues, not mine. Don't worry about me."

Ruby shook her head. "Don't apologize. So, he didn't like how close you were to your parents and siblings?"

Jasmine nodded. "It was so gradual. Like a look of irritation when I was on the phone, or complaining about the cost of flights, until I didn't see my family for a whole year." She exhaled. "It was a big wake-up call when Noor told me she didn't like to talk near her daddy. I realized the girls were holding back who they were because of him." She smiled, but it didn't quite reach her eyes. "I called Ayesha and Rashid and told them everything, and they were here within a few days. Anyway, enough about me. I should be telling my therapist this, not you. Should we take up Rashid's offer and watch a holiday rom-com? We both need it."

Ruby smiled. "Yeah, let's do that. And Jasmine, one thing…" Ruby exhaled. "If your husband *was* like my father, then thank you for leaving. For not letting your girls grow up like that. You gave them a huge, huge gift."

Jasmine looked at Ruby, speechless for a few seconds, then reached over and hugged her tightly. "You don't know how much that means to me," she said in Ruby's ear. Ruby hugged back—a little uncomfortable with the affection, but so happy she could make Jasmine feel better.

After she let Ruby go, Jasmine smiled. "Okay. My vote is *Love, Actually* or *Serendipity*."

Ruby grinned. She loved both those movies. She looked over to Rashid, expecting to see him scowling about having to watch a rom-com, but he had a small smile on his lips and, if Ruby wasn't mistaken, actual tears in his eyes. She smiled right back at him.

They decided on *Love, Actually*, because Jasmine and Ruby thought it was more likely Rashid would find something he liked about it since there were so many storylines and characters.

But they were wrong. Rashid hated everyone and everything in it.

"I mean, they may as well call this *Workplace Sexual Harassment, Actually*," he said. "Two of the supposed *romances* are boss/employee. The prime minister and the murder writer want to bang their staff! How is this heartwarming?"

"I mean, the catering manager doesn't actually work for the prime minister, does she?" Ruby asked. She frowned. Technically, there were *three* questionable employee/employer relationships—he hadn't mentioned Alan Rickman, who maybe slept with his secretary and made poor Emma Thompson cry to the Joni Mitchell song.

"That's what's charming about the movie," Jasmine said. "It's showcasing all the different kinds of love, not just healthy relationships. Sometimes love starts out messy."

He was quiet for a while, but Ruby could see him scowling as he continued to watch.

"The woman doesn't even speak English," he finally said. "And correct me if I'm wrong, but did her father first try to *sell* his other daughter or not?"

Ruby couldn't help it—she laughed. He was getting so worked up, and it was adorable.

"Don't mind my brother," Jasmine said. "I'll watch Christmas movies with you anytime. What are your thoughts on *The Holiday*?"

Ruby squealed. The Cameron Diaz, Jude Law, Jack Black, and Kate Winslet movie was her second favorite Christmas movie after *Love, Actually*. "Young Jude Law...I'd move across an ocean for him."

Which made Rashid roll his eyes.

After the movie, Jasmine said she was tired and said goodnight. Rashid ranted a bit more about the movie—about the stereotypes of American college girls and how terrible the guy who stalked his best friend's bride was. While he was ranting, Ruby called an Uber to take her home.

"Okay, lesson learned. Rashid only likes Victorian Christmas movies with heavy-handed lessons," she said, taking her mug to the kitchen. "My car will be here in five minutes."

"I can drive you," Rashid said.

Ruby shook her head as she walked toward the door to get her boots. He'd already done enough for her tonight. He'd rescued her with no hesitation when she called him in tears. He turned what was easily one of the worst days of her year into one of the best. Spending the evening with Rashid, Jasmine, and the girls was exactly what she'd needed.

"The car is almost here," she said. "The snow has stopped. I'll be fine. I had a great time tonight. I think I love your sister."

He chuckled. "Everyone likes my sisters more than me." He held out her red coat.

Ruby laughed as she buttoned the coat, then reached up to give him a tight hug. "I think both Hakim siblings I've met are pretty great," she said in his ear. He smelled so good—he wasn't wearing cologne, but just smelled clean, and like *him*. She inhaled deeply before letting him go. "Thank you so much. For dinner, for letting me vent, and for subjecting yourself to that movie. You…you don't know how much that helped."

He squeezed her hand a second, warm eyes locked on hers. "Anytime, Ruby. That's what friends are for."

18

WHEN WEDNESDAY CAME, RUBY rushed straight from work to the small Japanese restaurant where they'd decided to have dinner before the ballet. Her breath caught in her throat when she saw Rashid sitting between the girls in a round booth near the back of the restaurant. He seemed to be showing them pictures from the menu, helping them decide what to order, and he looked *devastatingly* handsome in a black suit with a charcoal dress shirt and no tie. For a man who claimed designer clothes were a waste of money, he certainly did know how to shop. Ruby watched the three of them for a few moments before joining them. She was just so *happy* to see them. It had only been three days since she'd had dinner at Jasmine's house, but Ruby was growing so attached to this little family. She felt a pang of sadness that it would all end so soon. This was their third outing, which meant there was only one left. And her flight was in less than three weeks.

She took a deep breath. She should be grateful she had them in her life now, instead of dwelling on the ending. She took out the small gifts she'd bought for the girls—brown-skinned ballerina Christmas ornaments—put a smile on her face, and joined them at their table.

The girls loved the ornaments and played with them all through the meal. After eating, the four of them walked over to the Four Seasons Centre for the Performing Arts and headed straight to their seats. There were a lot of families in the audience, and everyone was in festive clothes. Very soon after they sat, the house lights lowered, and the ballet started.

The show was spectacular. Ruby was mesmerized from the moment the first dancer leapt onto the stage. The music, the artistry, the beauty of it all gave her goose bumps. She loved being transported into the fantasy land with fairies, animals, and the most spectacular dancing she'd ever seen in front of her. She had no idea if Rashid was enjoying the show as much as she was. But gauging by how silent and focused he was for the first half of the show, he was either enjoying it even more than Ruby expected, or he was in absolute misery.

At intermission, before she could even ask if he was enjoying the show, Rashid leaned into Ruby and whispered, "Holy fuck, that was amazing."

Ruby grinned. "You enjoyed the Christmas ballet?"

He nodded vigorously. "The dancers are spectacular. I could've watched the Snow Queen all day. Girls, what did you think?" Ruby had Tara next to her, and Rashid had Noor next to him. He'd explained that they needed to be separated, otherwise they'd talk through the whole thing.

After the girls expressed their delight even though they'd seen the show last year, Rashid nodded, his face still full of awe.

"I wonder if we can get tickets to come back next week? Is all ballet like this?"

Ruby laughed as Rashid opened the program to see what other shows the National Ballet was performing. His enthusiasm was…Well, it was like hers when she found something she enjoyed. And the girls were excited, too.

After the intermission was spent with the girls talking about which characters were their favorite and which costume they wanted to wear for Christmas, the second half of the show started.

Now that Ruby knew that Rashid was loving the show, she watched him out of the corner of her eye while she also watched the ballet. He was so focused, but he had this tiny, almost imperceptible smile on his face—one that she'd seen a few times now. This was his content expression.

And it perfectly reflected how she was feeling, too. *Content.* December was her favorite month. No matter where she was, she'd be surrounded by joy, beautiful things, and happy families overflowing with love. And even though she didn't have a happy family or that overflowing love, she always felt good being around others who did.

But she didn't remember ever feeling like this *during* the holiday season—like she belonged. Like she was actually participating in the joy, instead of just witnessing it around her.

Was it only because of Rashid? Maybe. Or maybe it was because of Rashid, Jasmine, Tara, and Noor. And also, Marley, Reena, Nadim, Shayne, and Anderson. Her well was full this year—the fullest it had ever been.

But it was mostly Rashid.

How had this happened? How had she gone from disliking

this man so much, to only putting up with him because his father could help her, to feeling like he was the best gift that the universe had ever given her?

Him. Not his father or his hotel manager sister. How had Rashid come to mean more to her than almost anyone else in the world? With his crazy soft skin and tiny content smiles. She watched him enjoying *The Nutcracker* and was overcome with affection. Maybe even more than that. She was feeling things that she hadn't felt for someone in a long time. Maybe ever.

After that kiss, she had said they were better as friends, but why? True, she was leaving Toronto soon, but so was he. And maybe that was a reason to lean into this attraction instead of pretending it wasn't here. They both knew it would be temporary, so it wouldn't get in the way of their futures. Ruby should be making the best of her time now and not let her last days in Toronto slip through her fingers.

Without saying anything or even turning to face him, Ruby reached over and put her hand on Rashid's. He turned to her immediately, one brow raised in question. Ruby answered his unspoken question by lightly running one manicured fingernail down the back of his hand, then taking her hand back and resting it on her own leg, which was covered in a soft red Badgley Mischka dress.

Rashid leaned close to whisper in her ear. "What did that mean?"

His voice sent a shiver down her spine. Even in the dark theater she could see his eyes full of confusion…but also heat. She bit her lip, then leaned close so her lips were an inch from his ear. "It means I might be regretting the friends-only deal."

Rashid blinked, then immediately put his hand over Ruby's. But he didn't lightly stroke it like she'd done to his, or even just hold it. No, Rashid lavished her hand with attention, slowly rubbing it and tickling the tender skin between her fingers. He found the tiny bumps on the top of her hand and ran his fingertips over them. When his hand moved to her leg, it became downright erotic. His eyes were on the stage in front of them, but his fingers on her hand and thigh were making her feel things she shouldn't be feeling while at a family-friendly ballet performance.

The moment the dancers stepped forward to bow after the performance, Rashid's hand left Ruby's so he could clap. He still didn't look at her, which was fine. The house lights came on, and Ruby hoped no one noticed how warm and flushed she felt.

That hadn't been like any other handholding in a theater. That was foreplay. And Ruby had no idea if Rashid planned to finish the job his fingers had promised.

After navigating the crush of people leaving the theater, the four of them made their way to Rashid's car, and he strapped the girls into their seats. He seemed normal. Ruby's mind was going a mile a minute, analyzing that little dance their hands were doing and wondering what he was thinking now, but she played it cool and asked the girls who their favorite dancer in the second half of the show was.

As he'd done for their last two outings, Rashid drove silently and pulled up in front of Jasmine's house first instead of taking Ruby home, even though the girls were wide awake and talking animatedly about the ballet. He put the car in park, then turned to Ruby. "Stay put. I'll be right back." He helped the girls out, then took them inside.

Ruby bit her lip. What exactly was going to happen when he got back to the car? Was he going to drive her home and they'd continue exactly as they were before she'd realized that with the right man, her hand could be an erogenous zone? Thankfully Ruby didn't have to wait very long to get an answer to that question. He was back in the driver's seat in minutes. But he didn't start the car. He looked at her with an intense, almost sultry expression on his face. Her skin tingled with goose bumps. "Okay, Ms. Dhanji," he said, slowly. "I'm putting this completely in your hands. What happens now?"

She bit her lip. "What do you mean, what happens?"

"I mean," he said, running his finger over her thigh again. "Am I going to drive you home and drop you in front of your building, and then you'll say goodbye and we won't talk until next week's outing except for maybe a few texts? Or…" He smiled wide.

"Or what?"

"Or are you going to invite me up for a drink that we won't actually drink."

Ruby's eyes widened. It was getting hot in this car. She narrowed her eyes like she was thinking about her options. "I don't know, Dr. Hakim. It's a hard decision. Tell me, what exactly would we be doing instead of drinking that drink? Are you thinking…*conversation*?"

He shook his head. "No. The first thing I would do is tell you to take off that red dress. Because as stunning as you look in it, I suspect you would look even better out of it."

Ruby inhaled sharply. Somehow, she found her voice to ask another question. "Okay, then you'd take off your clothes, too?"

He shook his head. "Eventually, but first, I'd look at you." His voice was slow and smooth. "I'd run my fingers over the soft skin on your arms, then the sides of your ribs. I would finally touch those legs that I've been daydreaming about since I first saw you dragging a tree on the sidewalk. I would lick the soft skin under your ear and inhale that spicy sweet perfume you wear. I would worship you, Ruby Dhanji, like you deserve to be worshiped. So, your call. Do you want now what we both know is going to happen eventually, or do you want to wait?"

Ruby let out a shaky breath. She had no idea how he was so steady when Ruby felt like she was going to combust. There was no way on earth she could say no. Hell, she wasn't sure she could say anything at all. Instead, she leaned forward, took him behind the neck, and pulled him in for a deep kiss.

Rashid moaned as Ruby's tongue dipped into his mouth. It was as good as last time. Actually, better. His arms wrapped around her, and she almost climbed over the center console of the Volvo and onto his lap. Hell, she wondered if she should just get out of this dress now so she could feel the hands that made love to her fingers at the ballet on her bare skin.

But this was a nice neighborhood, and anyway, sex in a car was always better in theory than in practice. She pulled away from the kiss and put her lips to his ear. "Take me home. I want you in my bed now."

He laughed. "Yes, ma'am." He turned on his car.

It was a good thing that it was only a five-minute drive from Jasmine's house to Ruby's condo because she wasn't sure either of them could last much longer than that. Ruby had been with a number of guys before, but she honestly didn't remember wanting—no, *needing* someone this much. She needed to be consumed completely by him. She needed to feel nothing at all but Rashid Hakim.

He parked in a visitor spot, and they rushed inside to the elevator. Neither of them said a word until Ruby unlocked her door and they were in her tiny apartment with their shoes off. He walked to the window near the tree and closed the curtains. Then he turned to Ruby.

"Okay," Rashid said, eyes intense. "Take off the dress."

Oh. He'd been serious about telling her to just undress like that? She thought he was just being sexy. She'd assumed that things would carry on like normal. Like, they'd kiss a bit, move to the bed, take off each other's clothes, and go from there. But no. He was at least four feet away from her, and his eyes were locked onto her body. And he wanted her to take off her dress.

She swallowed. Had anyone looked at her like that before? He still had that content smile on his face, but his eyelids were heavy. Ugh—that expression on his face was breathtaking. He was so incredibly sexy.

"The dress, Red. Let me *see* you." He paused. "Please."

Well, since he was asking so nicely. She reached behind her to the zipper of her red dress. Every millimeter of her skin screamed to be touched as she slowly lowered the zipper, then slipped her arms out one at a time. She skimmed the dress over her hips, letting it puddle on the floor.

After stepping out of the dress, she leaned down and picked it up, folding it and putting it on the back of her couch. She didn't look at Rashid—for some reason this whole striptease was easier without making eye contact. She knew his eyes were on her, though. She hoped he liked what he saw. She assumed he was somewhat surprised by one particular thing on her body that she'd never told him about.

She finally looked at him. And yes, his eyes were wide with surprise.

"You have tattoos?" he asked.

She nodded. All she had on now was a simple black satin bra and matching panties, and her black lace tights. The bra was full coverage, but not full enough to hide that there was a large floral tattoo across her chest.

He didn't say anything else about her ink, and instead pointed to her legs. "Take off your tights."

She did as he asked, this time watching his face as she peeled off the stretchy black lace. Thank goodness she'd had a wax recently—not that she'd had any idea that this would happen.

Rashid inhaled sharply when she tossed her tights behind her and took one step closer to him in nothing but her bra and panties. She wasn't self-conscious about her body...not really. Having had major breast surgery meant she was used to people, mostly in the medical field, looking at her undressed. She smiled when she realized Rashid was yet another doctor studying her body. This didn't feel anything like when other doctors inspected her, though.

"You're beautiful, you know that?" he said, voice thick with emotion.

Feeling a little bold, she put one hand on her hip. She smiled cheekily. "I had an excellent plastic surgeon."

He laughed at that. "Now you don't have a problem with doctors?"

"I definitely don't have a problem with one doctor in particular." She reached out and ran her finger over his neck, right above the collar of his dress shirt. "I believe you promised to unleash those talented fingers on me?"

He's eyes closed briefly with her touch. "You think my fingers are talented?"

"Judging by what you were doing during the ballet, yes." She stepped over to her bed, which was only two steps away, and sat on the edge of it. "So, something about worshiping me?"

Rashid shook his head, grinning as he walked toward Ruby's bed, taking off his jacket and tossing it on the couch on the way. "I have no idea how you did that," he said, sitting next to her. His fingers immediately started trailing the skin on her bare thighs, making their way up her leg. The touch made Ruby shiver.

"Did what?" Ruby asked, arching her back.

He leaned close to her ear as his hand continued to trail the skin of her thighs ever so lightly. "I was all ready to take control, to turn you into a quivering ball desperate for me, but you've turned the tables and left me powerless." The hand that wasn't on her leg pulled Ruby's hair to one side, and he started planting soft kisses on her neck. Ruby turned her head to give him more access as her eyes instinctively closed. It all felt so, so good.

"Why does only one of us get to be in charge?" she asked. "Maybe we're so good together because we…complement… each…" Ruby lost her train of thought. Probably because Rashid's hand was now inside her underwear. She shuddered and leaned into him. His fingers really were magic.

"I got you," he whispered, guiding her body to lie down onto the bed. After pulling off her panties, Rashid showed her with his hands and his mouth exactly how talented he was. And holy *wow*. With his lips, tongue, and fingers, he brought her to an orgasm stronger than she'd ever felt. She held on to his shoulders, moaning his name as the pleasure seemed to go on forever.

As her consciousness floated back into her body, he scooted so he was next to her. He leaned down to plant soft kisses on her shoulders.

"Okay," Ruby said when she was finally able to speak again. "You win this round."

She heard him chuckle.

She wrapped her arms around him, holding him as close as she could. He was still in his dress pants and high thread-count shirt, and she could feel his erection on her leg. She'd take care of that—after she caught her breath.

His hands were soon trailing the skin on her belly and chest, like he couldn't resist touching her.

"You really have a thing for skin, don't you?"

"Not usually. But yours is so soft. And you glow."

"That's because I use an illuminating body cream with silk protein molecules."

He propped himself on his elbow to look at her face. "What does that even mean? Your cream is made of *silk*?" He still had his small smile. "How can silk penetrate the dermal layer? These ingredients are added because they sound luxurious without any evidence—"

"Shush." She put her finger over his mouth. "No skin care rants. Just enjoy the results of my expensive addiction."

He chuckled, then ran a finger along the base of her bra. That was the closest he'd come to touching her breasts. She was pretty sure he was avoiding them on purpose, which was actually very sweet, but unnecessary.

"It's okay. Don't be afraid. You can touch me."

"I wasn't sure how you'd feel about…I mean…"

She shrugged, then sat up and reached around to undo her bra. But before dropping it off her shoulders she looked at him. "They don't look like real breasts, and…there are tattoos instead of nipples. I don't have any sensation in them, either. But I'm not self-conscious about my reconstructed breasts. Beats getting sick."

He sat up and nodded, then reached up to pull the straps off her shoulders and removed her bra. And then he just looked.

Ruby meant it. She wasn't self-conscious about her silicone breasts. After watching her mother get sick and then die from breast cancer, Ruby had been glad to have a mastectomy so the same thing wouldn't happen to her.

"Wow," he said. Then he leaned closer. "This is…" He ran a finger over the intricate flowers in all shades cascading over her breasts in a watercolor style.

"Too much?" she asked. He was literally a dermatologist—healthy skin was important to him. Maybe he wouldn't find the riot of flowers on her chest attractive.

He shook his head, smiling. "No. Are you kidding? You're Ruby. I would expect nothing less than *too much* from you." His fingers trailed the outline of the water lily on her left breast. She couldn't feel it, but she could see his fingers' soft touch. "This is so beautiful. Why did you do this?"

Ruby chuckled. "Honestly? Impulsivity. I went to a tattoo shop in Montreal that has an artist who does excellent realistic-looking nipple tattoos, but when I was lying on her table, I saw some of her floral art pasted on the ceiling and decided to get flowers instead. I mean, I don't have nipples, so I had an empty canvas."

He nodded, still admiring the art on her breasts. "Is there any significance to the specific flowers?"

Ruby shook her head. "No. I thought about doing mine and my mother's birth flowers, but in the end, I didn't *want* it to mean anything. I went with what I thought was pretty and what would make me happy every day, not sad."

He smiled as he touched the big pink peony on the base of her right breast. "It's stunning. I could look at you all night."

Ruby raised a brow. "Seriously, dude? That's not what I signed up for when I invited you up here. And why are you still wearing clothes when I'm buck naked?" She reached into her nightstand and took out a box of condoms, then tossed it at Rashid.

He laughed and started unbuttoning his dress shirt. Ruby didn't remember ever feeling so comfortable with another person in bed. Laughing so much. As soon as his clothes were off, he climbed on top of her, kissing her deeply.

Honestly, the whole night exceeded all her expectations. She should never have put the brakes on this last week.

Because now Ruby was quite sure that thanks to the good Dr. Hakim, she was going to have the absolute best holiday season of her life.

19

AFTER RASHID THOROUGHLY WORSHIPED Ruby, and she gave him his fair share of worship, too, he spent the night in Ruby's tiny apartment. She hadn't expected him to—she assumed he'd go back to Jasmine's. But after they'd soaped each other in Ruby's shower—where he'd kindly bit his tongue about the shower gel she used on him—he got right back into her bed wearing nothing but his boxers and moisturizer (he gave in and used her illuminating body cream because he said he couldn't shower without hydrating his skin) and motioned her to join him. They were in constant contact as they slept—first spooned together, but when Ruby got a little warm and rolled over, he rested his hand lightly on her bare hip. Ruby was sure she'd never slept that soundly in years.

But when she woke up and felt him still sleeping next to her, she had a full moment of panic as everything they'd done the night before came back to her. What the hell had she been thinking? She couldn't blame getting caught up in a moment—she had been the one to instigate getting physical. What happened to keeping that solid line of friendship between them? To not jeopardizing the twins' holiday season by complicating their relationship?

Ruby exhaled. The heavy weight of his hand on her hip reminded her how spectacular the sex had been last night. Actually, better than spectacular. She shivered, remembering his intensity and the way he looked at her body. He'd not only accepted her somewhat lopsided reconstructed breasts, but called them beautiful, even with their tattoos.

But at no point between the hand foreplay during the ballet and passing out in each other's arms had they talked about what they were doing. She had no idea what he wanted. Was he expecting them to be a couple? Maybe this was going to be a friends-with-benefits situation? If circumstances were different, there was no question in Ruby's mind what she would want—she would happily jump headfirst into a relationship with Rashid. He was thoughtful, kind, and so incredibly sexy. He was complete boyfriend material.

But circumstances weren't different. She was leaving town in a few weeks. And even if she changed her plans (which she had no intention of doing), he was leaving a month after she did anyway. It was the absolute *worst* time to be getting into a relationship.

The hand on her hip was suddenly moving. And like at the ballet last night, the man's hands had the ability to turn her insides to complete goo. There was a definite plus to sleeping with someone who understood her anatomy.

But she knew she needed to put a stop to those talented

hands before she climbed on top of him for more of what they'd done last night. She couldn't be Impulsive Ruby now. She couldn't risk everything—the twins' holiday season, her mother's dream, or her friendship with Rashid—by not approaching this thoughtfully and with maturity. She put her hand over his wandering fingers, locking them in place.

"We should talk," she said. Then she exhaled. She probably should have started with *Good morning*. Maybe *Thank you for all the orgasms last night*. Instead, she awkwardly said the phrase that started most breakup conversations.

She heard him sigh. "Okay. Coffee first?" he asked, sitting up. "Wow. It's almost eleven. Brunch?"

Ruby hadn't realized how late it was. At least she wasn't working today.

Taking the bedsheet with her to cover herself, she got up and searched for a robe.

"You regret last night," Rashid said, voice flat. It was a statement rather than a question.

She looked at him. He was uncovered on her bed since she'd taken the sheet with her when she got up. She'd known he was athletic and he played hockey back in Calgary. It had been such a treat to feel his strength last night. But now, seeing his muscles and smooth skin on her pink bedsheets in daylight... she looked away. *Focus, Ruby*, she told herself.

"No," she said. "Honestly, I don't regret anything. I just...I want to regroup. Talk about our expectations before things get awkward. Brunch sounds perfect. We can probably get a table at that Egyptian place I was telling you about, if you're interested."

He swung himself out of bed and nodded. "Sounds perfect. I'll take a three-minute shower if you don't mind."

They were lucky to get a table at one of Ruby's favorite restaurants, a cute place that specialized in Egyptian brunches and was absolutely filled with natural light and plants. When they were seated, Ruby ordered a cardamom latte and Rashid an Americano. Ruby wasn't usually a coffee drinker, but after last night, she needed the energy boost.

While stirring a pale brown sugar cube into her fragrant coffee, she smiled at Rashid. They'd barely spoken on the way here—and when they did it was only about things like traffic and how lucky they were that the restaurant didn't have much of a line.

After ordering their meals, Ruby finally started the difficult conversation. "Okay...I mean, I wanted to talk...I feel we should—"

He smiled at her. "Relax, Ruby. It's me."

She exhaled. "Yeah. I'm not sure what you...you know... *expect*? Maybe last night was a mistake because I don't want—"

"You don't want to complicate things between us, you mean?"

Ruby nodded and took a sip of her coffee.

"So...does that mean you want a *long* engagement?"

Ruby literally spit cardamom coffee out of her mouth, which made Rashid laugh, and Ruby realized he was kidding. Ugh. Her grump was actually a shit disturber. She wiped her mouth and shook her head. "You're trouble, Rashid Hakim."

He laughed. "Look, Ruby. Last night was fantastic. If you want to do it again one night or every night, I'm down for that. But it's also okay if you want to put the brakes on this. We're kind of in a weird place. I'm just out of a long relationship, and you're on your way out of the country. Maybe it's the holiday season that's making us do things we wouldn't normally do."

Ruby's eyes widened. "Did Dr. Rashid Hakim seriously admit that there is a little bit of *magic* in the holiday season?"

He laughed. The server came to bring them their food—a date, honey, and caramelized onion grilled cheese sandwich for Ruby, and falafel eggs with fava beans and cumin potatoes for Rashid. He tore off a piece of bread and dipped it into the sauce for the beans. "Oh man, that's good," he said after eating it.

Ruby tilted her head. "Did you really mean what you said?"

He frowned. "Yeah, it's fantastic. You want a taste?"

"No, I mean, you'd be willing to put the brakes on you and me, and go back to just being friends?" Maybe his mind wasn't as blown last night as hers was, if he was willing to ignore their chemistry.

Rashid put his fork down and looked at her. "Ruby, I like you. *A lot.* And if the timing was different, I would want to see where this could go between us. But…"

"But the timing sucks," she said.

He nodded.

Ruby didn't know what to say. It sounded like they were on the same page—that last night was mind-blowing, and they wouldn't mind doing it again, but an actual relationship, with any level of commitment, probably wasn't a good idea.

But she was still here for almost three weeks. And so was

he. And they'd already decided to spend some of that time together…along with the girls, of course. But she wasn't sure casual was right, either—she liked him *way* too much for a friends-with-benefits arrangement. And she wasn't sure she could continue a physical relationship with him without a promise of exclusivity while they were together.

But a fling? Ruby was *excellent* at flings. She had them all the time, and she'd never had a problem walking away after a fling ran its course.

Ruby finished chewing before speaking. "What if we call this a little holiday fling? No strings, no promises for the future. Like we're a couple and do things together, not only sex, and we're exclusive, but not serious—like, no buying each other Christmas presents, or getting jealous, or anything like that. Then, after January first, we go back to being friends."

He smiled widely. "I like the sound of a holiday fling. Very fancy."

"Is that sarcasm?"

He laughed. "Not at all. Let's do it, Ruby. Let's have a fling."

Ruby grinned. Seemed she'd found herself a holiday boyfriend. Their first activity after making their holiday fling official was to agree to spend the day together, since neither of them was working. So, after paying the bill—Ruby insisted they split it since this wasn't one of the four outings that he was supposed to pay for—they headed back to Jasmine's house so Rashid could change. Ruby stayed in the car—the girls would be at school, but Jasmine would be home, and Ruby didn't want to see Rashid's sister the day after she had wild and passionate sex with the man.

Ruby had already planned to go shopping on her day off. After his comment last week about her not exchanging gifts with her friends, she had decided to get them something. Since the Caroling party was on Saturday, this was Ruby's last chance, and she still needed gifts for Reena and Shayne.

Rashid readily agreed to join her. "I should probably get something for Jasmine, anyway," he said. "The girls will expect Santa to bring her something Christmas morning."

"What about all that stuff you got at the artist market?"

He shrugged. "That was mostly for other people. Back home in Calgary."

"Okay, but what about the books I wrapped for you at Reid's? Weren't those for Jasmine and the girls?"

"Yeah, but I already gave them those."

Ruby frowned. Now that she thought about it, on Sunday Ruby had seen Jasmine reading one of the books Ruby had wrapped. Ruby suddenly smiled wide. "Wait. Did you buy those books *just* so you could come into Reid's and ask me to wrap them?"

Rashid's face transformed into an expression Ruby had never seen on him before. Embarrassment? Guilt?

Ruby laughed, pointing a finger at his face. "You did! You totally used that as an excuse to see me again! You *liked* me!"

Rashid took her hand that was pointing and kissed the back of it, making her shiver. "After what we did last night, isn't that obvious?" he asked.

"Okay, but you *always* liked me! Even back when I thought you hated me!" This was an unexpected discovery. She'd been so sure he thought she was a frivolous flake after their first meeting, but really, he already had a crush on her.

Also, Rashid blushing was just about the cutest thing in the world.

"Okay, fine," he said. "I thought you were strange and frustrating when we first met, but I couldn't stop thinking about you."

It made sense. "Last night you said you liked my legs from the first day you saw me."

He nodded. "I did like your legs. And your face. And your hair. Your personality, on the other hand…You're a bit of an acquired taste, Red."

Ruby chuckled. "That's what your sister said about you."

He rolled his eyes. "Remind me to thank her for that. So yes, I bought the books so I'd have an excuse to see you again. Are you happy now?"

Ruby beamed. "Yes. Very happy." And she meant it, too.

After brunch, they took a streetcar to the Eaton Centre, the same mall they'd taken the girls to to see the huge tree and the windows at the Hudson's Bay. It was even busier today, and Ruby could see that Rashid regretted agreeing to come shopping with her within ten minutes of walking into their first store.

"I don't get it," he said. "Why are there so many people here on a Thursday afternoon?"

Ruby was looking at the care labels in a sweater. She needed to make sure anything she got for Reena was machine washable since Reena was a baker. And had an infant. "Because

Christmas is in, like, two weeks? Come on, you must have noticed the pre-Christmas crowds in Calgary."

He shook his head scowling. "I never go to malls there."

Ruby squeezed her lips together. She picked a soft gray off-the-shoulder sweater for Reena. It would look fantastic with her breastfeeding boobs, and it was machine washable. Rashid grabbed the same one for Jasmine—probably because he didn't want to look around more. They went to a fancy menswear store next. Ruby wanted to get a tie clip for Shayne, since he'd said it was time for him to retire his aging club-kid look. But even this small, curated menswear store was absolutely packed.

Rashid frowned. "All these people are getting ties for their fathers-in-law, bosses, and uncles that will sit in a drawer for two decades before finally ending up in a thrift store where no one will buy them because they're two decades out of style, so they'll end up in a landfill. You could skip all this and go to Goodwill."

Several women in the store turned to look at Rashid. One gave Ruby a sympathetic look that she assumed meant *I'm so sorry your partner is such a Grinch*.

Ruby held in a laugh, quickly picking a silver and mother-of-pearl tie clip. After paying, she gave Rashid the out he probably wanted. "I'm done shopping. What do you want to do now?"

He looked at her for several long moments. She wished she knew what he was thinking when he looked at her like that. She knew him so much better now, but in so many ways he was still such a mystery. She knew all the things he didn't like—Christmas, consumerism, royalty, billionaires, and designer anything (except cologne)—but she still didn't know what he actually did like. Other than her, of course.

He was loyal to his family and loved them. Oh, and he loved hockey, which Ruby had never talked to him about because she was completely useless when it came to anything sporty.

She had an idea. She put her hand in his. "I know the girls aren't here, but it's Thursday. We're supposed to do festive, touristy things on Thursdays."

He raised a brow. "I think dealing with the insanity of this mall is pretty touristy."

"I mean, yeah, but I want to surprise you. Trust me, Dr. Rash. I know exactly where to take you. You'll *love* it."

He raised a brow again, skeptical. Ruby responded by turning her hand and lightly stroking his knuckles. She saw the minute that her light touch made his skin pebble. Last night she was delighted to discover that he wasn't just super talented at making her skin sing under his touch, but he himself had super-sensitive skin, too. Ruby was going to have a ton of fun discovering what reactions she could get from touching his body.

He smiled that small, private smile and nodded. "Okay. I'm all yours."

20

SHE GUIDED HIM TO the subway and took him straight to the Hockey Hall of Fame—which, as far as she remembered, was like a museum of hockey. He literally squealed when he realized that's where they were headed. She had no idea he even knew how to squeal.

"Oh my god! I've always wanted to come here! But it seemed weird to come alone. They keep the real Stanley Cup here, right? Unless it's touring or something. Do you know if it's here now? I mean, it doesn't matter to me—I want to go either way, but it would be *so cool* to get a picture of it! Thank you, Ruby!"

Ruby grinned ear to ear. Rashid was more like her than she'd realized. She just needed to find the thing he loved as much as she loved Christmas.

He was like an excited schoolboy as they went through the museum together. None of it was of any interest to Ruby—she'd been here as a teenager when she had a fling with a hockey bro, but coming with Rashid was so much more fun.

His enthusiasm was almost contagious. His reaction to the re-creation of the Montreal Canadiens' locker room was especially adorable. It was apparently his favorite team as a child. Ruby told him about seeing concerts at the Bell Centre in Montreal—where the team currently played—and about the old jerseys they had on display there. She refrained from mentioning the spoiled hockey wives she used to sell to at the boutique she worked at in Montreal. Ruby almost said they should take a trip to Montreal together—she would have loved to show him her favorite city in Canada, and she would have even been willing to go to a hockey game there if it made him this excited.

But then she remembered this was a fling—and a very short one. She was soon going to live too far for a weekend trip to Montreal.

Rashid was still in a great mood when they left the museum. "Thank you so much! It makes me want to get on skates. I don't know why I didn't bring mine with me. I keep seeing the skaters at Nathan Phillips Square. I wish I could join them."

"Why can't you? They rent skates there." Ruby was no skater, but even she knew that.

His brows raised with surprise. "They do?"

Ruby laughed. "Who's been showing you around Toronto since you got here? They did a terrible job."

"Let's go skating now," he said. "It's a perfect day for it." It had started snowing very lightly, but it wasn't particularly cold.

Ruby looked at him, blinking. "That's awfully impulsive of you, Dr. Hakim. I'm a terrible skater. I think I told you that."

"C'mon, Ruby. It doesn't matter if you're not good at it. It'll be fun."

She frowned. "You say that now, but I'll be holding on to you so tight that you'll bruise, or I'll end up on my ass the whole time."

He pulled her close and kissed her forehead. "I don't have a problem with you holding me tight. We can get hot chocolate after. Somewhere near there should have a gingerbread one."

Ruby couldn't say no, because one day she'd be looking back at this time with Rashid, and she didn't want to regret that she didn't do everything she possibly could with the man while she had the opportunity. Plus, skating at Nathan Phillips Square was such an iconic winter-in-Toronto activity—she kind of wanted to experience it, too.

They walked to the outdoor skating rink near city hall, and by the time they rented skates and laced them on, Ruby was quite sure she'd made a terrible mistake. She almost fell on the three steps from the bench to the ice. If Rashid's arm hadn't been around her waist, she would have been on her ass.

But he was a natural on skates. It was hilarious—the guy grew up in London, England, but with his blue beanie, plaid flannel, and jeans, he fit in more in Canada than most Torontonians. And with skates on, he may as well get a Tim Hortons coffee, a poutine, and add a few more *ehs* to his vocabulary.

Ruby clutched his strong forearm tightly as they stepped onto the ice together. She'd thought that the skates were hard to walk with on the rubber floor near the benches, but the rink itself? Whose idea was it to glide around on slippery ice on thin metal blades?

She shuffled along, moving her feet forward and back a tiny bit while holding on to Rashid for dear life. She was afraid to lift her feet because she'd fall on her ass. She was afraid to glide the way other people did, because she'd fall on her ass. She was pretty much afraid to breathe too hard because she'd fall on her ass.

All in all, she was pretty worried about her ass.

Rashid was effortless, though. He had one arm around Ruby's back, and one in front of her that she was grasping. Every time she lost her balance, her grip tightened. He was steady and strong, and he had her.

"I-I can't do this," Ruby said. This was such a bad idea.

He beamed at her. "What are you talking about, Ruby? You *are* doing this!"

Her eyes widened and she shook her head. Then she lost her balance because of the movement. This. This was proof she was living in the wrong country.

"Okay, put your arm around me here." He guided one of her arms to wrap around his back. "And use your other one to help you balance. I've got you." His arm wrapped around her waist. "I won't let you go. I promise."

Ruby panicked the moment her right hand wasn't on his, but he held her waist tight to keep her upright. He did have her.

Slowly they made a few circles around the ice—staying close to the outside edge of the rink, where the other beginner skaters were. Eventually, as Ruby found her footing, she started gliding a bit on the ice. It felt so strange—so foreign to be moving without moving her feet, but she eventually found her rhythm. Rashid tightened his grip on her whenever her balance wavered.

"I don't understand how you've never learned to skate," he

said. "I thought Canadians are supposed to skate before they walk?"

"Did Tara and Noor learn to skate before walking?"

He laughed. "No. My sister's a disgraceful Canadian. I signed them up for lessons starting in January. If it goes well, we're thinking of putting them in hockey."

Ruby frowned. It would be hard for Rashid if the girls did end up playing hockey—it would kill him that he wouldn't be there for all their games.

"Watch out, slowpokes!" someone behind them yelled. Rashid quickly pulled Ruby toward him, but it was too late. The person rushing past them—some bro on hockey skates—clipped Ruby on the arm as he passed her. It was enough to make her lose her balance again, and in what felt like excruciatingly comical slow motion, her legs started moving back and forth, unable to get any traction. Rashid couldn't hold her up this time, and she landed flat on her butt, her thin jeans not doing nearly enough to insulate her from the cold, hard ice.

"Ouch!" Ruby said. The hockey bro turned and said sorry—clearly a true Canadian—before whizzing away.

"Are you okay?" Rashid was bending over her with his arms out to help her get back up. He looked upset. Which, *fair*. He'd promised her she wouldn't fall. And she fell anyway. Her ass was cold and probably bruised, and a big part of her was telling herself that falling meant it was time to recognize her limitations and get off this damn ice.

Or maybe it was time to let someone who cared about her help her back up. Because one fall didn't mean that everything before now hadn't been fun. She smiled and took Rashid's arms to pull herself to her feet again. "That was hilarious," she said, wiping the snow off her butt. "Come on, they just started 'Last Christmas.' Let's skate to my favorite song."

Smiling widely, Rashid wrapped his arm around her, and they started making the rounds again. This time Ruby was a little braver—maybe because she had fallen once and she knew Rashid was here to help her back on her feet. She let him teach her how to use the side of the skates to push off. She fell a few more times—completely her own fault, not because of a polite douche. But soon enough she could skate without looking at her feet.

"You're a natural," Rashid said.

She frowned. "Hardly. I'm sure I look like a baby gazelle taking its first steps." She faltered a bit, but Rashid didn't let her fall.

He leaned in to whisper in her ears. "Nah, you're way sexier than an antelope."

Ruby laughed.

Eventually, she decided to stop skating to save her sore butt, and because she knew Rashid wasn't really getting the chance to do what he loved to do—actually skate. She told him she'd watch from the sidelines for a bit.

"Wait, before you go..." He leaned close to her. "There's something I've always wanted to do, but never have had the opportunity."

"Oh? What's that?"

He leaned forward. "Kiss someone on the ice." And then his lips were on hers.

It was magical. The holiday music playing. Light snow was falling. And the softest lips in the world were on hers. Ruby had never fantasized about kissing someone on skates—probably because she was so terrified of the death blades—but this soft, warm kiss combined with the cool air was beyond perfect. But that was probably because of who she was kissing, not the location. Every good memory Ruby had from Christmas seasons before this one paled in comparison to the memories she was making with Rashid Hakim.

He grinned at her after releasing her. He had such a great smile—she could get used to seeing it every day. She could get used to Rashid.

She exhaled. She wasn't supposed to get used to him. This was a fling. And for her own self-preservation, she needed to remember that.

Rashid spent the evening at Ruby's again on Thursday night. They ate Thai takeout and watched *Elf* because Rashid said he liked Will Ferrell. But they didn't really watch it; they ended up talking for hours, about his friends back in Calgary and even a bit about his ex. They'd been together for three years, and Ruby was curious about her.

"Your sister said she dumped you because you didn't propose," Ruby said.

He nodded. "Yeah, I guess, technically. Jackie's best friend getting a Tiffany engagement ring was the death knell to the relationship."

Oh. Was this woman the reason why he hated designer goods? "Was she into expensive things?"

He shook his head. "Not particularly when we met. But I guess she changed while we were together. Instagram didn't help. But I don't want to make her out to be materialistic." He exhaled. "Jackie was fine. We just weren't suited. I knew that long before we broke up. I'm not proud of it. I should have ended things earlier, but I was so busy. We both were. She's in finance."

Ruby frowned. "That's so sad. You were too busy to end the relationship?"

"To fix it or end it." He exhaled. "I don't come out as the good guy here. I wasn't ever really into Jackie, not like…not like I'd want to be before deciding to spend my life with someone. I think the right person would make me want to change for her…to sacrifice something to be a better person for her. Jackie wasn't that for me. And I wasn't it for her."

Ruby thought about that. She'd never in her life felt like that about anyone, and she wasn't sure she wanted to. "I'm happy with who I am. Why would I want to change for a man?"

Rashid looked at her for a moment. "I think it would be… nice…to find someone who inspires you to be a better person, both for yourself and because they deserve that."

Ruby exhaled. This conversation was getting altogether too deep for a fling. "Okay. I have a question," she said. "You don't have to answer it if you don't want to."

He nodded. "Go ahead."

"If I asked, would you eat spaghetti and meatballs with maple syrup? Like Buddy on *Elf*?"

He snorted a laugh, then buried his face in Ruby's neck, inhaling deeply. "There are limits to what I would do for you, Red."

That night the sex was slow and toe curling, the perfect end to a perfect day. They both had to work early Friday morning, though, so there was no time for a morning repeat. Or even breakfast.

"So, question for you," Rashid asked as he was putting on his shoes. "We are going to a celebration at Jamatkhana tonight. Jasmine is trying to introduce the girls to our culture and religion. I'm not super religious, but I said I'd go with her. Would you be interested in joining us?"

Ruby squeezed her lips together. That is not what she expected him to ask. Ruby wasn't religious, either, and had barely been to the prayer hall since her mother passed, even though her mother used to go several times a week. Should she go with Rashid, Jasmine, and the girls now?

Maybe it would be a good way to remember her mother before leaving Toronto. And an excuse to wear the one salwar kameez in her closet, which didn't get a lot of attention.

"The girls got matching lehengas to wear," Rashid added.

Ruby got off work at five, so she could go. "Okay. I'd love to come with you."

He smiled widely. And Ruby realized that she kind of *was* changing because of this man.

21

WHEN RUBY WALKED INTO the prayer hall Friday night, she knew she'd done the right thing by coming here with Rashid, Jasmine, and the girls. She'd forgotten how *moving* the place was, with its towering glass roof that made her feel like she was inside a crystal. She teared up a bit, remembered coming here with her mother, but the memories felt like a gift now, instead of feeling like something had been taken from her. Plus, all the women here were dressed in vibrant jewel-toned cultural clothing that was a feast for her fashion-loving eyes.

After prayers, the five of them went to the social hall for chai and cake. The girls were excited to see that sharbat was also being served—a pink milky drink flavored with rose essence and basil seeds that Ruby hadn't had in years. The first sip brought her right back to her childhood.

"Do you seriously like that stuff?" Rashid asked. He was drinking chai with no sugar. "Don't you think it tastes like rose soap?"

Ruby chuckled. "Why would a dermatologist use flowery-scented soaps?"

He smiled. "My mother likes scented soaps."

Ruby had been delighted to see him wearing the same suit he'd worn to the ballet, with a tie this time. He looked so good. She really wanted to ask him who made the suit—but she didn't want to ruin the illusion if she found out it was an off-the-rack suit from a discount store.

"Can I have more sharbat?" Noor asked, holding out her empty paper cup.

Tara immediately downed the rest of her cup and held it out, too. "Me too!"

Jasmine rolled her eyes. She looked gorgeous today in a simple pale pink salwar kameez with gold embroidery, and the girls were in matching bright pink lehengas, the long embroidered skirts skimming the floor. Ruby's salwar kameez was a muted turquoise with silver embroidery. Rashid hadn't said anything about it when he saw her come out to the car—which was probably because of the girls and Jasmine—but she hoped she would get a moment alone with him at some point tonight so she could tell him how much she liked that suit on him.

"I'll get it," Jasmine said. "They drink it so rarely. Why not?" She headed back over to the sharbat line, leaving Rashid, Ruby, and the twins alone near the wall of the social hall.

"There are more people here than I expected," Rashid said, looking uncomfortable. It seemed that he was uncomfortable in any crowded situation, not just Christmas events.

"Oh my, you're Rubina Dhanji, aren't you?" a voice next to Ruby said. She turned and saw an older woman, maybe in her fifties, wearing a light green sari. Ruby was almost positive she'd never seen the woman before.

"Um, yes? Do I know you?" Maybe she'd served her at Reid's? But she never went by Rubina at work, always Ruby.

"Neelam Premji—I was a friend of your mother's. You look *so* much like her." The woman was quite pretty, with large dark eyes and glowing skin. "You've grown up so beautiful." The woman put her hand out, and when Ruby went to shake it, she pulled Ruby in and kissed both her cheeks. She held on to Ruby's hand, her warm smile making Ruby feel a little exposed. Ruby forced a smile. She didn't remember this woman, but her mother had been quite religious and had lots of friends in the community.

"I had no idea you were in the city," the woman continued. She looked at Rashid and the twins, who were staying close to him. They were more comfortable with Ruby now, but their shyness came back around strangers. "Is this your family? What beautiful girls."

Ruby laughed awkwardly, taking her hand back. "Oh, no, this is my friend Rashid, and his nieces. Their mother just went to get sharbat."

The woman nodded. "I always thought…" she said. "I mean, I was so sorry that I didn't keep in touch with you after your mother passed. She would have wanted me to, but I had my own…" She smiled, clearly emotional. "Are you…okay? Happy?"

There was something there, like she was afraid that Ruby's life had turned out something like her mother's. Ruby wondered how close this woman had been to her mother. Ruby didn't know if it was the abusive husband or the genetic cancer that the woman was concerned about. But to ask if Ruby was *happy*? That was a strange question from a virtual stranger.

But the answer was very clear to Ruby. At this moment in time? A few weeks from fulfilling a dream she'd had for years? With a big circle of friends who looked out for her? And at the very beginning of a fling that was making her holiday season a whole lot of fun?

She looked up at Rashid and smiled wide. "Yes. Yes, I'm happy. Life is good." And the smile that Rashid gave back to her somehow made her happier.

Neelam smiled warmly and reached into her purse. She handed Ruby a business card. "Your mother meant so much to me. I wish she were here to see you, now. Keep in touch, okay? I would love to know how you're living your life now. And if you ever need anything in Toronto, please reach out. I told your mother I would always look out for you, and I have failed there."

After handing over the card, she hugged Ruby again.

Jasmine showed up then, balancing three cups of sharbat. Ruby was about to introduce Neelam to her, when Neelam smiled and told Ruby again that it was nice to see her, and then left.

Ruby frowned. That was weird. She looked at the business card. Neelam was apparently an investment banker. It had been a very long time since she'd met someone who knew her mother. And it felt like that woman knew her mother well, which meant that this stranger knew a lot more about Ruby than most strangers she met. It was the woman's warmth that left Ruby feeling off.

While Jasmine was helping the girls with their drinks and cake, Rashid stepped close to Ruby. "You okay, Red?"

He was so good at reading her moods. She tilted her head, looking at those dark eyes, which looked so warm with concern. "Yeah, I'm good. I'm glad you convinced me to come. Look at all the beautiful outfits! Did I mention how smoking hot you look in that suit?"

A slow smile transformed his face. "I'm glad you came, too." He leaned very close to her to speak in her ear. "I love you in Indian clothes. You are far and away the most beautiful person here," he whispered before letting her go.

That warm, small, contented smile on Rashid's face made Ruby's knees weak. And she realized that she'd told that woman the truth. She really was completely happy right now.

After they'd had their fill of cake, chai, and sharbat, they headed to the cloak room to put on their shoes and coats. After Ruby had slipped on her silver stilettos and her red coat, Rashid and Ruby waited outside the doors for Jasmine, who had taken the girls to the bathroom before helping them find their shoes. "Will I see you this weekend?" Rashid asked.

Ruby had to work early on Saturday, so even though she really wanted to invite Rashid for another sleepover, she needed a full night's sleep.

"I'm working Saturday and Sunday—but I'm leaving work early on Saturday for Marley and Shayne's party. You should come. It's their annual Caroling party." She hadn't asked them if she could bring Rashid, but she knew they'd say yes.

Rashid frowned, looking awkward. "Oh, um, I'm not

really into singing Christmas carols. I mean, you know I don't celebrate—"

Ruby laughed, tapping him on the chest. "Oh my god, *no*. I forgot you don't know Shayne that well. It's not a caroling party, as in singing Christmas carols. It's a holiday party, but the theme is the movie *Carol*. It's Shayne's all-time favorite movie, and it's set during the holidays, so he hosts a screening every year."

Rashid looked a little confused, so Ruby explained. "*Carol*? Have you seen it? It's a movie from like, 2015, I think. With Cate Blanchett and Rooney Mara. It's set in the fifties—very midcentury chic. It's about the secret romance between a divorced housewife and an aspiring photographer. It's sweet, but also super depressing. Shayne's obsessed with the movie, which makes sense because he's a photographer. It's a beautifully shot movie."

Rashid still looked confused.

"I went to the Caroling party last year," Ruby continued. "They go all out. Very glamorous. There'll be themed food, cocktails…the works. No singing. Probably."

Rashid finally laughed. "Okay, it sounds like fun. I like Shayne and Anderson a lot. And Reena and Nadim."

"You still need to meet Marley and Nik. Warning, though: Nik's an actor. I hope you're not the awkward starstruck type. Although you did meet Anderson, and he's on TV every day."

He chuckled. "I should be fine. I don't think I have any midcentury clothes. Do guests have to dress up?"

Ruby shook her head. "Nah. Just wear something festive and you'll be fine."

Ruby opened the text group the moment Rashid dropped her home.

Ruby: Can I bring Rashid to the Caroling party?

Nik: Who's Rashid?

Marley: Dr. Rash.

Nadim: I thought you hated him?

Ruby: No...

Reena: Oh my god, did you sleep with him?

Ruby: Where did you get that from?
All I said was no!

Reena: There was subtext in the no.
It was the three dots.

Shayne: Bravo, girl! Are you and he playing dermatologist and patient? Did he study ALL your skin?

Ruby: Never mind. You guys are weird.
I'm not bringing him.

Reena: No, bring him! He's HOT. Like...y'all need to see his skin. Softer than Aleem's.

Shayne: Has he even seen Carol? He'll need to watch it first.

Marley: Don't listen to Shayne, Ruby. He can come. I still haven't met Dr. Rash!

Nik: Okay, I think I've figured it out. Rashid is a dermatologist who Ruby is dating. But why go into dermatology if his name is Rash?

22

SHAYNE AND MARLEY'S HOUSE wasn't far, only about a ten-minute drive from Ruby's condo. Rashid drove to Ruby's place, but they'd decided to take an Uber to the party so they could have some cocktails.

When Rashid texted that he was downstairs, Ruby took the elevator down, carrying her bags of presents and the dessert she'd made for the party, and met him in the building lobby. She smiled warmly. It had only been a day since she saw Rashid, and she'd already missed him. But her jaw dropped when she saw what he was wearing.

"Um, are you wearing a Christmas sweater?"

He looked down at the bright blue Fair Isle knit that clearly had a pattern of snowflakes, snowmen, and snow-topped trees on it. "It's actually a holiday vest," he said. "You said to dress festive. I thought this is what people wore to Christmas parties. Aren't ugly sweaters a thing?"

Ruby huffed a laugh. "Yeah, maybe they're a thing for other people, but not for Mr. I Don't Celebrate Christmas. What happened to *the holiday isn't for us*?" She smiled and kissed him briefly on the lips, so he'd know that she was teasing him. The sweater wasn't *that* bad—the cool blue looked fantastic against his rich brown skin, but she wasn't used to seeing Rashid in a bright color. Ruby was wearing a soft cream cable-knit sweater with a full red skirt as a nod to the 1950s setting of the movie, along with her signature black lace tights and red lipstick.

"What's in the tin?" he asked, pointing to the round red container covered with snowflakes that Ruby was carrying.

She opened it to show him little white squares topped with crushed candy canes. "I woke up early to make these before work—peppermint burfi. My mom's invention." Burfi was a traditional Indian sweet—basically a milk fudge usually flavored with cardamom, pistachio, almonds, or saffron. Peppermint burfi was something Ruby's mother had come up with one Christmas when Ruby was a kid. Even though peppermint wasn't Ruby's favorite, she made it every year.

"Oh, wow, that sounds delicious." He leaned forward to smell them.

"Wait until you taste them." She closed the tin and checked her phone. "Car's here."

Once they were buckled in the back seat, Rashid turned to look at her with an unreadable expression. "I had an eventful day," he said.

Ruby nodded. "Buying a Christmas sweater...easily a once-in-a-lifetime experience for Dr. Christmas-Hating Rash. Did you feel the earth move when you paid for it?"

He shook his head. "That's not what I meant. I have news."

"Oh?" Ruby wondered why he hadn't said *good* or *bad* news. Just *news*.

"Jasmine and I usually go to the UK between Christmas and New Year's," he explained, "to spend the time with Mom, Dad, and Ayesha. But Derek has refused to allow Jasmine to take the girls out of the country. So, my parents and sister Ayesha decided to fly here instead. They'll be here December twenty-sixth."

"Oh, that's wonderful," Ruby said, smiling. But she wasn't sure if this *was* actually good news—at least for her. Ruby's ticket to London was for January 1, and her last day of work was December 27. She'd hoped she and Rashid could spend her last few days in Toronto together. But now he was probably going to spend it with his family.

She was being selfish. It was great that he could see them. Maybe this would be good for her, too. She could ween herself off Rashid instead of going cold turkey.

"There's more," Rashid said. He looked a little nervous. "I...I know that we talked about this, and we're supposed to be no-strings-attached, and you didn't want me to ask my father to hire you, but Jasmine mentioned your UK plans to Dad and Ayesha. They want to meet you while you're here."

"Oh." Ruby exhaled. Was that the only reason they wanted to meet her? "Do they, you know, know about us?"

He shook his head. "My parents don't know we're having a fling. Jasmine, Ayesha, and I have had a pact forever never to tell Mom and Dad about one another's love lives. You know how South Asian parents are. If they found out I even held your hand, they'd be planning our wedding."

Ruby chuckled. She did know—tangentially, of course—how wedding obsessed South Asian parents could be. That was one good thing about not having close family: She didn't have to deal with anyone else's expectations for her own life.

"But they know we're friends," Rashid continued, watching the road in front of him. He was clearly uncomfortable. "They know the girls adore you, so they want to take you out to dinner. Dad asked me if he thought you'd be suited for the hotel industry, and I said yes, you'd be fantastic, and you're very committed to your work and goals. He said he wanted to talk to you about your plans and see how they can help."

Ruby exhaled. She didn't know how she felt about this. On one hand, all she wanted a few weeks ago was to get an introduction to the Hakim family. But now, things were different. Ruby didn't want to complicate this relationship, even if it was supposed to be only a temporary fling. Mixing business and pleasure was always a bad idea. If something went wrong in either area, it could affect the other. She couldn't jeopardize her and her mother's lifelong dream like that.

She glanced at Rashid. There was a lot of uncertainty on his face, too—like he also wasn't sure this news of his was a good thing. Maybe he was afraid that his family wouldn't like Ruby, and it would mean the end of their fling.

But this was *just* a fling, and it always had an end date, anyway. There was no end date to her goal, and her goal should mean more to her than a three-day-old relationship with someone she'd known for a month.

And at the end of the day, it was pretty amazing that Rashid said those things to his father about her. That had been the whole point of Ruby getting close to this man—to show him that she was capable and responsible enough to work in his family's business. Before, he'd said she was too impulsive, too irresponsible for him to refer her to his family's business in good conscience. This meant she'd succeeded. He respected her now.

She smiled, put her hand on his, and squeezed. She saw the moment that content smile sneaked onto his face.

"Thank you," she said. "I really appreciate you saying that. I know you wouldn't have referred me if you didn't think I could do it, and I'm grateful. I'm so happy I met you." There was no other way to say it.

He turned his hand over and lifted hers so he could kiss the back of it.

As expected, Marley and Shayne's party was chic and stylish, with a vintage midcentury vibe to coordinate with the movie *Carol*. Marley was even wearing a teal dress with a fitted skirt and shawl collar almost exactly like the one that Cate Blanchett wore in the film.

"You look fantastic," Ruby said, kissing Marley on both cheeks.

"Of course she looks fantastic," Shayne said behind her. "You know *Carol* was nominated for best costume design at the Academy Awards, right?" He smiled at Rashid. "Nice to see you again, Doctor. And if you'd like to change out of that…*thing*, I have more reproduction costumes from the movie upstairs. Perhaps a beret might redeem that sweater? Some pearls?"

"Shayne, shush," Ruby said, handing him her coat. "He's

keeping the Christmas vest." Shayne was also wearing a vest—a black one over a button-up shirt with thin yellow and gray stripes. Also, a thin black tie and a red Santa hat. Most people would think this outfit was odd, but it was almost exactly what Rooney Mara wore in the first scene of *Carol*.

"Let's get you two some cocktails," Shayne said. "Put your presents under the tree."

After they each got martinis with big pimento-stuffed olives, Ruby started introducing Rashid to the people he hadn't met yet. He was surprisingly friendly and chatty with everyone. If someone had told Ruby a month ago that she'd be bringing the surly Dr. Rash to Marley's holiday party, and that he would be charming and personable, she would have laughed her face off. It wasn't a huge party—only about thirty people were squeezed into Marley and Shayne's house. Ruby had thought that Rashid's grump came out in big crowds, but apparently this crowd wasn't too big for him. He was like a whole different person.

And people seemed to genuinely like Rashid, too, which warmed Ruby's heart. He got along particularly well with Duncan, the red-bearded partner of one of Marley and Reena's old friends Amira, who lived about an hour out of town. It made sense—Duncan was a huge hockey fan. At one point Ruby came out of the bathroom, and Rashid wasn't where she'd left him on Marley's orange sofa. Ruby found Shayne in the dining room and asked if he knew where Rashid went.

Shayne rolled his eyes. "He went to look at Anderson's new *car*. Duncan and Nik went, too." Shayne suddenly handed Ruby the tin of peppermint burfi. "Ruby, these are evil. Take them before I eat them all. You need to screen your boyfriends better—the last thing we need in this group is another car bro. Who cares about cars!"

Ruby's father was literally a mechanic, and Ruby herself was a bit of a car bro. "Rashid isn't my boyfriend, and he isn't a car bro, either."

"What do you mean, he's not your boyfriend. I thought you two were a thing now?" Shayne asked.

"Oh, we're just, you know, having fun. Nothing serious. A fling."

Reena laughed, then looked lovingly at her husband, who was sitting in the living room holding a martini glass. "Hey Nadim, remember when we were *just having fun*?"

Ruby rolled her eyes at her friends. "You know I'm leaving town in two weeks, right? It isn't serious." She wasn't sure if she added that last sentence to tell her friends or to remind herself.

"Does he know that?" Marley asked taking a burfi from Ruby. "Because the way he looks at you isn't *not serious*." She took a bite. "Oh, man, these remind me of your mother."

"I agree," Reena said. "He's besotted. I can't believe that's the same man who scowled through the Santa Claus parade. He's wearing a Christmas sweater! Maybe he's hoping you'll stay in Toronto. Or come back."

"It's a holiday vest," Ruby said. "And he's leaving Toronto, too…probably a month after me. He's only helping his sister here temporarily."

Amira shrugged. "He told Duncan he'd come see his hockey tournament in Toronto at the end of February—so he expects to still be here until then. Also, weirdly, they were talking about going to the ballet together."

The front door opened then. "Looks like the men are back, smelling like motor oil and rubber," Shayne said loud enough for them to hear.

Anderson laughed as he walked over to Shayne and put his arm around his waist. "It's an electric vehicle, and you love the smell of motor oil, so what are you complaining about?" He kissed Shayne on the lips.

Rashid joined Ruby and casually put his hand on the small of her back. When she looked up at him, he kissed her on her forehead before taking a burfi from her tin, then whispering in her ear, "These are the best things I've ever tasted."

Shayne put the movie on soon after that, and people were mostly quiet while watching it. Rashid seemed to be enjoying *Carol*—but that could be because it was barely a Christmas movie. After the movie ended, Shayne put on some Christmas music. "Present time! I'll hand them out. Who needs a new martini first? We can do espresso or eggnog martinis."

Everyone found seats in the living or dining room. Still wearing his Santa hat, Shayne went through each gift under the tree and handed it out. Ruby was glad she'd decided to get things for her friends, because it seemed everyone got her something. Last year she'd only had gifts from Marley and Shayne.

Even Rashid had a gift. His eyes were wide as Shayne handed him an ornately wrapped package.

"Oh," Rashid said. "You didn't have to do this! You only found out I was coming yesterday!"

Shayne waved his hand. "Do you honestly think I would let someone leave my Caroling party empty-handed?"

Everyone opened their gifts at the same time. Shayne's gift to Rashid was a DVD copy of *Carol*. Ruby laughed at that, remembering that Shayne had given her the same thing last year. She wondered if he bought them in bulk.

The gifts Ruby received were all UK or travel themed, which was thoughtful. Some packing cubes, a tourist book on things to do in London, and a new toiletry travel bag with small fillable bottles that had tiny droppers.

"So you can have all your serums and lotions on the flight!" Marley said.

"You know," Rashid said. "All you'll need is a rich emollient cream with—"

Ruby put her hand over Rashid's mouth to shut him up. Okay, he wasn't a *completely* different person.

He kissed the hand that was on his mouth, making Ruby laugh. Everyone loved the gifts Ruby had bought, too. Shayne put his tie clip on immediately, and Marley squealed at the glass teapot and floral teas that Ruby had chosen for her.

It was pretty late by the time all the presents were opened. After helping clean up, Ruby called an Uber to take her and Rashid back to her house.

"Did Ebenezer enjoy that holiday party?" Ruby asked after they were in the car. "I see some seasonal glow on your face. Or that could be Shayne's glitter spray."

He laughed. "Yeah, actually I *did* enjoy myself. Your friends are a riot. They're a really eclectic bunch. I can see why you get along so well."

"Yeah, I only met most of them when I moved here just over a year ago. It's shocking how close we've all gotten."

"Why shocking? How much time do you think it takes to get attached to someone?"

Ruby didn't answer that question. She wasn't sure if he had intended the subtext—he and Ruby had only known each other just over a month, and they were clearly quite attached to each other. He may not have meant it about them, but that was all she heard. This was a fling, but she was already thinking about how hard it was going to be to walk away. When the car dropped them off in front of Ruby's building, Rashid paused instead of going inside with her.

"I haven't had a drink for a few hours," he said. "I can drive."

"So…you're not coming up?" Ruby frowned. That was why he'd left his car here, wasn't it? So he could spend the night.

"Do you want me to come up?" He looked at her with his intense gaze. What was he thinking? Did he know that Ruby had been terrified about how addicted to Rashid she already was?

She exhaled. "Yes, I want you to come up. If you want to."

"I do," he said. He hesitated a moment before he continued. "One question first. Jasmine wanted me to ask you if you'll come to her place for Christmas Day brunch. It will be me, her, and the girls. Maybe it's too soon, and you probably have plans, but—"

Ruby put her hand on his, stopping him. For all the love Ruby had for the season, she'd never actually spent Christmas Day with anyone since her mom died. Ruby didn't mind being alone on Christmas itself—for her it was all about the season, not the day.

But he was asking her to join him and his family for Christmas. "I would love to."

He smiled, then kissed her on the lips, lingering there a moment. "Okay. Good. Now let's go upstairs. I'm hoping there are more of those peppermint burfi up there, because Shayne ate all the ones you brought."

23

THE NEXT FEW DAYS went by in a whirlwind of long, chaotic shifts in the store and quiet cozy moments with Rashid.

Ruby developed callouses on her feet, her fingers were perpetually sticky from handling so much tape while wrapping, and she was finally, officially done with "All I Want for Christmas Is You" (but not "Last Christmas"; she'd never tire of Wham!). But her stolen moments with Rashid more than made up for her hectic job. They met for drinks in the Winter Market one night after she was done with work and had lunch together on another day when she didn't start until one, and he spent most nights sleeping pressed against her in her tiny apartment.

On Thursday, they had their final holiday outing with the girls. They'd decided on Casa Loma, an enormous castle-like property in the northwest end of the city that was fully decorated for Christmas and had a light display outside. Ruby had brought the girls a gift again: a combination kids' cookbook and storybook by a well-known South Asian cooking personality. They spent the whole drive going through all the pictures of food. Casa Loma was lovely—outside it looked like a castle, but inside it was like the English manor house of Ruby's dreams. They got some beautiful pictures, and the girls loved all the lights outside.

Finally, it was Christmas Eve. Ruby worked until ten, making sure the store was neat and tidy for the Boxing Day sale, then collapsed on her bed the moment she got home. About fifteen minutes later, her phone chimed with a text.

> **Rashid:** Buzz me in, I'm downstairs.
>
> **Ruby:** I didn't know you were coming over tonight. I'm exhausted. My feet hurt.
>
> **Rashid:** I have massage oil and ingredients to make ginger hot toddies.

Ruby buzzed him up into the building immediately.

Ten minutes later she was sitting on her sofa wearing her fuzzy bathrobe with a hot toddy in her hand. She'd showered, and her bare feet were in Rashid's hands on his lap.

"You're so good at that," she said. "I should have stayed with you all day instead of going to work. I forgot—why do I love this season so much?"

He laughed. "Now you're seeing things my way. The chaos is too much, right?"

She nodded, then sipped her drink. It was rich and fragrant with ginger, cloves, and whisky. "Retail is *brutal* this time of year." Hopefully this would be her last December working in a store. Hospitality would be busy, too, but she hoped less chaotic.

"You've had more to keep you busy this year than most years," he said as he slid closer so that her knees were on his lap instead of her feet. He started rubbing her calves.

He was right. She looked around her tiny apartment. She'd finally started packing—not that she had a lot to pack. Her two big suitcases were open near her closet, and about half of the clothes she was taking were in it. There were also empty boxes in her kitchen—she'd start packing up the rest of the apartment after her last day at work.

It wasn't just her big move keeping her busy, but Rashid. She'd spent every free moment with him. She'd been getting less sleep, she was behind on all her shows, and she didn't remember the last time she opened a book. Between work, packing, and this holiday fling, it was no wonder Ruby was on the edge of burning out. But she wouldn't trade it for anything. This holiday season might be her best one ever. She only wished there were more hours in a day to enjoy it.

But tomorrow was Christmas. Neither she nor Rashid was working. And they didn't have to be at Jasmine's until noon for brunch, so they could sleep in for the first time all week. Ruby drank the rest of her beverage in one sip, then slid onto Rashid's lap, straddling his thighs. The movement made her robe slip off one shoulder, revealing the top of the floral tattoo on her breast.

Rashid grinned, sliding his hands up her thighs to rest on her bare hips. "I thought you were tired?"

"It's Christmas Eve. I know we said we wouldn't buy each other anything, but you've been such a good boy. I think you deserve a present."

He pulled her robe off her other shoulder gently. "I like that idea. In fact, I'm wondering why I ever disliked this holiday."

Ruby was right. This *was* the best Christmas ever.

"Ruby Auntie! This one's for you!" Noor said, holding out a wrapped box.

Ruby leaned over to take the gift, suppressing a groan thanks to her sore muscles and full stomach. Jasmine had ordered their brunch from a local Pakistani restaurant instead of cooking, but the girls had insisted on supplementing the chicken tikka, naan, kebabs, and rice with mini strawberry pancakes with whipped cream. And Ruby had made eggnog chai and more peppermint burfi. Now they were all gathered in the living room for presents. Ruby was sitting next to Rashid on the white sofa—not so close as to be touching, but close enough.

The gift was from Tara, Noor, and Jasmine, and it turned out to be a pair of fuzzy socks and a rom-com novel set in London—clearly picked out by Jasmine.

"Thank you!" Ruby said. "These will be perfect for my flight."

"This one's for Ruby Auntie, too!" Tara said, handing Ruby a larger box. Ruby frowned. Who was this from? The box was wrapped horribly: thin, cheap paper; baggy corners; and more than one spot of the cardboard box showed under the paper. The label said TO RUBY FROM RASHID. Well, that explained the terrible wrap job.

She looked at him. "I thought we weren't going to exchange gifts?" The girls and Jasmine were preoccupied with opening more gifts from under the tree and weren't paying attention to Ruby.

He shook his head. "No, you said we wouldn't buy each other anything after we...you know. But I'd already bought these for you."

Ruby frowned. Now she felt bad. She'd stuck to the rules and hadn't got him anything. He must have seen the discomfort on her face. "It's not a big deal, Ruby. I didn't want you to have nothing under the tree, and I didn't know Jasmine and the girls got you anything."

Ruby unwrapped the box and pulled out a hideous pair of light blue mittens—clearly hand knit tightly out of scratchy acrylic yarn.

Ruby laughed. "You bought these at that craft market!" There were other things in the box—a mouse ornament made from a walnut shell and a wooden bead, some soap that smelled like cinnamon and marshmallows, a gorgeous fake-emerald vintage brooch, and a jar of spicy red pepper jelly.

"I thought this stuff was for your Calgary friends?" He'd already given her that necklace he bought that day.

"I did get stuff for other people that day, but these things were always intended for you."

She shook her head, amazed, and took the last thing out of the box—a small bag of sample-sized bottles of a drugstore skin care brand that advertised itself as being recommended by dermatologists. She rolled her eyes. Rashid had come a long way from the judgmental twat he was when they met, but she didn't think he'd ever stop judging her skin care choices.

Then again, if this was the stuff he used, maybe she shouldn't judge it without trying it. She grinned at him. "I love it. It's perfect."

They headed back to Ruby's not long after opening presents. The moment they walked into the apartment and dropped all their things on the sofa, Rashid put his arms around Ruby's waist.

"You seriously don't mind that I gave you presents?" he asked. There was a touch of uncertainty in his voice. She wondered if he was remembering how she freaked out when he gave her the necklace.

"Of course not. I wish I'd broken our rule, too." She wrapped her arms around his waist. He felt so strong and solid in her arms.

"I told you, I bought this stuff before we had the rule. And the skin care is just free samples from the clinic. I'm also not against regifting. You could give me that red pepper jelly back."

She shook her head. "Nope. I love that shit. It's mine." But she was only here one more week. Could she finish it in a week?

He leaned down to kiss her neck. "Or…there are other gifts you could give me. Less tangible ones."

She grinned, pulling his shirt to untuck it from his pants. "That I can do." She pulled him down for a long kiss.

That night was mind-blowing, just like every night with him had been. Ruby couldn't put her finger on why sex with Rashid felt so different compared to sex with others she'd been with. Yes, he was generous and considerate, but she'd had generous lovers before. He was skilled, but others had been skilled, too.

But mostly she felt content when they were together. She was comfortable with him. She didn't feel she had to suck in her stomach, hide her reconstructed breasts, or explain why she'd gotten floral tattoos instead of nipple tattoos. She could be herself. Every time they were together, it felt more and more like this was where they were supposed to be.

Walking away from this fling was going to be the hardest thing she'd ever done.

Ruby didn't see Rashid on the twenty-sixth or the twenty-seventh, since she was working long hours both days and he was with his family. They did text a few times. She sent him pictures of the grain bowl she'd grabbed for lunch, and he sent her pictures of all the UK chocolates his parents had brought for him, promising to share some with her—which seemed unnecessary since Ruby would be in the UK in a few days.

On the twenty-eighth, Ruby spent the whole day packing up her apartment. It was small, so she pretty much got it done in a few hours. She was bringing two large suitcases plus a carry-on bag to London, and everything else she owned was going to get picked up on the thirty-first to be donated to a charity for refugees.

At five, Rashid picked her up for dinner with his parents and sister Ayesha. Ruby was incredibly nervous about meeting them—not only because of Ruby and Rashid's fling (which his parents still didn't know about, but apparently Ayesha did) but also because this family was still Ruby's best chance to get a foot in the door in the UK hotel industry. Ruby dressed professionally for dinner—in wide-leg black dress pants and a dark red silk blouse. She really wanted to impress the Hakims tonight. But she was so nervous that she talked nonstop on the way to the restaurant in Little India. "Relax," Rashid said. "They'll be impressed by you, I promise."

She exhaled. "You weren't when we met." He did say he'd been drawn to her, but he definitely wasn't impressed by her professionally.

"Yeah, but I was an idiot. The rest of my family is much smarter."

"What are they like? Is Ayesha into cottagecore like you and Jasmine?"

He laughed at that. "No. Ayesha wouldn't be caught dead in flannel. My mom says that our family is split into country mice and city mice. Me, Jasmine, and Mom are the country mice. Dad and Ayesha are the city mice."

Oh. That was a surprise. "If your dad's a city mouse, why did he buy an inn in the countryside?"

"Because that's where Mom wants to spend their golden years. I think you'll get along well with Ayesha. She and I argue about designer versus drugstore skin care all the time."

When they got to the restaurant, the host took them to a large table, and Hakim and Farida Hakim stood to greet Ruby warmly. In their early sixties, Rashid's parents were a handsome couple. Farida looked a lot like Jasmine, while Hakim looked like what she'd imagine Rashid to look like at that age. Both seemed healthy and vibrant—which made sense since Rashid had mentioned they played tennis regularly. Ayesha's appearance almost made Ruby laugh, though. She looked exactly like Jasmine—if Jasmine had just had a makeover by Miranda Priestly. While Jasmine was prone to wearing floral sweaters and pale jeans, Ayesha was in shiny black slacks and a black mock-neck sleeveless sweater. Ruby was pretty sure the sweater was a Victoria Beckham. And instead of her sister's shoulder-length waves, Ayesha had a sleek and neat bob.

But Ayesha greeted Ruby as warmly as her parents had, kissing Ruby on both cheeks. There was a knowing twinkle in her eyes, and she grinned at Rashid after meeting Ruby. Yeah, she knew about their fling.

After ordering a selection of curries along with rice and naan for the table, Hakim grinned at Ruby. "So great to finally meet the Ruby Auntie that my granddaughters can't stop talking about."

Ruby frowned. "How much are they talking about me?"

"My dear, the girls are *obsessed* with you," Farida said, laughing. "Since the Santa Claus Parade, all I've heard when we call is Ruby Auntie has pretty hair, and Ruby Auntie likes hot chocolate, and Ruby Auntie always wears red. They are enchanted with you. They don't warm up to strangers easily. You should be flattered."

"Jasmine, too," Ayesha said. "She said I absolutely had to meet the woman who made my brother watch *Love, Actually*. I'm going to need all your secrets."

Ruby laughed while Rashid turned a cute shade of pink. "He didn't love everything Christmassy we did together. He was *not* a fan of Christmas shopping."

"Who is?" Hakim said. "I don't understand how you could work in a Christmas store. You must have nerves of steel."

"I love it there, but I'm also glad the season is done." She told them a bit about the store and what they sold there.

"We're planning to visit the Winter Market tomorrow evening," Farida said. "It looks like one we went to in Hamburg a few years ago. Have you ever been to the European holiday markets?"

Ruby shook her head. "I've always wanted to. I hope to go after I move to London."

Hakim nodded. "We're staying in the north now, but you must come visit us in London when we're there next. I understand you're intending to change careers to the hotel industry?"

Ruby nodded. "Yes, my long-term goal is to open a country inn, but first I need to get some hotel experience."

Hakim smiled widely. "Well, meeting this family has been lucky for you, because we should be able to help you with that. Let's leave business talk for later, though. Maybe you and Ayesha can find time in the next few days to meet alone? She can tell you all about the opportunities in the Hakim Group that are available, if you're interested."

Ayesha nodded. "Yes, let's talk alone. Send me your CV... sorry, résumé. Are you free tomorrow afternoon for a coffee?"

"Oh, my goodness, that would be fantastic! Yes, I'm free. Thank you!" Ruby beamed. This was going so well. She grabbed Rashid's hand under the table and squeezed it with excitement.

"No, Ruby, thank you," Farida said. "I don't think you realize the gift you've given this family. We weren't sure we'd see the girls smiling much this season. They've been through a lot, and so has Jasmine. It's been such a joy to hear excitement in their voices again. We're happy to repay your kindness to our family. Now, tell me more about the ballet. I can't believe Rashid is thinking of going again!"

Ruby grinned. She was more than happy to put the business talk aside and spend the evening getting to know this delightful family.

24

RUBY MET AYESHA AT a quiet coffee shop in the East End the next afternoon, and maybe because it was that weird time between Christmas and New Year's, they were pretty much the only two people in the dark wood-paneled café. After Ruby ordered a London fog and Ayesha a flat white, they slid into a booth. Ruby was dressed to impress again—in her Topshop suit with a red camisole underneath—because even in her power suit, she needed her good-luck color.

Ayesha was in all black again—this time a short skirt and black sweater with opaque black tights, along with a gorgeous felted coat with a wide shawl lapel. Ruby couldn't resist—she immediately asked Ayesha where the coat was from.

"Oh, there's this little boutique on High Street. Very snooty. It's fantastic." She told Ruby more about the store. Ruby liked Ayesha. In fact, after their big dinner yesterday, she was struck by how much Ayesha reminded Ruby of her cousin Marley, except Ayesha was much more extroverted. She was actually like a mix of Marley and Shayne. Ayesha would get along fabulously with Ruby's Toronto friends.

"I think my friend Shayne did a photo shoot there. He's a fashion photographer based here in Toronto."

"Oh, how cool! Rashid told me you have eclectic friends."

"Yeah, I met them all through my cousin Marley. She's a fashion stylist—she got me the job at Reid's but left to go freelance a few months ago. Her partner is an actor in LA. He's in a big superhero movie coming out next year. And Shayne, that's my photographer friend, his partner is a daytime talk show host here in Toronto. And of course, you know Nadim and Reena. Reena and Marley are actually cousins, too—on Marley's dad's side."

Ayesha grinned. "Yes, I've known Nadim *forever*...I still can't believe he's a responsible family man now. I adore it for him, though. I hope to get to know Reena better." She took a sip of her coffee. "You're so well connected in this city. It's surprising that you would pack up and leave. Do you have employment lined up in London yet?"

That was exactly what Rashid had said last month—he said it made Ruby seem irresponsible and impulsive. Ruby shook her head. "Not yet. I've applied to several boutiques, and even had phone interviews at a few. Most said they'd like to see me in person when I get there. I have extensive experience in luxury retail all over the country and excellent references from several stores."

"But selling luxury goods isn't what you want to do, correct?"

Ruby nodded. "My mother—sorry, I mean *my* goal is to one day purchase a property in the UK. England or Scotland. I've always dreamed of running an inn or small hotel in the country. Maybe with a little restaurant or tea house."

Ayesha tilted her head, a puzzled expression on her face. With that expression, she resembled her brother so much—much more than Jasmine did. "It's funny. I heard you wanted your own country inn, but after meeting you, I find it surprising. The countryside doesn't match your personality."

Ruby frowned. "Really?" Ruby had always thought her entire personality *was* the English countryside. She drank tea more than water. She had all the BBC adaptations of Jane Austen novels memorized. She loved chintz wallpaper. So what if she hung out with photographers and TV stars. That didn't mean her lifelong dream was wrong for her.

Ayesha laughed. "Ah, what do I know. I never would have imagined my brother enjoying the ballet. Or that he'd love living in a city like Toronto."

Ruby squeezed her lips together, trying not to laugh.

"By the way," Ayesha said. "Unlike my parents, I'm aware of this situationship you have with my big brother. It will have no impact on your possible employment. My family wants to help you because of what you've done for Tara, Noor, and Jasmine. The fact that you managed to get my brother into a Christmas jumper is beside the point...although I have mad respect for you for that one."

Ruby huffed a laugh. Yeah, she liked Ayesha a lot.

"Okay, tell me more about your role in the Christmas store," Ayesha said.

The conversation shifted to feel more like a job interview, as Ayesha asked her about her strengths, her transferable skills, and what attracted her to the hospitality industry, and to the Hakim Group in particular. Ruby answered all the questions the best she could, and she had honestly no idea how she was doing. She'd thought Ayesha and the whole Hakim family liked her yesterday. But even as she told Ayesha about her strengths and weaknesses, she worried about that comment that Ruby didn't seem like she would fit in the English countryside.

But maybe it didn't matter if Ayesha thought she was more city mouse than country mouse, because the Hakims had hotels in cities where Ruby could gain experience. After Ayesha peppered her with questions about her duties at Reid's, she nodded. "Rashid wasn't kidding. You *are* impressive. I think you'd be a great asset to the Hakim Group—if you're committed to it. I know you've changed jobs a lot, which is my main concern after looking at your CV. Of course, the fact that you've had no trouble securing employment after moving tells me that you're adaptable and a fast learner."

"I am committed." Ruby took a breath. "Can I be honest with you, Ayesha?"

"Please do."

"I've moved around because I feel like I haven't yet found what I'm supposed to do. I don't have any close family tying me to a place. My mother and I used to daydream about this move to England, and after she died when I was twenty, I've felt… restless. Like I haven't arrived *home* yet."

"You're originally from Toronto, aren't you?"

Ruby nodded. "Yes. And you're right, I do have friends and connections here. But it's still…" She exhaled. As nice as Ayesha was, this was a job interview. Ruby needed to remember to keep things professional. "I know my employment history makes it seem like I'm not committed to my career. And I guess that's one of the reasons why I want to change industries. I'm a little done with luxury retail. I'm ready to learn something new."

Ayesha smiled. "I have a good feeling about you, Ruby. Maybe it's because my brother and sister seem so taken with you, and I trust their opinions so much—especially Rashid's. Jasmine's so sweet, she adores pretty much anyone she meets, but Rashid is…quite particular about who he spends his time with. I trust his judgment immensely, which is why I'm comfortable making this offer now."

Ruby nodded, smiling, but inside she was screaming with joy. This was going even better than she expected.

"Let me give you some backstory on the company first," Ayesha said. "As you know, the Hakim Group has several hotels, and we've recently opened a few smaller boutique hotels, the Raj London, and the Raj Newcastle. The plan was always to grow the Raj hotels to be the main bread and butter of the company going forward. Do you know where the name Raj comes from?"

Ruby shook her head. "Raj means king, doesn't it?"

Ayesha nodded. "It does mean king, but R-A-J is for Rashid, Ayesha, and Jasmine. Despite my brother and sister not working in the company, we consider this business as belonging to all of us, and everything the family does is for the family." She chuckled. "I know it sounds like we're a mafia or something. We're a little codependent, but mostly normal. As you can probably tell, for all the Hakims, even the ones who don't work in the family business, family comes first. And that's why recent developments in the family have forced us to rethink our long-term plans to ensure we are doing what's best for *all* of our well-being, not just for the bottom line."

Ruby nodded. "Your commitment to each other is something I admire about you all so much."

Ayesha smiled. "Then surely you understand why my brother and I have decided to make these choices. Jasmine, Tara, and Noor need family nearby right now. I've signed the papers this morning to purchase a struggling hotel here in Toronto. In six months, I hope the Raj Toronto will be open for business."

What? The Hakims were opening a hotel *here*?

"I understand that your goal is to move to the UK," Ayesha continued, "but I think it would be a huge asset to have someone like you, with your familiarity with the city and your connections to major influencers, on board from the very beginning."

Ruby froze. Was she being offered a job…*here*? In Toronto? "I don't follow."

"I'm moving here," Ayesha said. "Once the immigration gets sorted. In the meantime, the Hakim Group will hire a project manager to oversee the construction and a hospitality manager to get some buzz going and to start staffing. I think you'd be wonderful in that role."

Ruby blinked. This was unexpected. She'd had no idea that Rashid's family was even thinking about expanding into Canada. But it made sense. Jasmine's soon-to-be ex-husband certainly wasn't making things easy for her, and Jasmine and Ayesha were twins. Ayesha wanted to be here for her sister and her nieces.

But this isn't what Ruby wanted. Like, at all. Not *now*. Maybe six months or a year ago she would have jumped at the opportunity to get hotel experience in Toronto. But her flight was literally days away.

If this opportunity had come up six months ago, would Ruby have still moved to London at all?

But she wouldn't have had this opportunity six months ago, because she didn't know Rashid then. And this opportunity—an opportunity of a lifetime to work in a hotel at the very beginning of its launch—wouldn't be hers if the eldest Hakim child didn't like her so much.

"Wait," Ruby said. "You said this was a decision that both you and your brother made. Is he…I mean, he isn't going to work in the hotel, is he?"

Ayesha paused, like she wasn't sure if she should tell Ruby this. "No, I was talking about him buying into Jasmine's dermatology practice and staying in the city."

Ruby exhaled. Rashid was staying. He wasn't going to leave Toronto in February like he said he would. Why didn't he tell her that his plans had changed?

Did this change of plans make a difference for her? Ruby was leaving; why did it matter if Rashid wasn't? Unless he was the one who'd asked Ayesha to do this so that Ruby would stay here with him.

They'd decided that this was just a fling. A *situationship*, not a relationship, because they were both supposed to be here temporarily. They were going to keep things casual—not even give each other Christmas presents.

But he broke that rule. He got her presents. And came back to her bed every night to sleep pressed against her. He made her hot drinks and gave her a foot rub. There had never been anything casual about their short relationship. Except for the fact that he didn't tell her that he was staying here in the city. Or that his family was buying a property here.

Ayesha told Ruby more about the hospitality manager role and why she wanted Ruby. "Look, I know it's a big decision," Ayesha said. "And if you're dead set on going to London, I may be able to find you a position there." She paused. "Why don't you think about it and let me know? Okay?"

Ruby smiled and nodded. She didn't want to ask her if this was her brother's idea, because she wasn't sure she wanted the answer to that question yet. But she was almost one hundred percent positive that she was going to turn down Ayesha's job offer here in Toronto. Giving up a lifelong dream because of a three-week situationship was the definition of *impulsive*—too impulsive even for Ruby. But she needed to talk to Rashid before she told Ayesha that.

After telling Ayesha she would consider her offer and thanking her again, Ruby left the café. The moment she was on the sidewalk, she called Rashid.

"Hey, Red!" he said after answering. "How'd your meeting with my sister go?"

"Um, how do *you* think it went?"

"I'm sure she loved you. What did she say?"

"You *really* don't know?"

"Know what? You're acting strange, Ruby. What's going on?"

Ruby exhaled. Was it possible he didn't know that his sister was going to offer her that job? But he had to have known his family had bought that failing Toronto hotel. And he of course knew that he wasn't moving back to Calgary in February, as planned. And he hadn't told her either of these things.

"We have to talk," she said. "I'm heading home now."

"Okay. Do you want to come to the house?"

Ruby exhaled. She couldn't have this talk with any of his family around. "Can you come to my place in about half an hour?"

"Sure," he said. "Do you want me to bring anything? My mother made a huge batch of biriyani today. I can bring some—"

"No. It's fine. I just need to talk to you."

Ruby's mind raced the whole subway and bus ride back to her apartment. Was she overreacting? Could Rashid have really pulled strings behind her back to make her stay with him? There were a lot of reasons why he may not have told her about his plan to stay in the city—not the least of which was the fact that it really wasn't any of her business. This was a fling with an end date, not a committed relationship. What he did after January first had nothing to do with Ruby.

But that thought hurt, too. Rashid meant so much to Ruby, and it was going to be torturous for her to go from this to no relationship at all in two days. She was going to miss him so much. If he wasn't opening up to her about his life, then maybe it meant he didn't feel the same way about her?

But it was also possible that her initial gut instinct was

right, and he told Ayesha to offer her that job to make her stay with him. That was manipulation, as far as Ruby was concerned. He was using something she wanted—a hotel job—to convince her to stay with him.

Just like her father had used something she wanted—the UK visa—to get her to come back to Toronto. Which he'd only done to get his hands on Ruby's money.

When Rashid arrived about ten minutes after she got home, Ruby had convinced herself that she was overreacting. That there was no way Rashid could be as manipulative as her father. And when she opened the door to see him standing there, she was even more sure.

Those kind eyes. That tiny smile whenever he saw her.

"Ruby, what's wrong? Did something happen in your meeting with Ayesha? She's hard to please sometimes, but I know she'll love—"

Ruby shook her head as she stepped aside for him to come in. "No. I like your sister. And I think she liked me fine, considering she offered me a job today."

A wide, surprised smile transformed his face. "Red! That's amazing! That's exactly what you wanted, isn't it?"

"Not really. Come and sit. I would offer you some tea or something, but the mugs are all packed." Ruby's whole life was packed up now. There were boxes and garbage bags everywhere.

He frowned as he sat on the sofa. "What do you mean, not really?"

Ruby sat next to him and put her hands in her lap. "Rashid, she offered me a job as hospitality manager *here*—at the new Raj Toronto hotel."

He grinned. "I knew she'd love you!"

Ruby frowned. "She said she wanted someone from here—a Canadian who understands the culture—who understands customers looking for luxury, which I do after working in luxury retail for so long. And she wants my connections—Marley and Shayne in the fashion industry, and their partners in entertainment media."

He smiled. "Ayesha is a smart cookie. She wouldn't offer if she didn't think you could do the job."

"Okay, but did you know she was going to offer it to me?"

"No. I did tell her how fantastic you are and told her she should consider you for the Toronto job after she told me about it, but I had no idea she'd make a decision on the spot. You must have really wowed her."

He knew. He told his sister to consider her.

"Why would you do that, Rashid? I'm leaving."

He blinked but didn't say anything to that. And maybe that was a good thing, because she really, really didn't want Dr. Rashid Hakim to ask her to stay here for him. Her answer would break both their hearts.

"There's something else Ayesha told me," Ruby said. "That you're buying into Jasmine's practice. Rashid, are you staying in Toronto?"

He nodded. "Yeah, I've decided not to move back to Calgary."

Ruby shook her head. She couldn't believe this. "Why wouldn't you tell me something so major? I know this was a fling or whatever, but we *are* friends, aren't we?"

"Of course we're friends, Ruby. We only finalized the

details this week." He rubbed the back of his neck. "I didn't tell you because I thought if you knew I was going to be here, then it would be harder for you to leave. I know it would be harder for me if I was in your position."

Ruby closed her eyes a moment, feeling a prickle behind them. When she opened them, she saw Rashid's kind face. He was so gorgeous. The last few weeks with him had been so perfect. Better than she ever imagined when she agreed to this supposed fling. Ruby had let herself be vulnerable with him. Leaned on him more, both physically and emotionally than she'd ever leaned on anyone. But she never let herself forget the end date. What if she knew from the beginning that he was going to be staying in this city for good? Would Ruby have been tempted to give up her dreams and stay here with him?

He didn't keep his plans from her because he wanted to keep her at arm's length, but because he cared for her and didn't want to make things harder for her.

She didn't know what to say. "If I'd known you were staying," she said slowly. "It wouldn't have made a difference for me."

Even now, knowing she could have a job in Toronto that would get her the hotel experience she needed, she was not tempted to stay. She'd planned this for so long. Hell, she'd even pretended to like her father for more than a year so she could get the visa. She couldn't—no, *wouldn't* give it up because she'd grown attached to a family she met literally a month and a half ago.

"But..." Rashid said. "If Ayesha wants you to work at the Raj Toronto, maybe you don't have to go *now*. Maybe you can get the hotel experience you want here in Toronto and go open your inn in the UK later. Or open it somewhere else."

She exhaled long. That was exactly what she was afraid he would say. "Rashid, I'm going. This was always my mother's and my dream. She left me that money so I could do this alone if she didn't survive long enough for us to do it together."

He took her hand in his. "But...what about *you*, Ruby? Whenever you talk about going, it's always 'this was my mother's and my dream.' I don't think you've really considered if it's *Ruby's* dream. Just Ruby's."

Ruby blinked. "It was *our* dream. Both of us. Forever." Ruby took her hand back. "I know she's gone, but she was my *mother*. I would think someone with a family as close as yours would understand why this is important."

He exhaled. "I have no idea what it would be like to lose a family member you loved so much, but—"

Ruby's teeth gritted. "Yeah, Rashid. You have *no* idea. You and your great big Hakim family who will literally drop everything when one of you is in trouble. You with two loving parents who guided you all to be your best possible selves but are still there to be your backup if something goes wrong. Not to mention a family with money. Homes in London, Spain, and Northern England. Hotels all over the UK. You're a literal doctor. I work retail. You can't ever understand what it's like to be me."

"Ruby, that's not fair. I think—"

"You think you can *buy* me to stay with you by getting me my dream job!"

He looked at her, and a familiar expression was back. Irritation. "I'm not trying to buy you, Ruby. This is another option that you should consider." His face softened. "You can go and do what you always planned. Or you can stay here...with me."

She shook her head. "Seriously? We've known each other, what...six weeks? You accused me of being impulsive and irresponsible when you found out I was going to England, and now you want me to stay, to throw away the dream I've been working toward for so long, for a three-week relationship? That's one hell of a risk you're asking me to take. Your sister Jasmine moved to Toronto for a man, and look how that turned out for her."

He shook his head. "How could you even think of me in the same breath as Derek?"

"I know, Rashid. You're not like him. But I'm not like your sister, either. I don't have a support system to come save me if something goes wrong. I'm all alone, remember?"

"You always say you're alone, but you're not! You have the best friends here—ones who would do anything for you! And that includes me, by the way. Even if we don't work out as a couple, I'll always—"

"We were *never* supposed to work out, Rashid! There was *always* an end date!"

He exhaled, looking at her. He looked sad. She hated the look on him. She was breaking his heart, and that was breaking hers. "But maybe it doesn't have to?" he said, voice small.

She shook her head, the tears falling down her cheeks. "I have to go. Toronto isn't my home anymore. I moved here because my father manipulated me, and I'm not going to stay because you manipulate me."

He exhaled long. "Okay, Ruby. I'm sorry." He didn't sound sorry. He sounded frustrated. "I wasn't manipulating you. I was trying to help you. But I'm not sure you know the difference. I wish you'd understand that you don't have to keep running to find a home. That maybe your home is where you want it to be."

"And maybe I'm going to where I *want* my home to be," she spat out.

He didn't say anything to that. Just stared at her with that intense gaze that she used to have trouble deciphering. Now she wondered if that look was Rashid upset that the world wasn't falling into place the way he expected it to.

Ruby took a deep breath. "I'm going, Rashid. In two days, I'm getting on a plane and making my lifelong dream come true. And maybe it's a good idea to move that end date for our…fling. I think it needs to end right now."

They were supposed to have two more days together, but she didn't want to spend those days with someone who didn't understand why she was going. Who didn't understand her.

He stood. "Okay. Ruby, I'm sorry I wasn't completely honest with you. I'm sorry you think I was trying to manipulate you—that wasn't my intention at all. Most of all, I'm sorry that you still feel that you're alone in this world, because that's the furthest thing from the truth. But I am really glad we met and that we had this time together. Even if this is how it's ending." He headed toward the door. Ruby didn't turn to see him go. She was afraid that if she looked at his face even one more time, she would give in. She would stop him from leaving and she would spend the next two days with him. But that would make it even harder to go.

And she was still leaving. There was nothing in the world that would make her change her mind. Not even Dr. Rashid Hakim.

25

RUBY EMAILED AYESHA THE moment Rashid left her apartment, writing that she was flattered and thankful for the job offer, but she was still planning to move to the UK. She wrote that if a position in any of the Hakim hotels in the UK should become available, she would be grateful for a chance to interview for it. By that evening Ayesha had written back thanking Ruby and saying no hard feelings and she understood. And that she would definitely look out for a position in the UK for her in the future.

Ruby was glad she could keep busy preparing for her move for the next two days so she could attempt to keep the Hakim family off her mind. She packed and repacked her suitcase a few times. She went shopping to buy all the things that she wasn't sure she'd be able to get right away in London. She booked a car to get her from the airport to the apartment hotel she'd reserved there. But staying busy wasn't enough to prevent her from thinking about Rashid and how upside down everything had gone in the last few days.

She didn't have one moment of regret for turning down the job in Toronto or for ending her relationship with him a few days early. She knew it was the right thing to do. But that didn't mean she wasn't devastated. And to add insult to injury, now she had to spend New Year's Eve alone. Her flight on January first wasn't until three p.m., but she needed to be out of her apartment on the thirty-first, so Rashid had booked a room in a hotel for their last night together, and then he'd planned to drive her to the airport. But now she was staying at Marley and Shayne's instead. Marley, Shayne, Nik, and Anderson were all going to some posh party downtown. They invited Ruby, but she was not in a clubbing mood.

It was almost six on New Year's Eve when Ruby was finally ready to leave her apartment. She called an Uber to take her to Marley and Shayne's house, grabbing her final mail from the mailbox in the lobby and leaving her keys with security on the way out.

When she got to her cousin's house, there was no answer. They must have already gone downtown. Ruby unlocked the door using the code they gave her, and immediately after opening the door, she heard a loud "Surprise!"

Ruby's hand went to her chest when she saw all her friends clapping and cheering in the living room. The strangest thing wasn't that they were all here when they were supposed to be partying, but their *outfits*. "What are you all…wearing?"

Reena and Nadim appeared to be in Victorian costumes—Reena in a long dark dress with a corset top, Nadim in tan pants tucked into tall boots, along with a pretty good period-appropriate jacket and even a freaking cravat. Anderson was dressed like…

maybe the seventies UK punk scene? Biker jacket, no shirt, and lots of chains and spiked hair. It was such a change from how he usually dressed that Ruby wasn't one hundred percent sure it was actually him. Shayne was easily recognizable as Freddie Mercury from the "I Want to Break Free" music video—pink sleeveless sweater, leather miniskirt, and black thigh-high boots. It worked because he already had a very Freddie Mercury mustache. Marley and Nik were dressed sixties mod—Marley in a psychedelic Twiggy-esque dress, and Nik wearing what looked like a cheap Austin Powers Halloween costume.

"This is your going-away party!" Shayne said. "We're dressed like the UK!"

Ruby smiled widely. Shayne had even decorated—there was a Union Jack bunting hanging on the wall and a big sign that said BON VOYAGE, which was French, not English, but it was the thought that counted. "When did you plan all this? Where did you get those clothes?"

"There *are* costume stores in this city, you know," Shayne said. "And we couldn't let one of our friends be alone on her last night in Canada."

"You needed a send-off party!" Reena added.

"But you guys all had New Year's Eve plans!"

Marley shook her head. "Believe me. Any excuse not to go to an industry party is welcome."

"We even left Aleem and some pumped milk with my parents!" Reena said. "I made trifle! And scones with clotted cream, and sausage rolls! Come on, we're going to drink Pimm's Cups and Beefeater gin. I don't have to breastfeed tonight!" It sounded like Reena had already started drinking.

This was so sweet of her friends. Ruby had a strong suspicion that this party wasn't just because she was leaving tomorrow, but also because of the implosion of her relationship with Rashid. But this was a much better way to spend her last night in Canada than crying alone with Marley's cat. She grinned and kicked off her shoes.

"There's a dress for you upstairs in the spare room," Shayne said. "I'll start mixing the cocktails."

Her friends knew her, so she expected the dress would be an Austen-esque Regency gown, but that's not what was draped over the bed. It was a Union Jack dress with red boots—a Ginger Spice costume—in Ruby's size. She changed into it before joining her friends downstairs, ready to celebrate.

Ruby's going-away party was hilarious. She should have known these guys would do something so extra. After pouring delicious gin martinis, they silly-danced to the Spice Girls, Queen, and the Sex Pistols, then played a goofy UK trivia game before crowding around the coffee table to eat. Reena had tossed off her corset, and Shayne made a pitcher of Pimm's cocktails for them all to share.

After her argument with Rashid, Ruby hadn't expected to have any joyful moments before her flight overseas. But her friends banded together to make sure her last night in the city was the definition of *joy*. They even, quite obviously, were staying far away from one topic—the Hakim family—because they didn't want to upset her more.

"I always forget details before trips like this," Nadim said. "Passport renewed? Keys turned in? Online check-in done? Mail forwarded?"

Ruby nodded. "I had a five-page checklist. I'm good." She looked at Marley. "Thanks for letting me forward my mail here. I don't expect it will be anything but junk. Oh wait, I didn't look at today's mail."

Ruby took out the small stack from her purse that she'd grabbed on her way out. She hadn't checked her mailbox since Christmas, and as expected, it was all junk—plus Christmas cards from her dentist and her bank. But…"What's this?" Ruby said, looking at a white envelope from a law office. She was immediately brought back to the last time a lawyer mailed her something unexpected—when she got notice of the trust from her mother. But this wasn't from the firm that handled her trust.

Could this be…? With shaking hands, Ruby opened the envelope. And then dropped it three seconds later. "Fuck," she said quietly, her eyes welling with tears.

"What is it?" Marley asked, voice laced with concern.

Ruby exhaled, blinking. Her father wasn't worth a single tear. "My fucking father is *suing* me for my inheritance."

There was silence in the room. She closed her eyes. She didn't think he would actually carry out his threat.

"What does the letter say?" Anderson asked gently.

She thought about telling them nothing, saying *Don't worry about it, this is a party*. She didn't want to burden them all with the messy bits of her life. But she remembered what Rashid had said a few days ago—these people were her friends. They did all this for her, threw her a party instead of going out on New Year's Eve. When shit hit the fan, Ruby wasn't actually alone.

She handed Anderson the letter. "Read it out loud. Maybe you all can make sense of the legalese."

Anderson read the letter, and then Nadim, who worked in the corporate world and understood legal jargon, translated. Basically, the letter was an intent to sue. It said that her father, Arif Dhanji, would be suing Rubina Dhanji for the full amount of the trust left to her by Maryam Dhanji plus interest, as the funds in the trust were acquired illegally from Arif's own assets.

Ruby frowned. "So, Dad's claiming that Mom stole the money from him, and therefore he's entitled to it all? Plus interest?" She couldn't believe this horrendous man was her father.

"I'm pretty sure he's not allowed to sue anymore," Nik said. "There are statutes of limitations on inheritances."

Nadim nodded. "Hang on, I'm looking it up."

"We know a lawyer," Reena added. "A good one. She handled my sister's divorce."

"I know one, too," Shayne said.

Everyone in the room started talking at once, analyzing the letter, looking through all their contacts, and even reading the relevant parts of Canadian law online to determine if Ruby's father had a case. Within half an hour, preliminary emails had been sent to three local attorneys, inquiring if they would consult with Ruby online in the next week about a threatening notice of intent to sue.

"Don't worry about this, Rubes," Shayne said. "Don't let it ruin your trip. I have no doubt we'll get this all sorted. He's trying to scare you, but we won't let him, right, guys?"

Ruby blinked. Rashid was right. Her friends did *have* her. The fact that they'd canceled their New Year's Eve plans and were now trying to become experts on Canadian inheritance laws for her was proof of that. They supported her. They accepted her. She was nowhere near as alone as she'd thought, and she suddenly felt terrible she hadn't appreciated them more.

"You guys are the best, you know that?" she said, feeling her eyes well with tears again. "First Rashid, now this stupid letter. Not sure my nerves could have handled it without you all. I'm going to miss you all so much."

"We're going to miss you, too," Anderson said. "But we'll still see you. Now we have a reason to go to England."

Shayne nodded. "Yes! Believe me, you're going to see too much of us. And we're keeping you in the chat group. It'll be like you never left Toronto."

She blinked. She couldn't believe all this drama right before she was leaving. Usually Ruby's first impulse when bad things happened was to want to get out of the city she was in. But not this time. She had all this *love* here.

She wiped her eyes. She blamed the Pimm's Cup. "Aren't you all curious about what actually happened with Rashid?"

Marley shrugged. "I mean, yes, but you don't have to tell us about it if you don't want to. I know you two were supposed to stay casual, so I figured it ran its course."

Ruby took a bite of a sausage roll, which of course reminded her of when she and Rashid ate sausages in the Winter Market. It wasn't fair. December was her favorite month—she wondered if it would be the month of painful memories now.

"I don't think it was casual for Rashid," Anderson said.

Ruby looked at him. "How could you tell?"

"The way he looked at you at the Christmas party. Plus, he kinda told me how into you he was when we were at that holiday craft market."

Ruby frowned. That was only their second outing. It was when he had bought her all those things so she wouldn't be empty-handed on Christmas. Ruby took another bite of sausage roll, mostly so she wouldn't start crying again.

"So what did happen between you?" Marley asked gently.

"Does it have anything to do with Ayesha being in town?" Nadim added. "Because Ayesha is a lot. We used to call her a chaos demon in uni."

"I *need* to meet this woman," Shayne said.

Ruby chuckled. Ayesha was the furthest thing from a chaos demon now, at least as far as Ruby could tell. She was a responsible executive in her family business. "Yeah, it was sort of because of Ayesha. Rashid asked her to offer me a job here in Toronto, to make me stay and not go to England. Because he's staying."

"Holy crap, he's *staying*?" Nadim asked, frowning.

"Why do men *always* get possessive and caveman-y?" Marley said, shaking her head. She kissed her boyfriend Nik on the cheek. "Except you, of course."

"Nah, I agree," Nik said, nodding. "We're really the worst." He grabbed Marley comically by the arm and said, "Woman mine!"

"I'm with Nik," Shayne said. "Men are the worst. But I don't get why he decided to stay here if he knew you were leaving?"

"He's not staying for me," Ruby said. "He's staying for his

sister Jasmine. Her soon-to-be ex-husband won't let her take the kids out of the country—"

"Now that's a possessive asshole," Nadim said.

Ruby nodded. "Yeah, totally. So both Rashid and Ayesha are moving to Toronto to help her out with the twins. Rashid is buying into Jasmine's dermatology practice, and Ayesha is opening a boutique hotel. The Raj Toronto."

"Oooooh," Shayne squealed. "This is not public knowledge yet, right? How cool. I've seen pictures of the Raj London... Will she need an exclusive photographer? Also, I know a ton of designers who would love to do a fashion shoot there if it will look anything like the Raj properties in the UK."

Ruby chuckled. Ayesha had said that she wanted access to Ruby's circle of friends, and apparently her circle of friends wanted access to Ayesha. But Nadim could introduce them; they didn't need Ruby.

And actually, since Nadim and Ayesha were old friends, they'd probably rekindle their friendship and hang out regularly after she moved here. And Rashid seemed to get along great with all these guys, so he might get absorbed into Ruby's friend group, too. Everyone she cared about could be meeting in this very house regularly for drinks, or movie nights, or whatever. Everyone but Ruby.

But leaving was what she wanted. She could meet new friends in London. And despite everything, she still held out hope that Ayesha would come through with a position for her in one of the Hakim hotels in the UK.

"I don't know," Anderson said. "I think Rashid's heart was in the right place. He wanted to help you."

"Maybe," Ruby said. "But he didn't even tell me he was staying. He thought that when he presented it all to me, the perfect job and the fact that he would be here, I would throw away my dreams and stay with him. It felt like he didn't understand me."

Everyone was silent for a while. Ruby felt another tear escape. She wiped it quickly, hoping her friends didn't see.

Anderson nodded. "Okay, but did he ask you to…I don't know. Commit to him? Like move in with him, or anything like that?"

She shook her head. "No. That would be ridiculous. We've only known each other for six weeks."

That made Reena snort. She and Nadim had eloped after dating only four weeks. "It's not the same as you and Nadim, Reena," Ruby said quickly.

"No, of course not," Reena said. "I would never advise anyone to commit after such a short time. It's incredibly stupid."

Nadim frowned. "Hey!"

Reena patted him on the leg. "Best stupid mistake I ever made. I get not wanting to take a risk like that, but feelings *can* get that big after a short time. So, I kind of get why he wanted to give you a way to stay with him. He's clearly smitten."

"But we should have had a conversation about it before he told his sister to offer me a job."

Marley nodded. "You're right. He should have talked to you. And when you said no, he should have accepted your decision."

Ruby squeezed her lips together. "Actually, he *did* accept my decision. He said it was my choice what I wanted to do, and he'd understand if I still needed to go. He said my staying was just another option."

"If he accepted your choice, then why aren't you two getting busy all night on your last night together?" Shayne asked.

Ruby shook her head. "Because asking his sister to hire me in Toronto without asking me first means he doesn't understand how important this move is for me! He shouldn't have put me in a position where I'd have to refuse a job from a company that I really want to work for. And I don't appreciate him making things harder for me right now..." Her voice cracked. "I've been working so long on this dream. I even had to see my father once a month to get the visa. Not to mention the money I've saved, jobs I've applied for, the research I've done...This has been something my mom and I have wanted to do *forever*. And Rashid giving me this other option at literally the last possible moment complicates everything. He's not making it easier for me to achieve my dreams. He's making it harder. Because he made me..." Her voice cracked again. She was going to ugly cry, and then she'd have puffy skin on her first day in London. Damn that Rashid Hakim.

"He made it so you're tempted to stay," Reena said gently.

Ruby nodded, then snorted inelegantly.

"And that's the clincher, isn't it?" Anderson said. "If this had stayed casual for him, he wouldn't have asked his sister to consider you for a job here. And if it had stayed casual for you, the fact that he gave you this option of staying wouldn't complicate anything because you wouldn't have been tempted to stay."

Ruby exhaled. As much as she pretended, it had never been

casual with Rashid. Hell, she'd been in deep even before they made it official the night they went to the ballet.

"Ruby, one question," Marley said after everyone was quiet awhile. "And before I ask, remember how much I loved your mother. She may as well have been my mother, too, and I'm still not over her dying on us." Marley's voice broke, and she paused a moment. "Is this dream of moving to the UK, of buying a property in the countryside…is this actually *your* dream, or are you trying to fulfill *her* dream? Because you and I know that she would have wanted you to follow your own path, not hers."

Well, there it was. Ruby had asked herself this question before. Because what Marley said was true—the last thing Mom would ever have wanted for Ruby or Marley was to put their own lives on hold for someone else's dreams.

"It *is* what I want," she said. "I know there are a lot of issues with England. I mean, colonialism sucks, but I've never felt that where I am now is where I'm supposed to be. But I'm not an idiot. I know that when I get there, this might be a case of the grass is always greener. Maybe I'll hate it. Maybe I'll realize my home isn't there, either, but I *have* to try. Now. While I'm young…and healthy enough to do it."

She looked at Marley. Her cousin understood her like no one else could. Marley and Ruby had both undergone mastectomies to lower their chances of developing cancer, but this mutation brought other cancer risks that weren't as easily prevented. There was no guarantee that they wouldn't get sick like their mothers had. Marley, more than anyone else, understood why Ruby needed to take advantage of the present, because they'd seen what the future could look like.

Marley nodded, smiling sadly. "I get it."

Nik put his arm around Marley then, supporting her. Ruby was so happy that Marley had Nik to lean on now.

Ruby exhaled. "If it doesn't feel right when I'm there, then I'll come back. Or I'll go somewhere else. Maybe I'm chasing a ghost, but I have to do this."

Marley nodded, holding up her glass. "You're doing the right thing, Ruby. Here's to seizing the day."

26

EVERYONE LEFT THE PARTY immediately after the countdown at midnight. Marley, Nik, Shayne, and Anderson went to some after-hours club downtown since Shayne said they couldn't waste their fabulous outfits, and Reena and Nadim headed home, probably to take advantage of the fact that the baby was at her mother's all night. Ruby went up to bed in the spare room and fell asleep immediately.

Fifteen minutes before the car was supposed to be at Marley's house to take Ruby to the airport the next day, there was a knock on the door. Assuming the driver was early, Ruby rushed to open it before the knocking woke Marley or Nik.

But it wasn't an airport limo driver at the door. It was Rashid.

He looked gorgeous. Of course he did. But what was he doing here?

"Rashid…I—"

He interrupted her. "Ruby, can we talk? All I need is ten minutes of your time before you go."

"My car to the airport..." She looked over his shoulder and saw the black car pull into the driveway.

He cringed. "I'm too late. Or can I drive you instead? Like..."

Like they'd originally intended. Ruby exhaled. It was about a thirty-minute drive to Pearson Airport, longer if there was traffic. Which there always was. Would he spend the whole drive begging her to stay with him?

She looked at his face. His eyes looked...sad. Sad that he hadn't been able to convince her to stay, or sad that he'd hurt her? That they'd hurt each other? But even if he'd tried to manipulate her, she didn't want to regret not letting him say his piece now. And she wanted to make sure he understood why she'd said no to staying.

She nodded. "Okay. You can drive me to the airport."

Rashid went to speak to the driver while Ruby brought her suitcases to the porch. He rushed back up to help her with her bags and put them into the back of the Volvo. Ruby belted herself into the passenger side.

How many times had they driven together like this? To all those Christmas dates that weren't technically dates, but really were. She remembered the time he showed up on a street corner during a snowstorm five minutes after she called him crying the day she'd argued with her father. Rashid had literally rescued her.

The streets were nearly deserted as Rashid drove toward the highway. Not surprisingly, he was quiet as he navigated. Why did he want to have a conversation in the car anyway?

The combination of the empty streets and the snow made

downtown Toronto look like a snow globe—a perfect, magical city. It was strange to think that Ruby came here a year ago because she had to—she needed her father's help to get a UK visa. And the whole time she was here, she told herself she was only passing through.

But she'd ended up in a job that she'd mostly enjoyed, and she'd made some great friends. Ruby felt connected to the city in a new way. It no longer only felt like the setting of her difficult childhood memories, or the place where her mother got sick and died, or where her father lived with his replacement family. It felt like a diverse, vibrant city where there was always something to do, and where Ruby had made both the best and the worst memories of her life. She was grateful to Rashid for making her appreciate her hometown in a new way.

When they'd been on the highway for two minutes, he finally spoke. "Thanks for letting me take you," he said.

"No problem. It beats awkward conversations with a cabdriver."

He chuckled. "Yeah."

He was still quiet. It reminded her a bit of when they didn't know each other well and she would ramble to fill the emptiness of his silence. "Are we actually going to talk?" she asked. "Because they won't let you past security at the airport without a ticket, so this is our last chance."

He sighed. "Yeah…I haven't thought this out. I knew I needed to see you…to apologize before you left, but now…I don't know what to say."

"You could start with an actual apology."

He nodded, his eyes not leaving the road in front of him.

"I'm sorry. I mean it, Ruby, I'm so sorry. I should have told you I decided to stay, and I should have talked to you before telling Ayesha to consider you for that job in Toronto. I was selfish. I was thinking only of myself. My sister knocked some sense into me last night."

"Which sister?"

"Both." He sighed. "They thought you knew I was thinking of staying, and they thought you told me that you'd be open to staying too if the right opportunity came. They didn't know how important this move is for you."

"Do *you* understand how important it is for me?"

He nodded, but Ruby wasn't sure.

"Rashid, you know what my father was like when I was a kid, right?"

"He was a yeller, right? Abusive."

Ruby nodded. "Yeah, but not only that. He was controlling. He didn't like my mother working outside the home. She used to work at this boutique in the mall, but he was jealous of the way customers talked to her, the way they respected her and treated her like an equal. He hated that she was spending time with these rich customers, so he made her quit. I think he was afraid she'd realize that she was too good to be with him. Anyway, when his auto garage started struggling, she started sewing to make ends meet. She made Indian and Western dresses, and she was good. I used to tell her she should go to fashion school and be a real designer. She even signed up for a clothing design night school class. But Dad withdrew her application without telling her."

"So, her dream was fashion design, not the English countryside?"

Ruby shook her head. "Fashion school wasn't really her dream. I just thought she'd be good at it. England was the dream, always. Mom and I were complete Anglophiles. Every Saturday when I was a kid, while Dad was at the garage, we'd watch the BBC *Pride and Prejudice*, the one with Colin Firth. And when I was in high school, we used to watch this show on PBS called *Find My Country House* or something. These real estate experts would help city people relocate to the countryside. We saw one once where a mother and daughter bought a place together to open a B and B after the mother's divorce, and my mom said we should do that. It was the first time I ever heard her mention leaving my father. We kept talking about that dream secretly for years. We researched where we could go, and how much money we'd need. She even told me that she'd opened a savings account and started putting money aside into it. But..." Ruby's voice cracked.

"That was the money she left you?"

Ruby nodded. "Yeah. Anyway, after her first chemo, she and Dad had a big fight, and Dad left because he said she couldn't be a wife if she was sick. Mom moved in with my aunt—Marley's mother. And then she died."

Rashid glanced at her, and Ruby could see glassiness in his eyes, like he was almost crying. "Oh, Ruby," he said as he looked back at the road. "I can't imagine anyone leaving their wife while she was sick. That's heartbreaking. And now you want to use the money she saved to make her dream come true."

"It's not just *her* dream, Rashid. It's mine, too. We used to watch these British dramas together...Austen stuff, but others, too. Our favorite was *Wives and Daughters*, but we even watched contemporary ones. I always felt like that setting, that *life*, that's where I'm supposed to be. I can't describe it, but when I watch that stuff, it's the closest I've ever felt to feeling at home. I want to see if I get the same feeling seeing…living in those places as I do when I read about them or see them in movies and TV."

He didn't say anything to that, so Ruby continued. "I know you think I'm flighty and impulsive, and it's not wise for me to leave everything and chase a half-baked dream, but that's not what this is. I'm going with my eyes wide open. If it's not right, I'll leave. But I have to try. You know I have the same cancer-causing genetic mutation as my mother."

"But you had a mastectomy."

"Rashid, you're a *doctor*. You know I can't remove all my risks. And it's not just illness. Life is full of risks. I have no idea—none of us do—what will happen tomorrow. I have to give this dream a fighting chance. In a year or two I'll know if it's possible, and if it's not, at least I'll know I gave it my best shot."

He nodded after a few long moments.

Ruby exhaled, remembering the letter from the lawyer. Her friends told her not to think about it until she was in London, but how could she not? "I might not even be able to do it now," she said bitterly. "My dad's suing me for my trust money."

"What?" Rashid asked, looking at Ruby a moment. "When did this happen? Can he do that?"

Ruby shrugged, then told him about the letter she got yesterday.

"That…that's terrible," he said. "Your father is a piece of work."

"I told you. The man is the *worst*."

"Do you think it's true? That your mother took money from *him* for that savings account?"

Ruby shrugged. "I have no idea. She told me it was money she earned sewing. But there was a lot more there than I would have imagined. Then again, I don't know. I'll talk to a lawyer soon. Reena apparently knows a great one used to dealing with manipulating families. My friends all think he doesn't have a leg to stand on with this lawsuit."

"How can I help? I know a local lawyer, too, or I can—"

She shook her head. "I don't want you to do anything, Rashid. My friends and I got this."

He exhaled. Rashid was a fixer. A *rescuer*. He came to Toronto a day after learning his sister's husband was abusive. This whole mess started because he tried to arrange a job for Ruby in Toronto. The whole Hakim family was used to bending over backward to rescue each other, and he would rescue Ruby, too, if she'd let him.

Ruby wasn't used to people helping her like this. If she let him save her, she'd never be able to walk away from him.

They were almost at the airport by then, and he merged into the Departures lane. He didn't say a word until he parked in a short-term parking lot. He finally turned to Ruby.

"I'm sorry," he said again. "I wish…I hate that he's doing this to you."

She smiled. "I know, Rashid. You're such a good man." She paused. "We were supposed to be casual, and I didn't want to go in too deep, but you supported me and cared about me like no one else has. There was no point in keeping things surface level, because my feelings were always deep."

He exhaled. "Me too. But I hate that I did what your father did. That I was controlling—"

"No, Rashid. You should have been honest with me, but you are not like my father. His goal was to get my money. Your goal was to—"

"Get you," he said softly. "I did it because I didn't want to lose you. I wanted you to stay with me."

And that was remarkable. Never in all the times Ruby had moved had anyone said they didn't want her to go. No one had ever asked her to stay.

A huge part of her wanted to stay with him, because she had no idea if she'd ever feel like this for someone again. Or if anyone would ever ask her to stay again.

She had to be touching this man. She unbuckled her seat belt, took off her gloves, and took his soft cheeks in her hands. They looked into each other's eyes for several long moments, then he put his arms around her waist and pulled her in for a deep kiss.

And it was perfect. It always had been. And knowing that this was a goodbye kiss and that she probably would never get a chance to explore his mouth and lips like this again didn't make the kiss any better than all the other kisses, because perfection couldn't be improved on. He pulled her closer until his arms were tight around her, and she could have stayed in his arms forever.

When they finally separated, he smiled and asked if he could walk her inside.

Ruby exhaled. She wished that she hadn't broken things off two days ago, because she could have had more of him in the last two days. But if that kiss told her anything, it was that the more she had of Rashid, the harder it would be to walk away.

And they both knew she *had* to walk away. She shook her head. "It's fine. I need to do this alone. Thank you, though, for the apology. And for everything else."

"I should be thanking you, Ruby. I was dreading being here at Christmas and…"

She grinned mischievously. "And you *loved* it, right?"

He laughed. "You, Ruby Dhanji, did the impossible. You made me *enjoy* the holiday season. Are we going to stay in touch?"

She wanted to. Ruby knew she was going to keep in touch with Jasmine and the girls, and probably Ayesha, too. She still was hoping to get a job with the Hakim Group in the UK, and she wanted to see his parents when they were in London. But Rashid…It would be harder to stay friends with Rashid. She wanted to one day—he was a good person, and honestly, he needed a fun friend like Ruby in his life.

But Ruby wasn't strong enough for that yet. She needed time to get settled in her new home. Time when she wasn't reminded of what she'd left in Toronto.

"Give me a few months in the UK. I don't know how long, but I need to get over us. Let me get settled there, and you get settled here, then, yeah. I'd like it if we could be friends." He would be coming to the UK regularly to visit his parents, and Ruby would be back in Toronto for visits, too. But she wasn't going to have a fling with him again. Casual wasn't possible with this man.

He nodded. "Okay. I'll wait for you to reach out when you're ready. I'll get you a luggage cart."

After he helped her put her luggage on the cart, Ruby smiled again. They were behind his car, both smiling like dorks who didn't know what to say. She didn't want another goodbye kiss, but she didn't know what else to say or do. Finally, he reached out and pulled her into his arms in a tight hug. She inhaled deeply at his cool winter-clean smell and planted a small kiss on his neck. "I'm going to miss you," she whispered.

"I'm going to miss you more." He tucked her hair behind her ear and then kissed her on the forehead. "Now go…make your dream come true."

Ruby smiled, then pushed her luggage cart toward the entrance, not turning back but knowing that Rashid's eyes were on her as she walked into the airport.

27

AFTER NINE GLORIOUS WEEKS of living in London (or close enough to London), Ruby was mostly acclimated to being a resident of the United Kingdom. She was long past her jet lag. She'd figured out which nearby supermarket had the best premade sticky toffee pudding and which chip shop's fish had the lightest batter, and she'd bought adorable pink rubber boots and a tan raincoat. She'd even made friends with some coworkers. A few of them had gone out for drinks last night, which had her hitting the snooze button on her alarm a few too many times this morning.

Ruby sat up with a start—she'd wanted to be a bit early for work today. She was convinced her manager Shahin didn't like her much—and she needed to step away from the front desk at four o'clock sharp for a call with her lawyer. She didn't want to be on the receiving end of Shahin's brand of British Indian condescension twice today. After practically crawling out of bed, Ruby turned on the kettle for some tea and hopped into the shower to jolt her awake.

So far, UK living exceeded her expectations in some areas and fell flat in others. Ruby was settled into an apartment—charmingly called a bedsit flat—that managed to be smaller but sunnier than her one back in Toronto. After a few interviews, she'd been offered three jobs—one in a department store, one in a High Street boutique, and one as a front desk supervisor at a Hakim hotel in Surrey, a suburb of London. Ayesha had emailed her about the role a few days after she'd arrived and arranged for Ruby to interview with the hospitality manager. It was one of the Hakim Group's older and bigger hotels—not one of the Raj boutique hotels. And Surrey wasn't quite city living or country living. She took the job, though. It was the foot in the door she needed.

Despite her coolness to Ruby, the hospitality manager Shahin was incredibly knowledgeable and experienced. Ruby was learning so much from her, even if she was a bit particular about how things should be done. Ruby's front desk supervisor role felt a lot like her role as manager of Reid's holiday store—without the designer fragrances and Christmas ornaments. She even had the same number of employees reporting to her. Her flat was close enough to the hotel that she could walk to work or to a few small restaurants and a supermarket. A bus could take her anywhere else she needed to go, including the train station if she wanted to go to London. She'd gone into town to go clubbing with her new friends once, and it was fabulous. Overall, Ruby was surprised at how easy it had been to settle in England. A big part of her had been scared that after looking forward to this move for so long, there was no way that the reality of UK living would live up to the hype in her head.

But she loved it here. Truly. The people she'd met were

kind, their accents were charming, and the food and shopping in London were excellent (not so much in Surrey, but it was a suburb; she couldn't expect much).

It wasn't that she didn't miss Toronto—because she did. The Shayne Freaking Loves Olives group chat was still very active, but Ruby had now replaced Nik's position as the one who had no idea what the others were talking about half the time. Reena sent pictures of Aleem regularly, and Ruby couldn't believe how much he'd changed in a few weeks. Her friends insisted on constant updates on her ye olde English relocation, and they'd been delighted with her pictures of double-decker buses and London taxis. They mentioned seeing Jasmine a few times, but none of the other Hakims.

Of course, Ruby missed Rashid. A lot. But being so far away, plus their agreement that they wouldn't contact each other for a few months, helped. And even though she was literally working for the Hakim family, she had no contact with any of them after she got the job. Hakim and Farida were working out of their country inn near Manchester. And Ayesha was in Toronto.

Everything wasn't perfect, but life rarely was. More than anything, though, Ruby was incredibly proud of herself. She was one step closer to making her dream a reality. And if the meeting with the lawyer today went as well as she expected, then nothing else would stand in her way.

At four, Ruby connected to the call from her laptop in the little office behind the front desk.

"Hi, Veronica," Ruby said when she saw her lawyer's face fill the screen. Veronica Ali was a referral from Reena, and so far Ruby was glad she'd put the fate of her mother's inheritance in Veronica's hands.

"I have news for you, my dear," Veronica said. She was in her fifties, with light brown skin and curls, and a booming, take-no-shit-from-anyone voice. In their first video conference meeting, only five days after Ruby had arrived in London, Veronica had rolled her eyes when Ruby told her the backstory with her father and showed her the notice of intent to sue. Veronica immediately sent Ruby's father a letter that basically said do what you need to do, but my client won't be paying.

Her father took the bait and sued. Veronica almost seemed gleeful and filed a countersuit to cover all Ruby's legal fees. The court date was soon, so now they were talking strategy.

"What news?" Ruby asked.

"As I expected, your father is starting to waver. I got a settlement offer. His lawyer said they would drop the suit for half the inheritance."

That was still a lot of money—money that Ruby didn't want to part with. "Do you think I should accept?" Ruby asked.

"Absolutely not. Not without negotiation. I think he's sweating. We could probably get him even lower. Maybe one quarter of the full amount."

Ruby frowned. She was surprised that Veronica thought she should settle at all. "You said there was no way he could win. Why do you think we should settle?"

Veronica sighed. "I'll be real with you, Ruby. I thought I'd be able to uncover something, but we still don't know where your mother acquired those funds. Her work as a seamstress was all cash—and under the table at that—so we can't know if that's where the money came from. And if what she told you was true, that she only started saving four or five years before her death, that's a lot of dresses…or she was charging Armani prices."

"Do you think she was stealing from my father?"

"I personally don't think she was, but without evidence, there's not much we can do. They were married, so their assets were joint at the time. So half of what was his was hers."

"But you don't think we'll win." Ruby couldn't believe it. Her father was going to take this from her.

"I really don't know. A sympathetic judge will see him for what he was: an abusive husband whose wife wanted to get away from him. But the fact that he's cleaned up now and is a model husband and stepfather doesn't help matters. I still believe we'll win, but I can't guarantee it. It's up to you if you want to gamble or take the deal. We have a week to decide on this settlement."

Ruby exhaled. At that moment, there was a knock on the door.

"Veronica, I'm going to have to go. I'll think on this and email you in a few days with my decision."

"Sounds good. Take care, Ruby."

As soon as the call disconnected, she stood and opened the door. It was Shahin, looking irritated, as usual.

"Mrs. Hakim is here to see you," Shahin said, walking back to the front desk. "She's in the GM's office. I suppose I'll stay on the front desk until you two are done."

Ruby froze. Rashid's mother was here?

"Oh. Did she say what she needed?"

Shahin waved her hand, clearly irritated. "How would I

know?" She started typing something on the computer. "They are *your* friends, not mine…" She said that last bit under her breath.

Ruby exhaled and packed up her laptop, taking it with her to the GM's office. The door was open, and she was surprised at who was working on a laptop behind the desk. Not Rashid's mother, but Ayesha.

Ayesha grinned widely, standing. "Ruby! Fantastic to see you!" She gave Ruby a hug.

Ruby laughed. "Shahin said *Mrs.* Hakim was here…I was expecting your mother!"

Ayesha rolled her eyes. "Oh god. I'll bet that was intended as a dig at me. Now sit." She gestured toward the chair across from the desk. Ruby sat awkwardly. "I want to hear *all* about how you're doing. I totally meant to text to check in, but *phew*, it's been busy. Going back and forth between Toronto and London has been a nightmare. I'll be here for a while now, so I have to remember to say *lift* instead of elevator. You should have seen the look I got this morning when I tried to order a double double at the café! So, how are you faring at the front desk?"

Ruby smiled, all the tension from the call with Veronica leaving her. Apparently, any member of the Hakim family had a calming effect on her. After talking for a while about how Ruby was settling in at the hotel, Ayesha grinned. "I knew you'd be fabulous. Everyone I've talked to *adores* you. Including Shahin, by the way. Okay, now enough of this work talk. How have you been *really* doing?" Ayesha grinned widely.

It was funny—Jasmine and Ayesha looked so similar. Even their smiles were pretty much identical. Except Jasmine had a sweetness behind hers, while Ayesha's always had a bit of mischief.

Like she was constantly sharing some inside joke. Ruby totally understood why Ayesha and Nadim had been such good friends.

"I'm good," Ruby said. "Made some friends. Did a bit of shopping."

"So, you've made friends. Any nice men?"

Ruby raised one brow. Was Ayesha trying to find out if Ruby was dating? Because...*awkward*. Ruby, of course, hadn't been anywhere near interested in dating anyone in the UK, thanks to Ayesha's own brother.

"Never mind," Ayesha said when Ruby didn't answer. "What's your schedule like? Jasmine said you're the best to shop with. I would love to hit High Street with you. We could go to that boutique I told you about."

Ruby grinned. This was great. She told Ayesha she was off tomorrow, and they arranged to meet in London in the morning.

Shopping with Ayesha was *everything*. They went to the bigger stores, like Harrods and Liberty, but also hit Ayesha's favorite High Street boutiques. Ruby, of course, couldn't afford to buy any designer things right now—especially with a pending lawsuit, but when Ayesha finally took her to a charity shop that had loads of secondhand designer goods, she knew she'd be coming back here again. Often.

"I honestly buy most of my things from charity shops," Ayesha said as they were going through the racks. "I *cannot* justify the prices otherwise, not to mention buying secondhand has a much better environmental impact."

Ruby grinned. Ayesha might be her soul mate. When they

finally stopped for dinner at an Indian-inspired pub, Ruby ordered a blackberry dry cider and a chicken tikka masala, while Ayesha went for their house biriyani with a glass of wine.

"This is really good," Ruby said, dipping her fluffy naan into the bright red curry.

"I think the Indian restaurants in London are the best in the world. Other than India, of course."

"Disagree," Ruby said. "Toronto has great restaurants. Which Indian places have you tried so far there?"

Ruby gave her recommendations for Indian restaurants better than the ones Ayesha had tried. Then they talked about other restaurants that Ayesha had been to in Toronto. She'd been to several of Ruby's favorites, including the pancake restaurant, and the Egyptian brunch place.

Those were both places she'd taken Rashid to. Had he taken his sister? Neither of them had mentioned Rashid yet. In fact, Ruby kind of forgot that it was Rashid's sister she was hanging out with today.

"So what restaurants have you tried in London?" Ayesha asked.

Ruby shrugged. "Not many. I had fast food a few times when I first got here, but I've only been in the city once since I moved to Surrey."

"Which is only a train ride to London! Come on, Ruby, this is *London*! The shopping and restaurants can't be beat!"

Ruby shrugged. "I'll come out more once I'm settled." It seemed wrong to come into town too much until her finances were sorted out. "I have this *thing* I'm dealing with. I don't want to overspend until it's sorted out."

Ayesha gave her a concerned look. "It's not your health, is it?"

Ruby shook her head. "No, my health is fine. Great, even." Could Ruby tell Ayesha about the lawsuit? Maybe it would be good if her boss—or rather, her boss's boss's boss—knew about her troubles in case Ruby needed to take more time off work, or even go back to Toronto. "The problem is my father."

God, she hoped she wouldn't have to leave her job because of the lawsuit.

Ayesha frowned. "Um, my brother mentioned he was…shady."

Ruby chuckled. Why wasn't she surprised that Rashid told Ayesha? "Yeah, he's suing me."

When Ayesha's eyes widened, Ruby told her all about her inheritance, the threatening letter, and, finally, the lawsuit.

"Holy shit. I can't even imagine a father doing something like that. I mean, I complain about my family being up in each other's arses too much."

Ruby smiled sadly. "You are extremely lucky to have your family."

Ayesha paused, then smiled. And it was a sweet, genuine smile, not her normal mischievous one. "I *am* lucky. I complain, but I adore them all."

Ruby understood. She kind of adored Ayesha's family, too.

"Speaking of family, it sounds like you could use a vacation," Ayesha said, that mischievous glint in her eyes coming back. "How about you come, as my personal guest, to my mother's birthday weekend at the end of the month? My treat. It's going to be at their inn in Cheshire County. Very pastoral. Sheep *everywhere*."

Ruby frowned. It was weird to go to her ex's mom's birthday party, wasn't it? Would Rashid be there?

"Come on, Rubes, this is a perfect opportunity for you to get out to see the countryside. It's your dream, isn't it? You can room with me, so it won't cost you anything. I'll even send you a train ticket. I'm the only one of my siblings going, so everyone else will be Mum and Dad's friends, and I would *love* to have someone under forty to talk to. It's near Lyme Park. I think they filmed one of those Austen movies there. You're a big Austen fan, aren't you?"

Holy shit—Lyme Park had the pond that Colin Firth jumped into before randomly bumping into Jennifer Ehle all wet, bothered, and sexy. If Rashid wasn't going to be there, how could Ruby say no?

The awe must have shown on Ruby's face, because the smirk got stronger on Ayesha's. "My mum's into those old houses and into Austen, too. I'm sure we could convince her to come with us for a tour of the grounds for her birthday."

A chance to visit the English countryside, see the actual house where her favorite *Pride and Prejudice* scene was filmed, and get a look at a country inn like what she wanted to own one day. Maybe Ayesha was right—she needed this. True, it would be hard to avoid thinking of Rashid if she spent the whole weekend with his family, but she'd deal.

"Okay. If I can get the time off, I mean."

"Ruby. I can get you the time off. Leave it with me. You'll take the train to Manchester and meet me there. We'll have the *best* time."

28

TWO WEEKS LATER, RUBY was startled awake by a phone call. A quick glance at her clock showed it was past eleven p.m. *Shit.* Whatever it was couldn't be good.

Ruby checked her phone and saw Veronica Ali's name on the display. She answered the call.

"Ruby! Sorry to call you so late! I forgot you're in London! We've had a development. Can you talk?"

"Yeah. What's up?"

"I just had the most interesting phone call. Does the name Neelam Premji mean anything to you?"

"Sounds vaguely familiar. A friend of my father's?"

"No, of your *mother's*. She said she met you recently—"

"Yes, in Jamatkhana! Sorry, that's our place of worship. I didn't remember her, but she knew me."

"Yes, well she had some interesting things to tell me. Apparently, years ago, she and your mother, along with three other women in the neighborhood, used to meet weekly."

"I remember. I think they were all running businesses out of their homes. Mom used to go while I was at school."

"Yes, well the group wasn't really a ladies' entrepreneur club. It was a kind of support group. All the women were in bad marriages, and they met every week to figure out how to get away from their spouses."

"What? Really?" Ruby had always assumed that her mother was alone. She had Ruby, of course. And she was close to Marley. But her mother hadn't been particularly close to her own sister, or any other family. Ruby thought her mother hadn't had anyone to vent to about her marriage. It was such a relief to know that wasn't true.

"Yes, and apparently it wasn't only moral support they gave each other—Neelam was particularly gifted at day trading. Another made a killing selling erotic stories on Amazon."

Ruby would have snorted out tea if she was drinking any. She hoped it wasn't her mother writing the spicy stories. "Are you serious?"

"Completely. Badass group of women, if you ask me. They determined that the only way for true freedom was *economic* freedom. All the money they earned was put into a pool and distributed among the five of them. They were raising their escape funds."

"Holy shit," Ruby said before her shoulders sunk with disappointment. "But then my mother died before she could escape."

"Yes. But one of the women helped your mother set up your trust after her cancer diagnosis so you'd get her share if she died before she could use it. They decided on the ten-year wait partially so it would be less likely that your father would find out about it, but they also wanted you to be a little older when you got it. Neelam said your mother told her that she wanted 'Ruby to know who Ruby was' before you had the money, so you could spend it wisely."

"Yeah, that's pretty much what the letter that came with the inheritance said." Ruby teared up. She couldn't believe that her mother had this whole secret life without her knowing. She was going to find that business card that Neelam had given her and call to thank her. "So, that's how Mom got the money. She didn't steal it from my father."

"Nope. The group continued to deposit your mother's share in the trust until they'd all divorced. Neelam called the other women before contacting me—all four are willing to sign affidavits they'd gifted Maryam Dhanji the money that made up the bulk of her savings account, along with her sewing money. Your father doesn't have a chance in hell of winning the lawsuit now. I think our countersuit for legal fees will be successful. Apparently, after creating the trust, your parents fought about something, and your mother told him about it, that the money was already in an ironclad trust for you. She told him that she was gifted the money. He always knew he wasn't entitled to any of it."

He knew. Her father knew that the money was never his, and he still wanted to take it from her. Ruby exhaled. She was disgusted. "One question: Why did they all want me to have the money? Why not use it to help the others get away from their husbands sooner?"

"Because they all knew that if your mother didn't survive, you wouldn't have a relationship with your father. They recognized the disadvantages that even adult children have without parents. No opportunities for generational wealth or even parental guidance. They didn't want Maryam's daughter to be economically disadvantaged. Neelam runs a grassroots charity now that raises money to help racialized and immigrant women in Toronto escape abuse. They named it after your mother—Help from Maryam. I've already offered them pro bono legal help, and I'm planning to write them a check after I get off the phone with you."

Ruby inhaled sharply, wiping her tears. Why didn't Ruby know about this? This organization with her mother's name was helping women escape bad situations. She couldn't imagine a better legacy. Ruby wished she could have been involved.

Veronica gave Ruby Neelam's contact information and told her that once she had the signed affidavits, she was going to prepare a settlement offer that if her father paid all of Ruby's legal fees up to now, they could avoid court. She said she'd have the paperwork ready for Ruby to sign early next week.

It wasn't until Ruby was off the phone, still weepy after what she'd learned, that she realized she hadn't asked Veronica how Neelam found out about the lawsuit and got Veronica's contact number. It could have been Reena—she was the one who referred Veronica to Ruby. But how would Reena have known Neelam?

She honestly didn't have the time to dwell on it right now. She was meeting Ayesha tomorrow for their trip to the countryside, and her train was at the crack of dawn. After learning more about where her trust money came from, she was more determined than ever to give Mom's English dream a fighting chance.

Ruby put Veronica's news out of her mind for now so she could enjoy her weekend. Her eyes were glued out the window for the entire train ride from London to Manchester. The views were *phenomenal*. The rolling hills, small farms, and tiny old villages—it felt like she was watching a movie. Ruby settled into her seat as a deep comfort blanketed her, just like she hoped it would. It was beautiful, and even though she'd never been here before, the terrain felt so familiar. Like the best warm memory.

It was ten in the morning when Ruby's train pulled into the Manchester train station. She texted Ayesha, who said to meet her in the passenger pick-up area. Ruby found Ayesha waiting near a car.

"There you are, Rubes. You look fantastic! You're going to fit right in at the Weeping Sparrow Inn," Ayesha said.

Ruby had curated a vaguely Regency-core outfit for her first trip to the countryside—wide pale blue jeans with beige sneakers, a light pink sweater with the slightest of puffy sleeves, a wide pink headband, and, uncharacteristically for Ruby, pale pink lipstick.

"Is it really called the Weeping Sparrow Inn?"

Ayesha nodded. "Ridiculous, right? Mom refuses to change it. Why would anyone want to stay in a place named after a bunch of crying birds? Go on and put your bags in the boot."

Ruby laughed as she dropped her overnight bag in the trunk of the car.

There was a lot of traffic as they left Manchester. Ruby wished she'd have more time to explore the city—it looked nothing like London. Maybe next time.

"Been a slight change of plans," Ayesha said as she turned onto the highway to the countryside. "Jasmine and the girls are here. They flew in yesterday."

"Oh my goodness!" Ruby grinned. "How did she manage that?"

"She had to get a court order to let her bring the girls overseas for her mother's birthday. Ridiculous. Can you believe Derek is now claiming that he should get half the future revenue from her new clinic because they were married while she was in med school? I mean, he wasn't even supporting her—Mum and Dad paid for her education. Her lawyer says there's no chance in hell of it happening."

Ruby exhaled. Jasmine could afford these legal nightmares, but other women couldn't. She smiled again, thinking of that fund with her mother's name.

"The guy is such a horse's bum," Ayesha continued. "I warned her back when they were dating—never trust a Derek. The name sounds too much like Dalek—oh, are you a *Doctor Who* fan? It's a British thing…Anyway, Jasmine is delighted you're joining us. You're still the twins' favorite auntie, by the way. I should be offended, but I think I like you better than me, too."

Ruby laughed. Ayesha talked a lot while she was driving, unlike her brother.

"Anyway, Mum *loved* the idea of going to Lyme Park today. She should be there with Jasmine and the girls by the time we get there."

"Oh, we're going to Lyme Park *today*?"

Ayesha nodded. "Just made sense. Most of Mum's friends won't be coming to the inn until dinnertime, and she didn't want to abandon them all tomorrow to go traipsing around a manor house. We can get some sandwiches and tea and have lunch in the garden there. Or the tea house. It's all equally idyllic. Then we'll head over to the inn for the birthday dinner and more picturesque fun. Mum's chuffed you're joining us, by the way." She snorted a laugh. "I'd told her I was bringing a date, but then had to admit it was you because about thirty questions followed about what you did for a living and if you'd be open to a big Indian wedding." Ayesha rolled her eyes. "Desi parents, amirite? They are literally caricatures of themselves."

Ruby laughed again. They were finally out of suburban Manchester, and the views around were as lovely as they had been on the train. It was making Ruby feel…*lighter*. Content. She couldn't believe she was finally here.

She'd been so excited about this weekend—and now knowing Jasmine and the twins would be here, too, she was even more excited. It was going to be weird to see the girls without Rashid, but it had been months since she'd seen him. The more time that had passed since she'd left Toronto, the more she wondered if maybe their fling wasn't as perfect as Ruby remembered. It had been over the holidays—she could have had the biggest holiday rose-colored glasses on. It was possible he wasn't even as good-looking as she remembered. As time passed, she hoped Rashid Hakim would be nothing to her but the brother of her friends Ayesha and Jasmine, and the son of the owner of the hotel she worked in, and nothing else.

When they got to Lyme Park, Ayesha parked in the parking lot and checked her phone. "They'll be here soon. Why don't we wander a bit."

It was a gorgeous, clear early spring day. They walked around to see the front of the main building, and Ruby's heart nearly stopped beating.

This was the house. *Pemberley.* She couldn't believe she was really here.

For so many years all she'd wanted was to come here. The wide-open space, the rolling countryside, and the manor house she'd seen with her mother so many times. Being in front of it now brought literal goose bumps to her skin and tears to her eyes. She wished her mother were here now, but she knew Mom would be so happy that Ruby finally made it. She wiped her eyes.

"It's beautiful, isn't it?" Ayesha asked. "I hate the reason these places exist, but I can't deny that I'm glad we *all* get to enjoy them now."

Ruby nodded. "My mom would have loved this." There were a fair number of other guests on the property, but that didn't take away from the magic at all. She understood Ayesha's point—Ruby hated that there was such a thing as nobility and people who were able to have this kind of wealth because of the luck of their birth, but she loved that all these visitors, no matter what family they were born into, were able to enjoy this space now. She couldn't take her eyes off the view in front of her.

Ayesha picked up her phone. "They're here. They are walking around the pond."

They started walking on the path toward the very pond where Darcy jumped in before seeing Elizabeth. *So cool.*

"Jasmine wants me to bring my iPad," Ayesha said, still looking at her phone. "The girls are fighting over hers. It's in the car—I'll whip back to get it. You go to the pond—imagine Mr. Darcy in his white shirt emerging like a siren…all that wet linen…" She turned and rushed back on the path toward the car park.

Ruby shrugged and continued toward the pond. She couldn't see Jasmine or the twins. There was a little picnic area to her right that looked like it had a lot of people sitting. Maybe they were there?

The day was almost completely without wind, so the pond was perfectly still. Ruby picked up her phone to snap some pictures. It was gorgeous. She was literally steps from where Darcy and Elizabeth first reunited at Pemberley—or at least where Colin Firth and Jennifer Ehle first reunited.

"Bloody hell, I'm going to *kill* my sisters," said a voice—most definitely not Darcy's—behind her.

She turned and saw Rashid, standing alone, wearing jeans, a flannel, a denim jacket, and his blue beanie pulled low on his head. He looked almost exactly like he did when they met, complete with the extremely annoyed expression.

Shocked, Ruby let out a snort of surprised laughter.

That made the annoyance leave his face; it was replaced by an exasperated chuckle. He rubbed the back of his neck. "I think we've been set up, Red."

29

"HI, RASHID," RUBY SAID, still laughing. She didn't know why seeing him was so funny. Probably because Ayesha and Jasmine clearly did all this so Ruby and Rashid could reunite exactly where Mr. Darcy and Elizabeth reunited. Which was equal parts charming, infuriating, and hilarious.

"Did you know about this?" he asked.

Ruby shook her head, still smiling. "I had no idea you were even in the country. Ayesha said Jasmine and the twins were here at the pond."

He rolled his eyes. "They're in the house. Jasmine told me Ayesha needed someone to take her picture for her Instagram." He shook his head. "I made my sisters promise they wouldn't secretly arrange for you and I to see each other while I'm in the UK. I should have known they'd lie through their teeth. I'm so sorry. My family are notorious meddlers."

Ruby couldn't help it—she laughed again. And there was nothing behind the laugh but joy. For years she'd dreamed of having a family who meddled like this. "Your family is adorable. They meddle because they care."

"Yeah, but…" He rubbed the back of his neck again. She knew that gesture. He was feeling unsure. Nervous. "You didn't want to see me."

Ruby looked at the breathtaking scenery around her. The perfectly situated manor house. The green lawns. The manicured garden. The pond.

She was here, in Lyme Park. The English countryside. Even Jasmine and Ayesha masterminding this meeting couldn't ruin this moment. She waved her hand. "It's fine. It's actually lovely to see you, Rashid."

His eyes widened. "Are you sure?"

Ruby nodded, smiling. "We can be friends again, can't we? I'm not Ayesha, but how about you take some pictures of me for my socials instead? I can't believe I'm actually at Lyme Park!"

He raised a brow. "You're not going to ask me to take my jacket off and jump in the water, are you?"

She laughed. It must be the air here up north, but Ruby was feeling lighter, happier, and more comfortable than she had in months. "I don't know. Would you do it?"

After they took several pictures, Ruby caught up with Rashid as they walked to the house to find his family. He was apparently well settled in Toronto. He'd bought a condo—ironically, in the building next to the one she'd lived in. He had his own patients in the practice he now shared with his sister, and was working part-time in a hospital, too. Jasmine had returned to work after hiring a nanny to help at home. Rashid said he was enjoying himself in Toronto, and he had even joined the hockey rec league that Reena's friend Duncan played in.

It sounded like Rashid and Ayesha were hanging out with Nadim and Reena a lot. And even sometimes with Marley, Nik, Shayne, and Anderson. Which was fine. Her friends back in Toronto had not mentioned that they'd seen Rashid, but she understood why. And she *wanted* Rashid to have a social life back in Toronto. She wasn't petty. She was the one who walked away from the possibility of a relationship with him.

They were walking with a casual foot of space and no awkwardness between them. Sure, he was still attractive, but it wasn't weird or even sad to see Rashid again. She was so happy and relieved that this could be easy. It seemed all she needed was ten weeks to get over him.

"How about you," he asked. "How are you liking your big move to London?"

Ruby smiled. "It's been wonderful. I'm learning so much about the hotel industry. I'm working a lot, but that was kind of the point, right? I've barely left Surrey since I moved there."

"Is England everything you hoped it would be?" he asked.

Ruby inhaled a lungful of clean country air. "It's beautiful. I feel so...content here."

He turned to her. His mouth was smiling, but she saw a hint of sadness in his eyes. And she understood. Because she was feeling the same thing. The sadness, because them both thriving, happy—without each other—took some of the magic from the memories of what they'd had.

But that was okay, too.

"You look good," he said. "I don't think I've ever seen you in that color. And your hair is different."

Ruby laughed, flipping her hair over her shoulder. She'd given up on her perfect flat iron waves because London was way too damp for heat-treated hair. She'd been enjoying her natural and somewhat unruly waves now.

"Not you," Ruby said. "You look exactly as you did the day we met."

When they got to the house, Tara and Noor ran for Ruby, yelling "Ruby Auntie!" After hugging the girls—she couldn't believe how different they looked after only a few months—Jasmine and Farida Hakim greeted Ruby warmly. Rashid made some snarky comments about meddling Brits never leaving anyone alone, but he was smiling. After the little reunion, they all took a guided tour of the Lyme Park manor house.

The house was lovely, but not familiar, as only the exterior was used for Pemberley in the BBC miniseries. The interiors were from some other manor house.

"We're actually not far from Chatsworth House," Rashid said while they were in the third sitting room with beautiful chintz wallpaper. "That's where they filmed Pemberley in the other *Pride and Prejudice* movie."

Ruby raised a brow at him. "And how would you know about local manor houses, Mr. Proletariat?"

"It's *Dr.* Proletariat," he said, smiling. "How long are you in town?"

"I'm taking the train back Monday."

"Well, if we can sneak away from the festivities tomorrow, this trip could be your grand tour of Pemberleys." He smiled, and Ruby saw the same mischievous sparkle that was normally in his sister's eyes. He also sounded a lot more British here than he had in Canada. "As friends, of course."

Ruby put her hand on her chest. "What a generous offer, Dr. Hakim. How could I turn down a chance to see a country house with a real British gentleman."

Ruby loved Lyme Park. It was everything she expected an English manor house to look like. But even better than the house were the tea and scones they had in the garden. The Hakim family was so charming when they were all together. Ayesha and Farida doted on the twins, and Ayesha, Jasmine, and Rashid teased each other nonstop. They even teased their mother when she couldn't read the tea menu because she forgot that her reading glasses were around her neck. And best of all, Tara and Noor were so chatty—miles away from how they'd been when Ruby first met them. When Ruby mentioned it privately to Jasmine, Jasmine said they were seeing a child psychologist now. They still dreaded visits with their father, but either Rashid or Ayesha went with them, and the girls felt safe with their aunt or uncle with them.

After they were done exploring Lyme Park, they all left at the same time. In the car, Ayesha asked Ruby if she was mad about them springing Rashid on her.

"I mean, it's his mother's birthday. I can't be mad he's here."

"But are you mad I didn't tell you?"

Ruby shook her head. It had been such a nice day, and none of this would have been possible without Ayesha, so she couldn't be mad at her. And she truly didn't mind that he was here. She'd been dreading seeing him, but it hadn't been scary, overly sad, or painful when she did. They *could* be friends now, which was great. "It's fine. It was...nice to see him again. There are no hard feelings. We're friends."

"Friends?"

"Yes, friends."

Ayesha snickered. "Sure. Friends who are madly in love."

"Ayesha!" She wasn't madly in love with Rashid. "Seriously, it was a casual fling, and I'm over it."

"Okay, fine. I don't know you that well, so maybe you are over it. But I do know my brother."

"You think he's still into me?" Ruby frowned. "Maybe I shouldn't be here." She didn't want to make his mother's birthday hard for him.

"Oh no, you're staying. Watching my brother squirm is the most fun Jasmine and I have had in months. He's had a stick up his arse too long—he deserves to be all flustered like this."

Ruby raised one eyebrow. "I always wanted siblings, but now I see that all they do is meddle and shit-talk each other."

"It's true!" Ayesha said, laughing. "But seriously, I love those two more than life. We shit-talk because we care." She paused a moment before continuing. "My brother's great, but he's always been a bit oblivious because of his convictions, you know? Doctors can be so sheltered—it comes from never leaving the hospital while training. He needed someone like you to knock him off his high horse. You've seriously done a huge service to this family."

Ruby chuckled. Was that what she'd done? Ruby had been so grateful for the big and maybe even lasting impact the Hakims had had on her life, but now she wondered if her fling with Rashid made an impact on his life. Had he changed for the better? And who was going to benefit from this new Rashid who rode a much shorter horse? His family, yes, but also the next woman who was lucky enough to date the man.

Ruby's stomach clenched at that thought. Not that she was jealous of this hypothetical woman. She wanted Rashid to be happy. She was sad that they probably wouldn't be friends like they said they would, since they lived on different continents.

Ruby was entranced when she first saw the Weeping Sparrow Inn. It was adorable—all quaint and comfortable, and just the right amount of shabby. Farida said they were planning a renovation soon but planned to keep the traditional country style. It was a touch bigger than what Ruby and her mother had envisioned buying themselves, but this was pretty darn close to Ruby's dream.

Farida's birthday party that night was a lot of fun. Ruby was introduced as Ayesha and Jasmine's Toronto friend and met aunties, uncles, old friends, and colleagues of Farida and Hakim. She ate biriyani and samosas, and talked until she literally lost her voice. Rashid seemed to be staying away from her but did smile and nod whenever their eyes caught. Ruby wondered if Ayesha had told him what Ruby said in the car, that she was over him.

The next morning, Ruby met Rashid downstairs before anyone else was awake. He was alone in the lobby, a couple of to-go cups and a paper sack in his hand. He wasn't in his Canadian flannel like yesterday, but instead in darker, better-fitting jeans, and a slim dark green Henley shirt, with a gray tweed sport coat over it. He looked hot. Devastatingly so, actually. This country gentleman vibe was even better than his urban doctor look. Ruby pushed down the fluttering in her stomach at seeing another side to him.

"You look nice," she said.

"So do you. All these new colors on you."

Ruby preened. She was wearing a gray wool miniskirt with tights and a pale lavender turtleneck sweater.

He held up the bag. "I had the cook make us breakfast. Egg and tomato baps and tea. A bap is a roll sandwich—"

"I know, Rashid. I've been living in the UK for almost three months." She took one of the cups from him. It was black tea with plenty of milk. "Thank you."

"Come on, I'm parked in the back lot," he said.

They were mostly silent on the forty-minute drive to Chatsworth. Which, of course, was completely normal because she was in a car with Rashid. It was strange; it felt kind of like they were back in Toronto, like the last few months hadn't happened and they were still in the middle of the hottest fling Ruby had ever had. Except now he was sitting on the opposite side of the car, and outside the grass was green. And their fling was over.

"The last time I was at Chatsworth was for this Christmas light thing Mum dragged us to," he said as he turned down a narrow road off the main highway.

Ruby chuckled. "That must have been torture for you."

He nodded solemnly. "I hated every moment of it. Each room was decorated with greenery and holly everywhere. Way overdone. Worse than that castle in Toronto. They even projected designs onto the outside of the building. You would have *loved* it."

"Christmas at an English manor house? Hell yeah, that's totally my scene."

He was quiet for a while. She wondered if he was going to say something about hating all the Christmas things they'd done in Toronto.

"It's funny, though," he finally said. "When I think back to that day at Chatsworth, my first thought isn't the gaudy decorations, or the conspicuous wealth gained from the exploitation of others. I remember my family. Jasmine was here with the girls. They were toddlers then, and the look of awe on their faces when they saw that light show outside was priceless. Ayesha brought a date —a woman she'd met at the gym. And Jasmine and I caught Mum googling the cost of an Indian wedding with two brides. Everyone teased me about being the only single one, and Mum said she would never pressure me to get married, but also told me about all their kids who'd started online dating and even offered to make a profile for me. Dad rolled his eyes while the rest of us all talked over each other. He said he had no idea how he'd ended up with such a ridiculous family."

Ruby smiled. "Your family is wonderful."

He nodded as he turned into the car park for Chatsworth House. "I know they are. I took them for granted. I always had them, so it never occurred to me that the reason people love the holiday season so much is because those memories, those moments, are rare for some people. I never thought about how hard it would be if I didn't have my family."

Ruby gave him a sad smile. "For some of us, the season reminds us of the moments we've never even had. Or will never have."

He didn't say anything. She half expected him to say that she *would* have those memories one day—that she would find someone on the right continent to grow old with and open her inn with and create all the holiday memories she wanted with. She didn't say anything, either, because she didn't know if she'd ever find that. She unbuckled her seat belt. "C'mon, let's go see how the exploitive nobility lived."

As they walked toward the enormous house, Ruby literally squealed and grabbed Rashid's arm. "Oh my god, it's the staircase that Darcy climbed down to chase Elizabeth! Come on, I can't wait to see the marble room."

Chatsworth House was way more opulent than Lyme Park. Ruby excitedly moved from room to room, pointing out places where the 2005 film was shot and soaking in the splendor of the house. Rashid probably wasn't wowed, but kept himself busy reading the historical placards without once mentioning the unethical way these noblemen acquired their wealth. They had afternoon tea—complete with little sandwiches, cakes, and Bakewell tarts in the tearoom. After lunch, they finally saw the marble room, and the exquisitely carved busts even put a look of awe on Rashid's face.

"I can't believe these were made with a chisel and hammer.

I don't know why, but I always assumed they were cast. Like bronzes."

Ruby gave him an incredulous look. "Seriously? Cast out of what, liquid marble?"

"Okay, but if it's done with a chisel, why is it so smooth?"

"Skill? Sandpaper?" She inspected a beautiful statue of a woman reading. Her skin was so, so smooth—as smooth as… well, Rashid's skin.

"She's beautiful," Rashid said.

"I know. I can't imagine looking that great just reading a book."

He looked at Ruby, tilting his head. She expected him to say she looked that great, but he didn't. "Red, can I ask you something?"

"Um, of course."

"You've…changed. Your hair is different, and longer, but also, you're not wearing any red. You have pink lipstick on, and your nails are pink, too."

"It's spring, so I'm wearing spring colors."

He chuckled. "Okay, but do I need to find you a new nickname?"

Ruby smiled. She didn't think she'd changed since moving here. She took his arm in hers. "Nah, I'm still me. C'mon, let's go to the gardens. There are apparently carved topiaries!"

On the drive back to the inn, Ruby expected Rashid to be silent like normal. But as soon as they got on the main highway with stunning vistas on either side of them, he spoke quietly without looking at her.

"That was nice," he said.

She wanted to make a snarky comment about how much *he'd* changed, because a few months ago he wouldn't have gone through a house like that without complaining about something, but she couldn't. It didn't feel right now. "It *was* nice," she said.

"I missed that. I mean, I missed doing things like that with you. Touristy things." He smiled. "I don't know how you manage to make the things I normally hate…fun."

Ruby exhaled. She meant what she'd said to Ayesha yesterday—she really did feel like she was over Rashid. She'd missed him so much at first. She'd thought about turning around and going back to him so many times when she first got to London. But she was settled here now. She had a great job. And she was so much closer to her and her mother's dream.

This whole weekend in the country, plus that call from Veronica on Friday night, had solidified something for Ruby: this dream, her goal, was more important than ever. This was a magical place, a place that felt so right for Ruby. It felt like it could be her home—the home she'd been looking for since her mom passed. After learning what those women had done for her mother, Ruby knew she had to fulfil the dream. She had to see this plan through.

"I missed it, too," Ruby said. "I've *missed* you. But, Rashid, I'm happy here." He'd understand what she meant, that missing him wasn't enough of a reason to give up on her dream. And it was the truth. Especially since the lawsuit was no longer hanging over her head, Ruby honestly had never felt better about her future.

He nodded, not looking at her. "I know. You *look* happy here. More content. I'm glad."

There was something in his voice then, like he was both sad and satisfied. Which made her wonder—could it have been Rashid who gave Neelam Premji Ruby's lawyer's information?

"Rashid, I had a call on Friday night. It was late, so I was kind of out of it, but…did you tell Neelam Premji, that woman we met at Jamatkhana, about my father's lawsuit?"

He didn't look at Ruby, only at the road in front of him, but Ruby knew this man. It was all over his face—it *was* him.

Finally, he rubbed the back of his neck. "I didn't want you to know I tracked her down, but of course I knew you'd find out eventually. I had no idea I'd be seeing you a few days after I spoke to her, though. Are you mad?"

Ruby nearly laughed at that. How could she be mad that he saved the day? She felt tears well in her eyes, so she looked out the window at the rolling hills in the distance. "How? Why? Tell me how it happened."

Rashid explained that Ayesha had told him that Ruby's defense wasn't going well because they hadn't found where the money initially came from. He remembered Neelam saying that she knew Ruby's mother well back then. So, he got Veronica's name from Reena, then went to Jamatkhana every evening for a few days until he found Neelam and asked her if she knew how Ruby's mother earned the money from her trust.

Ruby exhaled. It was so like Rashid not to ask first if she wanted him to help her, to meddle. But of course, Ruby couldn't have found the woman herself. She was in London. This was exactly what she got mad at him for in December, for involving himself in her life without talking to her about it first.

Ruby shook her head. "Did Neelam tell you where the money came from?"

"Yeah, she and her friends were secretly earning money to fund each other's divorces. She told me about the foundation she now runs in your mother's name."

"Badass women, don't you think?"

Rashid looked at Ruby, smiling small. "Total role models. Neelam sounds like an amazing person. So, are you mad at me?"

"Mom's old friends agreed to sign affidavits that they gifted her the money. My lawyer is positive there's no way my father can win the lawsuit now." She felt so torn. She should be grateful to Rashid, but she wished he'd told her what he was doing. Then again, she'd asked him not to contact her. And she suspected if he did ask first, she may have told him not to do it. Ruby had always been uncomfortable when people wanted to help her. She shook her head. "I'm not mad at you. I'm just…I kind of wished you'd told me."

He nodded. "I should have." He rubbed the back of his neck again. "After everything…but I didn't think you'd want to hear from me. Or would want me to do this."

He was probably right. She sighed. "I'm glad you did it. Truly. Thank you. You saved the day." She *was* grateful.

"That's what friends are for," he said, smiling small.

Ruby looked out the window again. The scenery was so beautiful here. She teared up again, wishing her mother could see it. "This makes me more determined than ever to open my own inn. It wasn't just her, but those women who supported her, who sacrificed for this dream. But I hope...I mean, I *never* want to lose you as a friend. I hope we'll stay in touch now."

He nodded. "I hope so, too." She couldn't miss the sadness in his voice. "It would be nice if we can do things like this whenever we're in the same country."

"Okay. Let's be tourist trap friends."

He smiled, looking at her briefly before his eyes returned to the road. "Deal."

30

RUBY WAS UNDERSTANDABLY EXHAUSTED by the time they got back to the inn that afternoon. She'd been up at the crack of dawn yesterday to catch her train to Manchester, and she'd done a lot of walking through manor houses in the last two days, plus working on her feet for the five days before this trip. She excused herself the moment she and Rashid walked in the door, telling him that she was going to take a nap.

As she started walking away, he put his hand on hers for half a second to get her attention. It was the first time they'd had skin-to-skin contact on this trip, and Ruby felt a millisecond of electricity flash between them. She flexed her hand. Maybe it was good that they hadn't hugged or even shaken hands—she was afraid her skin would combust, like her pores held muscle memory of the pleasure his touch used to give her.

"Thanks for today," he said, looking right into her eyes. Ruby couldn't read his expression again. He wasn't smiling—not even that small private smile—but he didn't have the look of disdain he used to have, either. Again, she wondered how much he had changed since they were together.

Ruby shook her head. "You shouldn't be thanking me. I should be thanking *you*. You took me to fucking Pemberley! Right after we went to another Pemberley yesterday! I know it's not really your thing. I appreciate it so much."

He chuckled. "I had fun. I kind of get the appeal now. Maybe I should watch those Austen movies?"

Ruby laughed as she walked toward the stairs up to the rooms. "Hear ye, hear ye," she called. "Be it known that Dr. Rashid Hakim has shown an interest in watching a period rom-com. What a joyous day."

Ruby heard him laughing as she climbed the stairs to the second floor of the inn.

After her much-needed nap, Ruby left her room in search of the others—and a cup of tea. The inn was pretty quiet. Most party guests had all left after breakfast; only Ayesha, Jasmine, the twins, and Rashid were still here. But Ruby couldn't find them in the dining room or the lounge. There were a few people in the pub: a couple of men talking to the bartender and Farida Hakim sitting alone near a window with a dark brown mug in front of her.

"Ruby!" She waved her over. "Come, join me." Ruby smiled and sat across from Farida. "Did you have a restful nap?"

"Very restful. Where is everyone?"

Farida pointed out the window. Out in the distance she

could make out a group of people near the fence bordering the neighboring property. "Cressida next door has ponies. She offered to take the girls out for a ride, and everyone went along to see them. My bartender, Ernie, makes a delicious masala chai. May I offer you a cup?"

Ruby nodded, so Farida called out to the bartender to bring another mug of chai.

"This is such a cute property," Ruby said. "I understand your husband bought it for you to retire in?"

Farida nodded. "Hakim *says* it's for me, but he's happy to be out of the city, too. We're both working, though. We're far from retired. But home base can be here instead of in London thanks to high-speed internet. And, of course, Ayesha is taking on more and more every year. She's essentially running the Raj hotels on her own."

Ruby looked out the window at the family again. She could make out the two small horses with riders in the middle of the group of people. Everyone had their phones out to take pictures. When the bartender brought over a steaming mug of chai, Ruby inhaled. Farida was right—this smelled perfect. The scent of cardamom and cloves was strong.

"I gave him my mother's chai recipe," Farida explained. "He keeps a pot on all day. The kitchen also makes excellent Indian food. I didn't have to teach them—there was already an Indian head chef. He has such a way with aubergine. We're hoping to open a tearoom soon and start serving an Indian-inspired afternoon tea."

"I thought the food yesterday was delicious." Ruby sipped her tea. "And this hotel is delightful. I can see why you love it so much."

"Is this the kind of property you and your mother dreamed about?"

Ruby shook her head. "Something smaller. We envisioned operating it just the two of us…or maybe with one or two employees." The Weeping Sparrow was much bigger than it seemed from the outside. There were even two restaurants—the pub and the dining room, plus the planned tearoom.

Farida nodded. "It's a challenging business, but it's rewarding, too. Smaller properties can be difficult, though." She paused, frowning. "I don't know much about your mother. I understand she passed when you were quite young?"

"Yes, of cancer. I was twenty."

Farida tilted her head with sympathy. "Such a difficult time for you to lose each other. She missed so much—she never got to see you as an adult."

Ruby blinked. She'd always thought about all *she'd* missed by losing her mother but hadn't really considered what her mother had missed out on. Would Mom have been proud of the adult Ruby had become?

"Hakim and I wanted our kids to follow in our footsteps," Farida said. "We dreamt they would all join us in the family business, but Ayesha was the only one interested in the hotels, once she'd sowed her wild oats. My other two are the black sheep. Imagine! Skin doctors! And *Canadians*!" She smiled with a hint of mischief in her eyes that was pure Ayesha. Hakim and Farida were probably the only Indian parents in the world that didn't want their kids to be doctors.

Ruby smiled. "But you must be proud of them."

She laughed. "We're exceedingly proud of them. I wasn't

surprised that Rashid and Jasmine wanted to be in a caring profession. Ayesha has the mind for cutthroat moneymaking. Jasmine and Rashid are my softies."

"Rashid said Jasmine used to bring home stray cats and injured birds."

"They both did. Rashid would never admit it, but he's even softer than Jasmine. My sweet boy—the way he used to take care of his little sisters! Remind me, I have pictures. Rashid hides all his sentimentalism under that gruff exterior, but he's got a heart like a gulab jamun. Soft and sweet."

Ruby chuckled. She'd never heard anyone compare someone to a gulab jamun before. And she'd never heard anyone call Rashid soft and sweet.

But he *was* soft and sweet. She'd seen that side of him at Christmas when he'd patiently talked to the girls to get them out of their shell, and when he helped Ruby skate. Hell, their whole deal in December was so he could give Tara and Noor a Christmas, even though he himself hated the holiday. He'd moved from Calgary to Toronto and figured out how to get his medical license transferred because his sister needed him. And he found Neelam Premji for Ruby, giving her a defense against the lawsuit so Ruby wouldn't lose her mother's inheritance. Rashid was so caring. All the people he cared about were so, so lucky to have him in their life.

Ruby felt a prickle behind her eyes. She quickly looked away so Farida wouldn't see. She didn't know how much Farida knew about Ruby and Rashid's relationship—she assumed not a lot, because otherwise Farida would be planning their wedding.

Ruby changed the subject by asking where the planned tearoom would be. Farida pointed out a room off the pub with large windows and told Ruby her vision for the space. When the conversation slowed, Farida smiled at Ruby. "Forgive me if I'm overstepping, but, as a mother…I feel I need to say this. I can see that you loved your mother very much, and I have no doubt that she would be very proud of the adult you are now. None of my kids are the people I thought they'd be when they were kids, but that doesn't mean I'm not incredibly delighted with the people they are now. I would never want my children to chase my dreams instead of their own. Now, if my dreams and their dreams were aligned, that would be wonderful. Hakim and I already have our own dreams. It is so much more interesting for our family if our children have their own unique aspirations."

Ruby looked at Farida, blinking. That wasn't far off from what her son had said to Ruby back in December when they broke up, that Ruby was chasing her mother's dreams instead of her own. It was also something Marley mentioned on New Year's Eve. Both times, Ruby had been adamant: This dream wasn't only Mom's; it was Ruby's, too.

And now that she'd been in the UK for a while, it was the best time to answer that question. Ruby was learning all about the hotel industry, working in Surrey, and she could see herself staying in the industry. She enjoyed it—more than retail, actually. She liked making guests' visits comfortable. She liked meeting people while they were traveling. There was less drama than luxury stores, and less chaos than retail. The well-oiled machine of a hotel was so satisfying. And this weekend had shown Ruby that the English countryside was everything she had hoped it would be and more. She'd never been more at peace in a place. She'd been here less than two days and couldn't wait to come back.

"I apologize," Farida said. "Maybe I shouldn't have said that. I'm meddling."

There was that word again. *Meddling.* Ruby only saw it as loving. She smiled at Farida. "No, I appreciate the advice. I love the way you all meddle. It shows you care about each other. No one meddles in my life. I'm so grateful for all you and your husband have done for me, have shown me. I love working in the hotel. And…" Ruby paused. She didn't know how to tell this woman how complicated this dream was for her. That walking away from it felt like walking away from her mother. Especially now, after learning how Mom got the money for the dream.

Farida put her hand on Ruby's. "It's *good* that you're taking your time to research and think about what you want to do. I hope you'll do what's best for Rubina, and not for anyone else." She smiled as she took her hand off Ruby's. "And it's a great honor to be on the receiving end of the Hakim meddling. Call me anytime you want someone to butt into your life. We're great at fussing, too. Did that son of mine get you lunch, or have you not eaten since breakfast? Because I can have Ernie put together a ploughman's lunch for you. We do a halal one with turkey sausage."

Ruby smiled. "That sounds perfect."

After a less elaborate but equally tasty dinner in the restaurant that evening, Farida and Hakim took the twins to get ready for bed while Ayesha dragged Rashid, Jasmine, and Ruby into the pub to get drinks and play cards, since Ruby had mentioned over dinner that she'd thought Jane Austen made up the card games in her books.

"I cannot believe you thought whist wasn't a real game," Ayesha said after they all had pints of English ale. "We'll teach you."

Ruby frowned. "You guys know how to play?"

Jasmine laughed. "Oh, the Hakim kids know *all* the card games. Comes from growing up in hotels—we would run wild and free while Mum and Dad worked late hours. I think it was that bartender José who taught us whist, right?"

Rashid shook his head. "No, José taught us blackjack. It was Vicky—remember the old restaurant host that smelled like cigarettes and cheese?"

Ayesha laughed as she grabbed a deck of cards from a little shelf in the corner that was filled with board games. They took their drinks to the private space that was the future home of the tearoom. "I'll deal."

They walked Ruby through the basics of the game. It reminded Ruby of euchre, which she played for hours with her roommates in Montreal years ago. But despite the rules being pretty simple, Ruby and Rashid were still losing after the first few hands of whist. Badly. Mostly because Ruby couldn't keep track of the cards already played. Or remember what trump was.

"Okay, now try to remember, Red," Rashid said, annoyed.

"*Clubs* are trump. Remember it like…you *clubbed* me with your tree when we first met."

Ayesha snickered. "Did you two really meet in a Christmas tree lot? Because that's hilarious."

"We met *outside* a tree lot," Ruby said. "I dropped my tree on him, then he carried it home for me."

Ayesha shook her head, amazed. "You two had a complete Hallmark movie Christmas, didn't you?"

Ruby nodded. "Yep. We drank buckets of eggnog and hot chocolate, and even went skating in the snow." She tried not to look at Rashid while she said it. She'd been intentional when she hadn't sat next to him at the card table—she didn't want to risk any unexpected touches. Knees accidently meeting. Elbows banging. But she hadn't realized that sitting across from him meant he would be her partner. And also…

He was right in front of her. She couldn't help but notice his content smile when she talked about their holiday outings.

"This weekend must also feel like a movie to you," Jasmine said. She also had a small smile on her lips. Jasmine seemed so different from how she'd been back in December. Ruby hadn't realized how much of her quietness, her solemnness, was actually a trauma response. Jasmine wasn't as outgoing as Ayesha, but she was much more alive now. Ruby was so happy to see it.

"Why do you say that?" Ruby asked.

Jasmine shrugged. "You wanted to come to Northern England for so long. You're a Jane Austen superfan, and you went to Lyme Park and Chatsworth. And now you're playing whist, just like they do in all the books and movies."

Ruby smiled. "Yeah, it does kind of feel like a fantasy." She looked out the window of the small room. It was dark, but she could make out some of the gardens surrounding the inn. "I'm having the best time here. Northern England has completely exceeded my expectations."

Ayesha shook her head. "Come in February and you'll change your tune. Besides, it's not the *north* that made this weekend great—it's because you're here with us. We're freaking amazeballs. Especially me."

Rashid rolled his eyes. "Modesty isn't my sister's strong suit."

Ruby laughed. "Girl knows her worth." She high-fived Ayesha.

But as they continued their game, Ruby realized something. Ayesha was right. This trip—her long-awaited pilgrimage to the English countryside, *was* the best because of the people she was with. Ruby had been in England for a while now, and yes, there was a lot to love about being in the UK. But honestly, it wasn't that different from Toronto. Actually, living in Surrey was arguably worse than living in Toronto—because in Toronto she'd lived in the city instead of the suburbs, so there was so much more to do.

She missed the hustle of living in a city. Being in London proper had been great. Fantastic, even. But Toronto was pretty great, too. Thanks to her holiday season with Rashid, she loved her hometown again. She missed the ease with which she could navigate, the casual diversity, and, of course, the amazing food thanks to that diversity. She missed her friends like crazy: Marley, Shayne, Anderson, Reena, and Nadim. She even missed baby Aleem. Despite loving her job, England itself hadn't lived up to her lofty expectations until this mini break in the countryside.

But this trip north had exceeded all of Ruby's expectations. It didn't feel like Toronto or London. She'd felt more at peace here, more comfortable than she'd felt since coming to the UK. She felt calmer, happier, and more at home than anywhere else. It could be thanks to this adorable inn, the tours of the manor houses, or the rugged beauty outside the window.

Or it could be because of the people at this table, plus Hakim, Farida, and the twins. Seeing Jasmine with a lightness to her after all her heaviness at Christmas. Watching the twins' faces light up when they saw Ruby for the first time at Lyme Park. Ayesha's snarkiness. Farida's motherly advice and warmth—even her meddling.

And Rashid. He brought her to Chatsworth House even though he'd hated the place the last time he was there. He brought breakfast and tea for her since they were getting on the road so early. He wasn't bitter about her breaking up with him, then not talking to him for almost three months. He understood why she pushed him away. Hell, he'd gone out of his way to help her with the lawsuit, so now she wasn't at risk of losing her mother's money anymore.

The realization rocked her to her core. What if she hadn't come to the countryside with the Hakims? Would she still have felt this magic if she'd come alone, as she'd initially intended to?

Ruby took a long gulp of her ale, her mind racing through the realizations. Why had she wanted to come to the English countryside in the first place? What was it about this place that spoke to both Ruby's and her mother's hearts? What had they been chasing?

Family. It was always family. When Dad was staying away from the house, or yelling at Ruby, or trying to control Mom, they'd watch that UK real estate show and see families leave their city life behind for a peaceful one in the country. Even their love of Austen…the stories they both loved to read and watch were love stories, but they were about family, too. The Bennet sisters and their chaotic love for each other. Emma visiting with Mrs. Weston and treating Harriet like a sister. Marianne and Elinor supporting each other even when they were frustrated with each other.

It wasn't the place—it was the *people*. Ruby, and maybe even her mother, had been chasing the feeling of belonging to a complicated, messy, but loving family. And that's why the last two days had been so magical for Ruby—because this complicated, messy family had welcomed her.

It had been so long since she had a family, and she'd never had a supportive one. She felt a truckload of gratitude for the Hakim family. But also, maybe Ruby should be rethinking her goals. Maybe she shouldn't be so fixated on a place to find her home. Maybe she'd find home when she found the right people. *Her* people.

"You okay, Red?" Rashid asked, eying her curiously.

She smiled. "Absolutely. I'm great. Just…really happy to be here." And she meant it. Her eyes welled with tears, but she blinked them away. "What was trump again? Hearts?"

His brows were furrowed with concern. "I'm happy you're here, too. And yes, it's hearts. Don't forget."

They continued the game, but Ruby only got worse. She was too distracted as her mind kept racing. Maybe she needed to think more about what Farida said, to really determine how many of the choices she'd made in her life were to make her mother happy, because Mom hadn't had a lot of happiness in the years before her death. Marley had said that Mom would want Ruby to follow her own dreams. But Ruby had been so fixated on doing what she and her mother wanted to do together that she didn't take the time to think if she wanted to do them alone. Because without family, without her people, was any of this worth it?

What had Mom said in her letter, and to Neelam Premji—she wanted "Ruby to know who Ruby was" before she got the money.

And did Ruby know who Ruby was? Other than Maryam's daughter?

"Ruby? Hey, earth to Ruby...I can see all your cards," Ayesha said.

Ugh. "Sorry." She lifted her hand higher.

"Maybe we should call it a night," Rashid said.

"You just want to stop because you're losing," Ayesha said.

"No," Jasmine said, shaking her head. "He's recognizing that Ruby's not in the right mind right now for a game that needs a lot of concentration because he's a considerate and generous person."

"Yes," Ruby said. That's exactly what Rashid was doing. "That's why I fell in love with him."

Ruby blinked. It was true. She loved his whole family, but she was *in love* with Rashid. She'd been denying it to herself and to others for so long. No one had ever treated Ruby as well as Rashid did, and it scared the hell out of her to rely on someone so much after being alone for so long. She fell in love with him during the holidays, and she was still in love with him now. Because he cared. Because he prioritized her well-being, even over his own enjoyment. Because he wanted to help her make her dreams come true, even if that pulled her away from him. Because he was sexy, and so fucking passionate, and so, so... beautiful. And he made *her* feel beautiful. She could be herself with him. With all her flaws and all her unresolved baggage, he still wanted her. And she wanted him. She was in love with Dr. Rashid Hakim.

Also...why was everyone staring at her like that? Holy shit...had she said that she loved him out loud? Ruby's hand shot to her mouth, mortified. She wondered if it was possible to will a sinkhole to open in the ground to suck her into the permafrost.

"What did you say?" Rashid asked. His eyes were wide.

"We should go," Jasmine said. It sounded like she was trying not to laugh. Ayesha looked like she was thinking of getting the bartender to make some popcorn for the show in front of her.

"Hell, no," Ayesha said, crossing her arms. "I'm not going anywhere. You said it was a casual fling. You actually *love* my brother? What happened to *we're friends*?"

Jasmine stood. "Ayesha, come." She walked around the table and literally pulled her sister out of her chair. Ayesha's cards fell to the floor.

"Fine," Ayesha said. "But I'm listening at the door."

"These doors are too thick to hear anything," Jasmine said. "Come with me."

Ruby didn't look at them when they left the room. She heard the door close, and she was alone with Rashid, and why the hell was that sinkhole taking so long?

"Red, what did you say?" Rashid asked again, his eyes locked on her. His jaw was set, but inside...inside he had a sweet and soft center. Just like gulab jamun. She'd seen it. She'd fallen in love with it.

And she definitely didn't mean to say that out loud.

"Oh, you know me..." Ruby said awkwardly. "Foot-in-mouth disease. I'm always rambling nonsense like that. But yeah, I've got a lot on my mind. Like I was wondering if I remembered to turn off my dehumidifier—"

"Ruby." That was all he said. Her name. She closed her eyes, and when she opened them the look on his face was clear as day. There was surprise, but also...maybe joy. Affection.

Ruby sighed. "I was having...an epiphany about my life."

"An epiphany that you're in love with me?"

Ruby waved her hand. "Among other things. I was wondering if maybe I need to stop chasing my mother's dreams and figure out what my own dreams are...who *I* am. And I was wondering how I can ever repay you and your family for all you've done for me. And I realized that I wouldn't have loved the English countryside without your family here, and maybe—"

"I love you, too, Ruby."

Ruby stopped rambling. She looked at him. Had he said he loved her? "What?"

"I said I love you." He put his cards down on the table. "I

fell in love with you in December. I haven't seen or talked to you in so long, I thought I was over you. But the moment I saw you standing near the pond at Lyme Park, it all came back. I knew I still loved you."

"The first thing you said when you saw me was 'Bloody hell, I'm going to kill my sisters.'"

He smiled. "Okay, that was my first thought. But then you laughed, and I thought *Ruby is still the most beautiful woman I've ever seen…and I am still so in love with her, and this weekend just got so much harder because I can never tell her how I feel.*"

She smiled. "But you just did."

He nodded. "I did. I'll do it again. I love you."

He loved her. Ruby, who always thought she was alone in the world, who never had anyone ask her to stay somewhere. This generous, brilliant, sexy man loved her.

And she loved him. She said it again, too. "I love you. I think I fell in love at the ballet, but I didn't realize it until today." Ruby took a deep breath. "So…what happens now?"

He reached across the table and put his open palm up. She immediately took his hand in hers, feeling that soft skin again. Her hand fit so well with his. The electricity between them crackled.

"We have a lot to talk about," Rashid said. "But…" He looked at her, those dark eyes soaking in her face. "Ruby, I want to *be* with you. Wherever you are, I want to be there. I'll come back to the UK or wherever you want to call home."

Ruby chuckled. "That's awfully impulsive of you."

He stood, then came around the table and pulled her up with their still clasped hands. He put his arms around her waist. How had she gone so long without being in his arms like this? How had she *ever* walked away from this man?

"I called you impulsive," he said, "and thought you had all the wrong values, but really, you were exactly what I needed. I've lived a boring life forever—planning everything, being there for my family, and doing the things that I thought were just and right for me and the world. But I was only going through the motions. It was like…I didn't know how to turn off my convictions and truly enjoy a moment. You taught me how to do that. But I was an idiot. I thought I could make plans for you the same way I planned my own life. I didn't *see* you, even though I loved you. I couldn't understand that everyone doesn't experience life the same way I do. But you opened my eyes, Rubina Dhanji. I see you now. I understand why you need to find your path. And whatever that path is, I want to be right next to you, holding your hand."

Ruby had tears running fully down her cheeks, but she didn't wipe them. That was the most beautiful thing anyone had ever said to her. "I want to be with you, too," Ruby said. She reached up so she could put her hands behind his soft neck. "But…" She took a deep breath. "I think…it's time for me to go home, Rashid. Back to Toronto. With you."

He smiled so wide, and it was so beautiful. And finally, he lowered his head and their lips met in a kiss.

It was perfect. It had been far too long. Every pore on her body sang for him. Her toes curled, her skin pebbled, and when he pulled her close, she felt like she was already home.

A banging on the window outside startled them. Rashid pulled away, and they looked out. Sure enough, Jasmine and

Ayesha were there, clapping and cheering. And they were joined by Hakim and Farida, who had surprised looks on their faces—happy looks, though.

Mortifying. Ruby buried her face in Rashid's chest.

Rashid leaned down to whisper in her ear. "You know, if you want me, you'll be stuck with them, too."

Ruby smiled, then got on her toes to press a quick kiss to his lips—quick because his bloody parents were watching. "I wouldn't have it any other way," Ruby said.

Rashid grinned and pulled her in for a tight hug. Ruby heard hooting and hollering and cheering from outside, but it only made this better. Ruby had found her people.

EPILOGUE

IT HAD BEEN A year since Ruby first met Rashid on her birthday while dragging a Christmas tree in the middle of Toronto Distillery District's Winter Market, and Ruby was going to learn from her mistakes that day. This year, she'd bring a car and not attempt to carry her tree home herself on the busy Toronto streets. And she was going to wear proper winterwear instead of her vintage red coat and heels. And, of course, she had *planned* to get a tree this time, instead of deciding to buy the Douglas fir on a whim after getting off work.

Not that she had any regrets for her impulsiveness on her thirty-third birthday, since she'd met a sexy lumberjack-looking doctor thanks to her miscalculations. But she didn't need a sexy lumberjack-looking doctor this year. She still had Rashid—now her boyfriend of eight months—and was bringing him with her to get their tree this year.

Rashid was driving—the roof rack on the Volvo was perfect for tying a Christmas tree to. But after leaving the underground parking of their condo, he headed toward the highway instead of the Winter Market where Ruby had worked last Christmas.

"Where are you going?" Ruby asked. She was glad she'd brought a to-go tea with her—she knew to be prepared to be in a car longer than expected whenever she went somewhere with Rashid.

"A patient told me about a farm that's already selling trees. I thought it would be fun to cut down our own tree this year."

Ruby grinned. That *would* be fun. This was just like Rashid: impulsive—but only about things he did with Ruby. He was a thoughtful planner in every other aspect of his life, but when it came to Ruby, he was prone to throwing caution to the wind and acting on both their whims. He loved trying new things—whether it was a new restaurant across town, checking out a museum exhibit without buying tickets ahead of time, or trying out new activities like curling or escape rooms. Ruby loved his newfound spontaneity, which had made her summer and fall full of unexpected fun. They'd had a last-minute weekend in Montreal and made new friends in their couples cooking class, and he even got an impulse tattoo on his upper arm after they walked by a shop and saw an illustration in the window of a water lily that looked a lot like one of the flowers tattooed on Ruby's breasts.

But their entire relationship hadn't been this easy or fun since they'd confessed their love for each other at his parents' inn near Manchester. Ruby had stayed in the UK for over two months before she moved back to Toronto just in time for the Raj Toronto's opening, where she was now the hospitality manager. Long distance had been hard—especially since they were both too busy with work to travel to see each other. But now she was back in her hometown, living in Rashid's condo near his dermatology practice, and things were closer to perfect than Ruby had ever imagined life could be.

They'd both been worried that moving in together was risky since they hadn't been together very long, but they threw caution to the wind and took the plunge anyway. But for Ruby, it wasn't really a risk—it wasn't like she was alone in Toronto if things didn't work out. Ruby could move in temporarily with Marley or Reena if she needed to. She had a big safety net here—friends and family who meant the world to her.

But things worked out fine. Rashid was happily settled in Toronto. He was playing recreational hockey and was also working part-time in the burn unit in a trauma hospital on top of seeing his own patients in the practice he shared with his sister. And Ruby loved working at the Raj Toronto with Ayesha.

Jasmine was officially divorced—she was able to expedite it on the grounds of abuse. Her ex-husband had a little hissy fit when the judge threw out his petition for spousal support and reminded him that his prenuptial agreement was ironclad. Derek stopped showing up to the supervised visits with his daughters out of spite, which was hard for the girls, but everyone—especially Ruby—knew that this was better for them in the long term.

Ruby's father had accepted Veronica's deal to pay Ruby's legal fees if he canceled the lawsuit, knowing that if it went to court, he would lose and the legal fees would be much higher. She hadn't seen or heard from her father since. Ruby did reach out to Neelam and had an emotional reunion with the other women who'd helped her mother. She and Jasmine were volunteering with the Help from Maryam fund, planning a gala at the hotel in February to raise money for the cause.

But easily the best thing about being back in her hometown was living with Rashid. They fell into such an easy comfort together. They didn't argue about how to decorate the condo, they always agreed on restaurants or who would cook dinner, and they loved seeing their huge group of friends and family in the city. Ruby had honestly never had a place she lived in feel more like home. Dropping everything in the UK and coming back to Toronto to be with Rashid was honestly the best thing Ruby had ever done.

It was a mostly silent drive to the tree farm an hour north of the city—Rashid was still a quiet driver, and Ruby didn't mind the silence at all. When they got to the farm it was exactly as she'd envisioned. Picturesque, quaint, and foresty. An adorable small man with a long red beard handed them a little piece of ribbon with their name on it. Apparently, they wouldn't be chopping down the tree themselves due to liability, but instead they would choose what tree they wanted and a more experienced lumberjack (instead of a dermatologist who liked to dress like one) would actually take the tree down. Which was fine with Ruby—the last thing either of them needed was an injury.

After they were set free in a little grouping of trees, she trudged through the snow in her boots and her new long red puffer coat the same shade as her favorite Ruby Woo lipstick. Ruby kept pointing out trees she liked—small ones, because their condo wasn't huge, and she'd given all her ornaments to charity last year.

"Too small," Rashid said, shaking his head.

"Since when would you want a big tree, Ebenezer? Isn't it a waste of resources…not to mention how much mess the needles will make, and how hard it will be to fit it in the elevator?"

He laughed and put his arm around her waist, pulling her closer to him. "Get in the Christmas spirit, Red. We have twelve-foot ceilings. That little tree will look ridiculous. All the trees on this path are too small."

"Okay, then, Dr. Needs His Christmas Decorations to Be Proportional to His Room, take me to where you think we'll find a tree."

Releasing her waist and taking her hand, he scanned the trees around them. Many of the larger ones already had red ribbons on them, which meant they were spoken for.

"There," Rashid said, pointing to a small grouping of trees away from the others. They went for a closer look. The trees in the grouping were all big—well over six feet tall. Ruby inhaled deeply, the cold winter pine smell going straight into her bones. She still absolutely *loved* this season and was so excited to be spending another Christmas with Rashid. She knew without a doubt that it would be even better than last year. And last year had been pretty great.

They had already made plans to see the Santa Claus parade next week with Jasmine, Tara, Noor, Reena, Nadim, and Aleem again. Ayesha and her new girlfriend Olivia were going to be joining them, too. And they'd already bought tickets to take the girls to *The Nutcracker* again later in December. Ruby had taken three skating lessons to be ready for a big skating party that Shayne and Anderson were hosting in a few weeks.

Shayne was renting an outdoor projector so they could still watch *Carol*, but outside.

"Okay," Rashid asked, "which one?" None of these trees had red ribbons on them. Ruby let go of Rashid's hand and inspected each tree until she found one that was just the right height and had just the right number of healthy-looking branches.

"This one," she said right before leaning into the needles of the tree to take a deep inhale of the scent. It was glorious. It was a deep rich green and would look fabulous in their living room. "I want this one," she said again, turning so she could get the ribbon from Rashid.

But she froze, mouth agape at what she saw. Rashid, with his jeans, flannel shirt, and blue beanie hat, was on one knee in front of her and holding out a little red box.

Tears welled in Ruby's eyes as she stepped closer. It was a ring. A gorgeous gold band with two little leaves wrapped around two clear stones, and a big red ruby right in the middle.

"Rashid," she said looking into his face. There was so much there. Hope. Respect. *Love.* "I...don't know what to say..."

"I think I'm the one who's supposed to say something." He smiled, then took a breath. "I don't have words for how much better my life has been since I met you a year ago. I thought I was happy—with friends and a wacky family that I would do anything for, plus a fulfilling job. But I was wrong. Everything was so empty when we were apart for those months. I don't ever want to do that again. So..." His voice cracked with emotion. "So maybe it's impulsive, but...Marry me, Ruby?"

With full-on tears falling down her cheeks, she dropped

onto the snow in front of him, and wrapped her arms around Rashid.

"Yes," she said into his ear. "A thousand yeses. Let's get married."

Rashid dropped his butt onto the snow and pulled Ruby into a tight hug.

This. This was why she was never going to leave this man. She wanted to make this feeling, this *comfort*, last forever.

Sitting on his lap, she put her left hand, with her new gold and red snowflake manicure, in front of him. He slipped the ruby ring on her ring finger, then pressed a kiss to her lips.

"I love you," he said.

"I love you, too. Your mother and sisters are going to take over wedding planning."

He nodded. "I know. Let's elope a minute past midnight on New Year's Eve."

Ruby laughed. She knew there was no way he would upset his family like that. And she knew that this, being in Rashid Hakim's arms, was exactly where Ruby was supposed to be.

Recipes

PEPPERMINT BURFI

Burfi is an Indian milk fudge traditionally flavored with rose, cardamom, pistachio, or saffron. Peppermint is an unusual flavor, but so perfect for the holiday season.

Makes 24 small squares

2 ½ cups milk powder (Instant skim milk powder works fine, but whole milk powder makes richer burfi)
¾ cup granulated sugar
1 cup milk
pinch of salt
¼ cup butter or ghee
½ teaspoon lemon juice or vinegar
¾ teaspoon peppermint extract
3 to 4 small candy canes, crushed finely

1. Line an 8-inch square pan with parchment paper.
2. In a large bowl, combine the milk powder, sugar, milk, and salt. Whisk until the milk powder dissolves and

the mixture is smooth. The mixture will start out thick and difficult to mix, but will loosen as the milk powder dissolves.

3. In a saucepan or wok (nonstick is best), melt the butter or ghee over medium heat. Once melted, reduce to medium-low and add the milk mixture. Stir with a silicone spatula until the butter is incorporated.
4. Continue to cook on medium-low heat, stirring and scraping the sides and bottom of the pan until the mixture starts to thicken. This can take anywhere from 8 to 15 minutes. If it gets thick quickly or browns at all, lower the temperature to the lowest setting. Use the silicone spatula to mash any lumps that form, keeping the mixture as smooth as possible.
5. When the mixture has thickened (but is not yet too thick to stir), add the lemon juice or vinegar and peppermint extract. Continue to stir vigorously for 5 minutes more, smoothing with the spatula, until the mixture is the texture of soft mashed potatoes and separates from the pan easily.
6. Remove the pan from the heat and dump the mixture into the prepared pan. Smooth and level the top with the spatula.
7. Sprinkle the crushed candy canes on top, then press them into the burfi with the spatula.
8. Refrigerate, uncovered, until cooled. The candy canes will melt a bit, and the colors will bleed into the burfi. Remove the burfi from the pan by pulling up on the parchment paper, and cut into squares.

Tips: *If the burfi is hard to cut, try wetting the knife with warm water. If the burfi squares are soft or wet after cutting, leave uncovered on a plate to dry out for a day—if you can stop yourself from eating them. These get soft if they are left covered but are still delicious.*

CHAI EGGNOG

Chai made with eggnog instead of milk. This is delicious served hot or cold. Try it chilled with an ounce of whisky!

Serves 2

  2 masala chai tea bags (Indian brands are better)
1 ½ cups eggnog
    cinnamon stick, for garnish
    nutmeg, for garnish

1. Pour 1 cup of boiling water over the 2 tea bags and let steep at least 10 minutes, to make a strong tea. Remove the tea bags and chill the tea.
2. Mix the chilled tea with the eggnog. Divide into 2 glasses and garnish with freshly grated nutmeg and a cinnamon stick.

Acknowledgments

Like Ruby in this book, I've always loved the holiday season and Jane Austen, and I worked for many years in luxury retail. Like Rashid, I come from a loving, supportive family, and have many extended family members in the hotel industry. I'm also the Canadian child of immigrants who was raised as a Muslim and as a hockey fan. I never saw an issue with making gingerbread houses, decorating my Christmas tree, or watching holiday rom-coms, but others with my exact background choose not to celebrate Christmas with the same enthusiasm. Of course, neither option is right or wrong, and it's a great example that even within immigrant and religious communities, there is a lot of diversity in how people identify with their faith, and with customs outside of their culture. Just like there is diversity in income levels and family dynamics and norms. I enjoyed writing Ruby and Rashid as two people who are culturally alike on the surface, but who actually have more differences than similarities—differences that complement each other beautifully.

There are many to thank for this book—my tenth published novel. First, my agent, Rachel Brooks, who is always in my corner and always so enthusiastic and supportive of my work. My editor at Forever, Leah Hultenschmidt, who I am convinced knows what I am trying to do with my books better than I do. Also, thanks to Jordyn Penner, Sabrina Flemming, Sam Brody, Luria Rittenberg, Estelle Hallick, Alli Rosenthal, and everyone else I have had the pleasure of working with at Forever. I have always been in the hands of an excellent team there. Thanks also to the art team for this perfect cover, to the sales team for getting my books in stores, to the audio team for the amazing audio edition, and to Lori Paximadis for the precise copy edit of the manuscript.

As always, thanks to all my amazing writing friends, with a special shout-out to Lindo Forbes, who brainstormed the plot of this book with me on a road trip from cottage country back to Scarborough.

And most importantly to my family. Tony, Anissa, and Khalil—thanks for your patience, enthusiasm, and endless support for this weird career. And thanks to Darcy and Matcha—behind every happy writer is a cat who won't get off her keyboard.

Praise for

Just Playing House

'An utter delight' *The Culturess*

'Heron's characters are lovingly drawn and richly layered'
Kirkus

Jana Goes Wild

'An enchanting story of love, family and self-acceptance. It was the perfect swoony escape'
Sara Desai, author of *The Singles Table*

'A beautiful, compelling romance celebrating second chances and forgiveness' *Kirkus*, starred review

'This satisfying, second-chance romance offers a big-hearted, clear-eyed examination of parenting and rekindling of old flames' *Library Journal*, starred review

'Heron continues her winning record of fun but deeply emotional romances' *Entertainment Weekly*

'This is a treat' *Publishers Weekly*

Kamila Knows Best

'This Bollywood-inspired retelling of Jane Austen's *Emma* is a fun, lighthearted binge from page one' *USA Today*

'Both Austenites and movie fans who fondly remember *Clueless* will be delighted' *Publishers Weekly*

'Heron's sensitive insights infuse this romance with both immense charm and emotional depth' *Booklist*

Accidentally Engaged

'Voraciously readable…fresh, warm, soft in all the right places… both its comedic and emotional moments sing. We dare readers not to devour it. Grade: A' *Entertainment Weekly*

'An engaging read with authentic characters who continue to surprise you' *USA Today*

'A mouthwatering romantic comedy…This book is undoubtedly what Heron would pull out during the Showstopper Challenge on a literary version of *The Great British Bake Off*.'
 BookPage

'Farah Heron balances the ingredients for a charming romance: a heroine finding her way, a swoonworthy love, a complicated but loving family and a happily ever after'

Shelf Awareness

'*Accidentally Engaged* does what all good romance novels do best: It's full of emotion, fun, and family, with that ultimately satisfying HEA that will settle in your stomach like a home-cooked meal'

Vulture

Do you love contemporary romance?

Want the chance to hear news about your favourite authors (and the chance to win free books)?

Kristen Ashley
Ashley Herring Blake
Meg Cabot
Olivia Dade
Rosie Danan
J. Daniels
Farah Heron
Talia Hibbert
Sarah Hogle
Helena Hunting
Abby Jimenez
Elle Kennedy
Christina Lauren
Alisha Rai
Sally Thorne
Lacie Waldon
Denise Williams
Meryl Wilsner
Samantha Young

Then visit the Piatkus website
www.yourswithlove.co.uk

And follow us on Facebook and Instagram
www.facebook.com/yourswithlovex | @yourswithlovex

PIATKUS